GOOD AS
DEAD

GOOD AS DEAD

Mark Billingham

Little, Brown

LITTLE, BROWN

First published in Great Britain in 2011 by Little, Brown
Reprinted 2011 (three times)

A CIP catalogue record for this book
is available from the British Library.

Hardback ISBN 978-1-84744-419-6
Trade Paperback ISBN 978-1-84744-420-2

Typeset in Plantin by M Rules
Printed and bound in Great Britain by
Clays Ltd, St Ives plc

Papers used by Little, Brown are from well-managed forests
and other responsible sources.

MIX
Paper from
responsible sources
FSC
www.fsc.org   FSC® C104740

Little, Brown
An imprint of
Little, Brown Book Group
100 Victoria Embankment
London EC4Y 0DY

An Hachette UK Company
www.hachette.co.uk

www.littlebrown.co.uk

To David Morrissey and Jolyon Symonds.

For bringing Thorne to the screen so brilliantly.

DAY ONE

WILD IN HIS SORROW

ONE

Chewing gum and chocolate, maybe a bottle of water on those hen's teeth days when the sun was shining. A paper for the journey into work and half a minute of meaningless chat while she was waiting for her change.

Nothing there worth dying for.

Helen Weeks would tell herself much the same thing many times before it was over. In the hours spent staring at the small black hole from which death could emerge in less time than it took for her heart to beat. Or stop beating. In those slow-motion moments of terror that measured out each day and in the sleepless nights that followed. While the man who might kill her at any moment was shouting at himself just a few feet away, or crying in the next room.

It is not my time to die.

Or my baby's time to lose his mother . . .

The chewing gum was a habitual thing, something to do and to help her stay off the cigarettes she'd given up two years before when she'd become pregnant. A newspaper ensured she would not have to look at the people sitting opposite her on the train, presuming she was lucky enough to get a seat and did not find herself pressed up against some lard-arse in a cheap suit who bought his aftershave from Poundstretcher. The chocolate was an addiction, pure and simple. One that had made the struggle to lose weight since her son was born no more than partially successful. She would try and eke it out; a chunk or two around eleven with a coffee, another after lunch and the rest as a treat at the end of the day. That was always the plan, but it was usually gone before she'd so much as logged on at her desk or, if the case she was working on was particularly unpleasant, by the time her train had finished its four-minute journey to Streatham station.

There were a lot of unpleasant cases.

She collected her paper from the rack near the door of the newsagent's, and by the time she reached the counter Mr Akhtar had already picked out her usual chewing gum and chocolate bar of choice. He smiled and brandished them as she approached.

Same as always. Their private joke.

'How is the little one?' he asked.

Mr Akhtar was a short, prematurely balding man who almost always had a smile on his face. He rarely wore anything other than dark trousers, a white shirt and a cardigan, though that might be blue or brown. Helen thought he was probably younger than he looked, but put him somewhere in his mid-fifties.

'He's good,' Helen said. She was aware of the customer she had seen browsing through the magazines on her way in, moving up to stand behind her. The man – tall, black, thirties – had been looking up at some of the covers in the top shelf's 'gentleman's interest' section and had quickly dropped his eyes down to the lifestyle and motoring mags when he'd seen Helen come in. 'Yeah, he's good.'

Mr Akhtar smiled and nodded and handed over the chewing gum and chocolate. 'Hard work though, yes?'

Helen rolled her eyes and said, 'Sometimes.'

Actually, Alfie was way better than good. He was indescribably brilliant. She grinned, thinking about her one-year-old son babbling happily as she had walked him to the childminder half an hour before. He was happy almost all of the time, as far as she could tell, but he certainly let her know when he wasn't. He had Paul's temper, Helen had decided, as well as his eyes.

Or was she kidding herself?

'Worth it though, yes?'

'Definitely,' she said.

'Trust me, it gets harder.'

'Oh, don't tell me that.' Laughing, Helen handed over two pound coins and waited for the forty-three pence she was given back every morning. As Mr Akhtar was digging her change from the till, she heard the bell on the door. She saw him glance up and heard the voices, braying and fearless, as a group of lads came into the shop.

She looked round. Three of them: one black, two white. All full of themselves.

'Here you are,' Mr Akhtar said. He held out Helen's change, but his eyes were on the three boys, and his voice was a little smaller than it had been a few seconds earlier. Before Helen turned back to him, she watched the boys amble across to the tall fridge and open the door, laughing and cursing.

Enjoying the attention of an audience, Helen thought.

'Looks like it might be nice today.'

'That's good,' Mr Akhtar said. Still quiet, looking towards the fridge.

'Won't last.' Helen put the coins into her purse and folded the newspaper into her bag. She heard the man behind her exhale loudly, clearly impatient to be served. She had just opened her mouth to say 'see you tomorrow' when Mr Akhtar leaned towards her and whispered, nodding towards the three boys.

'I hate those *bastards*,' he hissed.

Helen looked round again. They were rooting around inside the fridge, pulling out cans, then putting them back again. Laughing and pushing each other. One, who must have grabbed a paper on the way in, was leaning against a display of greeting cards, rifling through the pages.

The man standing behind Helen muttered, 'Christ's sake.' She could not be sure if it was frustration at being made to wait or irritation at the behaviour of the boys at the fridge.

5

'Hey,' Mr Akhtar said.

Helen turned back to the till, then heard the hiss of a can being opened and saw Mr Akhtar's expression darken suddenly.

'*Hey!*'

Another hiss, and now two boys were swigging from cans of Coke, while the third tossed the remains of his newspaper away and reached into the fridge for one of his own.

'You pay for those,' Mr Akhtar shouted.

'I forgot my wallet,' one of the boys said. The other two laughed, touched their fists together.

The white boy who had been reading the newspaper drained his can and crushed it. 'What are you going to do if we don't?' He held his arms out wide in challenge. 'Blow yourself up or something?'

'You need to pay.'

Helen looked at Mr Akhtar. She could see the muscles working in his jaw, his arms stiff at his sides, his fists clenched. She took a small step to her right, moved into his eyeline, and shook her head.

Leave it.

'Get out of my shop,' Mr Akhtar shouted.

The white boy's eyes looked small and dead as he dropped his empty can and walked slowly towards the till. One hand slid fast into the pocket of his hooded top. 'Make us,' he said. Behind him, his friends dropped their own cans, sending Coke fizzing across the floor of the shop.

'Sorry,' one of them said.

Suddenly, Helen had no spit in her mouth. She eased her hand into her bag and closed her fingers around the wallet that held both her Oyster and warrant cards. It was bravado, no more than that, she was almost certain. One flash of her ID and a few strong words and the gobby little sods would be out of there in a shot.

'I think Osama's shit himself.'

But an instant after Helen's professional instinct kicked in, another took hold that was far stronger. It could so easily be a knife in the kid's pocket, after all. She knew that she could take nothing for granted and

6

was aware of what could happen to have-a-go heroes. She knew one community police support officer in Forest Hill who had reprimanded a fourteen-year-old for dropping litter a few months before. He was still on a ventilator.

She had had more than her fair share of *this* a year or so before.

Now, she had a child . . .

'Your shop, but it ain't your country.'

The man who had been waiting to be served moved closer to her. Was he trying to protect her, or protect himself? Either way, he was breathing heavily and when she turned she could see that he was eyeing up the door, wondering if he should make a dash for it.

Trying to decide whether or not to make a move.

Same as she was.

'You lot are pussies without a bomb in your backpack.' The white boy took another step towards the counter. He was grinning and opened his mouth to say something else, then stopped when he saw Mr Akhtar reach quickly below the counter and come up with a baseball bat.

One of the boys at the fridge whistled, mock-impressed, and said, 'Oh, look out.'

The newsagent moved surprisingly quickly.

Helen took a step towards the end of the counter, but felt herself held back by the man next to her and could only watch as Mr Akhtar came charging from behind it, yelling and swinging the bat wildly.

'Get the hell out. Get out.'

The white boy backed quickly away, his hand still in his pocket, while the other two turned on their heels and ran for the door, their arms reaching out to send tins and packets of cereal scattering as they went. They screamed threats and promised that they would be back and one of them shouted something about the place stinking of curry anyway.

When the last one was out on the pavement – still swearing threats and making obscene gestures – Mr Akhtar slammed the door. He fumbled in his pocket for keys and locked it, then stood with his head against the glass, breathing heavily.

Helen took a step towards him, asked if he was all right.

Outside, one of the boys kicked at the window, then hawked up a gobbet of thick spittle on to the glass. It had just begun to dribble down past the ads for gardeners, guitar teachers and massage, when he was pulled away by his friends.

'I'm going to make a call,' Helen said. 'We've got it all on camera, so there's nothing to worry about.' She glanced up at the small camera above the till and realized it was almost certainly a dummy. 'I can give good descriptions of all three of them, OK? You know I'm a police officer, so . . .'

Still with his back to the shop, Mr Akhtar nodded and began fumbling in his pocket a second time.

'Mr Akhtar?'

When he turned round, the newsagent was pointing a gun.

'Oh, Jesus,' the man next to Helen said.

Helen swallowed hard, tried to control the shaking in her leg and in her voice when she spoke. 'What are you doing—?'

Mr Akhtar shouted then and swore as he told Helen and her fellow customer exactly what would happen if they did not do what he said. The curse sounded awkward in his mouth though, like something spoken by an actor who has over-rehearsed.

Like a white lie.

'Shut up,' he screamed. 'Shut up or I will fucking kill you.'

TWO

'It's *espresso*, for crying out loud,' Tom Thorne shouted. 'Espresso ...'

The man – who of course could not hear him – was talking enthusiastically about how he could not even think about starting his day without that all-important hit of caffeine. He said the offending word again and Thorne slapped his hand against the steering wheel.

'Not *ex*presso, you pillock. There's no bloody X in it ...'

Sitting in a long line of rush-hour traffic, crawling north towards lights on Haverstock Hill, Thorne glanced right and saw a woman staring across at him from behind the wheel of a sporty-looking Mercedes. He smiled and raised his eyebrows. Muttered, 'Sod you, then,' when she turned away. He had hoped that, having seen him talking to himself, she might presume that he was making a hands-free call, but she clearly had him marked down as a ranting nutter.

'I suppose that a nice strong *ex*presso gives you an *ex*pecially good start to the day, does it?'

Looking for something else, *anything* else to listen to, he stabbed at the pre-set buttons; settled eventually for something sweet and folksy, a soft, pure voice and a song he half recognised.

Shouting at the radio was probably just another sign of growing older, Thorne thought. One of the many. Up there on the list with losing a little hearing in his right ear and thinking that there was nothing worth watching on television any more. Wondering why teenagers thought it was cool to wear their trousers around their knees.

The song finished and the DJ cheerfully informed him which station he was tuned into.

Up there with listening to Radio 2!

Changes of opinion or temperament were inevitable of course, Thorne knew that, and on some days he might even admit that they were not necessarily a bad thing. When change happened gradually, its slow accretion of shifts and triggers could go almost unnoticed, but Thorne was rarely comfortable with anything that was more sudden. However necessary it might be. Too many things in his life had changed recently, or were in the process of changing, and he was still finding it hard to cope with any of them.

To adjust.

He pulled somewhat less than smoothly away from the lights, cursing as his foot slipped off the still unfamiliar accelerator pedal.

The bloody car, for a start.

He had finally traded in his beloved 1975 BMW CSi for a two-year-old 5 Series that was rather more reliable and for which he could at least obtain replacement parts when he needed them. The car had been the first and as yet only thing to go, but more major changes were imminent. His flat in Kentish Town had been on the market for a month, though he still had some repairs to do and buyers seemed thin on the ground. And, despite several weeks of quiet words and clandestine sniffing around, a suitable transfer to another squad had yet to become available.

Then there had been Louise ...

All these less than comfortable shifts in Thorne's life, important as they might seem, were secondary to that. The car, the flat, the job. The flurry of changes had come about, had been decided upon, as a direct result of what had happened with Louise.

He and Louise Porter had finally parted company a couple of

10

months before, after a relationship that had lasted just over two years. For half that time it had been better than either of them had expected; way better than most relationships between police officers, certainly. But as a team they had not been strong enough to cope with the loss of a baby. Neither had been able to give the other the particular form of comfort they needed and, while the relationship had limped on for a while, they had suffered separately and paid heavily for it. Louise had been understandably resentful that Thorne seemed more easily able to deal with the grief of strangers, while Thorne himself had struggled with guilt at not having been quite as devastated by the miscarriage as he thought he should have been. By the time that guilt had burned itself out and Thorne was able to admit just how much he had wanted to be a father, it was too late for both of them.

They had become lovers by numbers, and in the end it had simply fizzled away. It was Louise who finally plucked up the courage to say what needed saying, but Thorne had known for a while that the break had to come, before such feelings as were left between them darkened and became destructive.

They had both kept their own flats, which made the practicalities straightforward enough. Louise had taken away a bin-liner stuffed with clothes and cosmetics from Thorne's place in Kentish Town, while Thorne had left Louise's flat for the last time with a carrier bag, a few tins of beer and a box of CDs. It had ended with a hug, but it might just as well have been a handshake. Loading his boxes and bags into the back of his car, Thorne had decided that it might be a good idea to change a whole lot of other things.

To start again . . .

He turned towards Finchley and almost immediately hit a tailback. No more than five miles now, but still half an hour or so away from Hendon, and Becke House. The headquarters of the Area West Murder Squad.

'Why the hell do you need to change your job?'

He had been out drinking with Phil Hendricks a few weeks before, and, as always, the Mancunian had not fought shy of giving his opinion.

11

Thorne shook his head, but had listened anyway. Hendricks' opinion was the one he most valued professionally and the same thing usually applied when it came to his private life, because the pathologist was the nearest thing he had to a best friend.

'Only friend,' Hendricks never tired of saying.

'Why not?' Thorne had asked.

'Because it's not . . . relevant. It's not *necessary*. It would be like me doing a post-mortem on some poor bugger who'd been shot twelve times in the head, then saying the fact he had hardened arteries and a slight heart condition might have had something to do with his death.'

'You're drunk,' Thorne had said.

'It's too much, that's all. Just because you've split up with someone doesn't mean you have to change everything. I mean, car . . . yes! The bloody thing was a death-trap and I'm not saying there's anything wrong with moving to a new flat either. We'll find you somewhere much nicer than that dump you're in now *and* I'll take you shopping for some decent furniture, but do you really need to be looking for a new job as well?'

'It's all part of it.'

'Part of what?'

'New start,' Thorne said. 'New broom . . . leaf, whatever.'

'You're drunker than I am . . . '

They had moved on to football then and Thorne's desolate sex life, but Thorne could see that Hendricks had a point, and he had thought about little else since. Even though he still believed he was doing the right thing in looking for a new challenge, the thought of leaving Area West Homicide made him feel slightly sick. The nature of the job and the politics of arse-covering meant that it was often hard to build up real trust between members of a team. Thorne had come to value the relationships he had with a number of those he worked with every day. Men and women he liked and respected. Plenty of idiots as well of course, but even so.

Better the devil you know, all that.

On the radio, Chris Evans was making him almost as angry as

12

Expresso Man, so Thorne turned it off. He switched to CD and scanned through the ten discs he had mounted in the changer. He turned up the volume at the familiar guitar lick and that first lovely rumble of the man's voice.

Johnny Cash: 'Ain't No Grave'.

'While you're busy changing things,' Hendricks had said, 'you could always do something about that stupid cowboy music.'

Thorne grinned, remembering the pained look on his friend's face, and pushed on through the traffic towards the office.

It was not as if he was going to take the first thing that came along. Chances were nothing suitable would present itself for a good while anyway, and by the time it did he might feel differently.

For now he would just do his job, wait and see what turned up.

THREE

As Helen backed away from the gun, she could see a face at the window over Akhtar's shoulder. One of the boys he had chased from the shop, open-mouthed at seeing what was happening inside. He shouted something to one of his friends before tearing away, down towards the station. If Akhtar heard it, he did not seem unduly concerned. He just kept walking towards Helen and the man standing next to her.

Good, Helen thought, that's good. At least now someone on the outside will know what the situation is and will alert the police. This was provided they believed it, of course. She could barely believe what was happening herself.

Mr Akhtar.

She could not say honestly that she knew the man, not really, but she had been coming into his shop for over a year. They'd spoken every day, no more than pleasantries, but still . . .

What the hell was he up to?

Pointing with the gun, Akhtar ushered Helen and the other customer around the counter and through a low archway into a cluttered storeroom behind the shop. Sitting on a battered wooden desk was a

14

television showing *Daybreak* with the sound turned down. There was a single chair, a filing cabinet and a small fridge in the corner with a kettle, some mugs and a jar of coffee on top. Aside from a small sink, almost every inch of space on three of the walls was taken up with cardboard boxes and stacked plastic pallets containing replacement stock.

Tinned goods, crisps, kitchen towel, cigarettes.

There were two doors. The one with bolts top and bottom and a heavy padlock was clearly an exterior door which Helen presumed opened out on to the alleyway that ran along the back of the shops. She guessed that the unpainted plywood door led to a toilet.

Akhtar said he was sorry that things were a little cramped and told them to stand against the one bare wall. He asked Helen if she had a mobile phone. She told him it was in her handbag. He told her to slide the bag across the floor towards him and told the man to slowly do the same with his mobile phone. Then, once he had taken a seat at the desk, he ordered them both to sink down on to their backsides. Without taking his eyes from them, he rooted around in one of the desk drawers before tossing two pairs of metal handcuffs across to Helen.

'Off the internet,' he said. 'Top of the range. Same as the ones you use, I think.'

Helen reached across and picked the cuffs up from the floor. 'It's not too late to stop this,' she said. 'Whatever it is you're doing, things are not too serious yet, OK? I mean I can't say for sure you'll stay out of prison, because of the gun, but if you let us go now I'll do everything I can to make sure that it's not too bad. Are you listening, Mr Akhtar?'

He smiled at Helen, a little oddly. Said, 'I would like you to handcuff one another to the radiator pipes. There is one at either end, see?'

Helen exchanged a look with the man slumped next to her, and nodded. She reached across and cuffed his right hand to the small pipe that ran down into the floor. When she had finished, though it had now become somewhat awkward and took rather longer, he did the same to her left hand.

15

'Don't worry,' the newsagent said. 'The radiator is not on, so you will not get too hot.' He looked at Helen. 'Nice weather, like you said.'

Helen could see that he was trying to make a joke, but she could also see the tension in his face and hear the tremor in his voice. She could see how frightened he was.

This was not necessarily a good thing.

Satisfied that his prisoners were secure, Akhtar stood up and walked back out into the shop. The man handcuffed next to Helen stared at the archway for a few seconds, then, apparently satisfied that the newsagent was not coming straight back, he turned to her.

'You're a copper, then?' Perhaps it was because he was trying to talk quietly, but his voice was soft and high. He was well spoken with just a trace of a London accent.

Helen looked at him and nodded.

He had short hair and was wearing a blue suit and patterned tie. He reached up with his free hand and yanked the tie loose, tore at the top button of his shirt. He was sweating.

'So what are you going to do?' he asked.

'Sorry?'

'What are you going to do about *this*?'

Helen looked at him. 'Well, there's not really a lot I can do. Not right this minute.'

The man's head dropped. 'Shit.'

'The first thing is that we need to stay calm, OK?'

'You don't understand, I've got a meeting this morning,' he said. 'A really important meeting.'

Helen almost laughed, but the impulse vanished when she saw the desperation on the man's face. She knew that such a reaction was not uncommon. She had heard about some of the victims of the 7 July bombings, stumbling up on to the street covered in blood, keen to tell police and paramedics that they would skip the visit to the hospital, thank you very much, that they needed to get to this or that appointment. This 'inverted' panic was a natural instinct in some; a refusal to accept that a situation could really be as serious as it was.

16

It's only a little bit of blood. It's just a gun . . .

'I think your meeting's going to have to wait,' Helen said.

They stared at one another for a few seconds, until she saw the wash of acceptance slide across his face. He nodded slowly and sat back against the radiator. Said, 'I'm Stephen, by the way.'

'Helen,' she said.

They both turned at the sudden noise from the front of the shop. A loud grind and clatter. Stephen looked at Helen and she raised her voice over the drone. 'He's closing the shutters on the shop.' They listened in silence until the squeals and clanking had finished, which told them that the solid metal shutters were now down, completely covering the shopfront.

'We're locked in,' Stephen said.

Helen was watching the doorway. 'I think it's more a question of locking everyone else out.'

They had been locked in anyway, of course, but something in the lowering of the shop's shutters, a change in the light perhaps, provoked an increased panic in the man. He began yanking at the cuffs which rattled and scraped against the radiator pipe, grunting with the effort that Helen knew was pointless.

'Don't,' she said.

Stephen just yanked even harder. He moved on to his knees and began swearing and shouting as he used his free hand to try and pull the radiator away from the wall.

'Please don't—'

When Akhtar walked back into the room, he could see that Stephen had changed his position but he did not seem concerned. He clearly had faith in the quality of the handcuffs and the strength of his radiator pipes. He spent a few minutes wrestling the heavy metal filing cabinet from against a wall and inching it, corner by corner, across the room until it was pushed up against the back door.

He was sweating profusely by the time he had finished. He sat down at the desk and wiped his face with a handkerchief, then fished the gun from his pocket and laid it down on the desktop.

He turned to look at Helen. 'You have been in my shop hundreds of times,' he said, 'but I still don't know your name.'

Despite the situation and the fact that her mind was racing as she struggled to make sense of it, Helen felt a peculiar pang of guilt. She told herself she was being ridiculous. Life in a city like London was full of relationships such as theirs. A few words exchanged every day and a necessary distance maintained. Did this man want more than that? Did he feel ... slighted? Rejected even? Was he interested in her *romantically*?

'Helen,' she said. 'Detective Sergeant Helen Weeks.'

He nodded. 'My name is Javed.' He looked over at the man sitting at the other end of the radiator. 'I'm very sorry that you have been caught up in all this, Mr ... ?'

Stephen was still breathing heavily. He did not look up. 'Stephen Mitchell.'

'I can only apologise, Mr Mitchell.'

'Listen, Javed—'

Akhtar cut Helen off. 'What kind of police officer are you, Miss Weeks?'

Helen was thrown by the question. 'I'm sorry?'

'In which area do you work? Do you investigate robberies, fraud? Murder?'

'I work on a Child Protection Unit,' Helen said.

'So not murder?'

'Sometimes ... '

'I need to speak to a police officer urgently.'

'So speak to me.' She was careful to keep her tone even and reasonable. 'Tell me what it is you want and we can sort all this out. Whatever your problem is, the sooner you let us go, the easier things will be.'

'You don't understand. I need to speak to a particular police officer, so I need you to help me.'

'I want to help you, but I can't—' The words caught in Helen's throat when she saw Akhtar's expression change and watched him

18

scrabble for the gun. She could see that, for the moment at least, he was done with being apologetic or reasonable.

'I need you to use your phone,' he shouted. 'I need you to call whoever you have to call to get this policeman here.'

He was waving the gun at them as he ranted and Helen was aware that, next to her, Mitchell was flinching each time Akhtar used the weapon to emphasise his wishes.

'You get him here *now*, OK?' Akhtar threw Helen's handbag back at her and she had to raise her free hand to stop it hitting her in the face. 'Get him here and I will tell you what to say when he comes.'

Outside a siren began to sound, and grew louder.

For a few seconds, Akhtar and Mitchell were both staring intently at her. Helen could feel the rage and the fear radiating from both of them and from inside herself. The heater at her back was not turned on, but might just as well have been.

'Who?' she asked.

Akhtar told her the name.

'I know him,' she said. 'Not well, but . . .'

'Good,' Akhtar said. 'That might help both of us.'

Helen's hand was shaking as she reached into her handbag for her phone.

FOUR

Thorne had just picked up his own 'hit of caffeine' from the ancient and grubby machine in the Incident Room and was walking towards his office, when Detective Chief Inspector Russell Brigstocke stepped out into the corridor in front of him.

'Don't take your coat off,' Brigstocke said.

'Bloody hell, can I finish my coffee?' Thorne saw the look on his senior officer's face and stopped smiling. 'What?'

'We've got a situation in south London.'

'South?' Thorne's squad worked the north and west of the city and rarely, if ever, ventured south of the river. Even when he wasn't working, Thorne tried to avoid crossing the water whenever possible.

'A Child Protection Unit in Streatham got a call from one of their officers who claims she's being held at gunpoint in a newsagent's in Tulse Hill.' Brigstocke glanced down at the scrap of paper in his hand. 'Sergeant Helen Weeks.'

'I know the name,' Thorne said. He tried to remember.

'The CPU found us on the intranet system and the call got put through to me. So—'

'She was the woman whose boyfriend got run down at the bus stop.

20

A year and a bit ago.' Thorne tried to picture the woman who had sat in his office, to whom he had briefly spoken at her partner's funeral. 'He was Job too, remember?'

'No, but it might be relevant.' Brigstocke shook his head. 'I've no idea at the moment. Point is—'

'Hang on, what's this got to do with us?'

'Not *us*,' Brigstocke said. '*You.*'

Thorne waited, already feeling an unwelcome tingle at the nape of his neck and starting to wish that he'd rung in sick.

'The newsagent has apparently asked for you.' The DCI was still staring at the scrap of paper as though trying to gain some insight from what was clearly limited information. 'Better make that "demanded", seeing as he's holding a gun on a police officer.'

'Have we got a name?'

'Akhtar.'

It was another name Thorne recognized, as Brigstocke had known he would. A surname, at least.

'That manslaughter case last year,' Thorne said. 'Right?'

'He's the kid's father,' Brigstocke said.

Thorne tried to picture the man, but the face would not come. He remembered an uncontrolled anger though, when the sentence had been announced, a fury the man had taken out vociferously on Thorne and his fellow officers outside the court. Despite having a good deal of sympathy for him, Thorne had tried to calm the man down, pointing out that he should be taking up his dissatisfaction with the judge and not the police.

Thorne remembered the tears when the man had finally walked away.

'So is that what this is all about?'

Brigstocke's shrug said: your guess is as good as mine.

'Doesn't make sense,' Thorne said. 'The trial was what, eight months ago? Nine?'

'Look, you know as much as I do,' Brigstocke said, brandishing the scrap of paper. 'I'll try and find out as much as I can while you're on your way down there.'

'Can I take Holland?'

'Just go.'

Thorne walked quickly back into the Incident Room, told Detective Sergeant Dave Holland to follow him and took the stairs two at a time down to the car park. He grabbed a magnetic blue light from the boot and tossed it to Holland before they climbed into Thorne's car.

Holland dropped the light at his feet and reached for the seatbelt. 'Any chance you might tell me where we're going?'

Thorne had shared such information as he had by the time the car was pulling out of Becke House and turning towards the north circular.

'Something different,' Holland said.

Thorne had to agree, but was not at all sure that 'different' was what he needed right now.

With the traffic thickening as they hit Park Lane at the height of the rush hour, Thorne suddenly remembered that Helen Weeks had been pregnant the last time he'd seen her. About to pop, more or less.

She would have a one-year-old by now.

'Let's get the blues on,' he said.

Holland reached down for the light, and plugged one end of its curly lead into the car's cigarette lighter.

Thorne could imagine Helen Weeks staring at a gun and thinking about her child. He put his foot down, and as Holland leaned out to attach the blue light to the BMW's roof, Thorne accelerated south towards Victoria and Vauxhall Bridge beyond.

'This doesn't sound right,' Holland said. 'Why's Akhtar suddenly losing it now, and why take a hostage?'

It was much the same thing Thorne had said to Brigstocke half an hour before. Holland had worked the original manslaughter case too and could clearly sense, as Thorne did, that there was something wrong with the picture.

'It's stupid,' Holland said.

Thorne shrugged. 'We'd be out of work if people weren't stupid.'

22

'You reckon he still blames you for the sentence?'

Up until the judge's sentencing, the Akhtar manslaughter case had been run-of-the-mill, even if the exact details of the offence itself had remained a little vague. Amin Akhtar and a friend, aged sixteen and seventeen respectively, had been attacked by a group of three young men, all about the same age as they were, on a street in Islington. One of the attackers – Lee Slater – had been carrying a kitchen knife, and during the melee that had followed, while Amin had been trying to protect his friend, Slater had been fatally stabbed with it.

In an effort to avoid prosecution, the two surviving attackers were naturally keen to distance themselves from their dead friend, but their version of events had differed wildly from the account given by Amin and *his* friend. There had been snow on the ground that night and they insisted that a harmless exchange of snowballs had simply got out of hand. Denying any direct involvement in the attack, they were at least willing to admit that Slater had been the attacker, but claimed consistently that Amin had been equally aggressive in snatching Slater's knife when it was dropped and using it to stab Slater to death. This was not of course how Amin and his friend saw things and though theirs was the story that most believed, the conflicting testimonies led to the Crown Prosecution Service deciding it would not be in the public interest to pursue any charges of assault or GBH, despite the injuries to both Asian boys. In the end, they had decided to proceed only with a charge of manslaughter against Amin and it had been one of the easiest cases Thorne had ever had to put together.

With at least some of the evidence pointing towards self-defence and given the defendant's previously unblemished character, the prosecution had been expecting a sentence of four years or perhaps even less. Nobody had been more astonished than Thorne when Amin Akhtar had been sent down for eight. Or more outraged than the boy's father.

Though he could still not quite picture the man, the ferocity of his anger had become even clearer. Screaming in Thorne's face on the steps of the Old Bailey. Shouting over and over again that the law had let him down.

'It sounds like I'm the one he wants,' Thorne said. Ahead of him, cars swerved into the bus lane as he tore down South Lambeth Road into Stockwell. 'Maybe he's taken Helen Weeks so he can swap one copper for another.'

'Jesus,' Holland said.

She would have a one-year-old by now ...

Thorne would do it, if that's what it came to, and he spent the rest of the high-speed journey south thinking about how he would handle things and trying to keep his hands steady on the wheel.

Imagining himself staring at a gun.

Wondering who *he* would be thinking about.

The road had been sealed off one hundred yards either side of the newsagent's. Squad cars blocked side streets as well as the main routes in and out, which not only meant disruption for dozens of householders but also for commuters using the mainline station at Tulse Hill and the staff and children at a local junior school, both of which were well within the area that had been cordoned off.

Thorne showed his warrant card and was waved through the cordon. On the pavements either side of him, uniformed officers were ushering residents to safety. Some were still in nightclothes, having been hurriedly evacuated.

He drove slowly down the hill towards the target location.

There were a number of cars and motorbikes parked alongside the small parade of shops. Thorne guessed that most would belong to people who had caught the train into work, though it might now be a while before they could be claimed. He could see a police van and several more squad cars at the bottom of the hill on the far side of the station. He pulled over on the same side of the road as two Armed Response Vehicles and got out of the car.

He stared across at the shop.

The metal shutters were covered in graffiti though only the word *PAKI* was legible.

There were five or six armed officers standing around the two specially adapted BMWs, and, as Thorne and Holland walked towards them, it was clear from their stance and the almost casual conversations taking place that they had yet to be constructively deployed. With the shutters down there was nothing to take aim at and, with the shop based inside a single-storey unit, there was no possibility that the man inside could be taking aim at them.

They were waiting for orders.

Just before Thorne and Holland reached them, Thorne's mobile rang.

'I think I've got your "why",' Brigstocke said.

'I'm listening.'

'Amin Akhtar killed himself in Barndale Young Offenders Institution eight weeks ago. Tom . . . '

Holland looked at him, waiting to be told.

Thorne just swore under his breath and carried on walking towards the men with the guns, while Brigstocke gave him the sordid details.

FIVE

The leader of the CO19 Firearms Unit was a squat and surly individual named Chivers. He pointed Thorne and Holland towards the junior school at the far end of the street opposite, which had been designated as the RVP or Rendezvous Point and was being hurriedly transformed into a temporary Incident Room. Walking away, Thorne was thinking that Chivers had seemed irritated by the situation, bored even. One of those types for whom things were pretty tedious unless they were kicking in a door somewhere and spraying bullets around.

Thorne could only hope for everyone's sake that, as far as Inspector Chivers was concerned, this particular situation would remain as dull as ditchwater.

There was another gaggle of uniforms at the school gates. Staff and children were still being moved off the premises and, to his left, Thorne could see a small crowd behind the cordon, many angrily demanding to know what was happening. Some would be disgruntled parents, but the majority, he knew, were there for no other reason than to gawp and there would be plenty more of them as the day wore on and word spread.

It would not be long before the media arrived in numbers.

Thorne and Holland were escorted across the playground, through the main doors and into the echoing hall. Most of the plastic chairs had been stacked at one end and a series of trestle tables erected in front of the small stage. Uniformed and plain-clothes officers were shunting equipment about, their boots squeaking on the polished wooden floor, shouting and swearing as they rushed to get set up.

It still smelled like school though.

'That takes me back,' Holland said, breathing it in deep. 'Reminds me of crayons and sweaty socks.'

Thorne sighed theatrically. 'I was thinking about the dinner lady I was in love with,' he said. 'And a little tosser named Dean Turner who used to steal my milk. Until Margaret Thatcher stole everyone's, of course.'

Holland clearly did not understand the reference. 'You used to have milk at school?'

'Are you Thorne?'

They turned to see a tall man in full dress uniform walking towards them and Thorne did not need to see the crown on the man's shoulder to know that he was looking at a superintendent. He was in his early forties, with sandy hair cropped close to the scalp and a nose that looked to have been broken more than once. In a low voice and with a trace of a northern accent, the officer introduced himself as Mike Donnelly and explained that as the local superintendent on call that morning, he had by default become the Silver Commander; the head of the operation on-site. He did not sound overly thrilled about the fact. This could easily be due to a lack of experience in situations such as this, Thorne thought, but might simply be down to the shortage of information thus far.

'So, what do we think Akhtar wants?'

'Me, by all accounts,' Thorne said.

Donnelly nodded. He clearly had a habit of nodding and grunting in what sounded like agreement, whenever anybody else was talking. It was a strategy Thorne was familiar with, and one he had not been beyond adopting himself once or twice. It looked as though you were listening, paying attention. It gave the appearance of being thoughtful, even if all you were actually thinking was that you were out of your depth.

'You don't think this might be a Muslim thing?' Donnelly looked from Thorne to Holland and back again.

'A *thing*?'

'Come on, you know what I mean.'

'I don't think so.'

'Just throwing it out there,' Donnelly said. 'Got to consider every angle at this stage, right?'

Holland shrugged. 'Fair enough.'

'That's not what this is about,' Thorne said. He told Donnelly what Brigstocke had said on the phone.

Donnelly thought about it for a while. 'Now that's not good news for anyone. Least of all Detective Sergeant Weeks.' He excused himself, saying he needed to check on how the evacuation was going, then handed Thorne a transcript of the call made by Helen Weeks just over an hour before. There was a small CD player on the table and Donnelly leaned across to press *PLAY* before he turned and walked away.

Holland peered over Thorne's shoulder to read the transcript as they listened to the recording.

Call from 07785 455787. 08.17 am
– Child Protection Unit, Gill Bellinger.
– Gill, it's Helen, and I need you to just shut up and listen, OK?
   Pause.
   – I'm listening . . .
   – I need you to get hold of a DI Tom Thorne for me. He's Area West Murder Squad, or at least he was a year or so ago.
   Voice in the background. Indistinct.
   – It's very important that you get hold of him, OK? You need to do it now.
   – What's going on?

– I'm being held at gunpoint in a newsagent's on Norwood Road. Near the junction with Christchurch Road . . . just up from the station.

Voice in the background. Number 287.

– Number 287.

– Jesus—

– Make whatever calls you need to make, OK? But first get hold of DI Thorne. The man who's holding us wants him here.

– Who's holding you?

Voice in the background. Indistinct.

– I need to go, Gill . . . just get on the phone . . .

Call ends. 08.18 am.

'Akhtar seems happy enough to tell us exactly where he is,' Holland said.

'He wanted us here as fast as possible.'

'She sounds nervous.'

'Really, Dave? I can see why you sailed through those sergeant's exams.' Thorne saw Donnelly coming back and held up his mobile. 'Why don't I call her?'

Donnelly nodded, but was looking around. 'Let's make sure all the key people are listening in first, shall we?' He asked a passing uniform to go outside and fetch the CO19 team leader. Then he waved across a young woman from the other side of the hall. He turned back to Thorne. 'You met Chivers?'

Thorne nodded. 'Ex-military?'

'He told you?'

'Shot in the dark,' Thorne said.

The woman arrived at Donnelly's side. She was somewhere in her early thirties, Thorne guessed; above average height and skinny. Her dark hair was cut in a shaggy bob, and she wore a tailored leather jacket over jeans. She looked relaxed enough, but Thorne could not be sure how much of an effort she was making. Donnelly laid a hand on her arm. She glanced down at it for just a second, before smiling a little nervously at Thorne as the superintendent made the introductions.

29

'This is Sue Pascoe,' he said. 'She's here as our trained hostage negotiator and I hear very good things.'

Pascoe shook hands with Thorne and Holland. Donnelly told her they were just waiting for Chivers and she nodded.

'Done much of this?' Thorne asked.

'Enough,' Pascoe said.

Thorne was not aware of any full-time hostage negotiators in the Met and guessed that 'trained' just meant that Pascoe had been on the requisite course. He'd been on one himself a few years before, but one focused on how to cope should you find yourself being held hostage. A weekend at some cheap hotel off the M25, where for many, learning anything had come a poor second to heavy sessions in the bar or trying to pull. It was all the stuff you would expect: forging a bond with your captor; finding common ground; encouraging them to see you as a human being. All those techniques that might help keep you alive as long as possible.

He hoped that Helen Weeks had been on the same course, that she had not been one of those on the sniff or pissing it up the wall.

Chivers came through the doors and took off his helmet as he walked across to join them. Ignoring Thorne, Holland and Pascoe, he acknowledged Donnelly with a nod, his hand falling automatically to the handle of the Glock 17 on his belt, holstered next to a pair of 8 Bang stun grenades.

The superintendent told Thorne to make the call.

'Nice and easy,' Pascoe said. 'Obviously we need as much information as possible, but it's important to be reassuring. Nothing's a problem at this stage.'

'I'll try and remember that,' Thorne said. He checked the number on the sheet and dialled, then switched the phone on to speaker as it began to ring.

'Here we go,' Donnelly said.

It was answered almost immediately.

'Helen?'

'Yes?'

'It's Tom Thorne. Are you all right? Can you talk freely?'

Helen Weeks said that she could. That she was fine.

'Tell Mr Akhtar that I know about what happened to his son, and that I'm sorry.'

They listened as the message was relayed. Nothing was said in response.

'Helen? Can I talk to him?'

Helen asked the question, then said, 'He wants you to talk to me for the time being.'

'OK, listen. Tell him that I'm willing to trade places. It's me he asked for, so if he lets you walk out of there, he can take me instead.' Thorne became aware of Pascoe waving a 'no' at him, and of Donnelly gesticulating furiously, clearly annoyed that such an offer had not been discussed with him. He turned back to the phone. 'Helen ... ?'

'That's not what he wants,' Helen said.

Donnelly leaned in close to Thorne and whispered, 'Ask who's in there with her. We've got a witness who claims there was another customer in the shop.'

'Are there any other hostages?' Thorne asked.

'He's called Stephen Mitchell,' Helen said. A man's voice said something, then Helen gave out an address in Tulse Hill.

Donnelly scribbled it down and handed the piece of paper to a uniformed officer who hurried out of the hall.

'So, what does he want?' Thorne asked.

The exchange that followed was punctuated by a series of pauses and muffled conversations as Helen passed on Thorne's questions, listened to Akhtar, then relayed his responses. 'He says that his son did not kill himself ... that he would never kill himself. He says that the truth has been covered up. You are the one that sent his son to prison ... so you are the one who must find out who murdered him.'

Thorne glanced up. Saw that all eyes were on him. 'Tell him that we'll mount a full reinvestigation into his son's death, but that we need to end this situation now.'

While they were waiting for a response, Donnelly scribbled *RELEASE MITCHELL?* on a piece of paper and passed it to Thorne.

'He says it will end when you find out what happened to his son.'

'Tell him that we're happy to listen to him,' Thorne said. 'Tell him that I'll do what I can, but that we need an act of faith on his part. Tell him that he needs to let Mr Mitchell go.'

Next to him, Sue Pascoe was shaking her head. 'Never going to happen,' she said.

'He says no,' Helen said.

They could hear the newsagent shouting now.

'He says he *had* faith in the law, but not any more . . . so you need to do what he wants, or things will only get a lot worse.'

Thorne glanced up to see Donnelly and Chivers exchange a knowing look. Donnelly closed his eyes.

'You have to prove that Amin did not commit suicide,' Akhtar said. 'To find out who killed him and why. Or . . . '

'It's OK, Helen.' Thorne and everyone else had heard Akhtar clearly enough and Thorne did not want Helen to have to say it.

To hear the terror in her voice.

'Or I will shoot them both.'

SIX

When the call had ended, Helen laid her phone down on the floor in front of her and looked up at Akhtar sitting at the desk. He was breathing heavily and muttering to himself. He seemed pleased about how the conversation with Tom Thorne had gone. He looked back at her.

Said, 'Thank you.'

'So, what happens now?' Helen asked.

Akhtar stood up. He was holding the gun. Next to her, Helen felt Stephen Mitchell flinch.

'Turn the phone off,' Akhtar said.

'What if they want to talk to you? If there's news.'

'When I'm ready.'

He pointed the gun and Helen did as she was asked.

'Now you must try and make yourselves comfortable, and we will hope that Detective Thorne is as good as his word.'

'He will be,' Helen said.

'And is also good at his job.' Akhtar thought about this for a few moments then walked out through the archway into his shop.

Helen and Mitchell said nothing for a minute or more, then Mitchell spoke quietly, without raising his head.

'Why wouldn't he let me go?'

'I don't know.'

'This is all about you, right?' He looked up and glared at her. 'Because you're a copper and he knows they'll take it more seriously.' He spoke quickly, hissing out the words. 'So why the hell do *I* have to be here? What's the point of both of us going through this?'

'You need to shut up and stay calm,' Helen said. Mitchell looked away. Helen could see that he felt bad about what he had said, but that he was also terrified. 'Listen, it's OK. You're not the only one who's scared to death.'

Mitchell nodded slowly. They could hear Akhtar moving about in the shop.

'Will they tell my wife?' Mitchell asked.

'Course they will.'

'She'll be in bits.' He tried to smile. 'She's even less brave than I am.'

'They'll look after her,' Helen said.

Mitchell let out a long slow breath and straightened his legs.

'What do you do, Stephen?'

'I work in a bank,' he said. 'On Tottenham Court Road. I was up for a promotion today.'

'Sorry.'

'You think that something like this might happen in a bank, you know? Some nutter with a gun. Or a post office, maybe. Not a bloody newsagent's.'

'Wrong place, wrong time,' Helen said. She knew better than most that this was what actually lay behind the majority of violent crime. You walked into the wrong pub, turned the wrong corner, strolled blithely through an estate in the wrong postcode. It was understandable, being scared of boys with knives or men with bombs, but what people really needed to be frightened about was simply being unlucky.

'There'll be armed police outside by now, won't there?' Mitchell looked towards the back door. 'Snipers or whatever. I've seen this kind of thing on the news.'

Helen said that she thought there would be a Firearms Unit on standby, that they would probably be sealing off the shop. She told him that whoever was running things outside would know what they were doing.

'So what are they likely to do?' Mitchell lowered his voice still further. 'What's normally the plan with things like this?'

'There isn't one,' Helen said.

'Oh . . . OK.'

'It's always different and there isn't any set . . . protocol. They'll wait and see what happens.'

Mitchell seemed to take this on board, the idea that, in all probability, nothing would happen quickly. But Helen could see that he was far from reassured and she could hardly blame him. Aside from Akhtar unlocking their handcuffs, opening the shutters and letting them walk out of there, anything that happened was likely to be dangerous for all concerned.

She sat back and listened. Akhtar had stopped moving around, but then she heard the tell-tale sound of pages being turned.

'He's reading the paper,' Mitchell whispered. 'Looking through the paper like nothing's happening.'

Helen was still trying to decide how Akhtar himself was handling things, how *he* was coping. She knew it was important. Could this man who held a gun as though it were a poisonous snake really be that calm? Or was he making as much effort as possible to appear that way?

Whatever the truth was, and whatever Tom Thorne was up to on the outside, they needed Javed Akhtar to remain calm if they were going to stay safe. She and the man from the bank would need to do everything they could to keep him relaxed.

They stiffened when the newsagent appeared suddenly in the doorway. He raised a hand, as though apologising for worrying them. Then he calmly laid the gun down on the desk and asked if they wanted tea.

Thorne was in the playground, on the phone.

He had already called Brigstocke to bring him up to speed and to ensure that all the paperwork pertaining to the suicide at Barndale be sent across to his office at Becke House. He had also requested that a copy of the post-mortem be faxed to Phil Hendricks as soon as possible. Finally, Thorne had told Brigstocke to make contact with whoever had led the original inquiry into Amin Akhtar's death and ask the officer to call him immediately.

To his credit, DI Martin Dawes had called back within ten minutes.

'Did you not think it might be a good idea to let us know what had happened to Amin Akhtar?' Thorne asked.

'It wasn't connected with your manslaughter case.'

'Just as a courtesy, then.'

Dawes was clearly not the type to give ground. 'So you always need to know what's happened to everyone you've put away, do you?'

There were a few – the ones who had genuinely scared him – that Thorne would always keep a close eye on, but Dawes had a fair point. Besides, Thorne did not have time for a pissing contest.

'Can you run me through it?'

Dawes told Thorne that Amin Akhtar had killed himself with a drug overdose two months earlier, that he was found dead in Barndale's hospital wing. His body had been discovered first thing in the morning and he had been pronounced dead at the scene by the YOI doctor.

'What was he doing in the hospital wing?'

'He'd been assaulted four days before by another boy. Had his face sliced open, basically.'

'Enough reason to suddenly top himself?' Thorne asked. 'I mean he'd already been in there, what, seven months?'

'He'd also been raped,' Dawes said.

'In the *hospital* wing?'

'Could have been. The pathologist couldn't be sure exactly when the rape had taken place, but the CCTV camera that should have been covering the area the kid's room was in had been moved the week before, so anything's possible.'

'Why?'

'Why was he raped? How the hell should I know?'

36

'I meant why was the camera moved?'

Dawes laughed. 'Sorry ... apparently there'd been a lot of stuff going missing from the dispensary, heavy-duty painkillers or what have you, so they stuck the camera on that instead. Akhtar probably knew where the camera was. Knew nobody would be watching when he started popping his pills.'

Thorne thought about that. 'No other cameras?'

'One on the entrance to the wing and one inside another of the private rooms. Bugger all on any of them.'

Looking across the playground, Thorne could see Holland talking to Sue Pascoe by the main doors into the school. Holland said something and Pascoe laughed.

'What's the big drama anyway?' Dawes asked. 'Your DCI was a bit vague.'

Thorne guessed that Brigstocke had simply been in a hurry, but saw no reason to keep Dawes in the dark about what was happening. He gave him the highlights.

'I'd love to say I was surprised,' Dawes said.

'Sorry?'

'The father always looked to me like he was close to the edge. You know what I mean?'

'Why don't you tell me?'

'Well, for a kick-off he went a bit mental after the inquest, shouting and screaming at the coroner. At anybody who would listen, basically. Going on about a cover-up, telling us we'd got it wrong, all that.'

'When was this?'

'A couple of weeks ago. Yeah, he was definitely cracking up, I reckon.'

Pressed for time as he was, Thorne was not about to let this one go. 'Again, you didn't think it might be worth picking up the phone and letting us know?'

'Letting you know what exactly? That some newsagent was losing the plot? You're being stupid.'

'You're an idiot,' Thorne said. Dawes started to protest, but Thorne hung up, and went to meet Donnelly who was coming towards him across the playground.

'The wife's arrived,' Donnelly said. The superintendent nodded towards the main gates and Thorne turned to watch a WPC helping a middle-aged Indian woman out of a squad car. 'Nadira.'

Thorne remembered her. The woman looked every bit as dazed, as lost, as she had the last time he'd seen her. The day her son had been sent to prison. 'I could really do with talking to her,' Thorne said. He looked at his watch. It was more than half an hour since he had spoken to Helen Weeks and she had relayed Akhtar's instructions. 'Why don't I do it on the way to Barndale?'

Donnelly thought about it. 'What if we need her here? Sue Pascoe thinks she might be able to use her. Get her to talk to her husband.'

'So send a car to follow me and bring her back afterwards,' Thorne said. 'I only need ten minutes.'

They both looked up at the sound of a helicopter overhead. Thorne was impressed at the scale of the police operation until he saw the Sky logo on the aircraft's side. He looked at Donnelly.

'It was only a matter of time,' Donnelly said.

A few seconds later, Chivers came marching through the gates and across the playground. He was pointing angrily at the circling helicopter. 'You need to get them out of here now,' he said.

Donnelly muttered something about the freedom of the press, but Chivers was having none of it.

'Listen, we've not got a clue about what our target is up to behind those shutters, right? But if he's got a TV in there, thanks to those idiots he's going to know exactly what *we're* doing. Do I make my point?'

Donnelly nodded. 'I'll see what I can do.'

'So, what about the wife then?' Thorne asked.

Donnelly looked flustered. It was clear that Chivers hadn't finished with him yet. 'Ten minutes,' he said.

Thorne walked towards his car, beckoning Holland away from his conversation with Pascoe as he went. When Holland had caught him up, Thorne told him to get back to the office as quickly as he could. 'Get Yvonne Kitson on this. While I'm at Barndale, I want the two of you looking at anyone who might have wanted Amin killed. You might as well start with Lee Slater's family, they've got a decent enough motive, then talk to the other two kids who were with Slater the night Amin was attacked. We'll stay in touch by phone, OK?'

Holland ran a hand through his hair. 'I don't get it,' he said.

'Get what?'

'Why we're doing this.' Holland stopped walking. 'The kid killed himself. I mean it's a shame and all that, and I can see why his old man's upset, but we're not going to change anything by charging about looking for non-existent murderers.'

'You heard what he said.' Thorne took a few steps back towards Holland, put a heavy hand between his shoulder blades and pointed him towards the shuttered-up shop. 'What he wants and what he's threatening to do if he doesn't get it.'

'I heard, but we can't create a murder when there wasn't one.'

'What if he's right though?'

'What are the chances of that? He's a nutcase, you know he is.'

Thorne was starting to lose his temper, but did not raise his voice. 'So what, you think we should do nothing?'

'He doesn't know what we're doing, does he? Why can't we just tell him we've looked into it and that we couldn't find anything.'

'That might almost be a half-decent plan, Dave ... if Helen Weeks wasn't sitting in there with a gun pointed at her.'

Holland shook his head, still unconvinced.

'Just get on with it, *Sergeant*.'

Having signalled to the WPC who was looking after Nadira Akhtar, Thorne walked quickly out of the playground and down the street to his car. When the newsagent's wife had settled, somewhat nervously, into the passenger seat, Thorne nodded a hello then pulled away; driving slowly and saying nothing until he was through the cordon.

Then he put his foot down.

'Tell me about your son,' he said.

SEVEN

'Tell me about your son . . . '

Akhtar was perched awkwardly on the edge of the small chair. He looked down at Helen. He picked up his mug of tea from the desk, then put it down again. He straightened out some papers that were scattered around.

'Tell me what he was like, Javed.'

Akhtar started to speak, cleared his throat then started again. 'He was always good,' he said. 'You know?'

'Yes, I remember,' Helen said. She was not actually sure which of Akhtar's sons she remembered being served by on several occasions, but as things stood it did not really matter. 'Whenever he was in the shop he was always very polite. Very helpful.'

'He always tried to do the right thing,' Akhtar said. 'We all did. Now look where it's got us.'

'Why was he in prison?'

Akhtar shook his head as though it were a long story, or else one he could still not quite believe. 'He was trying to protect a friend, that's all. They were doing nothing wrong and they were set upon. It was all a mess, a big mess . . . '

Helen nodded, happy to let him continue. Next to her, Mitchell was still and silent. He had not drunk the tea Akhtar had made for him, not said a word since the newsagent had come back into the room. He sat staring at the floor, his chin on his chest, breathing deeply.

'We were told that he would be OK,' Akhtar said. 'They promised us, the police officers and the bloody lawyers. They said he would be OK and that they would be lenient. Liars, all of them. Lying bastards.' There was anger in his voice, but it was controlled. 'He was just a boy, for heaven's sake, and we trusted them because we were trying to do the right thing. You understand?'

'Of course I do,' Helen said.

He nodded. He seemed pleased, but he was studying her.

It was good that they were talking, Helen knew that. She needed to convince him that she did understand, and more, that she sympathised. She needed him to believe that she was on his side and that they would sort everything out together.

That when this was all over, they would walk out of the shop as friends.

'What happened to him?'

Akhtar grunted. 'Well, there is what happened and what they *say* happened and they are two very different things.'

'What do they say happened?'

'He was attacked, *again*. He was attacked and later on he took his own life, but I know my son, believe me. It is not true.'

'Had he been all right, up to then? When you visited him?'

'He was not happy, of course he wasn't. We talked about the appeal and all that and we tried to stay in good spirits, but it was clear enough in his face. He would not have been able to stand it in that place for so long.' He raised a hand, eager to make a point. 'But that did not mean he would ever do harm to himself, not at all.'

'Did he have friends in there?'

'There was one boy he spoke about, but I think he tried to keep to himself as much as possible. He was always quiet, you understand? Always studying, studying, studying.'

41

'Sounds like a bright lad,' Helen said.

'Yes, yes, very bright, but in my opinion that only makes it worse. It is more frustrating for someone like my son in one of those places. He did not belong there.'

'When did you see him last?'

Akhtar blinked slowly, remembering. 'One week before he died. He was cheerful and we talked about his sister's birthday and what I could buy for her. To give her as a gift from him, you know? He missed her and his elder brother very much ... *very* much, and this is another reason I know that he was not responsible for his own death.' He shook his head, waved the flat of his hand in front of him, the certainty bringing a half-smile to his face. 'He could never have chosen not to see them again.'

'Why do you think they say that he did?' Helen was careful to sound as incredulous as possible. She shook her head, as though the very notion were preposterous.

'You ask them.' Akhtar spat the words out. 'Because they are liars like the police officers and the lawyers from the bloody CPS. Maybe because it is easier and will cause less trouble. Nobody wants to admit that anyone could be killed in a place like that. That such things are allowed to happen.' He leaned towards her, the anger building again. 'But they are allowed to happen. They *were* allowed and now Amin will never see his sister get married, will never have the life he was working so hard for.'

He shook his head and bit back whatever was coming next. He reached across to the desktop and moved the gun a few inches closer to him. He leaned back in his chair. 'Now it is up to your friend Tom Thorne to find out the truth.'

Helen barely knew Thorne, though she had formed a good opinion about him based on how he had behaved during the investigation into Paul's death the year before. Now, she realised, she was counting on him every bit as much as Akhtar was. Tom Thorne had suddenly become the best friend she had.

'I know he'll do his best,' she said.

★

'My son is dead,' Nadira Akhtar said. She spoke quietly and without colour. 'That's all, it's finished.' She turned her head away and stared out at the concrete blur of the A40 moving past the window.

Thorne accelerated to overtake a white van, gave the driver a good hard look. 'Javed doesn't think it's finished.'

She turned to look at him. 'My husband is ...' She waved the thought away and went back to her view.

'Stupid? Stubborn?'

'He is not stupid. Never that.'

'What he's doing is stupid,' Thorne said. 'It's beyond stupid.' He waited for a response, but none was forthcoming. 'You know what's going on in the shop?'

She nodded. 'They told me.'

'Did you have any idea he was going to do something like this?'

'Of course not.'

'You knew he was angry though, right?'

'Javed has been angry for a long time.'

Barndale was a medium-sized Young Offenders Institution thirty-five miles north-west of London; its location in an area of lush Buckinghamshire countryside a constant source of irritation to the well-heeled residents in the nearby towns of Chorleywood and Amersham. From Javed Akhtar's shop, Thorne had driven north and crossed the river at Chelsea Bridge. The blue light cleared a path through the traffic into Earls Court and Kensington until he picked up the Westway at White City. Even without the flashing light, it was only ten minutes in the outside lane from there to the M40, then a couple of junctions on the M25 and they would be there. No more than forty minutes all told.

'Javed doesn't think that Amin killed himself,' Thorne said. 'He wants me to prove it. To find out what happened.'

Nadira laughed derisively. 'I want to win the lottery, so what?'

'You're not holding people at gunpoint until you do though.'

She turned to him. She was ashen. She said, 'What is it that you want?'

'You can start by telling me you think he's wrong. About what happened at Barndale.'

'My son took his own life,' she said. She might have been telling Thorne her son's name or how old he was. A simple statement of fact. 'He could not cope with what had happened to him. What was happening to him every day. He was not . . . a hard boy.'

'So why does your husband believe that he was killed?'

She thought about it for half a minute. 'It's easier for him to believe that, perhaps. He likes to think that everyone is lying to him.' She stretched her legs out, but they still did not reach the end of the footwell. 'He doesn't really sleep any more, so there is a lot of time for brooding on things and for foolish ideas to take hold.'

'What about you?' Thorne asked.

'Me, what?'

'How are you sleeping?'

She gave a small shrug, and smoothed out the material of her sari against her legs. 'I have some pills. It's fine.' She glanced at Thorne. 'You have to move on.'

Nadira Akhtar sounded fine. She spoke as if she had come to terms with what had happened to her son in a way that her husband had not, but Thorne could sense the anguish beneath the matter-of-fact exterior. He knew this was how couples coped sometimes. How they handled disaster. There was little point in both partners going to pieces and, if one did, the other had to at least maintain the pretence of getting on with things. Hadn't he and Louise done much the same thing after the miscarriage?

All a front, of course, but one that had served its purpose for a time.

Nadira had other children, a life to live, a business to keep afloat. It was understandable that she should at least seem to have adjusted to the death of her youngest child so much better than Javed.

'You'll need to help him,' Thorne said.

Before Nadira could answer, her mobile rang. She fished it from her bag, then spoke in Hindi for a few minutes. She sounded agitated, but had calmed down by the time she ended the call.

'My eldest son,' she explained. 'He is waiting for me back there, with the police. He is very upset.'

'I'll get you back as soon as I can.' Thorne checked in his rear-view and raised a hand to the driver of the squad car that had followed him from south London. The squad car flashed its lights in acknowledgement. 'There's an officer on the scene who specialises in these situations,' he said. 'She thinks you might be able to help. That it might be good if you talked to Javed.'

'We would only argue,' Nadira said. 'He won't listen to me.'

'Will you try?'

She took a deep breath and closed her eyes.

'There's a woman in there with your husband who has a young child. She's very scared.'

'He won't hurt anyone.'

'Are you certain about that?'

She reached into her bag and produced a wad of tissues. She clutched it in her fist. 'Before Amin died, I would have laughed out loud if you had told me what Javed was doing. Like it was some practical joke off a TV show or something. He would never hurt anyone, you know? If there were boys in the shop stealing things or messing around, he would talk to them. He would ask them very quietly why they were wasting their time taking chocolate bars or what have you, until they felt guilty and most of the time they would not do it again. He taught them respect. He was always calm and he would never raise his hand.' She pressed the tissues to the corner of each eye. 'Now though, I cannot be so sure . . . '

They were approaching the turnoff and Thorne told her that he would pull over as soon as they had left the motorway. That the car behind would take her back to her eldest son.

She shook her head. 'I want to go with you. I want to see the place.'

Thorne looked at her.

'I never visited him,' she said, quietly. 'I could not do it. I made food for him and sent it along with Javed, but I did not want to see him in there.'

'I understand,' Thorne said.

'Do you?'

Thorne's mother came suddenly into his mind. It was, as always, a pleasant surprise, for even though she was always lurking somewhere, it was Jim and not Maureen whose ghost usually shouted the loudest, who demanded the lion's share of headspace. That made sense of course. After all, had it not been for Thorne, his father would not be a ghost at all.

He remembered them coming home from some party or other. The key in the door as they and another couple arrived back, shushing and giggling, the goodbyes as the babysitter left and then the music starting. She crept into his room, and he recalled the wine on her breath as she bent to kiss him, the guitars and the voices from downstairs.

'It's nice here,' Nadira said.

They were driving through countryside within a few minutes of leaving the motorway. They passed Chorleywood Common, then turned north across the canal into an area with dense woodland on both sides and carpets of bluebells along the edge of the narrow road.

'I never thought it would be.'

Unable to sleep, he had crept down in his pyjamas, no more than nine or ten, and she had come out to use the toilet and found him sitting on the stairs. She had brought him into the living room and he had sat between her and his father on the sofa for half an hour while they and their friends talked and drank some more. She had sung along with Patsy Cline and George Jones, singing the words to him, and he had seen his father rolling his eyes, the same way Holland and Kitson did now, and he had never told them that he had got it from her.

Football from the old man and the music from her. Gilzean, Perryman and Jennings from Jim. Hank, Merle and Johnny from Maureen. The beat and the fiddles and the hairs on his neck standing up beneath his pyjama top at the cry of what he would later learn was called the pedal steel.

All those voices and the wine on her breath.

'You know, as green as this,' Nadira said. 'I wasn't expecting so many trees.'

She did not speak again until they drew within sight of Barndale, but when they did, her expression was enough to tell Thorne that she did not think the view was particularly nice any more.

As the BMW slowed for the security gate, she asked Thorne to pull over and she climbed out as soon as the car had stopped.

The prison had been established on Ministry of Defence land on the site of an old RAF base. The original building had been added to many times over the years, each new block seemingly greyer and more depressing than the last, as though the budgets had not run to anything as flash and fancy as imagination. Acres of brick and metal loomed beyond the barrier, and coils of razor wire ran along the top of the green fence that stretched away in each direction from the main entrance.

Nadira stared, unblinking, through the wire. The wind had picked up and was coming hard and noisy across the fields of stubbled corn on either side. When she spoke, Thorne had to lean in close to hear what she was saying.

'I can't blame him . . .'

She said something else, but Thorne lost it on the wind and it was clear enough that it was meant for no one but herself.

After another minute or so, she turned to Thorne and nodded. She had seen all she needed to see. She turned to walk back towards the waiting squad car, then, after a few steps, she stopped just for a moment and said, 'I will try and think about what to say to Javed.'

Thorne watched the car turn round and head back towards the motorway, then got back into the BMW and drove up to the checkpoint. He was quickly waved through and directed towards the visitors' car park, but parked in one of the staff places instead, because it was slightly closer and because he felt like it.

Then he walked towards the building where Amin Akhtar had died.

EIGHT

Roger Bracewell, the governor, was younger than Thorne had been expecting, floppy-haired and well spoken. Hugh Grant with trendy spectacles. He pushed a collection of files across the desk, bound with a thick elastic band and labelled.

A name, date of birth, prisoner number.

'This is everything on Amin Akhtar,' he said. 'Admission papers, progress reports, course assessments and so on.' He sat back from his desk. 'I was asked to get everything together in a hurry, so ...' He waited, as if expecting thanks or explanation, but none was forthcoming. 'Nobody's seen fit to let me know the reason for all the rush, but ours is not to question why, I suppose.'

Thorne lifted the files from the desk and dropped them on the floor by the side of his chair. 'We're investigating Amin Akhtar's death,' he said. '*Re*-investigating.' He saw no reason to explain anything to Bracewell. He did not want anyone he would be talking to at Barndale knowing what his agenda might be, besides which they would all know soon enough, when they switched on a television or opened the evening paper.

'Right,' Bracewell said.

The governor's office lay at the far end of a warren of interconnected offices in the prison's administration block. With modern furniture and venetian blinds at the windows, it was rather less imposing than some Thorne had visited. There were no antique clocks or dusty paintings of hunting scenes on the wall. There was no portrait of the Queen.

'Horrible business,' Bracewell said. He reached for the mug of coffee that had been brought in soon after Thorne had arrived. 'Sure I can't offer you some biscuits or something?'

Thorne said that he was fine. Took a sip of his own coffee.

'Worst thing that can happen, obviously.' Bracewell tapped at the edge of the wooden desk. 'Thankfully we've got a pretty good record as far as suicides go, but it's always a possibility. They'll always find some way of doing it if they're determined enough.'

'Tell me about Amin,' Thorne said.

Bracewell leaned back again, cradling his mug. 'Kept himself to himself,' he said. 'Studied hard, did as he was asked. Stayed away from trouble.' He pointed down to the files on the floor. 'It's all in there.'

'I'll go through them later on.'

'We run a mentoring scheme here, something I introduced a year or so ago. We team up the more trusted of the older boys with some of the younger ones who look like they might be having a problem adjusting. A buddy system, if you want to call it that. Amin was certainly one of those I would have asked to do some mentoring for me.'

'Why didn't you?'

'Not much point as he was moving on.'

'Over there?' Thorne nodded towards the window, the building a hundred yards away on the other side of a large, well-maintained courtyard. Barndale was a split-site prison, with three separate estates whose inmates were divided by age. The Juvenile site, where Amin Akhtar had been held, housed boys between fifteen and eighteen. The population was fed from a Secure Training Unit holding younger boys and itself fed directly on to the Young Offenders Institution for those aged eighteen to twenty-one. The three sites had different governors and management teams, but while each prison was autonomous, key members of staff moved between them on a regular basis and they shared sports facilities, a reception area and a hospital wing.

'No,' Bracewell said. 'He was being transferred.'

'Where?'

'He wanted to do an A-level course in Pure Maths, whatever that is, and unfortunately we don't do an awful lot beyond woodwork here. He'd applied to do the course at a YOI in the East Midlands. Long Minster?'

Thorne shook his head. He didn't know it.

'Anyway, I was happy to approve the application despite some stupidly strong opposition from the Youth Justice Board, and he was scheduled to be transferred ... some time this month, I think.'

Thorne made a note of it.

'He was doing well here,' Bracewell said. 'And I can't say that for too many of the boys. He spent almost all his time on our Gold wing, with better rooms and extra privileges and so on, and presuming things had carried on the same way he would probably have been looking at an open prison well before his sentence was up.' Bracewell smiled and shook his head. 'Tragically, all speculation now of course.'

'It's very helpful.'

'Is it?'

'Building up a picture of him, you know?'

The governor nodded and looked at Thorne. 'Well, I'd certainly have been sorry to see him go.'

'But you still approved his move?'

'Because it was the best thing for him, and it was what he wanted.'

'So why was the Youth Justice Board opposed to it?'

'Well, I suppose it would have been a little further from his family than he was here, but sometimes these pen-pushers who allocate placements just like to try and make things awkward, if you ask me. I'm sure you've met the type.'

Thorne said that he'd met plenty. That it sounded like a detective chief superintendent of his acquaintance. He glanced at the white-board behind Bracewell's desk. Various headings had been scribbled: *Re-offending Rates*; *Justification for Remand*; *Age/Offence/Ethnicity*. At the bottom of the board, somewhat incongruously, it said, *Buy milk, eggs, smoothies*.

'How did he end up in the hospital wing?' Thorne asked.

Bracewell shrugged. 'Looked at someone for a few seconds too long. Or someone didn't like the fact that he was awarded certain privileges for good behaviour. Sometimes these kids don't need any reason at all.'

'What happened?'

'Someone walked into his cell and slashed his face. In and out, no sign of a weapon.'

'You had a damn good look though.'

'We followed all the normal search procedures.'

Thorne nodded. The sharpness of the governor's response had probably been justified. Thorne knew how hard it was to find any weapon, when a boy determined enough could fashion one from almost anything that came to hand.

'Amin was taken to the local A&E to get stitched up, then brought back here the same evening. It's all in the police report.'

'I haven't seen it yet,' Thorne said. He had already decided that the constraints placed upon him by time might be no bad thing in terms of his investigation. Not having had a chance to look at the notes, he would be unprejudiced by the findings of the original inquiry and would have no choice but to investigate Amin Akhtar's death as if it had just happened. If he came to the same conclusions as Martin Dawes then so be it, but this way he might just be giving himself the best chance of getting at the truth and that was what Javed Akhtar wanted. 'Best to start with a clean slate anyway, I reckon,' he said. 'Compare what I find out today with what my predecessor found out eight weeks ago.'

Bracewell smiled, knowing. 'See if anyone changes their story.'

Thorne smiled back. 'That's always a possibility.' He kept his eyes on the governor as he drank the last of his coffee. 'Any idea who was responsible for the attack on Amin?'

'A couple of my officers reckon they've got a very good idea,' Bracewell said. 'But proving it is something else entirely. The boy concerned denied it of course. Amin refused to tell us who it was and it's very hard to find witnesses in a place like this. I'm sure you know what it's like.'

'I'll need to speak to him,' Thorne said. 'Proof or no proof.'

'Unfortunately, he was released a couple of months ago. Just a few days after the attack on Amin, in fact. Annoying, but without evidence there was nothing we could do to prevent it.'

'I'll need a name, then. The address on his release papers.'

Bracewell said that shouldn't be a problem, but with sufficient hesitation for Thorne to point out that, as far as this inquiry was concerned, the normal procedures did not, could not apply. There was simply no time for niceties, or ethics. Bracewell said he understood, and though Thorne could see that he did not, that the man was still desperate to know the reason for what was happening, he could also see that the situation was making him uneasy.

'I need to speak to whoever found the body as well.'

'That was Ian McCarthy,' Bracewell said. '*Dr* McCarthy. I think he should be in by now, so I can get one of my officers to take you down there. If that's OK?'

Thorne thanked him for his help and Bracewell phoned out to make the arrangements. Almost as soon as he had hung up, the phone rang and Bracewell took the call. He said, 'For Pete's sake,' and 'Right,' and when the call was finished, he sat back shaking his head as though the weight of the world had just settled on his smartly suited shoulders. 'One of the boys has smashed his cell up. Seventeen-year-old Polish lad, doesn't speak a word of bloody English.'

'Can't be easy.'

'It isn't. My officers are doing their best, but they've got their work cut out as it is.'

'I meant for the boy.'

Thorne remembered the colourful sign he had seen at the entrance to the prison. A single word written in dozens of languages. It was a nice idea, but a shame that the effort at translation had not gone a little further. The inmates probably thought it was a sick joke anyway, considering where they were and what that one word was.

Welcome.

'Well no,' Bracewell stammered. 'Of course not ... I mean, *obviously*. It's a very tricky situation for everyone.'

When the prison officer arrived, Thorne stood to gather up the files and Bracewell moved quickly from behind his desk to assure him that he would remain available if there was anything else he could help with. With his hand pressed firmly between the governor's two, Thorne said that he would bear the offer in mind.

Then he turned and followed his escort out of the office.

Decided, on reflection, that perhaps there was a miniature portrait of the Queen tucked away in one of the drawers.

In the school's assembly hall, the temporary Incident Room was up and running. A communications team had set up fax and phone lines and had tapped into a local CCTV feed. Monitors showed live, black and white images of the shopfront from two different angles, while a hastily erected camera in the alleyway behind the property broadcast a picture of the shop's back door. There was no sound and precious little movement. Occasionally an emergency vehicle moved through shot, or a stray dog that nobody had yet been able to catch. A member of the CO19 team wandered between the two Armed Response Vehicles which were still parked on the street across from the newsagent's.

Still waiting for instructions.

There were more than two dozen officers working inside the school. Most sat at computers, feeding back any information they could find about the layout of the shop and the man who owned it to the team from Specialist Crime. A few more had come down from Helen Weeks' unit in Streatham, volunteering to help, but now found themselves with little to do.

Donnelly was at the monitors with Sue Pascoe when Chivers walked across to join them.

They studied the pictures for a while.

'Phones?' Chivers said.

Pascoe shook her head. 'He's making us wait.'

They had quickly established that there was a landline in the shop, but just as quickly discovered that Akhtar had taken the phone off the hook. Calls being made every fifteen minutes to the mobiles registered to both Helen Weeks and Stephen Mitchell were going straight to voicemail.

'In for the long haul, I reckon,' Donnelly said.

Chivers shrugged. 'Up to you.'

'Up to Mr Akhtar, I would have thought.'

'Only if we let him have control of the situation.'

Donnelly stared at the screen. 'I'm open to suggestions.'

'Look at those shutters.' Chivers pointed at the monitor. 'They've already been twisted up at the bottom, see? That's just kids or what have you. Wouldn't take us long to get through those.'

'Long enough for him to do something.'

'We need to get this sorted quickly,' Chivers said.

'What we *need*,' Pascoe said, 'is to open a channel of communication with our hostage taker.'

'At least let us get Tech Support in here.' Chivers was looking at Donnelly. 'Get some microphones up on the roof, take a listen to what's going on in there.'

'Too risky,' Pascoe said. 'If he thinks there's anything like that going on, he might do something stupid.'

'We don't even know the gun is loaded.' Chivers stabbed at the monitor again. 'He's a *newsagent*, for Christ's sake.'

Donnelly looked at Pascoe. She shook her head.

'We do something without really thinking it through,' she said, 'and he'll be the one making the news.'

NINE

Helen listened, waiting and hoping for some reaction.

Akhtar had been in his shop for ten minutes or more, while for most of that time, from the front of the building, a woman's voice had echoed – crackling and tinny – through a loudhailer.

'We just want to talk, Mr Akhtar. We need to know that everyone's all right in there. If we could start some kind of dialogue on the phone, we could begin talking about how we're going to resolve this. How we can get you what you want without anybody getting hurt.'

When he finally came back into the storeroom, Akhtar was carrying an armful of chocolate bars and bags of crisps. He stood a few steps away from where Helen and Mitchell were chained to the radiator and stared down at them.

'So, what do you think?' Helen asked.

'What do I think about what?'

'Should we maybe just switch my phone on at least?'

Akhtar blinked, licked his lips.

'If you don't communicate with them—'

'I already *said*,' he shouted. 'When I'm *ready*.' He stamped his foot like a petulant schoolboy and shook his head as if clearing it or trying to refocus. Then he smiled suddenly at Helen and Mitchell, calmly opened his arms and dropped the crisps and chocolate at their feet. 'It's lunchtime,' he said. 'I'm afraid this is the best I can do.'

Helen watched him walk back to the desk and pick up the gun. As far as her stomach was concerned, she did not know where fear ended and hunger began.

'It's time to eat,' he said.

She slowly pulled a chocolate bar towards her with her free hand and tore at the wrapper with her teeth. She bit into it, then nodded towards a packet of crisps. 'I don't think I can open that with one hand,' she said.

Akhtar said, 'Sorry.' With the gun still pointed at them, he bent down slowly, opened the two bags of crisps that were closest to him then nudged them across the dirty linoleum floor with his foot.

Mitchell did not seem interested in the food. He never took his eyes off the gun.

'Can we have something to drink?' Helen asked.

Akhtar apologised again, the anger having seemingly given way to embarrassment and concern, and hurried back into the shop.

'You should eat something,' Helen said to Mitchell.

'I don't think I can.'

'Just a bar of chocolate.'

'I'd probably be sick anyway,' he said. He blew out his cheeks and rubbed at his stomach. 'Butterflies, you know?'

'Yeah, I know.' She reached across and laid a hand on his arm.

Akhtar came back in with three cans: Coke, Diet Coke and Sprite. He held them up so that Helen and Mitchell could take their pick.

'I'll have the Diet Coke,' Helen said, 'if that's all right. Probably wasting my time worrying about calories while I'm stuffing my face with chocolate, mind you.' She tried to smile. 'Might as well make the effort though.'

Akhtar nodded and laughed. He opened the can and laid it down within Helen's reach, then he raised up the other two, one in each hand. 'Mr Mitchell?'

Mitchell said he was happy with either.

'You can have the Coke,' Akhtar said. He opened the drink and placed it on the floor, then sat back down at the desk. He laid the gun on the desktop and popped the ring-pull on his own can. He looked across at Helen and patted his paunch. 'I gave up worrying about weight a long time ago,' he said. 'All that ghee in everything my wife cooks.'

'I can't afford to give up,' Helen said. She looked at him and swallowed hard. 'Been struggling with it ever since Alfie was born. Can't seem to get rid of those few extra pounds, even though I spend half my life running round after the little bugger like a lunatic. Well, you've seen how much energy he's got.'

Akhtar looked away and took a long swig from his can.

Helen was happy to see that Akhtar was feeling uncomfortable. Had she managed to provoke a pang of guilt, or remorse? Perhaps she had simply succeeded in reminding him of his own son. She decided that this could not be helped, that whatever she said, the man would not need to be reminded of the child he had lost.

It was the reason they were there, after all.

She finished the chocolate and started on the crisps. 'Where did you get the gun, Javed?'

'What?'

She asked again, kept it nice and casual, as though she were enquiring where he had bought his shoes.

Akhtar reached for the gun and picked it up, felt the weight of it as if holding it for the first time. It looked old. A revolver. 'A man who came into the shop,' he said.

Helen waited.

'I knew he was involved in certain sorts of business, you know? The way he looked and some of the things he said. Same way I got to know the business *you* were in.' He slowly turned the gun over in his hand, as though curious himself as to how it had got there. 'I told this man some made-up stories, told him I was having real trouble with kids in the shop, all that kind of nonsense. He said there were things I could do to protect myself, that it would be easy to get what I needed if I was happy to pay for it. He said there was a pub I could go to, people I could ask. So, for several nights, when I had told my wife I was at the cash-and-carry, I sat in this pub that stank of God-knows-what, trying to look as though I had a good reason to be there, and I asked questions. Eventually I found a man who was keen to take my money and give me what I wanted.'

'You must have been frightened,' Helen said.

'I was *terrified*, Miss Weeks, I don't mind telling you. More scared than I have ever been. But in the end it was so easy, that is the terrible thing. Those boys who were in my shop this morning? They can get guns any time they want.' He snapped his fingers. 'Like *that*.' He shook his head. 'I thought it would be difficult and dangerous, but it was really no different to buying anything else. No different.' He nodded down to the floor in front of Helen. 'Like buying crisps or bloody Coca-Cola ...'

Helen knew that Javed Akhtar was right, of course. The war on knives was all but lost, and it was hard to imagine the attempt to tackle gun crime going any other way, when you could buy one in a pub car park as easily as a box or two of dodgy fags.

He might just as well have been at the cash-and-carry.

'Why don't you just get rid of the gun?' Helen asked.

'No, I don't think so.'

'*Please*,' Mitchell said. The single word was said quietly but was thick with desperation. 'You don't need it.' He rattled the handcuffs against the radiator pipe. 'We can't go anywhere.'

'You don't have to do anything else,' Helen said. 'We can carry on just like this if you want. It's only the gun that's making things dangerous. For all of us.' She nodded reassuringly. 'You can see that, Javed, can't you? Just put the gun away ...'

'My son never carried a weapon in his life,' Akhtar said, 'and look what happened to him.'

'I know, but isn't one terrible incident enough? Just put—'

'"Dangerous".' Akhtar spat the word out. 'That's what they said about Amin in court. That he demonstrated a "degree of dangerous-ness". What kind of word is that? What does that even mean?'

It was a legal term that Helen was well familiar with. It had been applied to many offenders she had dealt with over her years in Child Protection. It was invoked as justification for harsher sentencing, and for increasing the period an individual had to spend on licence once that sentence had been completed.

'So what do you think, Javed? About the gun.'

Akhtar stood up and looked at her as though he had no idea what she was talking about. 'What kind of word is that, I ask you?'

'I don't know,' Helen said. 'But it's just a word.'

Akhtar shook his head and shouted. 'No, no, no! Not *just* anything!' His face was flushed suddenly and he was waving the gun about.

Next to her, Helen felt Mitchell flinch and whimper.

'What kind of *bastard*, stupid word?' He looked from Helen to Mitchell for an answer and, when none came, he shook his head again and stormed quickly out into the shop.

A few seconds later, the noise started, things crashing and breaking.

Helen shuffled across and, once again, dropped a hand gently on to Mitchell's shoulder. 'It's going to be OK, Stephen,' she said.

He turned slowly towards her. His skin was clammy and his lips looked pale.

He said, 'I can't do this.'

A woman approached Donnelly as he was walking back into the hall from the boys' toilets. She introduced herself as DC Gill Bellinger. Said, 'I work with Helen.'

'Right,' Donnelly said. 'Well, we're doing everything we can, but right now it's a sodding big plate of wait-and-see pudding, I'm afraid.'

'I was wondering what you were doing about Helen's little boy.'

Donnelly said, 'Right,' again and nodded, as though he had just been wondering exactly the same thing.

Bellinger nodded back, but she could see that this was the first time he had so much as thought about Alfie Weeks. 'He goes to a local childminder,' she said. 'I just thought we should make some arrangement to have him picked up?'

'Yes, of course. Is there any family?'

'There's a sister, Jenny. Lives in Maida Vale, I think. I'm not sure they're particularly close, but . . .'

'OK, I'll try and get that organized, thanks, Gill.' Donnelly looked around. 'I'm not sure—'

'You want me to do it?'

'That would be great,' Donnelly said, taking a step away. 'Might all work out very well, seeing as you're a friend of Helen's, I mean.'

He was already on his way back to the monitors as Gill Bellinger was telling him that she would let him know what she'd managed to organise. He raised a hand in acknowledgement and sat back down.

'Takes me back,' he said.

Sue Pascoe looked up at him. 'What?'

'Boys' toilets.' Donnelly smiled. 'I remember, we used to go charging into the girls' toilets every so often. A big gang of us, just running in there shouting and screaming, trying to see what it was like. What the hell you got up to in there.' He looked at Pascoe. 'Funny that the girls never seemed particularly interested in what our toilets were like.'

'Yeah, funny that,' Pascoe said.

'Anything momentous happen while I was pointing Percy at the porcelain?'

Pascoe shook her head. 'Well, he hasn't given himself up or shot anyone, if that's what you mean. But it might not be too far away.' She nodded across to where Chivers was talking to somebody on the far side of the hall. 'He was looking for you.'

'What does he want?'

'Says his boys can hear a load of crashing and banging coming from inside the shop,' Pascoe said. 'Bottles breaking and what have you, like he's smashing the place up.' She stared at the monitor, let out a slow breath. 'Sounds like he might be losing it.'

'So what do you think?' Donnelly asked.

'I think we really need to talk to him.'

60

Donnelly watched Chivers finish his conversation and start walking quickly towards him. It was hard to be sure, as the man's expression never changed a great deal, but even from a distance the CO19 team leader appeared rather pleased with developments.

TEN

It was as ridiculous to generalise about a group of people as diverse as prison officers as it was about anybody else – pointless and ultimately reductive – but it saved time, so Thorne did it anyway.

They were, so Thorne imagined, either no-nonsense, by-the-book types or those slightly more sensitive sorts who could easily have become teachers if they didn't like the uniforms quite so much. 'Old school' or 'reconstructed' might have been more accurate labels, but Thorne found it easier to think of them as 'Mackays' or 'Barracloughs'; the archetypes named in honour of the two very different types of screw on the sitcom *Porridge* that he had adored as a kid.

Which he still thought about sometimes, in the middle of a particularly tedious trial.

Norman Stanley Fletcher . . .

The PO that escorted him from Bracewell's office to the hospital wing was a thickset and balding fifty-something named Dobson. Like all the officers, he was wearing dark trousers and a black polo shirt with his name stitched into it, but it was not until Thorne commented on what the *boys* were wearing that Dobson revealed his true colours. At other YOIs Thorne had visited, the boys had worn tracksuit bottoms, and he was surprised that those he had seen that morning were wearing cargo pants beneath their dark blue sweatshirts or T-shirts.

'That was the governor's idea,' Dobson said, nodding towards one of the boys. 'Bloody good one, as well. They used to strut about with their hands shoved down the front of their tracksuit bottoms, grabbing their bollocks like wannabe gangsters. These days, we have to shake hands with the little bastards a hundred times a day.' He pulled a face. 'So . . .'

To the likes of Dobson, the boys they banged up every night were no more than adult prisoners waiting to happen, whether they had started shaving or not and whatever he and his colleagues were required to wear as part of a more casual and caring regime. Thorne knew that there were those within the Prison Service who requested the posting to a YOI. Officers who enjoyed working with young offenders, because they felt there was a chance to make a real difference. There were others, however – a small minority, thankfully – who were unhappy to find themselves assigned to kids and saw no reason to treat the prisoners in their charge any differently to those who might previously have been subject to their less than tender mercies in Long Lartin or the Scrubs.

It was not hard to work out which category Dobson belonged to.

Ian McCarthy was waiting for them outside the doors when they arrived at the hospital wing. Dobson said, 'Here you go,' then turned and walked away.

'He's a charmer,' Thorne said.

McCarthy opened the door for Thorne and ushered him through. 'Bark's worse than his bite,' he said. 'Like a lot of them.'

Thorne had naively imagined that Barndale's chief medical officer would be older. That he might possibly be wearing a white coat. As it turned out, the man who showed him into his large, bright office and dropped into a chair behind a cluttered desk was, like the governor, a few years younger than Thorne himself and considerably better dressed. He was stocky with thick, dark hair and a well-trimmed goatee. There was a trace of a northern accent.

'Roger said you're looking into Amin Akhtar's suicide.'

Thorne nodded and held up the stack of files he'd brought with him from Bracewell's office. 'Got to work my way through this lot as soon as I can, but I wanted to have a quick look around in here first.'

'That's fine—'

'Just get my bearings, you know?'

'Not a problem.'

'You found Amin, right?'

McCarthy stood up, removed his jacket and hung it across the back of his chair before sitting down again. A heavy sigh made it clear that he was going to find talking about Amin Akhtar's death hard work.

'I've not been here that long,' he said. 'Only a year or so, and this is like the worst nightmare. There was a kid who cut his wrists in his cell a few months before I got the job, and I know this kind of stuff goes on in prisons, but Amin was *here*.' He held out his arms. 'On my watch, so ...'

'Tell me what happened.'

'I got here about seven-thirty,' McCarthy said. 'A bit earlier than usual because the governor had called a senior management meeting for eight o'clock and I needed to get a few things dictated in the office. I decided to do a quick round before the meeting and Amin's was the first room I checked.'

'Why was that?'

'I always check the private rooms first,' McCarthy said. 'And his was the only one that was occupied.' He looked down and straightened some papers on his desk. 'Well, you know what I found.'

Thorne was thinking: clean slate. 'I haven't had an opportunity to see the police report yet,' he said.

'Really?'

'Or the post-mortem. So I'd be grateful if you could tell me.'

McCarthy cleared his throat. 'Amin had taken an overdose of Tramadol, which is the same drug he was being treated with. It's related to morphine ...'

Thorne nodded.

'He'd been checked twice on the rounds between six-thirty and seven a.m. and although the hospital officer on duty was rightly suspended, I don't think we can really blame her for not noticing that anything was wrong. I mean, I can't honestly say I'd have done anything different. He was just lying there in bed, so anyone looking in through the window for a few seconds could easily have thought he was asleep and that everything was OK.' He held up his hands. 'She didn't notice the plastic cup and the few spilled tablets lying on the floor by his bed. Simple as that.' He shook his head, looked to see if Thorne needed any more detail.

Thorne waited.

'There was some blood where he'd bitten through his tongue and he'd ... soiled himself, though obviously that couldn't be seen from outside the room.' He looked at Thorne again. 'Yes, we *might* have been able to save him if the officer on duty had been a little more observant, but as it was, Amin was dead by the time I went into his room. He was still ... warm, but I checked and there was clearly no hope of resuscitation. So—'

'Still warm? So what time did he take the overdose?'

'Well, I haven't seen the PM report either, but I spoke to the Home Office pathologist when he arrived and he put the time of death at somewhere between six and seven a.m. The hour after he was given that last dose of medication.' McCarthy smiled sadly. 'Right about the time I was rolling out of bed at home and coming downstairs to put the kettle on.' He swallowed. 'Looking forward to the day.'

'That was your first mistake,' Thorne said.

'Sorry?'

'I stopped looking forward to work years ago.' He leaned forward, mock-conspiratorial. 'You should always assume that things are going to be *really bad*. That way, even if it's just an averagely shitty day, you feel like you've had a result.'

McCarthy's gaze drifted towards the large window that looked out on to the corridor. He smiled weakly, but looked as confused as he did upset. 'I said all this a fortnight ago at the inquest,' he said. 'Told them what had happened.'

Thorne shrugged. 'Another set of papers I haven't seen.'

'I don't understand.'

'A . . . situation has developed very suddenly, which means that we're looking at Amin's death again.' Thorne let that hang for a second or two. 'That *I* am. Starting pretty much from scratch, I'm afraid.'

McCarthy sat back, thinking, then raised his arms. 'Right, well I'm still none the wiser, but if there's anything I can do . . . '

Thorne stood up. 'A guided tour would be very helpful,' he said.

McCarthy said that would not be a problem, so Thorne walked out on to the ward, waiting by the door for a few moments while the doctor grabbed his jacket.

Waiting, and thinking that for once he knew what might be causing that tickle in the soft hairs at the back of his neck; that something McCarthy had told him would need looking at more closely.

'All set?' McCarthy said, closing the door to his office behind him.

'Absolutely.'

Thinking that six o'clock in the morning was a very strange time to kill yourself.

Gavin Slater did not seem inclined to let Holland and Kitson into his house. He had glowered at their warrant cards and drawn the front door a little closer towards him. From inside came the sounds of a television at high volume and somewhere upstairs a woman was shouting, raising her voice above the barking of a dog.

Holland and Kitson were not overly keen on going inside themselves.

'You may or may not know that Amin Akhtar died two months ago,' Holland said.

Slater blinked, then smiled. 'I didn't, but thanks. Not too often you lot knock on my door with good news.'

'We just need to ask you a few questions.'

Slater laughed. 'Right, like where I was when it happened? Was I breaking into whatever prison the little shitbag ended up in, something like that?'

'Something like that,' Kitson said.

'So what happened?' Slater sniffed. 'Somebody take a knife to him or what?'

'We're not at liberty to reveal the circumstances—'

'Yeah, yeah, whatever.' Slater began to pick away at a patch of paint that was peeling from his front door. 'Just let me know when you've got a name, so I can send him a box of chocolates or something.'

'Maybe you can help us with that,' Holland said.

Slater laughed again. Inside, the woman was screaming at the dog to shut up.

Kitson brushed away a sliver of white paint that had blown on to her jacket. 'So you're not exactly heartbroken that Amin is dead then?'

Slater turned and studied her for a few moments. 'The Met really is taking on the brightest and the best, isn't it?' He looked away and up towards the main road where heavy traffic was pouring east towards the Angel and west towards King's Cross. A few streets from where, just over a year before, his eldest son had been fatally stabbed with his own knife by Amin Akhtar.

'You still in touch with either of the boys who were involved in the incident with Lee?' Kitson asked.

'The "incident"?'

'Yes or no?'

'Not seen them since Lee's funeral.'

'You sure about that?'

'They helped to carry his coffin, them and a few of Lee's other mates.' Slater narrowed his eyes at Kitson. 'You might have known that, if any of your lot had actually bothered to come. Don't you normally do that, show up to pay your respects when a victim of violent crime is buried? Or does it depend on what colour they are?'

'It depends on how you define "victim",' Kitson said.

Slater breathed in deep, then smacked his palms together hard to get rid of the dried paint. 'Well, thanks again for dropping by to cheer me up. If I think of anything that might help, I'll be sure and keep it to myself.' He turned away and walked back inside. Said, 'Now piss off,' before slamming the door shut.

Holland and Kitson walked back towards their car.

'He was lying,' Kitson said. 'About not seeing those other two.'

'Doesn't mean anything.' Holland said. 'Careful,' and stepped around a smear of dog shit. 'It's the default position with rubbish like him, lying to coppers.'

Kitson reached into her bag for the keys. Pressed the remote to unlock the car.

'I still don't know what he wants us to do,' Holland said. 'What he thinks we *can* do.' He saw the questioning look from Kitson. 'Thorne.' They climbed into the car and Kitson started the engine. 'I mean, we've got no good reason to think *anyone* killed Amin.'

They sat there for a few moments. They could still hear Slater's dog barking from the other end of the street. Holland could see that Kitson clearly found something funny.

'What?'

'You,' she said. 'Doesn't seem like five minutes since you were all fresh-faced and floppy-haired and thought the sun shone out of Tom Thorne's arse. You'd have jumped off a cliff if he'd told you to.'

Holland said, 'Yeah, well,' and ran a hand through blond hair that was somewhat shorter these days. Nobody's fresh-faced anything.

'Then you found out he was fallible,' Kitson said. 'Like everyone else.'

Holland looked at her, thinking that he was not the only one who had changed. That she had ... softened, while, for whatever reason, he had moved the other way. Thinking: yes, if *fallible* means being everyone's sure thing for youngest female commander in the Met, until you sleep with a senior officer and screw up your marriage and have to start all over again. 'Like everyone else,' he said.

Kitson angled the rear-view mirror down to check her reflection. She pursed her lips and opened her eyes wide. 'We have addresses for the other two?' she asked.

'Yeah, for all the good it's going to do us.'

'You got anything else on?'

'I'm just saying . . .'

Kitson readjusted the mirror then looked back towards Gavin Slater's house. 'His youngest's inside, isn't he?'

Holland nodded. Following in the criminal footsteps of both his father and elder brother, Wayne Slater was serving four months in a YOI near Manchester for breaking and entering.

'So there might be something useful there, right? Someone in that YOI knows someone in Barndale, you know how it works.' Kitson moved out into the traffic and turned towards the main road. 'It's not beyond the realms of possibility, is it?'

Holland shrugged, said, 'I suppose not.'

Thinking that the only thing they could usefully do would be to turn the car round, pick up that piece of dog shit he had almost stepped in and pop it through Gavin Slater's letterbox.

ELEVEN

Prisons smelled bad enough, but hospitals were a lot worse. Blood and bandages or maybe just the stink of the stuff they used to sterilise everything, but whatever the source, it always triggered bad memories and made Thorne uncomfortable. Oddly, he was far more at home in a mortuary, less affected by the stench of the bone-saw at work and the freshly harvested organs than he was by bedpans and rotting fruit.

Perhaps it was because the only people suffering in a mortuary were the ones throwing up over their shoes.

From McCarthy's office near the main doors, they walked past the prison hospital officers and nurses' station, an examination room, a surgery and a large storage cupboard that had been converted into a small tea room. The dispensary was at the far end, opposite another set of doors.

Thorne stopped and searched for the CCTV camera Dawes had mentioned. Unable to see one, he asked McCarthy where it was.

'There was one, yes. We'd had a few thefts from the DDA cupboard.'

'DDA?'

'Dangerous Drugs Act. Morphine, methadone, what have you.'

'And that camera was moved there from somewhere else just before Amin died, yes?'

McCarthy thought about it. 'That's right ... a couple of months ago, somewhere around there.' He sighed, exasperated. 'And now it's been moved again.'

'Because?'

'Because some bright spark suggested we might be better off putting the camera inside the dispensary. That way we might see the culprit coming in. *From the front.*' He smacked the side of his head. 'Clever, eh?'

'Caught anybody?'

'Not as yet,' McCarthy said.

'So where are the monitors?'

'In the nurses' station.'

Thorne nodded and looked around. 'There's another camera at the main doors.'

'Right.'

'And inside one of the rooms?'

McCarthy nodded, grim. 'The room next door to the one Amin was in.'

'Why just that one?'

'That's what's so bloody ironic,' McCarthy said. 'It's the room we put any patient in who's on suicide watch.'

The medical officer used his pass-key to take them through the set of white metal doors on to the first of two interconnecting wards. Each ward contained half a dozen beds, three on each side. All were occupied.

'You always this busy?' Thorne asked.

'God, yes,' McCarthy said. 'And seriously understaffed. Even if I'm here I'm usually up to my neck in medical reports for parole hearings, organising rehab programmes, all that stuff. So I need locum GPs to come in for the daily sick parades or to dole out the Ritalin and we still have a contract with the local primary healthcare trust to provide extra nursing staff. The PHOs do a good job, don't get me wrong, and even with them we're run off our feet, but most of them have only had very basic medical training.'

'Like the one who thought Amin was asleep, right?'

'Unfortunately, yes.'

They walked slowly up and down the two wards. Each had its own small toilet and shower block at the far end. There were glass walls and no locks. Passing each bed, the looks Thorne received from those patients who were not asleep or reading magazines were considerably less aggressive than he might expect from the boys in the main body of the prison. Out there, if you weren't wearing a uniform of some sort you were almost certainly a solicitor or a copper.

And Thorne did not look like a solicitor.

Perhaps the kids in here were just too drugged up to care, he thought. Or maybe he made a more convincing doctor than he did a brief.

He was sure that Phil Hendricks would have something to say about that.

Somebody turned a radio up and was quickly told to turn it down as Thorne nodded towards the bunch of keys in McCarthy's hand. 'Who has keys in and out of here?'

McCarthy looked at him as though it were a very inappropriate question.

'I need to ask.'

'You think so?'

Thorne looked at him. 'Didn't DI Dawes?'

McCarthy nodded slowly, which made Thorne think that the man who had led the original inquiry might not have been quite as much of an idiot as he'd taken him for.

'Well, myself, obviously. The PHOs. All the officers . . . '

They walked through an open doorway at the far end of the second ward, on to the corridor that contained the wing's three private rooms.

'And the pass-key opens these as well, does it?'

McCarthy shook his head and lifted his keys up, selecting two different ones for Thorne to look at. 'The pass-key is for all the main doors, but you need this one to open any of these cells.'

'Cells?'

'*Rooms*, I mean.' He reddened slightly and waved his embarrassment away. 'Room, cell. Patient, prisoner.'

Thorne understood. Boy, little bastard. It all depended who you were talking to and what kind of mood they were in.

'Which one was Amin's?'

McCarthy pointed and moved to open the door furthest to their left. While he was doing that, Thorne took a few paces towards the room next door to the one being unlocked. The room reserved for potential suicides in which the remaining CCTV camera was installed. Once past it, he turned and walked slowly back towards the door McCarthy had opened for him, taking care to stay as close as possible to the wall.

McCarthy watched him, but Thorne saw no need to explain what he was doing if the doctor was not bright enough to work it out. He would stop off at the nurses' station to review the footage on his way out.

'Here we are,' McCarthy said.

The doctor's indecision as to what to call it was understandable, as the space with which Thorne was confronted was somewhere between a room and a cell, albeit one of those on the Gold wing. Ten feet by eight, with plain white walls, an alcove cordoned off containing toilet and sink. The room was dominated by a traditional hospital bed with sides that could be raised if necessary, an IV stand on one side and a small melamine-topped table on the other. There was no window, save for the one in the metal door through which a PHO had looked, though for not quite long enough to establish that the room's occupant was not breathing.

'Not exactly BUPA, I know,' McCarthy said.

Thorne walked across to the bed. It smelled clean but there was a yellow-brown stain on the pillow. He wondered if anyone had slept in it since Amin Akhtar. 'Well, if it was any nicer you'd only get stick from the "prisons are holiday camps" brigade,' he said. 'You'd have the *Daily Mail* complaining that your patients were too comfortable.'

McCarthy nodded, gave a small laugh. 'A few months back, our head of PE ordered a pitch-and-putt set for the boys and a week later one of the papers claimed that we were building an eighteen-hole golf course.'

'So what kind of dosage was Amin on?' Thorne asked. He walked across to the far wall. Just a few steps. 'The Tramadol.'

'Two fifty-milligram tablets, four times a day. It's a medium-strength painkiller.'

'And nothing else?'

'Only a low-dose antibiotic. A drip, you know?'

'And how many tablets would he have needed to OD? Just roughly.'

'I don't know, thirty or more at least.'

Thorne thought for a few seconds. 'Plus the few you said got spilled on the floor, right? So that's thirty-something tablets he somehow managed to avoid taking during his routine medication and stashed away. Does that sound about right?'

McCarthy nodded, said, 'More or less.'

'Right, and he'd been in here four days, so in order to get enough to do the job properly, he would have had to be palming virtually all his pills almost every time he was given them. Sorry, I'm just thinking out loud here ... but the staff are supposed to watch and make sure med-ication gets taken, aren't they?'

'Yes, they're supposed to.'

'Well, someone screwed up rather badly by the sound of it.'

'I gave him several doses of the tablets myself,' McCarthy said, 'and I certainly didn't screw up.'

'I wasn't trying to say you had, but can you think of any other explanation?' Thorne walked slowly back across the room, turned and leaned against the door.

'Perhaps someone brought them in for him,' McCarthy suggested.

'From the outside?'

'Why not?'

'Because that would mean Amin had suicidal feelings even before he got attacked.' Thorne shook his head. 'It would have to have been after he was admitted to the hospital wing. Was he allowed visits from other boys while he was in here?'

'Yes, at least one lad came in, I think. I can get you the name.'

'That would be helpful,' Thorne said. 'But we've still got the same question to answer. Where did whoever gave Amin enough tablets to kill himself get them from?' Thorne had already figured out the most likely answer, but waited for McCarthy to catch him up. It only took a few seconds.

'What about the thefts from the dispensary?'

'Sounds good to me,' Thorne said.

The doctor nodded, looking highly delighted with himself and his powers of deduction. 'Shouldn't be a problem to find out if and when any Tramadol tablets were taken. Everything is noted down in the DDA book, so—' He stopped at the noise from Thorne's pocket. 'Is that yours?'

Thorne was unsurprised at McCarthy's shocked expression when his mobile rang. They were strictly forbidden inside the prison and that applied to members of staff every bit as much as to prisoners themselves. It was another protocol Thorne had been obliged to ignore, and dispensation had been granted after a senior officer at the Yard had spoken to the governor by phone and made it clear that they were dealing with a serious live-time incident.

Thorne took the phone from his jacket and saw who was calling. 'I need to take this,' he said.

McCarthy stayed where he was, then seeing that Thorne was not about to answer while anyone was around to listen, indicated that he would wait outside and stepped into the hall.

Thorne pushed the door shut after him and answered the phone.

'Helen?'

'He wants to know what's happening.'

Thorne pressed the handset to his chest and swore quietly. He could still hear the radio that was playing on the ward across the corridor. 'Tell him I'm doing what he asked me to do,' he said. 'I'm working as quickly as I can, all right?'

'I'll tell him.'

'That this might take some time.'

There was a pause. 'I'll tell him . . .'

'I'm talking to all the people I need to talk to.' He looked down at the bed in which Amin Akhtar had died. He reached out and touched the metal bedstead. 'I'm in the right place. Tell him we're taking everything he said very seriously, OK?'

'The truth, that's what he wants.'

'I know . . . I know it is, and I'm going to find out what happened, one way or the other.' He sat down on the edge of the bed. 'You make sure he knows that.'

'I will.'

'Helen . . . ?'

'That's good.'

She was breathless and he could hear the tightness in her voice, the effort to sound upbeat. He guessed that Akhtar was listening. 'How are you and Mitchell doing, Helen? How's Akhtar doing?'

There was another pause, longer this time. Thorne could hear Helen Weeks breathing, imagined he could also hear the breathing of the man who was probably pointing a gun at her.

'None of us are doing very well,' she said.

TWELVE

Once he had finished in the hospital wing, Thorne decided that he should spend half an hour going through Amin Akhtar's paperwork. In his experience, the library was rarely the busiest part of any prison, so it seemed as good a place as any to get some peace and quiet.

He called Donnelly on his way there to see what was happening in Tulse Hill. He told him about the meetings with Bracewell and McCarthy and then about the call he had received from Helen Weeks.

'Thank God for that,' Donnelly said. 'Pascoe's been desperate to get a line of communication open.' He asked Thorne how Helen Weeks had sounded on the phone.

'She's holding up, but she doesn't sound great.'

'I think Akhtar had a bit of a wobble,' Donnelly said. 'He seems to have calmed down now.'

'What do you mean, a wobble?'

'Smashing the shop up, shouting and screaming. We've got no idea what set him off, so everyone's still a bit jumpy.'

'Chivers?'

'Inspector Chivers is responding ... appropriately.'

'You need to keep on top of him.'

'I don't need anyone to tell me how to run this operation, thank you very much.'

Thorne took a few seconds. Donnelly was a detective superintendent, but he was not Thorne's detective superintendent. That said, it would not be doing anyone any favours, least of all Helen Weeks, to alienate the man running the operation. He would need to observe at least a few of the niceties.

'That's what I'm trying to say, sir.' Thorne dug deep to find a reasonable tone of voice. 'You know what some of these ex-army types are like. Once there's any kind of weapon involved, they tend to think they're calling the shots. Sir.'

That seemed to do the trick.

'I'll consult with whomever I need to,' Donnelly said, 'but *I'm* calling the shots. Not that it's a particularly suitable phrase, considering the circumstances.'

'Probably not,' Thorne said. He thought, considering the circumstances, that nobody should give a tuppenny toss about whether a phrase was suitable or not, but he bit his tongue. He just hoped he had made his point about Chivers. He'd come across that sort enough times to worry that the man leading the Tactical Firearms Unit could prove every bit as dangerous to Helen Weeks' safety as a newsagent with a gun.

'I need to go and get this call set up,' Donnelly said.

'You're sure he's calmed down?'

'That's why Pascoe's keen to do it now. We need to talk to him, or if not then at least talk to him through DS Weeks. We want to let him know that we're doing everything we can to get this resolved, but above all we need to make sure he's stable.'

'Up to you, obviously, but isn't Helen under enough pressure as it is?'

'Like it or not she's our go-between, so we don't have a lot of choice.'

'I suppose not.' Thorne could hear voices in the background. Sue Pascoe's and Nadira Akhtar's.

'If it all goes well,' Donnelly said, 'we're going to see if he'll talk to his wife.'

Thorne remembered Nadira Akhtar's face when he'd talked to her in the car a couple of hours before, when she'd considered the possibility of her husband ever hurting anyone. Thinking about it, the wad of damp tissue squeezed in her fist.

Now I cannot be so sure . . .

'Are you saying you're worried about her?'

'His wife?'

'DS Weeks.'

'No more so than I would be about any other officer,' Thorne said.

A clatter echoed down the corridor from somewhere deep on the wing, followed swiftly by jeering and catcalls. There were whistles and a few seconds of clapping until it was silenced by the voice of a prison officer.

'I spoke to a couple of her colleagues,' Donnelly said, 'and as far as they're aware, she's never been in a seriously threatening situation before. They weren't altogether sure how she'd handle it.'

'She's not going to do anything stupid.'

'You're sure about that?'

'She's got a child.'

'Yes, I know, but that means she could well react . . . emotionally, which might not be the best thing for anyone.'

'She'll be fine.'

'I hope you're right,' Donnelly said. 'I know you've had some dealings with her in the past.'

Thorne doubted that anyone Helen Weeks worked with would know too much about what she had been through a year before. Her partner's murder and the risks she had run to find out who had been responsible. He did not know all the facts himself, but he knew what an ordeal it had been.

He knew that she had come through it.

'I think we need to trust her,' Thorne said.

As much as she'll be trusting us.

Trusting me.

Thorne glanced up as a small group of boys ambled past, escorted by a prison officer. Teeth were sucked and curses muttered. Thorne met the eyes of the angriest-looking and held them. 'I honestly don't think we could ask for anyone better in there,' he said.

Akhtar had not said much when he had reappeared in the storeroom after his bout of destruction in the shop. He had been sweating and had taken off his cardigan to mop his face and neck. Though most of the hair on top of his head had gone, there were silver-streaked tufts above his ears that were sticking up and he smoothed them down with small, delicate hands. When he had finally sat down, Helen could see that the redness in his face was as much the result of embarrassment as exertion.

'Stupid,' he'd said.

Then he had passed Helen her mobile phone and told her to call Tom Thorne . . .

He sat thinking for a few minutes after the call was finished, then stood up and fetched a broom that was leaning against a stack of shelves. He put the gun down on the desk, then, careful not to get too close, he swept the empty crisp packets, cans and chocolate wrappers towards him. He stuffed them into a plastic bag and carried it across to a black rubbish bin in the corner.

He sat down again and picked up the gun.

'Seems a bit daft to go on a cleaning spree,' Helen said. 'Considering the mess you must have made out there.'

The redness returned to Akhtar's face. 'I know, but that foolishness is no reason you should have to sit in here with rubbish stinking every-where.'

Helen was still wearing her jacket. Her underarms were clammy and her blouse was pasted to her back. 'I think that might be me,' she said. She held up her free arm. 'Can I . . . ?'

'Yes, of course,' Akhtar said. 'Slowly, please.'

Helen moved her shoulder until she had enough room to pull the arm that was free up through the sleeve of her jacket. Then she shuf-fled it behind her back and shook it down until finally the jacket was gathered around the hand that was cuffed to the radiator pipe. 'Thanks,' she said. 'Shame you were right about the weather.'

Akhtar asked Mitchell if he would like to do the same.

'I'm OK,' Mitchell said. 'Thank you.'

'I'm sorry you can't be more comfortable,' Akhtar said. 'But we are stuck with things as they are, so . . .'

'We don't have to be stuck with anything,' Helen said. 'You heard what Thorne said.'

'I heard what *you* said.'

'He's doing everything he can to find out what happened to Amin. He's talking to people.'

Akhtar smiled. 'People lie to policemen as often as they lie to anyone else. More, I think. People lie all the time.'

'How about if *I* promise not to lie to you, Javed?' Helen looked at him. 'How about that?'

The newsagent shrugged. 'You will say whatever you think I want to hear, because I am pointing a gun at you.'

'I won't lie, OK? I need you to trust me.'

Akhtar turned away, apparently uninterested, but Helen could see that he was considering what she had said.

When he looked back, he nodded down at Mitchell. 'Is he all right?'

Other than refusing the chance to remove his jacket, Mitchell had not spoken in almost half an hour. He was staring at the floor between his knees. He was shaking.

'He's frightened,' Helen said. 'That's all.'

'Are you?'

'I'm frightened for my son.'

Akhtar nodded and turned away again. He folded his arms. Helen could see that he was doing his best to appear hard-bitten and unconcerned, but he was not even close to carrying it off.

'You get used to it,' he said.

There were plenty more hard looks and insults as Thorne walked through the wing towards the library. It was not a novelty and he

81

heard nothing he had not heard many times before, though he was a little surprised to find that it was the youngest boys who were the worst. One particular double-act who could not have been older than fourteen got extremely worked up; telling Thorne exactly what they thought of him, what they would happily do to his wife and mother, before being gently admonished by a prison officer who was clearly more of a Barraclough than a Mackay.

All par for the course.

Approaching the library, Thorne saw two more likely lads hanging around outside the doors and prepared himself for another bout of industrial-strength badinage. He was pleasantly surprised to see them hurrying away as he got closer. Then, hearing footsteps behind him, he turned, and saw that he was not the one they were keen to avoid.

There were a dozen or so boys, sixteen and upwards, in step and walking close together. They were black, white, Asian. They all wore regulation blue T-shirts and cargos, but each also wore a simple grey skullcap. As they drew closer, Thorne saw that there was a middle-aged Asian man in the middle of the group, wearing a plain white robe and embroidered velvet *kufi*. The boys flanking him moved aside when the group was within a few feet of Thorne, allowing the man to move ahead.

He placed one hand over his heart and extended the other one towards Thorne. 'I am Imam Mir Hamid Shakir,' he said. 'I am the visiting imam here at Barndale.'

Thorne shook the man's hand, nodded over his shoulder. 'Got your own bodyguards, I see.'

The boys standing behind Shakir gave no more of a reaction than the imam himself did.

'I hear you are asking questions about Amin Akhtar.'

Thorne said that he was.

'Then we need to talk.'

THIRTEEN

The address that Holland and Kitson had been given for Scott Clarkson – one of the other two boys alleged to have attacked Amin Akhtar on the night of Lee Slater's death – turned out to be a fifth-floor flat in a block behind Highbury and Islington station. The lift was predictably out of action and, after the climb up five flights of stone stairs that apparently doubled as a communal toilet and rubbish dump, there was no reply when Holland and Kitson knocked.

'We should get some cards printed up,' Holland said. '"We called while you were out. To ask if you, or any other waste of DNA you know, had anything to do with a death that may or may not have been a suicide. Please contact us on the number below if you can help." That kind of thing.'

'Or we could just move on to the next one,' Kitson said.

'Can we grab some lunch first? I'm bloody starving.'

Kitson turned and began walking back towards the stairs. 'We'll get a sandwich or something on the way.' She peered over the wall and was pleased to see the car was where she'd left it. That it still had the requisite number of wheels. 'I don't think taking the full hour would go down too well under the circumstances, do you?'

'Probably not.'

Holland followed, stayed a few steps behind her as they trudged back down the stairs. 'Where's Armstrong live?'

'Luckily we've got a work address for this one, so I suggest we try that first.' Kitson dug into her bag for a piece of paper. 'Might be hopelessly optimistic of course.'

'Theme for the day,' Holland said, quietly.

Kitson looked at her notes and smiled. 'Well that's a bit of luck. He works in a takeaway on Essex Road, so we can kill two birds with one stone and pick you up a burger or something at the same time.'

'Not unless I want extra spit in it,' Holland said. 'Or worse.'

'Well if you're going to get picky.'

Holland caught her up on the next flight. 'Seriously though, Yvonne—'

'I know, but let's just get on with it, shall we?' Kitson's tone was suddenly a little less matey. A simple reminder that she was a rank above him. 'Yes, we'll almost certainly turn up jack shit, but it's not like Thorne's got a lot of choice, and it's the least we can do for that poor cow with the gun at her head, don't you reckon?'

Holland appeared to have got the message, said he supposed it was.

'Besides, it's nice to have a day away from the office,' Kitson said. They emerged from the stairwell on to the scrubby patch of grass in front of the block. There were two newly painted benches, and an old bike leaning against a yellowing fridge-freezer. 'Get out and about, see a few of the sights.'

They both turned at the noise of a car backfiring and saw two figures fifty yards away to their left, huddled in the shadows of a concrete overhang. They watched something change hands that almost certainly wasn't a set of Pokémon cards, before one of the figures looked in their direction, suddenly aware that they were being observed. Each shoved their hands into their pockets, but neither showed any inclination to move away.

'Such a shame we're in a hurry,' Kitson said, then turned and began walking quickly towards the car. 'See, Dave?' she said. 'If we weren't so up against it, and we actually gave a monkey's, we might have had *that* nonsense to deal with. So, every cloud . . . '

They both knew very well that, busy or not, the chances of them choosing to intervene in a petty drug deal were slim to non-existent. But Holland was happy to play along for the sake of the joke.

'I didn't see a thing,' he said, a step or two behind.

Thorne followed Mir Hamid Shakir and his friends in a slow, ten-minute procession to the other end of the wing. At each set of heavy metal gates they waited patiently for a prison officer to let them through, until eventually, after descending to the ground floor, they turned into a narrow corridor and arrived at a plain wooden door.

A sign outside said *Faith Suite*.

The imam unlocked the door and invited Thorne across the threshold, leaving his followers to wait outside. The room was the largest Thorne had been in since he'd arrived, white and windowless. There were half a dozen wooden benches against the walls, a wide-screen TV on a stand and a scattering of plastic chairs across a thin blue carpet. At the far end, a simple altar draped in purple sat beneath a large metal cross.

Shakir sat on one of the benches and Thorne took a chair a few feet away.

'Yes, it *is* rather strange,' Shakir said, watching Thorne take in his surroundings. 'At the moment this is the only place of worship we have, so we are forced to share it.' The imam was somewhere in his mid-fifties with a wispy grey beard. He was slight, birdlike, and the eyes that shone behind rimless glasses were almost as bright as the perfect teeth that flashed when he smiled. 'There is rather more work for us than for my fellow priests as we have a little more . . . *paraphernalia* than they do to remove when it is our turn.' He fluttered a hand towards the altar. 'We need nothing but our prayer mats.'

'Nice and easy,' Thorne said.

'And of course, we pray rather more often.' He smiled at Thorne.

'I am hoping that we will have our own place of worship very soon. It would be more convenient for everyone.'

'You wanted to talk about Amin Akhtar.'

Shakir nodded and lowered his head. Muttered, 'Yes, yes . . .'

Thorne waited a few seconds. 'Is there something you can tell me about his death?'

Shakir looked up. 'Why he did it, perhaps?'

'That would certainly be helpful.'

Another fifteen seconds passed. Thorne glanced at his watch, hoping that the imam might catch it.

'Most of the young men who come to this place are looking for something,' Shakir said. 'The fact that they have not found it might explain why they have turned to violence or drugs to fill the holes in their lives. In here, those options are of course denied them, so they search for something else. There are gangs of course, even inside these walls, but those who wish to change their lives will seek out something they can belong to that nourishes them and shows them a different path. I believe passionately that Islam offers them that. I have no idea if you are a man of faith at all, it does not matter, but does what I'm saying make sense to you?'

Up to a point, Thorne thought. He just nodded.

'You only have to look at the numbers. In an hour's time I will have twenty or more boys in this room. Black, white, whatever, all praying and reading from the Qu'ran. I can assure you that is many more than the Catholic priest might expect. Or the . . . *vicar*.' He enunciated the word very precisely, smiling as though he found it amusing. 'Muslims are less than three per cent of the population outside,' he said, holding up fingers to make his point. '*Four* times that number in here, and at other institutions such as this one. Many finding their faith, you see?'

Thorne tried to look impressed, but in truth he was not surprised.

He had read about the increase in the Muslim population in UK prisons, which to a large extent was due to the numbers of those converting to Islam while behind bars. There were those who were every bit as concerned at these figures as Shakir was delighted; pointing to what they saw

86

as a troubling degree of radicalisation going on at the same time. They held up the example of Richard Reid – the so-called 'shoe bomber' – who had become radicalised at Feltham YOI, and of Muktar Said Ibrahim – one of the leaders of the failed 21/7 attacks in London – who had spent two and a half years in Huntercombe YOI. Numerous reports now openly declared that those the imam believed to be searching for something were finding it in the more extreme elements of the Islamic faith.

Fuel to the fire, sadly, for those with an ultra-right-wing agenda, and to the simply ignorant who imagined plots being hatched beneath every minaret.

Worrying reading, nonetheless.

Shakir clearly saw the way Thorne's mind was working and nodded. 'Of course, I know how this ... *blossoming* is being interpreted in certain quarters. I am familiar with all the predictable scaremongering. "Breeding grounds for Jihad." "Universities of terror."' He shook his head. 'It is a shame that boys who have been called gangsters and jailbirds are now called terrorists, when all they are doing is sitting peacefully and reading, and I don't need to remind you that none of those studying the Bible seem to be labelled in the same way.'

'Was Amin one of those boys?'

'Amin was ... lost,' Shakir said. 'That was very obvious.'

Thorne thought about how the governor had described Amin. Studious and quiet, with a small group of friends. 'That's not the impression I've been given,' he said.

'Whatever your impression, he had that same emptiness inside him that so many others in this place have. I reached out to him, but sadly I could do nothing to help.'

Thorne remembered a boy who, though raised as a Muslim, had shown no inclination whatsoever towards profound religious belief.

He said as much to Shakir.

'I am aware of that, but what better opportunity could he have had to rediscover the faith he had lost? A guiding force which would offer hope and comfort. And believe me, such things are in short supply around here.'

'So, when you say you "reached out" ...'

'Approaches were made to him by several boys whose lives have already been changed.'

Thorne pictured the posse of Shakir's acolytes waiting just outside the door. He could not help but ask himself how gentle these 'approaches' had been and if one or two of the boys in grey skullcaps would be altogether welcome when they came knocking on a cell door. He wondered if one of them might even have been responsible for the attack that had put Amin Akhtar in hospital.

Had his rejection of the faith been taken too personally?

Once again, Shakir appeared to have seen something in Thorne's face. 'I also spoke to him myself,' he said. 'Several times, in fact. But as I have already said, I could not get through to him. I could see that he was lost and, if I am honest, I was not surprised at what eventually happened.' He raised a hand and laid it against his narrow chest. 'I must accept that my failure was at least partially to blame for ... what he did.'

The distaste had been plain enough in the imam's reedy voice. 'You don't like the fact that he killed himself?'

'Of all the bounties bestowed on human beings by Allah, the most precious gift is life.' Shakir leaned towards Thorne. 'It has been granted to us, but it is not our possession and is not ours to throw away. The Qu'ran makes it perfectly plain, I'm afraid. To take one's life is as sinful as taking any other.'

Thorne asked himself what Mohammad Sidique Khan or any of the other 7/7 suicide bombers would have thought about that, but he said nothing.

'Most other faiths believe this too, I think you'll find. Suicide was illegal in this country, once upon a time.'

'Right,' Thorne said. 'And in theory you can still be banged up for not practising archery twice a week.'

Shakir smiled, a few less teeth on display. 'You used to bury their bodies at a crossroads,' he said.

'Sorry?'

'Those who had taken their own lives. At night, with a stake through the heart.'

'I didn't know that.' Thorne smiled back. 'You think we should have done that with Amin's body?' He gathered up the files that he had set down next to the chair. 'Maybe asked his mother and father to do it?'

The imam chuckled and stood up slowly. Said, 'You are being rather facetious now, I think, but that is fine, and I can tell that you are keen to get on.'

Thorne thanked Shakir for his time, though even as they shook hands he remained unsure as to exactly why the imam had thought their conversation would be of any use. He felt rather as though he had just seen muscle being flexed. He opened the door and, with no more than the odd brush of shoulders, eased his way through the devoted gathering outside, which had now grown to more than a dozen.

As he walked away, he was aware of Shakir beckoning them into the chapel. Without a word, they trooped inside. Thorne guessed that afternoon prayers were imminent and there was unwelcome paraphernalia to be cleared away.

89

FOURTEEN

She hadn't stopped thinking about Alfie of course, not for one second, but there had been practicalities to consider. A relationship to establish with Javed Akhtar and the worrying condition of the man sitting next to her.

A situation to try and get on top of.

Now, as Helen looked at her watch, the image of her son's face knocked the breath from her, and she pictured the childminder trying to get him to sleep for half an hour after his lunch. Janine, holding him and shushing while she rubbed his back. The way Helen had shown her – small circles, low down on his back – even though Janine had three kids of her own and knew perfectly well what to do.

The way he liked.

Panic-stricken suddenly, she tried to reassure herself that she had packed the soft toy he liked to clutch when he was sleeping. The raggedy, greenish-brown thing that might have been a frog and might have been a bear.

Yes, she had packed it. She had packed everything.

The same chaotic routine every morning, struggling to get herself and Alfie ready and out of the flat. Snatching bites of toast while she got dressed and made up and Alfie crawled unerringly towards every sharp corner he could find or reached up for any heavy object he might just be able to pull down on top of himself. Stuffing things into her own bag, and into his. Court reports and photographs of bruised and bleeding children. Nappies, toys and teething gel.

Then the struggle with the pushchair on those sodding stairs. Ten minutes' walk to Janine's and that last cuddle, then on towards the station. Chewing gum and chocolate.

That last cuddle . . .

She thought about the catch in his voice that killed her when he cried and the way he gummed at her chin, fastening on like a limpet as he tangled his fingers in her hair.

The smell when she nuzzled at the back of his neck.

Akhtar was next door in the shop. Helen could hear him moving things around and the noise of glass being swept. She guessed that he was trying to clear away the mess he had made earlier.

That was a good sign, she thought. A desire for order.

Stephen Mitchell sat bolt upright at her side, running with sweat and scratching at himself. His eyes were closed and he was mouthing words she could not make out clearly.

Alfie would need picking up in a couple of hours' time. Janine was always strict about that, with a school run to take care of and a husband coming home from work. Helen would always call, even if she was going to be just a few minutes past pick-up time . . .

Sweating, as she ran from the station.

They would have organised something, she was sure about that. Maybe Janine had already heard about it, seen something on the news. Helen hoped it would not be a uniformed officer knocking on Janine's door. Some big awkward oaf scooping Alfie up and carrying him out to a squad car. No, they would have told Jenny, surely . . . which was probably the best thing.

Good in a crisis, her younger sister. Organised. Cold.

She rolled her wrist around inside the metal cuff.

Proof positive, of course, that Jenny had been right all along. Had

91

known best, as usual. Hard enough to cope on your own, never mind going back to a job like that. Not so quickly anyway. Think about the baby.

Now look where you've got your bloody self!

She wondered if they were outside. Jenny and her dad. The old man nagging every copper he could get hold of, demanding to be told what was being done, with Jenny trying to keep him calm. Taking charge and finding out where the tea and biscuits were.

Being Mum.

She tried not to think about it, but it was like trying not to breathe.

At least Jenny knew the best way to get Alfie off. Helen had shown her plenty of times, *enjoyed* showing her.

Small circles, low down on his back—

'It's going to be OK, isn't it?' Mitchell asked suddenly. 'You said so before. I mean, you're not just saying it, are you?'

She looked at him. He was blinking quickly and trying to smile. He looked like a little boy.

Her phone rang.

She stared at it – the vibration causing the handset to inch across the floor between her legs – until Akhtar came hurrying back in.

'Is it Thorne?'

Helen shook her head. She did not recognise the number. She pointed towards the front of the shop. 'Probably them,' she said. 'They'll want to talk to you.'

Akhtar sat down and picked up the gun. He let the phone ring for another few seconds, then nodded.

'Answer it.'

On his way back towards the library, Thorne slipped into one of the prison officers' tea rooms to call Holland. He walked into the corner and took out his phone, smiling at the two occupants, despite stares only marginally less aggressive than those he'd received out on the landing.

'Any joy?'

'Slater's old man was as much of an arsehole as you'd expect,' Holland said. 'But he was surprised enough to hear that Amin was dead.'

Thorne wasn't surprised to hear it. A result that fast was way too much to hope for. 'What about Lee Slater's mates?'

'Clarkson wasn't in and we're just on our way to see Armstrong.'

'OK. Quick as you can, Dave.' Thorne heard Kitson in the background, saying she couldn't find a place to park. 'Just park *anywhere*,' he shouted.

Holland said something, but Thorne lost it in the blare of a passing siren.

'Dave?'

'I said, what about you?'

'What?'

'Any joy?'

Thorne was still struggling to process everything he'd heard and seen since he'd arrived at Barndale. The reactions to Amin Akhtar's death from Bracewell and McCarthy. The psychological analysis from Shakir. He looked at his watch, then glanced across at the two POs cradling mugs of tea and looking as though they could not wait for the day to end.

'Precious little in here,' Thorne said.

FIFTEEN

Sue Pascoe was grateful – despite the speakers that had been set up to listen in – that the microphone on her handset was not sensitive enough to pick up the sound of her heart beating.

The phone continued to ring out . . .

She had done everything required of her up to this point, gathering all available information about both hostages and hostage taker and working to formulate a negotiation strategy, but that would be worth next to nothing if this first call did not go well. The initial contact with the hostage taker was always the most delicate part of any operation. The foundation on which, if it went according to the textbook, everything else could be built.

The problem was that Javed Akhtar was anything but a textbook hostage taker.

Outside of situations involving domestic disputes or disgruntled employees, hostage takers usually fitted neatly into one of four categories: criminals, the mentally disturbed, prisoners or terrorists. They were part of structured groups or they were unstable individuals and the actual taking of hostages was either well planned or spontaneous.

It was easy enough to see which of these boxes Akhtar ticked, but from that point on he had ceased to be predictable.

To be someone you could be trained to deal with.

The received wisdom was that any hostage taker was faced with three options. He could surrender to the police. He could lessen his demands and continue to negotiate. Or he could choose martyrdom by killing the hostages and/or himself. Akhtar could yet choose to do any of these of course, but trying to predict which and guiding him towards an outcome in which nobody was harmed depended almost entirely on what he was demanding.

There were well-structured reactions to demands for money, or drugs, or the release of comrades in arms. There was an accepted response to a simple need for attention. This time though, Sue Pascoe listened to the phone ring inside the newsagent's shop and felt as though she would be making it up as she went along, because the man who was holding two hostages at gunpoint appeared to want nothing but answers.

And she could not be sure Tom Thorne would be able to provide the ones he was looking for.

Done much of this? he had asked her. Cheeky bastard obviously thought he was God's gift.

All those gathered around the speakers in the school hall leaned that little bit closer when the call was answered. Donnelly gave Sue Pascoe the nod and the hostage negotiator spoke softly into the phone.

'Helen?'

'Who's this?'

Pascoe looked at Donnelly who quickly nodded his understanding. It was clear from the echo that Helen Weeks' phone was also on speaker. That Akhtar was listening in.

'I'm Detective Sergeant Sue Pascoe and I'm working here with the team that's trying to get this situation resolved, OK?'

'OK ...'

'First of all, how are you doing in there?'

'I've been better, obviously.'

Pascoe gave Donnelly a thumbs-up. Always a good sign if the hostage felt able to make light of their predicament. That they were permitted to by the person holding them. 'Well, I can promise you that everything's being done to get this sorted out as fast as possible.'

'What about my son?'

Another look to Donnelly, who shrugged. It had been agreed that Pascoe would try to avoid talking about Helen Weeks' child, but clearly the subject could not be avoided if Helen Weeks brought it up.

'That's all taken care of, Helen. You don't need to worry about that.' Pascoe knew at once that it was a stupid thing to say. Of course she would be worried. 'We've made all the arrangements, OK?'

'OK ...'

'How's Stephen?'

'He's ... doing OK.'

Pascoe took a deep breath. 'Can I talk to Javed, Helen?'

There was a pause. Pascoe imagined Helen looking towards Akhtar for a response. Looking at the gun. She listened for his voice, prepared herself.

Thinking: active listening, validation, reassurance.

'He doesn't want to,' Helen said.

Pascoe raised her voice. 'Javed, can you hear me? If you can hear me, I'd really like to speak to you, if that's all right.'

'I only want to speak to Thorne,' Akhtar shouted.

'I understand that, Javed,' Pascoe said. 'You only want to speak to Tom Thorne.' She took care to repeat the hostage taker's words, just as she had been taught, to focus the attention on him and make it clear that she had understood his wishes. 'We will definitely make sure that happens, but right now he's not here. He's busy trying to gather the information you wanted.'

'Not "information",' Akhtar shouted. '*Truth*. They are not the same thing ... not the same thing at all.'

'No, of course they aren't,' Pascoe said, careful to show concern, but not to talk down. To let him know she felt the same way about these things as he did. 'We do understand what you want, Javed.'

96

Akhtar said nothing.

'Nadira's here, Javed.' She paused for a few seconds, deliberately. 'She's here and she wants to talk to you.'

'*No.*'

Pascoe had to move quickly, before Akhtar had a chance to hang up. She beckoned his wife across and nodded to her. The woman glanced at the listening officers as she took the phone. Donnelly raised two hands and mouthed, 'Nice and calm.'

'Javed ...' Nadira Akhtar sounded as nervous as she looked. She gave a hesitant smile when Pascoe reached out to lay a hand on her arm. 'It's me.'

'I can't talk now,' Akhtar said.

'You need to talk to me, OK?'

'No, I *don't.*'

'This is ridiculous, Javee.'

Akhtar said something in Hindi then and Nadira said, 'No, you need to tell me.' He spoke in Hindi again, for longer this time. Pascoe looked across at Donnelly and shrugged. Even though there was a translator standing within earshot – a young woman poised with notepad and pencil – it had been agreed that Nadira would try and talk to her husband in English. Nadira looked at Pascoe, panic-stricken. She put her hand over the mouthpiece and whispered, 'He won't talk to me in English.'

'It's OK,' Pascoe said. 'Just keep talking to him.'

They spoke for several minutes more. Akhtar did most of the talking, shouting at first, then growing calmer as he said the same thing over and over, while his wife tried and failed to interject, until eventually she gave up and began to weep.

When Akhtar ended the call, Pascoe took the phone and stood up to put an arm around the woman's shoulders. She looked at Donnelly as she told her how well she had done, while Nadira shook her head and dabbed at her eyes with a tissue. Donnelly nodded the translator across, but Nadira waved her away. She wanted to tell them herself.

'He says he loves us all very much and that he's sorry.' She fought back a sob. 'This is for Amin, he says. All for Amin. He says that he owes it to him to do this.' She lowered her head. 'He is happy to offer his life back to Allah if need be, but he has no choice. *Everyone's* life ...'

The tears came again and she made no effort to stop them. Donnelly quickly beckoned the WPC who was working as family liaison officer to escort her away. Nadira turned to say sorry one more time as she was led from the hall, but Donnelly, Pascoe and Chivers had already moved into a huddle.

'I didn't like the sound of that last bit,' Chivers said. 'Offering his life back. Heard that a few too many times.'

'He's not a terrorist,' Pascoe said.

'Isn't he?'

Donnelly raised his hands and tried to speak, but Pascoe was not about to let Chivers have the last word.

'He's just a father who's lost his son, so let's not go throwing labels around.' Her responsibility as a negotiator began and ended with the safety of the hostages. That meant maintaining an atmosphere of calm and making sure that nobody – fellow officers included – got over-excited.

Chivers made no attempt to hide a sneer. Donnelly asked both of them if they had quite finished. Pascoe – calling on every ounce of training and experience when it came to reading people and making judgements about personality and state of mind – decided that Chivers was a twat.

'Right ...' Donnelly said.

They all turned at the sound of raised voices in the corridor, and moved quickly when somebody screamed and what sounded like a full-blown slanging match began to erupt. Donnelly led the way, charging out of the hall and towards the classroom that had been set up as a family liaison area.

They entered the classroom to see a WPC struggling to hold back a young black woman who was raging at a terrified Nadira Akhtar. She called her a bitch and swore that if anything happened to her husband, she would make her and her family pay for it.

Donnelly shouted, demanding to know what was going on.

'Sorry, sir.' The red-faced WPC finally managed to gain some control over the woman. 'This is Stephen Mitchell's wife. I didn't know where else to put her.'

Pascoe took Nadira's arm and led her from the room. Chivers raised an eyebrow and followed them.

Donnelly glared at the WPC. 'Nice job,' he said.

SIXTEEN

When Thorne eventually got to the library, he spread the files out across a table in the corner and spent fifteen minutes tracing Amin Akhtar's journey, from first court appearance to funeral.

As was the case with all young offenders sent down from the Old Bailey, Amin had been transferred to Feltham YOI, the same place in which he had spent five months on remand after his arrest. From there, he was eventually assigned to Barndale to serve what would be the first half of his eight-year sentence, before moving into the adult prison system.

Despite the circumstances of the offence and the nature of the boy who had committed it, the court had handed down a sentence at the high end of the scale. It had clearly been Amin's misfortune to come up in front of a judge determined to be tough on knife crime. Even so, it was little wonder that Amin's legal team had spent six months mounting a vigorous appeal, which would now of course never be heard.

Arguably, Helen Weeks was now a victim of that same misfortune.

Thorne made a mental note to talk to Amin's solicitor and sent Brigstocke a text asking him to get hold of the phone number.

He looked up from the paperwork at the sound of laughter from two boys huddled around a computer at the far end of the library. Along with an older boy who sat engrossed in a book near the door, they were the only inmates in the place and thankfully seemed uninterested in Thorne's presence. The boys at the computer giggled again and the female PO at the desk raised her eyes from a copy of *Closer*. Told them to keep the noise down.

Thorne guessed that Amin Akhtar had spent a good deal of time in this room that smelled of polish and something else. Damp, perhaps. He opened the police report and took out the photographs of the boy's body that lay on top of the file; the lips drawn back across the teeth, the blood caked around his chin and dried like streaks of rust on his neck.

He wondered what kind of books Amin had liked to read.

Once Thorne had done some reading of his own, it became clear that the original investigation had – with one notable exception – been less sloppy than he had initially feared. Dawes had done just about all that was required of him to ascertain that there had been no suspicious circumstances around the sudden death of Amin Akhtar.

He had reviewed the CCTV footage and asked all the right questions about keys. He had looked at the possibility that the drugs taken by Amin had been brought in from outside the hospital wing and interviewed the boy who had visited him. He had even checked the plastic cup found on the floor of the room for fingerprints. Only Amin's and those of the PHO who had given him his final dose of meds had been found.

Dawes had also taken statements from all the patients on the two wards the night that Amin had died. Eleven boys from across the three prison sites with a variety of conditions and dependencies; a few with broken bones and several recovering from minor operations performed at the local hospital.

Predictably, none had seen or heard anything. Having seen how drugged-up many of the patients currently in residence were, Thorne was almost tempted to believe the statements, but he had to agree with Dawes' assertion that looking for witnesses was a lost cause.

Something was still missing though.

Thorne looked through the report one more time. There was no reference anywhere to the thefts from the dispensary, or the possibility that one of them had been the source of the Tramadol that had killed Amin.

Not quite a job well done then, but one with a nice neat line drawn under it nonetheless, ensuring a speedy resolution to the formalities that followed.

Based on the information he had gathered, Dawes had come to a perfectly reasonable conclusion, and with a post-mortem to support it, the coroner would have been happy enough to release the body to the family for burial within a few days. In the apparent absence of any new evidence, the formal inquest that had taken place a fortnight ago would have been straightforward enough. There was little reason for the jury to deliver any other verdict than the one it did. No reason to harbour doubts, or for anyone to take the concerns of a grief-stricken father seriously.

But now, Thorne had a few concerns of his own.

There were others he needed to talk to, of course, and perhaps it was all because he *wanted* to find something he could take back to Javed Akhtar. To give Amin's father what he was asking for and get Helen Weeks out of that shop in one piece. Perhaps Holland had been right and Thorne was looking for a murder where there was none ...

He closed the file when he saw the two boys get up from the computer and start walking towards him. He slid the photographs underneath.

'You the one asking questions about the kid that topped himself?'

Thorne caught the eye of the PO who was clearly wondering whether or not to intervene. He shook his head to let her know there was not a problem.

The boy who had asked the question was a tall, skinny Asian, eighteen or so. He sniffed and reached to nudge glasses back up his nose, then went back to holding the DVD he was clutching to his chest. The boy next to him was younger, shorter and thickset. White, with a shaved head and bad teeth which Thorne saw a good deal of, as he had not stopped smiling since he arrived at the table.

Thorne said, 'Yes, I am.'

The Asian boy pulled out a chair and sat down and his friend was quick to do the same. The PO looked across again, but Thorne ignored her.

'My name's Tom Thorne. I'm a police officer.'

The Asian boy shrugged, like he'd worked that much out already. 'Aziz,' he said. He nodded towards his friend. 'This is Darren.'

Darren smiled.

'He was called Amin,' Thorne said. 'The boy that killed himself. Did you know him?'

'Seen him around,' Aziz said. 'Wouldn't say I knew him though.'

Thorne looked at Darren.

'Same,' Darren said.

'Thing is, you never really get to know anyone, if you understand what I'm saying.' Aziz spoke quickly with a London accent and the merest suggestion of a stammer. 'People in here are all trying to be something they're not or something they want you to think they are. Easier that way, yeah?'

Thorne nodded. 'What about you?'

Aziz laughed and leaned back until the front legs of his chair had left the ground. 'Nah, too much effort, all that, and I've been here a while anyway so I know how to be myself and keep out of trouble.' He spread out his arms, the DVD in one hand. 'What you see is what you get.'

Darren leaned forward to Thorne suddenly. 'So, you like the library then?'

'It's good,' Thorne said. 'Quiet.'

'Yeah, it's quiet.'

'You like it?'

Darren pointed across at Aziz, grinning. '*He* does, and that's a fact. He's in here all the time, I swear. Reading this weird shit about space and all stuff that's been invented. Science and that, like a professor or something.'

Thorne looked at Aziz who reddened slightly, then shrugged, happy enough with the description.

'Go on, ask him something,' Darren said, excited. 'He knows everything about science and that, I'm telling you. He could go on *Mastermind,* I swear, and thrash any of them, piece of piss. Go on, ask him a question. Hard as you like.'

Aziz eased his chair gently back down and told his friend to shut up.

'No point anyway,' Thorne said. 'I'm rubbish at science.'

'*He's* not rubbish,' Darren said, pointing at Aziz again. 'Honest to God, he's like that bloke in the wheelchair who sounds like a Dalek ... except the bloke in the wheelchair's not a Paki.'

'You should talk to that black kid,' Aziz said. He nodded Thorne across towards the boy who was reading by the door. Aware of the attention, the boy glanced up from his book for a second or two. His face was expressionless; handsome and hard.

'Why?' Thorne asked.

'He was that dead kid's mate. I saw them together a fair bit, talking in their cells, all that. In here too, sometimes.' Aziz lowered his voice, and not just because the PO was scowling at him. 'He got in big trouble for punching someone a few weeks back, got chucked off the Gold wing and all that. I reckon that was because they said something sick about his mate killing himself and he didn't like it, you know what I'm saying?'

Thorne looked over at the boy by the door again, but saw no more than the top of his head.

'You want to see something funny?' Darren asked.

Thorne turned back, his mind still on the boy. 'What?'

'Show him,' Darren said. Laughing, he reached across and tried to grab the DVD, but Aziz snatched it away.

'What have you been watching?' Thorne asked.

Aziz tossed the DVD on to the table. There was a picture of a human foetus in the womb on the cover. 'Been showing him some stuff about reproduction and all that. Basic human biology, how it all works, whatever. He wanted to know, so ... '

'I told you,' Darren said. 'He knows everything about all that.'

'What did you think of it?'

Darren shook his head, though the smile never wavered. 'There's some seriously strange shit on there, I tell you. Test-tube babies and weird rubbish like that. I swear, I'd never want no test-tube baby.'

Aziz looked at Thorne and rolled his eyes.

'They've got like . . . webbed hands and feet,' Darren said. He held up his hands and wiggled his fingers. 'No word of a lie.'

Aziz shook his head. 'Why do you think they've got webbed feet?'

'That's how they swim out of the test tube.'

Thorne fought to control a smile, but couldn't manage it.

'He's not normally quite this mental,' Aziz said. 'He's just a bit over-excited.'

'Tell him why.'

'*You* tell him.'

'I'm getting out in two weeks,' Darren said, beaming. 'And I'm going to be a dad. My girlfriend's having our baby.' He smacked his chest proudly, then pointed at the DVD, to the picture of the foetus in the womb. 'Our own little baby, just like this one.'

'That's good,' Thorne said. 'Best make sure you don't come back then.'

Darren nodded, solemn.

'How long have you been inside?'

'Eighteen months,' Darren said. He looked at Thorne and then at his friend. 'What . . . ?'

Aziz was still laughing as Thorne gathered up all the files, and the PO was smirking behind her magazine. Darren looked confused but continued to smile. Thorne turned round again, just in time to see the boy in the corner walking out through the library doors.

SEVENTEEN

The takeaway where Danny Armstrong worked was fifty yards from Essex Road railway station, between a dry cleaners' and a shop that seemed deserted but still had a few old vacuum cleaners on display. Holland and Kitson stared in through the steamy window and spotted a likely-looking teenager chopping tomatoes behind the counter. He looked up when they entered, pushed the tomatoes into a plastic container and wiped his hands on the back of his jeans.

'Yes, mate?'

The place sold kebabs, burgers, chicken; pretty much anything that could be deep-fried and stuck inside a bun. Come half past eleven at night with a few drinks inside you, it probably smelled like heaven, but, stone cold sober at lunchtime, Holland was suddenly feeling a little less hungry than he had been.

He produced his warrant card.

'Just a quick word, Danny.'

Armstrong looked nervously towards a doorway to his right and, on cue, a burly, middle-aged man appeared carrying a metal tray piled high with chicken wings. He was Greek, Holland guessed, or Turkish, and he watched as Kitson went to the door and turned the sign to CLOSED.

106

'Hey . . .'

Holland flashed his ID again, but the man shook his head and shouted at Kitson. 'You can't do that.'

'Yes, I can,' Kitson said.

Holland said that he was sorry for the inconvenience, but that they would only need a few minutes of the boy's time. The man laid his tray down and pointed at Armstrong. He said, 'It's coming out your wages,' then turned and walked out.

Armstrong looked at Holland. 'Cheers.'

Kitson walked across and placed a five-pound note on the counter. 'We'll have a couple of bags of chips then,' she said. 'Keep your boss happy, OK?'

Armstrong grunted, moved to the deep-fat fryer and pushed up the lid.

'Amin Akhtar,' Holland said. 'Remember him? He died in prison a few months back and we were wondering if you'd heard about it.'

Armstrong didn't look up. 'News to me.'

'You sure?'

'Yeah, I told you.' He raised his head. 'I swear . . . I didn't know that.'

'Not spoken to Scott Clarkson about it, maybe?' Kitson asked. 'Or Lee Slater's dad?'

'Don't really see them.'

'You might see them now though, right? Have a few drinks to celebrate.'

'Yeah, why not?' Armstrong shovelled chips out and into a styrofoam container. 'Be a year soon enough anyway, since Lee was killed. So yeah, we might get together.'

'Lee's brother might be out by then,' Holland said. 'I imagine he'll be pretty pleased to hear about Amin, too. Don't you reckon?' It was clear enough from Armstrong's expression that not only was the answer blindingly obvious, but that he did not understand why he was being asked the question. Holland glanced at Kitson and saw that she'd seen it too. However many insinuations they made or however

107

hard they tried to dig for something, the kid was every bit as surprised as Slater's father had been to hear about Amin Akhtar's death.

Armstrong dug out a second portion of chips. 'You want salt and vinegar?'

Kitson leaned across and helped herself, then pushed the containers back for Armstrong to wrap. 'He killed himself, just so you know. So you know *exactly* what you'll be drinking to. After he was attacked and put in hospital. After he was raped.'

'Yeah, well, he'd have enjoyed that,' Armstrong muttered.

'Sorry?'

'Nothing, just ... ' Armstrong reddened and quickly wrapped another sheet of paper around the takeaway cartons. He shoved them into a plastic bag and looked at Kitson. 'Look, he deserved it, all right? Not dying I mean, I didn't even ... know about that. Getting banged up, though, that was fair enough.'

'You reckon?'

'For what he done to Lee.'

'What, after you and your mates attacked him, you mean?'

'It wasn't like that.'

Armstrong tried to protest but Holland cut him off. 'I know, just a harmless bit of snowballing, right?'

'He stabbed Lee.'

'Yeah, well,' Kitson said. 'That's what happens when you take a knife to a snowball fight.'

'Hey, when can I open my bloody shop?'

They all turned to see that the owner had reappeared in the doorway.

'That's three pounds for the chips,' Armstrong said. He took the note and put it into the till, laid two pound coins down on the counter.

Holland pushed Kitson's change towards her and snatched the bag. He nodded across at the conical slab of grey meat turning slowly on a spit in the corner. 'You're as full of shit as that is, Danny,' he said.

*

108

Helen had drifted away. Her eyes closed and her head back against the cool metal of the radiator.

Alfie was laughing and Paul was there and he was laughing too. The way she had almost forgotten, because she was unable to call his face quickly and clearly to mind. The features blurring, until she was left with nothing but the shape of him. A muddy image of his mouth half open while he slept, or that thunderous scowl when he was pissed off. Each expression growing fuzzier with every week that passed, while she searched desperately for the ghosts of them in her son's face.

It was clear enough now though.

A daydream that she wished more than anything was a memory, or better yet a vision of the future.

Jammy little bugger's got my looks.

You reckon?

Come on, he's bloody gorgeous!

He's a damn sight less moody than you, that's for sure.

'I need a drink.'

Helen opened her eyes, astonished to hear Mitchell finally talking. She turned to look at him and saw him nodding towards Akhtar who was sitting at the desk and staring at the wall above their heads.

'I need a drink,' Mitchell said again. 'Can I please have something to drink?'

Akhtar nodded and stood up. 'Coke or something?'

'That's fine, thank you.'

The newsagent walked out into the shop and as soon as he was gone Mitchell leaned across to Helen. 'We have to do something now,' he said.

'*What?*'

'I can't do this, I told you.'

'Just calm down, Stephen, all right?'

'I can't.' He shook his head. 'Who knows how long we could be stuck here and he might just kill us anyway.'

'He won't kill us if we do as he says.'

'Come on, you're a copper. You should be working out a way to get us out of this.'

'Trust me, I am.'

'We can't just sit here.'

'Yes we can,' Helen said. 'We don't have to do anything.'

'We could try and get the gun.'

'Please, just—'

'I've thought about it.'

'*No . . .*'

She leaned quickly away from him as Akhtar came back in. She hoped he would not notice that she was suddenly breathing heavily. With the gun in his right hand, Akhtar leaned down and handed Mitchell the can with his left.

'Thanks,' Mitchell said. He opened the can and took a drink. 'It's just so hot, that's all.' He smiled, too wide and wavering a little at the corners of his mouth. 'We're never happy about the weather in this country, are we?'

Akhtar went back to the desk and sat down.

Helen listened to Mitchell gulping down the drink. She could not look at him. She kept her eyes on the gun that Akhtar had once again laid down on the desk, praying that Mitchell had listened to her. That he would not do anything stupid.

'Sorry,' Mitchell said. 'Now I need the toilet.'

Helen turned and looked hard at him, but Mitchell would not meet her eye. She said his name quietly, but he ignored her.

Akhtar thought about Mitchell's request for a few seconds, then nodded. He stood up slowly and reached for the gun. Then he picked up the key to the handcuffs.

'Thanks,' Mitchell said. 'Bursting . . .'

Akhtar tossed the key across to Helen, then pointed the revolver at her. 'Please do it slowly,' he said.

She picked up the key, inched over to her right and gradually leaned across Mitchell's lap. She could smell the sweat as she pressed against him. He kept his eyes on Akhtar, refusing to engage with her though their faces were only inches apart.

Her hand shook as she struggled to fit the tiny key into the lock.

110

'OK, now stand up slowly, please.'

Mitchell climbed to his feet, rolling his wrist around and groaning as he stretched his legs. He let out a long breath and pointed towards the toilet door. 'OK?'

Akhtar nodded. The hand that was holding the gun shifted to track Mitchell's movements as he took the few steps across and opened the toilet door. Helen caught a glimpse of the grubby-looking bowl and black plastic seat just before Mitchell turned to pull the door closed behind him. He finally looked at her, only for a second or two, but she could not read the expression.

Blank or focused, it was hard to tell, but the eyes were empty.

Helen and Akhtar looked at one another as fifteen seconds passed without any noise from inside the toilet. Helen listened for the sound of Mitchell pissing, but heard nothing until, a minute or more after he had gone inside, he began to sob.

They both turned and stared at the scarred wooden door. The noise from behind it was deep and regular. It could almost have been a laugh were it not for the high catch in the throat as Mitchell struggled to find the breath between each tattoo of sobs.

It subsided after a minute or so. There were sniffs then and a bout of coughing, until the toilet flushed and the door finally opened.

'OK, Stephen?' Helen asked.

Mitchell did not respond, standing perfectly still just outside the toilet door and making no attempt to conceal what had been happening inside. He stared, unblinking, at Akhtar, until the newsagent raised the gun and told him to sit down.

Mitchell did not move. Akhtar took a small step in his direction and told him again.

'Better out than in, eh?' Helen said, trying to laugh. 'Stephen?'

Mitchell turned to look at her as if he had only just noticed she was there. He closed his eyes for a few seconds, then opened them again and began walking slowly back towards the radiator.

'Nice and easy,' Helen said.

Akhtar glanced at her. 'Yes . . . please.'

Helen held her breath – keeping her eyes fixed on Mitchell's, searching for the desire, the intent to make any sudden move – and did not release it until her weight was once again across him and she was leaning over to fasten the handcuff back around his wrist.

EIGHTEEN

'He's got someone with him.'

The secretary's warning was somewhat half-hearted, so after giving her the nicest smile he could summon up, Thorne went ahead and knocked on the governor's door anyway.

He walked in without waiting to be invited.

Bracewell was talking to Shakir.

They were standing close together in front of the governor's desk and both turned to stare at Thorne when they saw him come in. Thorne said he was sorry to interrupt, that he just needed a moment. There were a few seconds of silent nodding.

Then the governor and the imam spoke at the same time.

'It's really not a problem . . . '

'We were just finishing up . . . '

Thorne said that he was about ready to go and that he'd just come to thank the governor for all his help before he left. He looked at Shakir, thanked him too.

'Really, there is no need,' Shakir said. 'It would have been nice to talk for longer.'

'Absolutely.' Thorne smiled and wondered which of them was being the less sincere.

The governor stepped forward to shake Thorne's hand. 'And if there's anything else you need, you have my direct line?'

Thorne said that he did and gave the governor a card with his mobile number and home email address on it. 'Oh, I do need that name before I go. The boy you thought was responsible for the attack on Amin?'

'Yes, of course. I meant to ...' The governor walked back to his desk and picked up a piece of paper. He handed it to Thorne. 'Name, address and a contact at the local probation office if you need it.'

Thorne said thanks and slipped the piece of paper into one of the files. He turned to go, then stopped and turned back. 'By the way, Dr McCarthy was going to let me know about the thefts from the Dispensary,' he said. 'The DDA cupboard.'

The governor nodded, said, 'Right.'

'I'm sure he's busy, but I'd be grateful if you could chase that up for me. Get him to give me a call.'

'Of course.'

'And an address for the prison hospital officer who was suspended would be good. I've got her name but, you know, it would save me the trouble of finding her.'

'I'll get him to dig it out,' the governor said.

'Anything that might save a bit of time.'

'Yes, well, I can understand now why this is such a kick-bollock scramble.'

Thorne looked at him.

'One of my officers saw something about this siege business in the early edition of the *Standard*. Not many details, but he recognised the name and we put two and two together.' He puffed out his cheeks. 'Bloody awful.'

'Grief can do very strange things to people,' Shakir said. 'It can affect their ... judgement.'

Thorne said nothing, but the imam was right of course. Thorne

114

knew the way that the loss of a loved one could play havoc with the lives of those left behind. He had watched absurdly cheerful denial become uncontrollable rage and seen rage turn in on itself and fester into self-loathing. Not as quick perhaps as a blade or a bullet, but just as dangerous.

So it made sense to question Javed Akhtar's judgement. To put his accusations down to grief – pure, simple and terrible – and to dismiss the suggestions of a bereaved parent as paranoia, just as police, coroner and jury had done.

None of that helped Helen Weeks though.

'I'll leave you to it,' Thorne said.

Behind him the governor wished him luck and Shakir said, 'Go well.'

Thorne reached for the door. Thinking: nothing wrong with *my* judgement.

Back on the wing, there were dozens of boys engaged in afternoon association. For some, this meant the gym or table tennis, but the majority seemed to prefer hanging around doing nothing in particular. Thorne had heard their voices and those of the prison officers echoing from the landings as he had walked out of the admin block. Now, turning towards the main entrance, he saw that he would need to make his way between small groups of boys huddled in corners, drifting in twos and threes along the main corridor or gathered in larger numbers at the tops and bottoms of staircases.

Whatever the numbers, the gatherings appeared to be strictly divided.

White. Black. Asian.

As a couple of the younger ones stepped out of the way ahead of him, Thorne recognised the boy he had seen in the library. He was probably eighteen or so, with close-cropped hair and a physique that suggested he spent more time working out than he did reading. He was leaning against a wall opposite as though he'd been waiting, and looked away when Thorne spotted him.

Thorne walked across the corridor.

He remembered what Aziz had told him and guessed this was the same boy that Dawes had questioned two months earlier. The boy who had visited Amin in the hospital wing.

'You're Antoine Daniels, right?'

The boy was not looking at him. He sniffed and gave a small nod.

'I'd like to talk to you about Amin.'

'I don't want to talk about him.' The voice was deep, the accent straight out of Hackney or Harlesden.

'Yes, you do,' Thorne said. 'That's why you were waiting for me.' He waited until it was clear that he was not going anywhere; until the boy finally turned and looked at him. 'You were Amin's friend. You're the one person I should be talking to.'

Daniels carefully watched the comings and goings for another half a minute, then pushed himself from the wall. He brushed Thorne's shoulder as he went past, and cast the smallest of backward glances as he walked away.

The invitation to follow him seemed obvious enough.

They walked for five minutes or more, Thorne ten or so steps behind, and Daniels staying close to the walls as they moved into a recreation area and through a large group gathered around a pool table. All the boys were wearing their cargos and Ts, the only badge of individuality being the training shoes each had chosen to wear. Many had these sent in by family from outside and could have them taken away for bad behaviour, but for those who kept them, the cost and style told others a great deal about the wearer.

The trainers, and how you chose to walk in them.

You strutted, you shuffled, you pimp-rolled.

I'm confident. I'm harmless. I'm a bad-man.

With the squeals of rubber soles against the vinyl floor fading behind them, they climbed up to a second-floor landing and along a corridor until, after a few minutes, Daniels calmly turned and walked into a cell.

When Thorne arrived at the doorway, Daniels was standing in the corner, urinating into the metal toilet bowl. Thorne said, 'Sorry,' and turned away. He waited until he heard the flush and when he turned around again and stepped inside, Daniels was sitting on the edge of his bunk.

'Push the door to,' he said.

Thorne did as he was asked, then leaned back against the door. The cell was the same size as the room he had seen in the hospital wing, but the bricks had been painted rather than plastered. The bed was cemented to the wall – a blue, rubberised mattress and neatly folded grey blanket – as was the desk, no bigger than a tea tray. The same 'robust' furnishings as could be found in all but those few rooms assigned to the orderlies or those on the Gold wing. Thorne wondered how the Polish boy he had heard about earlier could possibly have smashed up such a room without the use of a sledgehammer.

'Antoine's an interesting name,' he said. 'French?'

Daniels shrugged. 'Only bit of French in me is fries, far as I know.'

There were a few pictures stuck to the pin-board above the bed, animals and ships, painted by numbers. Thorne noticed that along the edge of the small desk, cartons of juice and sachets of jam hoarded from breakfast grab-bags had been lined up meticulously, the labels all facing the same way. He saw the same order displayed in the rows of small shampoo bottles and squares of soap that had been arranged above the sink. It might have been pride or a simple method of telling if anyone had been inside the room. It might have been both.

'How long you been in?'

'Two years and a bit.' Daniels glanced up. 'One more to go.'

Thorne knew better than to ask what the boy was in for. He guessed, with a sentence that long, that he'd done more than steal a car or get caught with a bit of blow. 'So did you and Amin become friends quickly after he came in?'

'I suppose.'

'You looked after him.'

'Just showed him the ropes, that's all.' Daniels' face gave little away.

117

He was very dark-skinned and, up close, Thorne could see the skin was pitted with acne scars. 'He didn't need looking after.'

'No?'

'He was no threat to anyone.'

'What about the kid who attacked him?'

'Yeah, that was strange,' he said. 'Usually in this place you hear whispers, you know? You hear when something's likely to kick off or if someone's after someone else. That just came out of nowhere.'

'You hear any whispers about who might have done it?'

'Maybe,' Daniels said, after a few seconds. 'One name, but as far as I know he wasn't even someone Amin had ever spoken to and anyway he was out of here two days after it happened, so ...'

'So no time for you to do anything about it.'

Daniels said nothing.

'Any chance it was one of the imam's boys?'

Daniels grunted. 'They're not happy when they get knocked back, that's for sure. Like it's an ... affront or something, you know?' He thought for a few seconds then shook his head. 'Amin wasn't inter-ested in any of that stuff, but I don't think they'd take it quite that personally.'

'Why wasn't he interested?'

'Just wasn't.'

'In religion, you mean? Or in joining Shakir's little gang?'

'Neither,' Daniels said. 'Didn't suit him, that's all.'

'Sounds like you knew him pretty well.'

Daniels looked up at him. His fingers crept around to grip the edge of the bunk. He said, 'Yeah.'

'How was he?' Thorne asked. 'When you went to see him in the hospital wing.'

'How d'you think he was? Some toe-rag cut him up.'

'Was he depressed though? Did he say anything that made you feel like he was thinking about killing himself?'

'No chance,' Daniels said. 'He was upset, you know? But he was still himself at the end of the day. Joking about the scar he was going to

118

have on his face. He was feeling good about how the appeal was shaping up and all that stuff.'

'And the transfer to Long Minster.'

'Yeah, that.'

'Listen, I need to ask you if you took anything in,' Thorne said. 'When you went to see him. There's no way he could have got all those tablets himself. You understand?'

'No way.' Daniels shook his head, kicked out with one foot. 'I swear.'

'Fair enough.'

'Just some books, that's it.'

'Anyone else visit him?'

'Just staff, that's all. The governor, Shakir, them lot.' He looked up at Thorne with a twisted smile. 'All the assorted God-botherers.'

'Yeah, that makes sense.' Thorne smiled back, guessing that for a majority of the patients such visits would be right up there in the popularity stakes with injections or enemas. He took the few small steps across to the adjacent wall, so that he was directly facing Daniels. 'Did Amin tell you anything else had happened to him?'

'Like what?'

'They say he was raped.'

For fifteen seconds or more the only sound came from outside the cell. A series of shouts from further along the landing. A TV set blaring somewhere nearby. Daniels slowly shook his head and Thorne saw the fingers tighten still further around the metal frame of the bed.

'You didn't know, or . . . ?'

Daniels looked at the floor.

'I heard you got into a fight,' Thorne said. 'Over what happened to Amin.' He looked at the empty space above a corner shelf where in other cells a television would have been, a PlayStation even. 'Lost your TV, lost your nice room on the Gold wing.'

'I'll get it back.'

'Tell me about the fight.'

'Not a fight.'

'You punched someone.'

119

'That was the end of it.'

Looking again at the size of Antoine Daniels, Thorne could well imagine that it was. 'What happened?'

'Just some smartarse, saying stuff to wind me up. No big deal, OK?' He stood up. 'Listen, I've got a class, so—'

'Stuff about Amin?'

Daniels moved to gather up some exercise books and a pencil case from the small desk. He looked sideways at Thorne and stared, as though he were willing him to leave. Thorne stayed where he was.

'You and him were close, right?'

Daniels' chest was heaving against his T-shirt. He tried to hold Thorne's eyes, but could not.

He gave the smallest of nods and said, 'Yeah.'

Just one word, whispered, but Thorne felt as though he were being pushed back hard against the whitewashed bricks. The breath pressed from him. One small affirmation that screamed a barrage of questions.

Yeah, like have you not been listening?

Like how good a detective are you anyway?

Yeah, like how long have you fucking got?

The cell door swung inwards, nudged a few inches then booted wide open by a gleaming white Nike. The same pair of young boys who had given Thorne such a hard time earlier stood grinning in the doorway. The gobbiest looked at Thorne and then at Daniels. 'What's happening, batty-boy? You like them a bit older these days?'

His mate laughed and slapped him on the shoulder.

'Why don't you both fuck off?' Thorne said.

Thorne's words had little effect, but one hard stare from Daniels was enough to send the pair scurrying away, shouting and laughing at their comic genius. Oddly, the look – the dead eyes and the muscles working beneath the jaw – had seemed even more menacing than it otherwise might, with tears coursing freely down Antoine Daniels' face.

NINETEEN

Holland and Kitson stood leaning against Kitson's Mondeo eating their chips. They watched parents collecting their kids from a primary school opposite and Holland called his girlfriend to see what kind of a day their daughter had had at nursery. A boy in her class had taken to biting the other kids and he and Sophie were both a little concerned.

'Everything OK with Chloe?' Kitson asked, when Holland had hung up.

'Still got all her fingers,' Holland said.

The afternoon was starting to cool off a little as the sky clouded over and the first delicate spatters of drizzle were coming down.

'Should we knock this on the head?' Holland asked.

Kitson swallowed. 'Maybe we should try Clarkson again. Or call the DCI, see if he's got any bright ideas.'

'Up to you,' Holland said.

'We've got to do *something*.'

Holland looked down at his chips. 'These are pretty good actually.' He stuffed a handful into his mouth. 'Should have got something to drink though. Maybe a sausage or something.'

Kitson nodded ahead. 'Let's walk up towards Islington Green.'

'It's raining.'

'It's only ten minutes away.'

'What is?'

'The place where Amin Akhtar and his mate were attacked.'

'And?'

Kitson began to walk. 'And I don't want my car to stink of chips.'

Helen leaned down towards the wrist that was handcuffed to the radiator and checked her watch. They had been there for the best part of eight hours already. By rights she should be stepping off the train about now, getting excited about seeing Alfie again and putting whatever darkness the day had thrown up out of her head until tomorrow.

Her stomach lurched.

He would need collecting from Janine's in less than ten minutes.

Would Jenny take him home, she wondered. Or would she drop him round at their dad's place then come back to Tulse Hill? Yes, that's what she would do, Helen decided, what Helen would prefer her to do. Her sister always enjoyed being where the action was.

A typical car-crash watcher, if ever there was one.

Maybe that's why she was so bloody fascinated with me and Paul, Helen thought. What we laughably called our 'relationship'. Yes, there was always plenty of advice and offers of help, but her sister always seemed to ... relish it somehow. The fact that Helen needed those things. It made Jenny's own perfect life that much more perfect, never mind the fact that she was actually neurotic as hell, or that the tedious tosser she was married to thought life began and ended with fishing and fixing up old cars.

Helen took a deep breath.

God, I am such a bitch, she thought. Jenny will be in pieces, and she and her perfectly nice husband will love my son if I don't make it out of this, and I am *such* a bitch ...

She turned to Stephen Mitchell and said, 'Tell me about your wife.'

Mitchell opened his eyes and looked a little panic-stricken, as though it might be a trick question. They had spoken a little since he had come back from the toilet and Helen was relieved that he seemed to have settled down. To have become resigned to what was happening.

'What's her name?'

Akhtar had gone out into the shop ten minutes before. Helen could not hear him moving about. He was spending longer and longer out there, leaving her and Mitchell alone in the storeroom, and Helen imagined him sitting quietly behind the till. Trying to keep calm and explain to himself, or to his dead son perhaps, why things had gone as far as they had.

Why there could be no turning back from them.

He was alone out there, she thought, because he could not bear to look at what he had done.

'She's called Denise,' Mitchell said. 'She works in the same bank as me, only she's out front and I'm sitting upstairs.' He smiled, more easily than she had seen him do before. 'Tied to a computer, playing with other people's money. Your money, maybe.'

'No money to play with,' Helen said.

'She's pretty ... fiery.' He nodded, thinking. 'Doesn't take any crap, you know?'

'Sounds like we'd get on. I can't wait to meet her.'

'Yeah, she's definitely got a temper on her. Probably because she cares about stuff, well more than me anyway. Politics, animals ... the environment, all that. She has a right go at me sometimes, says I should get more worked up about things ... but I just like a quiet life, I suppose.'

'Nothing wrong with that.'

'Right.' He raised an arm. 'And look what I get.'

They laughed, and Helen thought, I hope he hears that. Out there in the semi-dark, staring at his shutters and thinking that nobody has ever felt pain the way he's feeling it. Or hate. She wondered if she should show Akhtar some of the pictures in her bag, read him some of the witness statements from people whose children had been through a damn sight worse than prison.

123

They did not go out and buy guns. They did not do ... this.

'We were supposed to be going out tonight,' Mitchell said. 'You know, presuming I didn't mess up my interview. Nothing flashy, just a decent steak or something and a nice bottle of wine. Steak for me anyway, she's a vegetarian.'

'I tried that a few years ago,' Helen said. 'Couldn't live without bacon sandwiches.'

Mitchell nodded. 'She likes a glass of wine, Denise does. Neither of us knows a thing about wine, mind you. Only what we like to drink. She says all that "what wine goes with what" and sniffing it and stuff is just about trying to look clever. She said that to one of the managers at the bank once, when he was banging on about some Château some-thing-or-other he'd had with his hundred-pound lunch.' He smiled again, remembering. 'No, she's definitely not shy about telling people what she thinks.'

'That's good.'

'Plus, she's seriously gorgeous.' He swallowed hard. 'You know?' He was suddenly having to work harder to keep that smile in place. 'So ...'

'How long have you been married?' Helen asked.

'Three years next month.' His eyes widened. 'I can't believe it's gone so fast.'

'You got any kids?'

Mitchell shook his head. 'We've been talking about it quite a lot lately though, trying to work out the best time and all that. I'd love it, you know? I mean we both would, but Denise wants to keep working for a little bit and she's really brilliant at her job, so ...'

'It's not easy.'

'*You* have though, right? I heard you and him talking about it ... before.'

'Yes, I've got a little boy.' Now she was the one struggling to keep the smile from slipping. 'And trust me, if anyone ever picked the wrong time to have a baby it was me. So don't worry about it.'

'OK.'

Helen reached across, took Mitchell's left hand in her right and squeezed.

'Denise is out there waiting for you,' she said. 'So let's just do what we have to, all right, Stephen?' She waited until he looked at her, squeezed his hand again. 'Make sure we get out of here so you can have that steak. And those kids.'

From Upper Street they walked west, crossing Liverpool Road and cutting through side streets until they came to Barnard Park. It had been here, between the football pitch and the adventure playground, that Lee Slater, Scott Clarkson and Daniel Armstrong had attacked Amin Akhtar and his friend a year before.

'What was he doing all the way up here anyway?' Kitson asked.

It had become obvious fairly quickly that Amin Akhtar was lying about where he had been on the evening he was attacked. At first he had tried to claim that the pub quiz he was supposed to have taken part in near his home had finished early, but later said that he and his friend had gone to a party. Neither could provide an address, however, claiming that they'd just heard about the party through someone else and gone along to see what it was like. Both boys had strict parents, so the subterfuge had seemed reasonable enough, and not particularly relevant to the inquiry. The salient fact remained that they had ended up in Islington, fighting for their lives on snow-covered ground in Barnard Park. Exactly how they had come to be almost ten miles from home, on the other side of London at 11.30 at night, was really only a matter for them and their parents.

'Didn't you ever lie to your mum and dad?' Holland asked.

'I suppose so, yeah.'

They walked towards the large playground decorated with brightly painted murals. There was a climbing area with high wooden walk-ways, rope bridges, a paddling pool. 'I think Amin's parents were pretty hard on him,' Holland said. 'So you can hardly blame him for telling porkies when he wanted to sneak off to a party. Probably some dope around or whatever.'

125

'I certainly didn't do any of that,' Kitson said.

'Different for boys, maybe.'

'It was strictly underage sex and heroin for me.'

The drizzle had got no worse, so for a few minutes they watched a couple of kids clambering over an enormous wooden dragon, while the children's mothers sat smoking on a bench nearby. Holland was impressed with the place and said he might try and come back with Chloe some time. He said that the play facilities near his place at Elephant and Castle left a lot to be desired, unless you enjoyed games of dodge-the-wino or thought playing with used syringes was educational.

'North–south divide for you,' Kitson said.

They walked out on to Copenhagen Street and, crossing the road to head back towards the car, they passed a large pub on the corner opposite the entrance to the park. Loud music spilled out on to the street, where a group of lads sat drinking at a table outside, seemingly oblivious to the drizzle.

A large sign in the window advertised various themed evenings.

Thursday: Wild West Night (with rodeo bull!)
Friday: Eighties Night!
Saturday: Gay Night.

Kitson pointed to the sign. 'Maybe you should bring Chloe down to the playground on a Saturday. You can always pop in here for a quick one while she's playing. Maybe get a drink as well.'

'You're hilarious,' Holland said.

'Denial's a terrible thing, Dave.'

They walked back to Upper Street, then cut behind the green on to Essex Road. They had almost reached the car and were still trying to decide where to go next when Holland's mobile rang.

'I've just come out of Barndale,' Thorne said.

'And?'

'And I'm starting to see why Javed Akhtar thought the police got it wrong. Why they all got it wrong.'

126

'You're joking.' Holland looked at Kitson who raised her eyebrows. He mouthed, 'Tell you in a minute.'

'Look, there's still people I've got to talk to,' Thorne said. 'I'm not saying I've got anything solid to tell him about yet, and it might be that stuff comes out of this he doesn't want to hear anyway.'

'Like what?' Holland stopped at the kerb, waiting for a gap in the traffic.

'It's probably got sod all to do with anything,' Thorne said, 'but I think Amin might have been gay.'

Holland looked at Kitson again. He remembered something Danny Armstrong had said when they had told him Amin had been raped. A snide remark about how much he would have enjoyed it. He thought about that pub opposite the entrance to Barnard Park.

'You still there, Dave?'

'What night of the week was it, when Lee Slater got stabbed?'

'Saturday. Why?'

'I think I might know what Amin and his mate were doing in Islington,' Holland said. 'And why they were attacked.'

TWENTY

Thorne knew he would hit the rush hour coming off the M40, but he would use the blue light to get through it. With luck he would be back in Tulse Hill within forty minutes or so, though if there had been any major developments he felt sure Donnelly would have let him know.

Now he needed to let Javed Akhtar know that he was doing as he had been asked.

He reached for his phone and dialled. One day he would get around to putting a hands-free kit in the car, but right now getting stopped for driving while using a mobile was the least of his worries.

Helen's phone rang out and after half a minute went to voicemail. He listened to the message, hung up and tried again. This time she answered almost immediately.

'Sorry,' she said. 'He was in the next room, so I couldn't pick up.'

Thorne thought about the confident voice he had heard on Helen's answerphone and compared it to the one he was hearing now. They might have been two different people.

'Is he there now?'

'Yes.'

'Can I speak to him?'

He waited while Helen asked the question.

'He wants you to talk to me,' she said.

'OK ... tell him I've spent the day at Barndale, that I've been talk-ing to people about what happened to Amin. The governor, the doctor that treated Amin. Amin's friends. Tell him that.'

He waited again, easing the BMW into the outside lane and push-ing it up to ninety, while he listened to Helen Weeks relaying the information to Akhtar.

'OK, he's got that.'

'But you also need to keep telling him that this is going to take time. I'm going flat out here, but it's not like anybody's confessing to any-thing. He needs to understand that.'

Helen started to talk to Akhtar, but Thorne cut her off.

'But I will find out what happened,' he said. 'Tell him that. No, *promise* him that.'

Helen passed on what Thorne had said.

'And this is the most important thing, Helen. Are you listening?'

'I'm listening.'

'Tell him I believe him, OK?'

TWENTY-ONE

'Jesus, that's terrible. Sorry if I was a bit . . .'

'It's fine.'

'So, what can I do to help?'

The man who had spent six months putting together an appeal that would never be heard had not sounded best pleased to be receiving a phone call from a police officer at eight-thirty in the evening. But as soon as Thorne had told Carl Oldman who he was and explained the circumstances, the solicitor was only too keen to answer his questions.

'I saw Amin a week or so before he died,' Oldman said. 'The day before he was attacked. Actually, I think I might well have been the last person to visit him.'

'And how was he?'

'He was in pretty good spirits as I remember. I ran through our appeal with him and he had every reason to be happy about it. I think we had a hell of a good chance of getting his sentence reduced.'

'On what grounds?'

'On the grounds that the bloody judge went way over the top, pure and simple. Based on the circumstances and all the pre-sentencing reports, Amin should have got three years tops, and then the judge starts banging on about this ridiculous "dangerousness" business. There's no basis for that in any of the reports he was given, not a whisper. It was quite clearly a self-defence incident, Amin's character was nigh-on spotless and any fool could see that he wasn't a danger to anyone.' Oldman sighed heavily. 'Some of these idiots see a knife involved and start reaching for an imaginary black cap, you know what I mean?'

'Yeah, I've come across a few of those,' Thorne said.

'Right. Well, I was definitely up for going after this one, I tell you that.'

The solicitor was clearly angry, though whether it was aimed at the judge in question, or the fact that Oldman would never now have the chance to challenge the sentence he had handed down, was hard to tell.

'So you wouldn't say he was depressed when you saw him?'

'Not even close.'

'Or showing any signs that he was feeling suicidal?'

'Look, I'm not a psychiatrist,' Oldman said. 'And I can't possibly know what that attack did to him, but he seemed fine to me. He was excited about the appeal and he was pleased that he had this move coming up. I think there were some friends he was going to miss and he was a bit upset about that, but he was keen to get this qualification, so . . .'

'So were you surprised at what happened?'

There was a pause, and Thorne heard Oldman take a drink of something. He suddenly imagined the solicitor on a designer sofa with a glass of wine, while an angry wife or girlfriend pointed towards a plate of dinner that was getting cold. Mind you, he also knew plenty of briefs who lived alone in grubby flats and survived on Stella and pot noodles.

'I was gutted,' Oldman said. 'And pissed off. I spend half my bloody life looking after scumbags, but Amin was a good lad.'

When Thorne had thanked Oldman and hung up, he walked across to the stereo and slid a Willie Nelson disc into the CD player. Then he sat down on the floor and leaned back against the sofa, looking up at

131

Phil Hendricks who was sitting there studying the PM report. He held up the phone that he was still carrying. Said, 'No way did that kid top himself.'

Hendricks held up the report. 'It certainly looks like he did.'

'*Looks* like it,' Thorne said. 'That's the point.'

Hendricks cast his eyes back down to the report and flicked through the pages. 'This bloke seems to have done a reasonable job as far as I can see. I mean obviously his prose style isn't as good as mine.'

'Come on, Phil.'

Hendricks had picked up a takeaway from the Bengal Lancer on his way over. He leaned down now to scoop up what was left of a cold onion bhaji from the plate on the floor and took a bite. 'There's a shed-load of Tramadol in the boy's blood. The remains of a few tablets in his stomach. All the evidence of an overdose and nothing that suggests it wasn't suicide.' He looked at Thorne. 'So why do you think it wasn't?'

'The timings don't work for a start,' Thorne said.

'Go on.'

'People don't kill themselves first thing in the morning. They do it in the early hours, in the middle of the night.'

'What, you got that off an episode of *Morse*, did you?'

'I read it somewhere.'

'Well you're wrong,' Hendricks said. 'The most common time is around four o'clock in the afternoon. If you're interested, March, April and May are the favourite months for suicides and the most popular method worldwide is hanging, except in America obviously where they tend to prefer guns. It's also cobblers that suicide is more common among young people than old people and that more people kill themselves at Christmas. It's actually below average.' He popped what was left of the bhaji into his mouth. 'I went to a seminar.'

'Course you did,' Thorne said. 'So I suppose there's no point me mentioning the absence of a suicide note is there?'

'Less than twenty per cent leave a note,' Hendricks said. 'I'm not really helping, am I?'

Thorne let out a noisy breath. 'He had no *motive*, Phil. Nothing at all. His appeal was going well and every person who saw him said he was full of the joys of spring.'

'People who are depressed can be pretty good at putting up a front. I've seen you do it.'

Thorne shook his head. 'These were people who knew him, OK? His father, his lawyer, his friend. And what reason did he have to be depressed in the first place?' He pointed down at the report on Hendricks' lap. 'Forget about the pills for a minute, OK? As far as I can make out, this whole "suicidal state of mind" thing seems to stand or fall on the knife attack and the idea that he was raped, so I need you to tell me if what it says in there is conclusive.'

Hendricks sighed theatrically and turned to the appropriate page in the report. He read, while Thorne waited and Willie Nelson sang in a cracked, world-weary voice about a preacher crying like a baby.

'OK, so the word "rape" isn't actually used,' Hendricks said. 'But we just record what we find when we examine the body, so that doesn't mean a great deal. It's not a pathologist's job to draw conclusions from this stuff . . . Come on, you know all this.'

'Yeah, I know. Now shut up and draw a conclusion for me, would you?'

Hendricks read on. 'There's clear evidence that the boy had been sodomised,' he said.

'No semen though, right?'

'Rapists do know about DNA. A lot of them wear condoms.'

'In prison?'

'There are some signs of internal tearing and some damage to the soft tissues . . .'

'Does that rule out the possibility that it was consensual though?'

'Consensual or not, it was certainly . . . aggressive.'

'Is it possible that this was not rape?'

Hendricks thought about it. 'Well, if you're suggesting this was the result of sex with a regular partner, then I *suppose* it's feasible his boyfriend was hung like a donkey. Or maybe he just liked it rough.' He smiled. 'Some of us do, you know?'

'Too much information, Phil.'

'Yeah, OK . . . it's possible. But—'

'Right,' Thorne said. 'Well, there's your motive for suicide shot to shit.'

Hendricks glanced down to see if there were any more leftovers he liked the look of, then swung his legs up on to the sofa and lay back. 'So where's your motive for murder, smartarse?'

Thorne reached across and tore off a piece of nan bread. 'I don't have all the answers.'

'Don't have any of them as far as I can see.'

'Yeah, well, that's where I stupidly thought you might be able to help.'

'It's a radical idea, I know,' Hendricks said, 'but evidence might be a good place to start. You've got bugger all on the CCTV.'

'Because whoever did this knew how to stay clear of the cameras. It's not difficult to do. I checked.'

'OK, what about the lack of prints on that cup the pills were supposed to have been in?'

'Easy enough to get plastic gloves in a hospital wing, I would have thought.'

'You should do this for a living,' Hendricks said.

'Those pills were *given* to him.' Thorne tossed the bread back on to the plate. 'No question.'

'And you don't think that might be down to this Antoine kid?'

'Antoine loved him.'

'Enough to help him kill himself, maybe?'

Thorne shook his head. 'It's got to be someone who was in the hospital wing. Someone with access to that DDA cabinet.'

'One of the other patients?'

'No chance.' Thorne had not bothered talking to any of those boys who had been patients on the night Amin was killed. He knew that some would have been released by now anyway and that he would get no more out of those who were still serving sentences than Dawes had done.

134

That he would only have been wasting time he did not have.

'Think about why Amin was in hospital in the first place,' Thorne said. 'If these kids want to hurt someone, they do it with fists or home-made knives. The lid off a tin of peaches. They don't bother getting elaborate. Anyway, this had to be someone with keys.'

'What about that PHO? I mean she conveniently saw nothing when she checked his room.'

'She's first on the list.'

'Still can't see a motive though.'

They said nothing for a few minutes. The album finished, but Thorne did not bother getting up to change it. He had stayed off the beer in case he needed to get somewhere in a hurry, but Hendricks climbed off the sofa and went into the kitchen to fetch himself another can.

'Actually, I reckon the pills are your biggest problem,' he said, coming back.

'Why?'

'You ever tried giving people tablets against their will? Ever tried giving a *cat* a fucking tablet?'

'Amin was half asleep,' Thorne said. 'Already drugged up.'

'Even harder to do it. Look, even if we accept the possibility that someone gave him that overdose, I honestly don't see how they could have done it. They'd have needed thirty, forty of those tablets at least, and there's no way they could have got them down Amin's throat without causing one hell of a bloody racket. Whoever did it would have needed to get in and out fast, right?'

'Yeah, before the patients were checked again.'

Hendricks shook his head. 'No way it could have been done that quickly. Sorry, Tom.'

Thorne said, 'Shit,' closed his eyes and let his head fall back.

'Look—'

'There's got to be a way,' Thorne said. 'The man who's holding Helen Weeks is not going to want to listen to anything else. I can't go back there with nothing. I can't just say, "I think you're right, will that

135

do you? Yeah, your son probably *was* murdered, but God knows why or by who and there's no way I can prove it anyway, so why don't you stop pissing about and put the gun away?" I can't . . . *do* that, all right, Phil?'

The look on Hendricks' face made it clear he could see there was no point arguing. Not when Thorne was in this mood. 'Fair enough,' he said. 'I'll have a think about it.'

'Well, think fast.'

'Calm down, mate, I've got the message.' Hendricks opened his beer. 'You concentrate on who and why, all right?' He took a swig. 'I'll try and figure out how.'

When Hendricks had gone, Thorne sat down at his laptop and saw that an email had arrived from Ian McCarthy. The doctor apologised for not getting the information Thorne had asked for to him sooner. Said that he had been swamped all afternoon. He gave him the name of the prison hospital officer who had been suspended, an address in Potters Bar. He told him that, having checked in the DDA book, he could confirm that sixty Tramadol tablets had been stolen from the dispensary the day after Amin Akhtar had been admitted.

Thorne closed the laptop and heard himself say, 'That's very bloody convenient.'

He called the RVP.

Donnelly told him everything there was quiet. That the overnight team would be coming on at 11.30 and that Pascoe had scheduled another call to the newsagent's in an hour, just before the handover.

The overnight team . . .

A fresh set of officers was vital of course, Thorne understood that. A new SIO, a wide-awake hostage negotiator and, crucially, a unit of firearms officers with eight hours' rest behind them. He hoped that the man or woman leading them was a little less excitable than Chivers.

'We'll let you know how it goes,' Donnelly said. 'Now get some sleep. *I'm* certainly going to.'

Thorne put *Red Headed Stranger* on again, turned out the lights and took his friend's place on the sofa. He held his phone to his chest and closed his eyes. The music – sparse and simple – curled around fragments of the day's conversations; the pictures that bloomed and swam as he tried and failed to take Donnelly's advice.

The catch in Helen Weeks' voice.

The tears on Antoine Daniels' face.

The blood caked around a dead boy's mouth . . .

And, as those images finally began to blur and blacken, and the tiredness gained sway, Willie Nelson whispered to him about a man who was 'wild in his sorrow' and Thorne remembered his promise to Amin Akhtar's father.

TWENTY-TWO

Helen watched as Akhtar moved boxes and stacked them on top of pallets that were piled up against one another. Made some space. He opened a low cupboard and hauled out a green canvas camp bed which he unfolded and pushed against the wall, then went back and took out a couple of ratty-looking cushions. He smacked the dust from them and held them up for examination.

'We should all try and get a little sleep,' he said. He tossed the cushions on to the floor in front of Helen and Mitchell. 'I'm sorry you can't be more comfortable, but we will have to make do.'

Helen reached for the cushion and nodded towards the camp bed, six or seven feet away. 'You've slept in here before then?'

'Oh yes, many nights,' Akhtar said. 'The shop was broken into three times in one month. Three times!' He pointed. 'They smashed straight through that door, took all my stock, everything.'

'You were insured though, right?'

He shook his head. 'I lost thirty thousand pounds' worth of cigarettes in one go and the insurance company refused to pay a penny, because they said I should have had a proper alarm.' He sat down on the edge of the camp bed. 'Bloody thieves. Insurance companies, banks, all of them.'

Helen turned to Mitchell. 'Banks? What have you got to say to that, Stephen?'

Mitchell smiled weakly and said, 'No comment.' He was looking exhausted suddenly.

'So I slept in here for weeks in case they came back.' He patted the grubby canvas next to him. 'It was perfectly comfortable, but then Nadira told me to come home and stop being silly.'

'I didn't know that was your wife's name,' Helen said.

He nodded. 'Nadira, yes. It means "One who is rare and hard to find". Like a diamond or something, you know?' His hand bounced nervously against his knee. 'It's a good name for her . . . '

Helen had spoken to Akhtar's wife on many occasions when he was not in the shop. She had been shy and soft-spoken and had not smiled as much as her husband. 'What will she be thinking about all this, Javed?'

Akhtar looked at her.

'Will she be proud, do you reckon? Or ashamed?'

She waited, but Akhtar showed no desire to answer her question. She reached for the cushion and tucked it behind her head. It smelled of mould and mice. Seeing that Mitchell had not moved to retrieve his own cushion, she leaned forward to pick it up and held it towards him. After a few seconds he bowed his head and, without a word, she gently tucked the cushion behind it, holding it in position until he leaned back.

'Here you go. That's better . . . ' There was no noise, just the small-est of shudders across Stephen Mitchell's shoulders, but Helen could tell that he had begun to cry again.

'Sorry,' he said.

'Don't be silly.'

They sat for a few minutes, still and silent, until Helen could no longer ignore the pressure in her bladder. She told Akhtar that she was sorry and nodded towards the toilet door.

Akhtar stood and picked up the gun from the desk. As he reached for the key to the handcuffs, he said, 'My wife understands why this needs to be done, and she will not judge me. Nadira will not condemn me for this.'

Sue Pascoe sipped from a styrofoam cup of strong coffee. She would be heading home in half an hour or so, after putting in her final call of the shift to Helen Weeks, but wanted to make sure she was on her toes for the remaining time until she was relieved.

There was no movement on any of the monitors, but the phone remained hot in her hand.

She could not help wondering who would be replacing her overnight and if they would be better qualified for the job than she was. Someone who had been to Virginia, maybe. She had applied months before to attend the Advanced Hostage Negotiation course at the FBI Academy at Quantico.

She was still waiting to hear about a vacancy.

The buzz had kicked in from the moment she had received the call first thing and had not gone away. She relished the coppery kick of the adrenalin that coffee could not wash from her mouth; the rush that came from doing something she knew she was cut out for. Those moments when it was just her voice and the hostage taker's. When the success of the operation was down to her and nobody else.

Certainly not to the likes of Chivers anyway. Not the sort of tosser who thought women did not really belong in high-pressure situations. Who would talk at you instead of to you, then still try it on after work given half a chance. Who still called female officers 'plonks' when they weren't listening.

Nine out of ten hostage situations were resolved through negotiation, she told herself for the umpteenth time.

By people like her.

Why on earth was she worrying about how well qualified she or anybody else was? She knew her superiors thought well of her and that her record was as good as anyone's. Other negotiators were busy being assigned to talk nutters down off car-park roofs and only the best in the field got called in when weapons were involved.

'About ten minutes, Sue?'

Donnelly was pulling out the chair next to her. She looked up at him and nodded. For a second she considered asking him who would be taking her place overnight, but thought better of it. Then, when she was sure he wasn't looking, she lowered the phone and wiped it and her palm against her trouser leg.

As she and Donnelly began a pre-call briefing, Pascoe chided herself again for those fleeting moments of insecurity. She had done a good job, she told herself, had acted and *re*acted as per all her training. Most importantly of all, the hostages remained safe.

Donnelly talked and she nodded.

As long as they were still safe by the time she walked out of that school hall at the end of her shift, she could sleep well.

Helen had used the toilet twice since Mitchell had been that first time and the routine was now well established. When the newsagent gave the nod, Mitchell picked up the small key which Akhtar had tossed to the floor in front of him then leaned across Helen's lap and attempted to unfasten her cuff.

Akhtar stood safely out of reach, the gun trained on the pair of them.

It was not easy, as Mitchell was right-handed and was forced to try and unlock the cuffs with his left. He had managed it after a minute or two the first couple of times, but on this occasion he seemed to be struggling.

'Just go easy,' Helen said.

His hand was shaking and he cursed under his breath.

'You really don't want me to piss myself.'

Mitchell took a deep breath and made another attempt, the key grasped between his thumb and forefinger as he stretched awkwardly to manoeuvre it into the tiny lock. Just as it looked as though he had succeeded, the key slipped from his grasp and dropped to the floor.

'Can I not just do it myself?' Helen asked. 'Please.'

Akhtar shook his head. Said, 'The same way as before.'

Groaning with the effort, Mitchell strained to pick up the key. He pushed clumsily at the lock and missed. He tried again, then sat back up and threw the key down hard.

'I can't *do* this.'

The key settled on the scarred and dirty lino a few feet in front of him.

'Just relax, Stephen,' Helen said. 'Give it another go.'

'No . . .'

Helen watched Akhtar take two steps forward, the gun held out in front of him, and something cold fluttered in her chest. From the corner of her eye she caught the look on Mitchell's face, but even as she saw what was coming, it was too late to do anything about it.

Akhtar let his eyes drop to where the key had fallen, just for a moment, but long enough for Mitchell to launch himself forward, stretch out his arm and get a hand on the gun.

Helen screamed Mitchell's name.

Mitchell pulled hard at the gun, dragging Akhtar towards him and on to his knees. The newsagent gasped in panic. He shook his head. Then they were both shouting, 'No, please,' and 'Give it to me,' and the metal handcuff clattered against the radiator pipe as Mitchell fought to wrench the gun from Akhtar's hand.

Helen leaned across and clawed at Mitchell's arm.

She opened her mouth to say his name again, then the explosion forced her back hard against the radiator and down on to her side.

She kept her eyes closed while the gunshot's report sang in her ears.

TWENTY-THREE

Every officer in the hall was silent, frozen at their station. Donnelly was on his feet. 'Was that what I think it was?'

He and Pascoe stared at the monitors. They watched as firearms officers who had been leaning casually against their vehicles scrambled to take up combat stances and trained their weapons on the shop. They turned to see Chivers pick up his helmet and his Heckler and Koch carbine and rush from the hall to join his team, then turned back to the monitors to see him appear on screen twenty seconds later and take up a position himself.

'Oh, Jesus,' Pascoe said.

Donnelly studied the monitor for half a minute. There was no further movement. He pointed to the phone in Pascoe's hand.

Said, 'Call.'

The number had been programmed into speed dial. Pascoe hit the button and waited. The click of connection popped from the speakers and, a few seconds later, the ringing of Helen Weeks' phone began to echo, tinny and grating, around the hall.

The call went to voicemail.

Hi, this is Helen. Up to my eyes in something or other, so please—

'Again,' Donnelly said.

Pascoe ended the call and hit redial. The phone rang three times, then was answered.

'Helen?'

There was a long pause before Helen Weeks said, 'Yeah.'

'It's Sue Pascoe.' Pascoe waited. 'Helen?'

'Yes ... I'm here.'

'Is everything OK in there? We heard what sounded like a gunshot.'

'Sorry.'

'Was it a gunshot, Helen?'

'It was a stupid accident—'

'Are you all right?' Pascoe asked. 'Is Mr Mitchell all right?'

'We're both fine. It was just ... an accident, that's all, so no need to panic.'

Pascoe felt the tension in her shoulders, in the *room*, lift a little. She watched Donnelly let out a breath as he leaned against the table. The next question was obvious enough. There was still the possibility that the hostage taker had turned the gun on himself.

'Mr Akhtar?'

'He's fine too,' Helen said.

There were more than a few in the hall who struggled to hide their disappointment.

'What happened?'

'The gun went off, that's all. No harm done and nobody hurt. Well, except for the bloody ringing in my ears.'

'As long as everything's OK.'

'Yes ... look, I'm sorry if you were worried. I'm sure everyone started getting a bit jumpy out there.'

Pascoe put a laugh into her voice. 'Yeah, just a bit.'

There was a longer pause before Helen said, 'This is going to sound a bit pathetic, but I *really* need the loo, so ... '

'OK,' Pascoe said. 'We'll talk again soon.'

The line went dead.

Pascoe looked at Donnelly, but he was already on the radio, reporting the conversation to Chivers. A minute later, the CO19 man came marching back into the hall. He dropped his helmet on the table next to the monitor and grabbed a bottle of water. He looked rather less relieved than everyone else in the room. 'Up to me, we'd be going in,' he said.

Donnelly nodded, picked at one of the buttons on his jacket.

'*What?*' Pascoe said.

'How do we know it was just an accident?'

'I spoke to Sergeant Weeks.'

'I'm well aware of what she *said*, but how the hell can we be sure she wasn't made to say it? How can we trust anything she tells us?'

'There was nothing to indicate any form of coercion,' Pascoe said.

Chivers shook his head, then took out his Glock and held it against his temple. 'It was just a silly accident, nothing to worry about.' He widened his eyes, spoke in a robotic monotone. 'We're all fine, honestly, having a lovely time—'

'That's enough,' Donnelly said.

'Her speech patterns were normal,' Pascoe said. 'The rhythms, the way she was breathing. I know about all that stuff.'

Chivers holstered his weapon, but the look he gave Pascoe made it clear he was unimpressed. As though she had just admitted to studying crop circles or reading tea leaves.

Donnelly sat down. 'So, in your professional opinion . . . ?'

'It's fine, sir,' Pascoe said. 'No harm done.'

Chivers took a long swig from his water bottle. 'Well, at least we know the gun's loaded,' he said.

Thorne was torn from a dream, something vaguely sad and sexual which evaporated almost immediately with the clamour of the phone against his chest. He saw the time on the small, brightly lit screen and realised that he had been asleep for less than half an hour.

'There was a gunshot inside the newsagent's,' Donnelly said.

'*What?*' Thorne sat up fast.

'The gun went off for some reason, but nobody's hurt. Sue Pascoe spoke to DS Weeks and assures us that everything's fine.'

A pungent scrap of the dream drifted across Thorne's mind, just for a second or two. A woman he had briefly known called Anna Carpenter. Alive again, with skin that tasted of salt.

'I'll come down,' Thorne said.

'There's no need.'

'I wasn't asleep anyway.'

'Look, it's up to you, but I think you'll be more use to us if you try and get your head down. More use to *her*.'

It made sense. Thorne knew he would struggle to get back to sleep, but could not pretend that he was not exhausted.

'We're handing over to the night shift,' Donnelly said. 'And I've briefed the SIO to call you if anything else happens, OK?' He told Thorne he would see him first thing the following morning at the RVP, assured him they were leaving the safety of Helen Weeks in good hands.

Thorne sat in the dark for a while afterwards, thinking about the handful of occasions in the last twenty years when he had thought he might be about to die. Those slow-motion, shit-yourself seconds. Each moment was pin-sharp and terrible, though oddly more comfortable lying curled in his memory than those mercifully fewer times when he had felt himself capable of killing.

Thorne hoped that Helen was keeping such feelings at bay, though he knew they might well come along later on.

He pushed the idea from his mind, tried to focus instead on what he might do to help her. He thought about what Hendricks had said and imagined himself trying to shovel pills into Amin Akhtar's mouth. Forcing him to swallow, his hand over the boy's nose as he retched and kicked and bit.

He knew Hendricks was right. However perfect the timing of that theft from the dispensary was, it had to have been done another way.

He got up and switched on the light, then gathered together the papers that were spread out across the small table. Was the answer somewhere in those reports? Or would he come face to face with the person responsible for Amin's death tomorrow?

146

If he had not done so already.

He turned the television on and picked up the dirty plates that were still lying on the floor. He carried them out to the kitchen. He ran hot water across the dried food and left them in the sink. Then he opened the fridge.

Presuming Hendricks had left any, Thorne decided there was no reason to deny himself that beer any longer.

TWENTY-FOUR

Five minutes on from it, Helen could no longer be sure that the noise in her head was the result of the gunshot. That it was not simply a silent scream of alarm at what had happened: the head slamming back against the radiator, the light leaving the eyes, the body slumping slowly down across her own.

And at what had happened afterwards.

The things she had said on the phone . . .

She had dragged herself, wailing, from beneath the dead weight of Stephen Mitchell. She had pushed his body away in disgust – her hands slick with him – and flinched when his head had cracked against the floor. She had turned, as the cry died to a ragged groan that bubbled in her throat, and seen Akhtar shuffle backwards to press himself against the wall.

She had listened to him murmur in a language she did not understand.

She had wondered if he was praying.

Then, when it had begun to ring, they had become still and stared at the phone. The handset juddering across the linoleum between Helen's leg and Mitchell's head. Its bright blue casing spattered with red.

It was not until it had rung a second time that her brain was able to do what was needed. Then, it had calmly told her hand to move and pick it up. Told her mouth to say what it needed to . . .

Now, she lifted the cushion from behind her by one sodden corner and tossed it towards the toilet door. She leaned back and tried to control her breathing. She could feel the sticky wetness on her blouse. The blood, livid against the ivory, pressing the material against her skin, and her chest rising upwards to push the skin against the wetness.

'Can I please put my jacket back on?'

Akhtar was examining his hand, the gun that lay in his open palm.

'*Please*. I don't want to look at the blood.'

Still, Akhtar did not raise his head. Just shook it, as though pushing it through water or treacle-thick air. 'What have I done?' he said, the whisper gaining in strength with each repetition. 'What have I done, what have I done, what have I done?'

Helen could just make out her own voice, cracked and nervous, below the high-pitched whine in her head.

Asking the same question.

The party is shaping up nicely, and he bloody well needs it after a long day dealing with idiots. There are plenty of good bodies on display and the drugs are top quality as always. The first joint – in his hand before he had removed his jacket – has helped him relax a little, taken the edge off, and he will move on to some of the harder stuff later on, once things really start to get serious.

When the lights are dimmed and the bedroom doors begin to close.

He has already met one or two he might go back to see later and made more than casual eye contact with someone he hopes is as keen as he is to take things further. Just a look, but that is usually more than enough early on, and he had needed to step out into the hallway afterwards, slip a hand into his underpants and make the necessary adjustments.

The feel of things down there had got him even more excited of course. The smoothness of it, and the weight in his hand. He had spent a few minutes in the bathroom after that.

He is pouring Glenlivet into a glass when his phone rings. He sees the caller ID and hesitates for just a second as he reaches for the water jug. He lets the phone ring. Then, once he has taken a sip and helped himself to a nibble or two, he carries his drink out on to the balcony and calls back.

It is a warm night, if a little breezy, and there are three or four boys out there laughing and smoking. They smile, but he ignores them and walks to the furthest corner; stares out across the rooftops towards the winking light on top of Canary Wharf.

'It's me.'

There is a noisy breath at the other end of the phone. 'Listen ... you should know that some questions are being asked about one of our old friends.'

150

He takes a gulp of whisky. 'You might need to be a little more specific than that.'

'Don't be stupid.'

'Are we talking about an old friend we haven't seen for a while?'

'For heaven's sake. Yes.'

'I thought that had all been dealt with.'

'When was the last time you watched the news?'

The conversation continues for another few minutes. All perfectly casual, at least from his end, and as far as those boys eavesdropping from the other side of the balcony are concerned.

A little business, no more than that.

When he goes back inside, he tops up his drink and sits down across from a group he recognises from one of the parties the month before. He has encountered one of them professionally once or twice, but here that counts for nothing. Nods are exchanged, that is all.

He holds the whisky in his mouth, then swallows, closing his eyes and letting the warmth spread through his chest. He needs to think, for a few minutes at least, about what he has just been told. It is problematic, certainly, but it is manageable, and he will not let it spoil his enjoyment.

Stop him satisfying himself.

He will have a couple more and a snort or two of something to liven him up. Get the juices flowing. Then he will get good and sweaty giving some lucky so-and-so the seeing-to of their lives.

DAY TWO

LIES HAVE DONE
THESE THINGS

TWENTY-FIVE

Thorne left the house just before seven-thirty, still eating toast as he turned the BMW on to Kentish Town Road and headed north. He wanted to avoid the worst of the morning rush hour on his way to Potters Bar, but also thought it might be a good idea to call on Susan Hughes nice and early. There was every possibility, he thought, that some helpful officer from Barndale had thought fit to let her know Thorne had been asking questions.

She might well be expecting his visit.

He was over the M25 before eight, and ten minutes later he was pulling up opposite a small, neat-looking house in a modern terrace just behind the High Street. The curtains were still drawn, upstairs and down. There was a Honda Civic parked on the road outside with a *Nurse On Call* sticker in the window. Thorne wondered if Susan Hughes had found herself another job yet, or just left the sticker there to avoid parking tickets. He had done the same thing himself often enough.

If she had been expecting him, the woman had not gone to a great deal of effort in tarting herself up for the occasion. The white towelling dressing gown was not wholly surprising at this time in the morning, but the tracksuit bottoms and grey T-shirt beneath suggested that she was not thinking about changing any time soon. Thorne could smell the fags as soon as the door was opened and, once he had told her who he was and why he needed to speak to her, it looked very much as though Susan Hughes needed another one.

Thorne accepted the monosyllabic offer of tea and followed her inside.

The house was divided somewhat clumsily into two flats and Hughes lived on the ground floor. Once through her own front door, she led Thorne through her living room and into a small kitchen. There was a laminated wooden floor, plain white cupboards and a grey, granite countertop. It was as spotless and uncluttered as everywhere else.

Susan Hughes was the untidiest thing in the place.

She was short and full-figured, somewhere in her mid-thirties, with a dark-rooted blonde bob that had seen better days. 'You been to Barndale, have you?' She flicked the kettle on and tightened the belt on her dressing gown. 'Spoken to McCarthy, I suppose.'

The distaste had been clear enough in her voice. 'Not a fan, then?'

She shrugged. 'Would you be? If you were the one that been made into a scapegoat?'

'Probably not.'

'Don't you think he should have taken some responsibility?'

'He wasn't there when it happened.'

'Doesn't matter.' She shook her head, her mind made up. 'As chief medical officer, the buck stops with him.'

Though it was clearly in Hughes' own interest to think as she did, Thorne had some sympathy. He had seen plenty of hard-working friends and colleagues sacrificed by senior officers who had refused to take ultimate responsibility. He had been hung out to dry enough times himself. 'Actually, he was defending you,' Thorne said. 'He told me you couldn't really be blamed for what happened.'

'Did he?' she scoffed. 'Shame he didn't say that when I was being suspended.'

The kettle was starting to grumble loudly and save for the necessary questions and answers about how Thorne wanted his tea, they said no more until it had boiled. When the tea was ready, she walked back into the living room. She sat down on the edge of the sofa and lit a cigarette. Thorne took his tea across to the window and peered out through a gap in the curtains. A woman was walking a small dog on the pavement opposite. She stopped to say something to a man who looked as though he was leaving for work. A smart suit and a pinched expression.

'Open them if you want,' Hughes said.

Thorne turned away from the window. 'It's fine,' he said.

She sat back and drew her legs up beneath her. A decent enough attempt to appear relaxed. 'So what else did he say then? McCarthy.'

'He told me that you checked Amin,' Thorne said. 'Twice. That you looked into the room and you thought he was OK.'

She pulled on her cigarette. Leaned forward to knock away a worm of ash.

'I take it you should have gone into the room. You should have done a bit more than glance through the window, right?'

'I'd already been working for twelve hours straight.' She looked away, took another drag and let the smoke out on a muttered curse. 'I know that's not an excuse.'

'It sounds like one.'

'It's all I've got,' she said. She ran clawed fingers through her hair. 'There's going to be some pointless disciplinary hearing in a few weeks and believe me, I really wish I had something better. Because there isn't a cat's chance in hell they're going to reinstate me and that's fifteen years of nursing up the swanee.' She carried on as she stubbed out the half a cigarette that was left. 'People talk to one another in this job, you know? Word gets round, so it's not like anyone's going to be banging on my door offering me anything else.'

Thorne drank his tea. He sat there, finding it hard to care a great deal, and waited for her to say something else. Then, when she spoke again, he could see that the bitterness in her voice up to that point had been nothing but bravado.

He watched her blink slowly and saw the mask slip.

'I thought he was sleeping,' she said. 'He'd been doing so well, you know? He would probably have been out of there in a day or two, so when I looked . . . I thought everything was fine. It had been fine, just before, so I assumed . . .'

'He'd bitten through his tongue,' Thorne said.

'I know—'

'There was blood all over his face.'

'His head was turned the other way, so I couldn't see it. I didn't . . . see it, all right? I just saw a boy, asleep in bed.' She leaned forward and fumbled for another cigarette from the pack on the table. 'Do you really think I haven't thought about what I should have done? That I've thought about anything else?' She grabbed at the material of her dressing gown then raised her arms, the unlit cigarette held between her fingers. 'You reckon I've had a good night's sleep, do you? That I've had one since? Look at me, for God's sake.'

Thorne did as he was asked, but only for a second or two, a little uncomfortable with the fact that Susan Hughes was looking right back at him. He might have been dressed rather more formally than she was, but he guessed that his own face was every bit as drawn, as grey as hers.

'Listen, Susan . . . I didn't come here because you were negligent.'

'So why *did* you come?'

'I presume you knew about the thefts from the dispensary.'

She nodded, lighting her cigarette. 'You think those might have been my fault as well?'

'Did you know that sixty tablets of Tramadol were taken the day after Amin came in?'

'You think he stole them?'

'No, I don't.'

'What, so someone took them for him?'

'I'm not convinced he even swallowed those tablets,' Thorne said. 'I think someone murdered him.'

The nurse stared at him and released smoke from the side of her mouth. 'Why would anyone . . . ?'

158

'That's my problem,' Thorne said.

'He was a decent enough kid,' she said. 'I mean I hadn't come across him before he was admitted to the wing, but that's what I'd heard. Good-looking lad too. At least he was until some little twat took a knife to him.' She thought for a few seconds then leaned forward, shaking her head in realisation. 'That's why you're here, isn't it? I was prime suspect, was I?'

Thorne drained the last of his tea. 'I can't think of too many other people who could have done it,' he said.

'Jesus.'

Thorne did not rely on instincts, not any more. They had got him into trouble too often. Cost as many lives as they had saved. He had been played by killers – male and female – too many times to place trust solely in the gut feeling or that insistent voice in his head. Both were every bit as capricious as they were convincing.

And yet, was his belief that Amin Akhtar had been murdered based on anything more than a nagging doubt?

Wary as he was of these things, he looked at this woman in a dressing gown, saw her glaring at him through a plume of cigarette smoke and knew that she had not murdered anyone. She had not done her job as well as she might, and she was clearly living with that, but she was not directly responsible for Amin Akhtar's death.

He was sure of it, and he told her so.

'I *know* I'm not,' she said, the anger returning to her voice. 'But that's not going to get me my job back, is it?'

TWENTY-SIX

When Helen woke suddenly, it seemed as though one corner of the room was alive with light. She blinked and saw that Akhtar was watching television in the dark, his shoulders slumped and his hands clasped together in his lap. The colours danced across his face. The flickering reds and blues gave expression to his face where there was none and showed up the wetness around his eyes.

They flicked to hers, and he seemed shocked that Helen was awake.

He said, 'I'm sorry.'

Helen said nothing. Thinking: sorry for waking me up? For the dried blood on my neck?

For this? For all of . . . *this*?

She closed her eyes again, and though she could not be sure how long she had slept or what had been a dream and what had not, the next thing she was fully aware of was the shape of him standing over her with a mug of hot tea and a packet of biscuits. A polite cough and him saying, 'Some breakfast.'

He stepped away, left the tea and biscuits on the floor within reach of her, and sat down.

The gun was on the table.

'I meant to say thank you,' he said. 'For what you said on the phone last night, I mean. For not telling them what had happened.'

Helen reached for the tea. Her mouth tasted foul and she was glad of the scalding liquid to wash it away. She glanced down at the spatters of blood dried brown against the linoleum next to her, and the broad smear of it that led out into the shop. Akhtar had still been questioning himself the night before as he had unlocked the handcuffs and dragged Stephen Mitchell's body out of the storeroom. He had stayed in the shop with it, while Helen sat shivering, with one arm hugging her legs to her chest, wishing that she had both hands free to block out the noise of him muttering in Hindi or shouting at himself. He was weeping, high-pitched like a woman, when sleep had finally overtaken her.

'I am very grateful,' he said now.

Helen nodded, but the smile was much harder to plaster on and keep in place than before. An innocent man was lying dead among yesterday's newspapers because Javed Akhtar believed the world was conspiring against him. Because he had gone out and bought a gun. Helen would still say and do whatever it took to stay safe, of course. She would do her best to sympathise and forge a bond with this man who held her prisoner, to convince him that she could help, that she was on his side. She would take his side if need be.

But she would never forgive him for Stephen Mitchell.

'Why did you lie to them?' he asked.

'I didn't really think about it,' Helen said.

It was almost the truth. Instinct had certainly kicked in quickly, but she had known very well what might happen if the officers running the operation outside thought that a hostage had been killed or injured. She knew that there would suddenly be huge pressure to intervene, to use such force as was necessary to resolve the situation quickly, before the second hostage was also killed.

Before they lost one of their own.

She knew what could happen once that kind of intervention was authorised. Once the bullets started flying. She had done the only thing she could think of to prevent that happening, and though she

161

had been well aware that the lie she was telling could end up costing her career, she had also known that it might just save her life.

It is not my time to die.

Or my baby's time to lose his mother.

'It was the sensible thing to do,' she said.

Akhtar drank his tea and began to talk about how, by this time on an ordinary day, he would normally have been up for four hours already. He told her that he would have driven to work, then delivered the papers and laid out any new stock that was needed before opening the shop. He talked quickly, trying a little too hard to keep things light, while Helen tucked into the biscuits. She realised suddenly that she was ravenous.

Alfie would be up and about by now, she thought, full of beans and demanding to be fed. Would Jenny have been shopping? Would she have the things in that he liked best?

'So, what do you think will be happening?' Akhtar asked, suddenly.

Helen looked up. She had not really been listening. 'Sorry?'

'Out there.'

He sounded genuinely anxious now, and looking at the tightness around his mouth Helen felt a peculiar rush of elation. Thinking that he damned well deserved to be. She was a trained police officer, for God's sake, and there were dozens more outside his poxy shop who would happily tear his head off given half a chance . . .

The feeling was short-lived. She needed him calm and reassured, and her bring-it-on confidence evaporated when she saw the speckles of blood on her tights and thought about Stephen Mitchell's wife, waiting and hoping somewhere outside.

Denise, who liked a glass of wine and didn't mind telling people what she thought. Who wanted to wait just a little while longer before she and Stephen had their kids.

'I don't know what's happening out there,' Helen said. 'Sorry.'

'It's OK.'

'I'm sure they'll be calling soon.'

Akhtar smiled and reached for the remote. 'We can find out,

162

maybe.' He turned the sound up on the television, then stood to angle the set so that Helen could see the screen. 'Good idea?'

They watched for a few minutes until, on the half-hour, *Breakfast Time* handed over to BBC London for what the smarmy presenter called the 'news where you are'. The local anchor looked serious as a stock shot of an armed police officer appeared behind her.

'There are no new developments this morning in the armed siege at a newsagent's in south London. Overnight, there had been uncon-firmed reports of a gunshot from inside the premises, but police have so far refused to comment. They have assured reporters in the last few minutes that both hostages, including an unnamed police officer, are alive and well, and that everything possible is being done to resolve the situation quickly and peacefully.'

Another picture. A different expression. An interview with a local gymnast.

'So,' Helen said.

Akhtar grunted and went back to his tea, as though the story they had just heard about had nothing whatsoever to do with him. He nodded towards the television. 'Shall I leave it on?'

'I don't mind.'

'We might as well.'

It was almost surreal, Helen thought. As though he were trying to restore some level of *normality* to the situation. However incongruous that notion might be with one of them handcuffed to a radiator, one armed with a gun and another growing cold in the next room.

'I can never usually watch at this time,' he said. 'The shop is always so busy, you know?'

So Helen brushed the crumbs from her bloodied skirt and they sat, like any other two people enjoying their breakfast, and watched the rest of the morning's news.

TWENTY-SEVEN

Thorne was back at the RVP by nine-thirty. In the playground, the small catering van known to all and sundry as 'Teapot One' was still serving hot bacon rolls and Thorne could not resist. He saw Sue Pascoe smoking at the side of the main school building and wandered over.

'You'll get a detention for that,' he said.

She took another drag, nodding towards what was left of the roll in Thorne's hand. 'And you'll get hardened arteries.' She touched a little finger to the side of her mouth. 'You've got . . .'

Thorne wiped away the ketchup. 'So what happened last night? This gunshot.'

Pascoe shook her head. 'The gun went off, that's all she said. Maybe he dropped it or something.'

'Or fired it to prove it was loaded?'

'Helen said it was an accident and I'm convinced she was saying that of her own free will.' She turned and crushed the cigarette butt against the wall behind her. 'Whatever happened, it was enough to give Chivers a stiffy.'

'I don't think it takes much,' Thorne said.

The look on Pascoe's face told him she was every bit as wary of the CO19 team leader as he was. Another one of many who thought that a significant number of firearms officers took themselves a little too seriously and were rather too enamoured of the alpha-male canteen culture. There had been a minor scandal the year before, when one of their number was accused of slipping song titles into the evidence he was giving at an inquest. This had generated plenty of comic mileage throughout the Met, but sadly, many of those tough-as-old-boots alpha males in CO19 had shown themselves unable to take a joke.

'So, all quiet overnight then?'

Pascoe explained that an agreement had been reached late the night before between the outgoing team and those replacing them to make no further calls to Helen Weeks until the morning. Nobody believed that anyone inside would be getting a lot of sleep, but it had been decided that it would be best for everyone concerned to let hostages, and hostage taker get as much rest as possible. While the replacement negotiator and firearms officers had remained on high alert throughout the night, there had been no proactive moves made from an operational standpoint, and no calls had been received from inside the newsagent's.

'Always good to come through the first night,' Pascoe said. 'Thing is though, as time goes on and everyone inside there gets more and more exhausted, they also get less predictable. And that's more ammunition for those that want to get this resolved sooner rather than later.'

As if on cue, Chivers appeared. He gave Thorne a nod, then focused on Pascoe. 'Donnelly's looking for you,' he said. 'Time to put another call in.'

Pascoe hurried back towards the entrance and Thorne and Chivers followed a few steps behind.

'So how's it going your end?' Chivers asked. He lowered his voice as though he did not want Pascoe to overhear.

Thorne looked at him. 'Well, I've not made an arrest as yet, if that's what you want to know.'

'What I want to know is how likely it is that you can give the man in that shop what he's asking for. How *likely* and how *long*.'

'There's no way I can answer that.'

'Well, you might have to think of one.'

Thorne kept smiling. 'I'll do my best.'

'Listen, I need to think about what my options are,' Chivers said. 'Do you understand?' He jabbed a finger in the direction of the newsagent's. 'When he runs out of patience.'

'Oh, I understand,' Thorne said. 'Because I'm not an idiot, you know?' He shouldered open the doors and turned towards the hall. 'Sounds to me though like you're the one that's getting impatient.' He took a few steps. 'Maybe you should *relax* a little, mate. *Take it easy*, you know, instead of *living on a prayer. One day at a time, sweet Jesus.*'

Chivers stared for a few seconds, until the penny dropped. 'Song titles,' he said. 'Funny.'

Donnelly was waiting at the monitors and as soon as he saw Thorne and Chivers approaching, he gave Pascoe the go-ahead to make the call. Pascoe nodded and made final adjustments to the headset she had connected via Bluetooth to her mobile.

Thorne saw that photographs of the two hostages had been taped to the edges of the monitor. He presumed that Pascoe had done it. A reminder to herself that they were dealing with human beings.

Stephen Mitchell was grinning in sunglasses and a garish shirt. A holiday snap, presumably provided by his wife.

The picture of Helen Weeks had clearly been faxed over from the Met's HR department. A straightforward ID photograph, but Thorne recognised the woman he had last seen at a funeral more than a year before. The soft features and ash-blonde hair. She looked serious in the picture, but this too was how he remembered her. Heavily pregnant with a dead boyfriend, there had not been much to smile about back then.

Next to him, Pascoe dialled. She moved the small microphone into position and cleared her throat.

Not an awful lot to smile about now, Thorne thought.

Helen Weeks' phone rang three times, then Akhtar answered. They all looked at one another anxiously as the newsagent's voice rang out from the speakers.

'Hello.'

'Javed . . . this is Sue Pascoe. I spoke to you yesterday.'

'I know who you are.'

'I need to speak to Helen. Is that possible?'

'What, you need to speak to her because you have something to say or you need to check that she is all right?'

'Can I speak to her?'

Akhtar's voice faded a little as he said, 'They want to know that you are all right.' Then, after a second or two, Helen shouted, 'We're both fine, Sue. I could murder a decent cup of coffee and a sausage sandwich though.'

Pascoe said, 'I'll see what I can do,' but Akhtar had come back to the phone.

'Is that acceptable?'

'Yes, thanks, Javed.' She glanced at Thorne. There was an odd formality to Akhtar's voice that she had often heard in those who spoke English as a second language. But there was an unmistakable tightness there too. 'So how was your night?'

'It was fine,' Akhtar said. There was a long pause. 'How was yours?'

'It was good, thanks. Listen, is there anything we can do to make you all a little more comfortable in there? Anything—'

'We're fine,' Akhtar said. 'Nobody's coming in, OK? No policemen dressed as pizza delivery men or any of that.'

'I understand,' Pascoe said. 'Nobody's coming in, Javed. We just want to do anything we can to help while we try and get everything sorted out the way you want.'

'Is Thorne there?'

Pascoe looked to Donnelly. He nodded. 'Yes, he's here.'

'Let me talk to him.'

Pascoe took off her headset and handed it to Thorne. He sat down and adjusted the microphone. Said, 'I'm here.' Pascoe made 'calm, calm' gestures with her hands and Thorne nodded, thinking that there was someone else he needed to tell that he wasn't an idiot. 'I'm listening, Javed.'

167

'No, *I'm* the one that is listening. I want to know what you have found out about my son. About what really happened to him.'

'Did you get my message?' Thorne asked. 'Did Helen tell you what I said?'

'That you believe me? Yes, she told me.'

'That's good.'

'So now it's up to you to make people believe us. The fact is, I don't care one way or another what you believe as long as you find out who murdered my son. And I am not a fool, so please do not keep telling me that these things take time.' The voice was tighter still now, the anger surfacing fast. 'It did not seem to take very long for your colleagues to decide that Amin had killed himself. It took *less than an hour* for the jury at that ridiculous inquest to confirm it. I only hope that you can prove that they were wrong just as quickly.'

'I'm doing everything I can, Javed. I'm—'

'You are sitting out there, talking on the phone,' Akhtar said. 'How is that going to help either of us? How is it going to help your friend Miss Weeks?'

Thorne looked at Pascoe and searched for something to say, but before he could come up with anything the line had gone dead.

TWENTY-EIGHT

Thorne asked Donnelly if he could speak to Nadira Akhtar again before he left. Told him that, with luck, she might be able to suggest where he should be going.

'You think she knows something that will help?'

'Not a clue,' Thorne said. 'But I haven't got any better ideas.'

'Listen, wherever you go, make sure you stay in touch, OK?' The superintendent was walking with him to the classroom that had been set aside as a family liaison area. Donnelly was rather more casually dressed today, in short-sleeved white shirt and black tie. Dispensing with the jacket and hat gave the impression to fellow officers and interested civilians alike that he was mucking in with the rest of his team, rolling up his sleeves. Though it might just have been because he was sweating. 'And obviously, if you have any communication with Helen Weeks, you let me know straight away.'

'I have been,' Thorne said.

'So what was all that about on the phone?'

'All what about?'

'Your *message*.'

'You know what it was.'

'Is it true?' Donnelly stopped outside the classroom. 'Do you think he's right about what happened to his son?'

'Yes, I do,' Thorne said. 'But whether I can prove it and give him what he wants in time is a different question.'

'He hasn't given us any kind of time limit.'

'You heard him just now.' Thorne nodded back towards the hall. 'And a certain firearms officer with his cock where his Glock should be is getting decidedly twitchy, if you ask me.'

Donnelly flashed him a warning look as he knocked on the window in the classroom door and beckoned to the WPC inside. He told her that Thorne needed to talk to Mrs Akhtar and the officer stepped out, looking grateful for the chance of some air, or perhaps just a change of company.

The desks had been pushed back against the walls and a few plastic seats set up in a circle in the middle of the room. There was a low table with tea and biscuits. A few magazines were scattered about, but Nadira Akhtar did not look as if she felt much like flicking through *Take a Break* or *OK!*

She was sitting on a chair near the window.

Thorne saw the open holdall beneath one of the desks as he carried a chair across to join her. Clothes and a flowery washbag. 'Did you sleep here last night?'

'I wanted to,' she said. 'The house is empty anyway.'

'Where's your son?'

'He has a family of his own to take care of.' She looked at Thorne for the first time. 'He will come back later but I am happier being on my own, to be honest with you. We argue.'

'About what?'

She waved the question away.

'Couldn't your daughter stay with you?'

'I told her to keep away.' She shook her head, then tucked a strand of greying hair back beneath her embroidered headscarf. 'I do not want her to see her father like this. To see how much he is frightening everyone.' She looked towards the door. 'To be around all these people who hate him.'

'Nobody hates him,' Thorne said. 'They're just doing their jobs.'

Nadira turned away and stared out again at the empty playground. A group of uniformed officers was gathered in one corner near a climbing frame, and on the far side it was just possible to see a row of emergency vehicles parked up beyond the tree line: the ARVs, the squad cars, an ambulance.

'Do you still see Rahim Jaffer?' Thorne asked.

Something tightened, just momentarily, in Nadira's face.

The boy who had been with Amin the night of the attack.

The boy he had been trying to defend when he had stabbed Lee Slater to death.

'He came to Amin's funeral, of course,' Nadira said. 'Lots of his friends came, some I had never even met before.' She nodded, proud. 'He had a great many friends.'

'So what about seeing Rahim?'

'Not since then, no.'

'Any particular reason?'

Another small wave of the hand, as though what she were about to say was silly and unimportant. 'We used to be friendly with his parents, but after what happened there was some ... awkwardness. Perhaps they thought we would blame their son. Perhaps because he was free and ours was rotting in that place. So we have not seen them in a while. We sometimes hear about Rahim, but only because one of his cousins still comes into the shop now and again.'

'What's he doing?'

'He is studying hard, I think.' Her hands were in her lap, one rubbing at the other as she spoke. 'At the South Bank University. Accountancy or economics or what have you. He was a very clever boy, same as Amin.'

Thorne thanked her for her time, grateful too that she had not seemed keen to know how things had gone the day before at Barndale. Whether or not she secretly shared any of her husband's concerns about what had happened to her son, it was obvious that she preferred to remember him simply as a popular and bright boy.

171

Not one who had died alone and unhappy in prison.

Thorne considered asking Nadira Akhtar there and then if she had known her son was gay. Perhaps she had known – would a mother not always know? – and kept the truth from her husband. He felt sure the time would come when he would have to tell both of them, but in the end he decided that it could wait. Thorne knew that where there was one secret though, there were usually others. That they bred easily. He guessed that Rahim Jaffer had shared the secret of Amin's sexuality at the very least, so now Thorne had a place to start looking.

'If you see Rahim,' Nadira said, 'please would you be sure to tell him that we never blamed him for anything?' She had turned to the window again, her eyes closed against the sunlight that was suddenly streaming into the room.

Thorne said that he would, but carrying his chair back to the centre of the classroom, he was thinking about something Nadira had said a few minutes before. About the boy who so many had told him kept himself to himself.

Wondering where he had got all those friends from.

TWENTY-NINE

As Holland and Kitson reversed into a parking space a few doors down from the address they had been given in Hackney, they saw a young man step out on to the pavement and start walking towards them. Nineteen or twenty, with dark hair that seemed pasted to his scalp and tattoos clearly visible on the arm outstretched to yank a bull terrier puppy along behind him.

Holland checked the black and white headshot clipped to the folder in his lap. 'That'll be our boy, then.'

'Bless him,' Kitson said. She nodded down to the file. 'Say anything in there about him being an animal lover?'

The file detailed the assorted crimes and misdemeanours that had resulted in Peter David Allen serving various sentences in three different Young Offenders Institutions since he was fourteen years old: actual bodily harm, burglary, threatening behaviour, sexual assault. Up until nine weeks previously, he had been a prisoner at Barndale, serving eight months out of thirteen after attacking a woman with a fence post when she had dared to try and stop him stealing her car.

Holland tossed the folder on to the back seat. 'Pete seems to like animals rather more than people.'

They watched Allen haul his dog past the car, waited a minute or two, then got out and followed.

'Just makes him typically British,' Kitson said. They walked a hundred yards behind Allen on the opposite side of the road. 'More money gets given to the RSPCA every year than the NSPCC, did you know that? Makes you proud, doesn't it?'

'Country's going to the dogs,' Holland said.

'Funny . . .'

At the end of the street, Allen turned left on to Dalston Lane. He ducked briefly into a grocer's and came out chugging from a can of Red Bull and tearing the wrapping from a packet of Marlboro. A hundred yards further on, he stopped to tie the dog to a lamppost and disappeared into a bookmaker's.

When he emerged a few minutes later clutching his betting slip, Kitson was leaning against the lamppost checking her phone. Holland was on his haunches making a fuss of the puppy, who was happily chewing at his sleeve.

'Fuck you doing?' Allen asked.

Holland looked up. 'Nice dog,' he said. 'Course it almost certainly won't be by the time you've finished with it.' He gave the puppy's belly one last rub then stood up. 'It's all about how you bring them up, isn't it? Same as kids really, but I don't have to tell you that, do I?'

'You what?'

Allen's stance was still aggressive, but he was clearly confused. His mouth opened then closed again, before his eyes flicked to the warrant card Kitson was waving at him and his shoulders slumped. Without a word he stepped across to untie his dog, then turned and walked back the way he'd come.

Holland and Kitson fell into step either side of him.

'Got yourself a job then, Pete?' Kitson asked.

'What's it got to do with you?'

'Just making conversation. I mean either you have, or you're just pissing your dole money away on the gee-gees.'

'It's my money.'

They paused as the dog stopped and squatted outside the same grocer's Allen had been into a few minutes earlier. Allen dragged the puppy across the pavement, lit a cigarette and watched as the dog went about its business in the gutter.

'You'd better hope you win,' Holland said. 'There's a two-hundred-quid fine for that.'

Allen smirked. They carried on walking.

'You been out what, a couple of months?' Holland asked.

Allen shrugged. 'Something like that.'

'Back on your feet?'

'Getting there.'

'More than Amin Akhtar is, that's for sure.'

Allen said, 'Who?'

They turned into the street where Allen lived. A row of old artisans' cottages ran for almost half its length, but at the far end the Victorian terraces had been knocked down and replaced by blocks of council-owned maisonettes. The small front gardens were nicely maintained for the most part, but there were bars on almost all the doors and windows. Allen had moved a few feet ahead of Kitson and Holland as he approached his front door. He reached for his key then turned to see them following him up the front path. He shook his head. 'No chance.'

'We only want a chat,' Kitson said. 'What are you so jumpy about?'

'Not without a warrant. That's harassment, whatever.'

'Don't need one if you invite us in.'

'Yeah, right.'

Allen opened the door, but when he turned to close it he found Holland's foot in the way.

'That's very kind of you, Pete.' Holland pushed his way inside and Kitson followed. 'But we can only stay a few minutes ...'

A small hallway-cum-porch led straight into a living room. Allen marched past Holland and Kitson and took the dog through into the kitchen. They watched as he opened a back door and let the puppy out on to a tiny, turd-covered patio at the back. Kitson opened another door on to a narrow corridor with what she presumed were a bedroom and bathroom running off it, while Holland walked across to examine the sleek black stereo and the rows of CDs and DVDs on the shelves above it.

Allen came back in to see Kitson emerging through the doorway and Holland rifling through his collection of thrash metal and torture porn. He stood in the centre of the living room and raised his arms in outrage.

Said, 'This is taking the piss.'

Holland nodded towards the stereo system: a Denon CD and Blu-Ray player; the big Bose speakers at either end of the room and the smaller ones mounted high up on the walls. 'This is decent gear, Pete. I wouldn't mind something like this myself.' He turned to look at the plasma TV that took up most of one wall. 'Have to put in a bit more overtime though.'

'I've got receipts,' Allen said. 'All right?'

Holland looked impressed. 'You must be getting some good tips then.'

'What?'

'On the horses.'

'Yeah, I've had a few winners.'

'And we can check that, can we?' Kitson asked. 'Obviously your bookie up the road keeps records of all his payouts.' She sat down on a faded brown armchair. 'For tax reasons, you know?'

Allen seemed to grow agitated suddenly. He walked over to the wall and leaned back hard against it. 'Is there any point to this?' He pushed his hands into his pockets. 'Because if you're waiting for tea and biscuits you can stick them up your arse.'

Holland dropped into the chair that was in front of the TV and turned it round so that he and Kitson were both facing Allen. 'Why did you put Amin Akhtar in hospital?' he asked.

'I didn't,' Allen said.

'Sure?' Kitson asked. 'Five minutes ago you didn't even know who he was.'

176

'I just meant ... I never knew him very well, that's all. You know how many kids there are in there?'

'Why does it matter if you knew him or not?' Holland asked. 'How well did you know that woman you battered with the fence post?'

'It wasn't me.'

'Some of the prison officers think it was.'

'Well they can kiss my arse, same as you can.' Allen was doing his very best to look cocky, but there was still nervousness around the eyes as he tried and failed to stare Holland and Kitson out. 'Look, I never took a knife to that kid, what else can I tell you?'

'Who said anything about a knife?'

Allen looked flustered, but only for a second or two. Then he smiled, pleased with himself. 'Everybody knew he'd been slashed, so you're not being clever. Something like that happens, word gets round before the poor bastard's finished bleeding. Besides, the screws turned my cell over looking for it, didn't they? And they found sod all.'

'It's a fair point, Pete,' Kitson said. 'There isn't a scrap of evidence and the fact is that even if you told us right here and now that it *was* you, we're far too busy to do a great deal about it. I mean the kid's dead now, right, and it wasn't like you had anything to do with that.' She waited, studied his face. 'But let's just say hypothetically that it was you who attacked him—'

'It wasn't.'

Kitson held her hand up. 'For the sake of argument, all right? If it *was* you, then why might you have done it? Like you say, you barely knew the kid, right? It wasn't like it was revenge for some fight you'd had with him or he'd said something to piss you off in the canteen, was it? Not a kid like him. I mean ... fair play to you, you did a very nice job, you got away with it somehow. You managed to stash the knife somewhere, got yourself cleaned up, but it was still a hell of a risk.' She turned to Holland. 'Don't you reckon?'

Holland nodded. 'You'd have to be an idiot.'

'What were you, just a few days from being released? Something like that would have put plenty more time on your sentence, so there's no way you'd have done it without a seriously good reason, is there? Without something decent in it for you, I mean. You're not Brain of Britain, but you're not an idiot, are you, Pete?'

Allen struggled for something to say. Settled for: 'This is bollocks.'

'Maybe you did it because someone asked you to.'

'What?' Allen shook his head and tried to laugh, but it was tight, strangled.

'Where did the money come from for all this?' Holland asked. The dog was whimpering outside the kitchen, scratching at the back door. 'And don't tell us it was the three-thirty at Kempton Park, because we're certainly not idiots.'

Allen sniffed and looked as though he was considering spitting on the floor, until he remembered he was in his own living room. He pushed himself away from the wall and said, 'I've got to feed my dog.'

Holland and Kitson watched as Allen sauntered into the kitchen and closed the door behind him. They heard him open the back door, then listened to the skitter of the puppy's claws on the tiles and Allen fussing over it, his voice deliberately raised so that they could hear just how unconcerned he was.

'If you tell us who put you up to it, we can guarantee you won't be prosecuted for the attack,' Kitson shouted.

Holland looked at her. They had been authorised to give no such guarantee. Kitson shrugged.

There was no response from the kitchen.

After half a minute they stood up to leave, but as Kitson moved back towards the porch, Holland walked across and leaned in close to the kitchen door. 'Good luck.'

There was a pause before Allen answered. 'What?'

'I was talking to the dog,' Holland said.

THIRTY

Good people who snapped, they were always tricky to deal with. It was what they did that counted of course, the havoc no different to that wrought by multiple killers with no discernible conscience, the grief of those left behind no less crippling. But still . . .

Hard to treat them the same way.

As Thorne drove north, he thought about a Russian he had read about in a magazine, a man who had tracked down the Swiss air traffic controller whose negligence had cost the lives of his wife and children in a plane crash. The Russian had gone to the man's door holding a photograph of his dead family and when the air traffic controller had knocked the picture from his hands, the man had lost his reason, burst into the house and stabbed the owner to death.

'It was as if he had taken them from me all over again,' the Russian had said, and years later, when he was finally released from prison, there had been a parade held in his honour.

Good people who snapped.

He remembered a teacher – the 'best in the school', according to parents and other members of staff – who had put a fifteen-year-old boy into a coma with a cricket stump after being baited once too often.

Thorne had watched the man break down in the interview room, weeping like a child for two lives wiped out in a few seconds of madness. 'The red mist,' the teacher had said to him. 'One of my kids put that in an English essay once and I crossed it out and put "cliché", but that's exactly what it's like. I was watching this arm clutching that stump and then I realised it was mine, but I just couldn't stop swinging it. It was like there was blood in my eyes.'

Thorne could not foresee a parade when the teacher completed his sentence for attempted murder, but neither had there been any team celebration in the pub the day he was sent down. He guessed that it would be much the same when things had played themselves out in Tulse Hill, unless Javed Akhtar did something very stupid.

Negotiating his way across the main roundabout at Elephant and Castle, Thorne knew that he was somewhere close to where Holland lived. One of the turnings off St George's Road. He'd only been there a couple of times, on the last occasion just after Chloe was born, but Sophie had not been shy about making her feelings towards him obvious, and there had certainly not been an invitation to return.

He wondered if it was something Holland and his girlfriend argued about.

Or did Holland think he was a prick as well?

Half a mile further on and he was in Southwark, looking for somewhere to park, when his phone rang. He pulled over.

'How's it going then?'

DI Martin Dawes was trying to sound cheery and no more than curious, but Thorne knew better. 'Checking up on me?' he asked. 'Worried that I might find something you didn't?'

'Don't be stupid.'

'How do you think Amin got hold of those drugs?' There was a pause, as though Dawes was trying to work out if it was a trick question or not, so Thorne ploughed on. 'Were they brought in by someone else, d'you reckon? Or maybe he nicked them himself.'

'Well, either's possible.'

'What about those thefts from the DDA cupboard, do you think they might be important?'

'Listen, I took all that into account.'

'Really? Including the fact that the Tramadol was stolen the *day after he was admitted*?'

Another pause.

'You never thought to check that, did you?'

'Well, I did find out later on,' Dawes said, flustered. 'It was mentioned at the inquest, as a matter of fact, so it's not like you've found Shergar or anything. Didn't make any difference in the end, so to be honest, I don't see quite what you're getting so worked up about.'

'Don't you?'

'If he took them it's still suicide, isn't it?'

'*If* he took them.'

Dawes clearly wasn't listening. 'It doesn't change anything.'

'Actually it does,' Thorne said. 'I was wrong yesterday when I said you were an idiot. You're a fuckwit.'

He parked behind the Local History Library on Borough Road and walked back across Keyworth Street, which neatly bisected the Southwark campus of South Bank University.

Thorne had called the office before he'd left Tulse Hill and asked DS Samir Karim to do some checking for him. Karim had spoken to the university registrar and discovered that Rahim was in the first of a three-year Marketing and Accountancy course. A second call to his tutor had established the day's lecture schedule.

10.30-12.00: Quantitative Literacy.

Thorne stopped to ask directions from a couple of girls who tried their best to help, despite having little English. He knew which building he was looking for, but it still took him another quarter of an hour to find it.

He checked his watch. He still had fifteen minutes.

It was striking, the way that Rahim Jaffer's expression changed twice after he had spotted Thorne on the way out of the lecture theatre. He was talking to another student who was laughing at whatever was being said, when his eye was caught by the man in the leather jacket standing up from a chair in the corridor. The smile was instinctive, a natural enough reaction on seeing someone he recognised, but it lingered no more than a second or two, until Rahim remembered where he had met the man before.

When he had last seen him.

Thorne knew that none of this was necessarily significant, of course. As investigating officer in the manslaughter of Lee Slater, Thorne had been giving evidence for the prosecution, while Rahim had been a key witness in his friend's defence. It was nine months ago, so understandable that Rahim had been unable to place Thorne for a few seconds. It was also very likely that the circumstances in which their paths had last crossed would be the reason that he did not seem overjoyed to see him again.

'Remember me?' Thorne asked. He could see that Rahim did, but it was always worth trying to elicit a lie immediately. It told you something straight away. Brigstocke called it 'getting the lie of the land'.

Rahim nodded and put out his hand.

Thorne shook and said he needed a word. 'It won't take long and you're not due at your Digital Marketing seminar until one o'clock, so there's plenty of time.'

Rahim blinked, taken aback. 'Right . . . '

Again, it was a simple enough trick, but when you weren't sure where a conversation with someone was going to lead, the back foot was usually the best place for them to start.

Thorne led the way to a small seating area where he had spent most of the previous fifteen minutes drinking coffee and flicking through a student newspaper. A few metal tables and chairs, vending machines for snacks, hot and cold drinks. He sat Rahim down and asked him if he wanted anything. He bought him a bottle of still water, then took the chair opposite.

He saw Rahim looking around and told him not to worry.

He had been careful to select a table where they would not be over-heard.

'So come on then,' Thorne said. 'What the hell is "quantitative lit-eracy" when it's at home?'

'It's just about being comfortable with numbers really,' Rahim said. 'How we use them in our everyday lives. So ... logic and reasoning, algebra, geometry, probability, statistics. It's basically just a pretentious way of saying maths.'

'Enjoy it?'

'Yeah.'

Thorne nodded. 'Take away the algebra and geometry bits and it's the same kind of stuff I use. Reasoning, probability, all that. Maybe I should start calling myself a quantitative detective.' He stumbled over the words and smiled. 'Well, I would if I could say it.'

Rahim smiled too, but it was as short-lived as before. He fiddled with the cap from his water bottle.

'What are you now, eighteen?'

Rahim nodded.

Thorne had recognised Rahim straight away, but the boy had cer-tainly changed a good deal since he had last seen him. Perhaps it was just that jump from sixth-former to undergraduate. The neatly combed hair was now gelled up into a fin and the simple grey suit had been replaced with baggy jeans and a tight-fitting T-shirt. A tattoo was just visible on his forearm and he wore a diamond stud in each ear.

Before he had clapped eyes on Thorne, he had seemed comfortable and happy.

'You know what this is about?' Thorne asked. 'Right?'

'What's going on with Amin's dad, you mean? Yeah, I saw it on the news.' Rahim sat back. 'Is everybody OK?'

'At the moment.'

'So, what's it got to do with me?'

'You lied about where you were,' Thorne said. 'The night you and Amin got attacked.' He waited, but Rahim said nothing. 'I mean we

183

knew you were lying back then, but we didn't think it was very important. Now, it might be.'

Rahim took a long swig of water.

'I know you're gay, Rahim.' Thorne knew no such thing, but the look on the boy's face told him he was right.

'So?'

'And so was Amin.'

'Look ...' Rahim put down the bottle. 'We couldn't say anything because our parents didn't know. Mine still don't know. They're pretty strict ... *very* strict, and there's no way I can tell them that isn't going to be a nightmare. It's an Indian thing, OK? You wouldn't understand.'

'I do understand,' Thorne said. 'And for what it's worth I've got no intention of telling them.' He studied the boy's face, looking for a sign of reassurance or relief, but there was none. He was clearly worried about something else.

'I still don't see—'

'Javed Akhtar doesn't think Amin killed himself.'

'Sorry, I don't—'

'He believes that Amin was murdered.'

'What?'

'And I think he's right.'

'Jesus ... !'

It could easily have been an exclamation of shock, but it had taken just a second too long and to Thorne it looked more like fear. 'Here's the thing, Rahim,' he said, leaning across the table. 'Right now, I don't have a motive and if I'm going to catch the person responsible for this, I really need to find one. So ... using "logic" and "reasoning" and a bit of bog-standard guesswork, there's a fair chance that there are other things about Amin that I don't know and maybe one of them got him killed.' He let his words hang for a moment, waiting until the boy looked up and met his eyes. 'Now, you'd know way more than me about the *probability*, but I'm betting that he had more than one secret, and I need you to tell me what they were.'

184

Rahim leaned away and raised his hands. 'There's ... nothing.'

'You quite sure about that?' Thorne's tone was sharp suddenly. He had given up expecting anything on a plate, but was content to take out his frustration at the last day and a half on the young man sitting opposite.

'I can't think of anything, I swear.'

'You might want to try a bit harder,' Thorne said. He spat the words out, happy enough for them to be overheard by the group of students two tables away. 'Because he was your friend, and he wouldn't even have been in prison if he hadn't been trying to stop some thug sticking a knife in you.'

'I know that. Don't you think I know that?'

'Good, so rack that fucking big brain of yours and do it sharpish.' He grabbed the half-empty water bottle and threw it hard into the plastic bin by the side of the vending machine. 'You've seen what's happening at his dad's shop, so you know that we're kind of against the clock on this one.'

'Yeah, I know ...'

Thorne gave him a card with his mobile number on. 'Call me any time, OK? Now you give me yours.'

Rahim gave Thorne the number, then reached down for his bag. He looked close to tears. He said, 'I need to have lunch before my next class.'

Thorne watched him walk away without a word.

He felt a brief pang of sympathy for Rahim Jaffer, of regret at his outburst. The boy was guilty of nothing, he was almost certain of that. As he reached for his phone and dialled, he knew losing his temper had been justifiable – given the circumstances, given his desperation – but that he should be saving all his anger for those deserving of it.

If he ever got the chance.

'Dave?' He could hear that Holland and Kitson were driving. 'How did it go with Allen?'

'I managed to stop myself punching him,' Holland said.

Thorne heard Kitson laughing. 'You fancy him for the attack on Amin, then?'

'Oh yeah, but there's definitely something else going on.'

'He was shitting himself,' Kitson shouted.

'When we talked about someone putting him up to it, he was as nervous as hell.'

'Any bright ideas?'

'Well, he's rather more minted than your average ex-con, I know that much,' Holland said. 'He's got seven or eight grand's worth of hi-fi and TV in his front room.'

Thorne told Holland that he might as well get himself and Kitson back to the office, then asked them to run a name through the Police National Computer as soon as they had a chance. 'It's Rahim Jaffer,' Thorne said. 'J-A-F-F-E-R.'

When he stood up, he could see that the group of students were eyeing him suspiciously. Most stared quickly down at their Cokes and lattes when they saw him looking. He smiled as he walked past them on his way to the exit, toyed with announcing that he was a visiting Criminology professor, but decided against it.

There's definitely something else going on.

It might well have been the two coffees he'd drunk waiting for Rahim, but was more likely the conversation he'd just had with Dave Holland and Yvonne Kitson. The implication, the possibilities.

Either way, Thorne was fired up suddenly. Full of energy.

All he needed now was something, or someone, to focus it on.

THIRTY-ONE

'What happens if Thorne doesn't find what you want him to find?' Helen asked. 'What do you do then, Javed?'

Akhtar was sitting at the desk. He had been to fetch an assortment of reading material from the shop, and had been staring at the same page of a motoring magazine for half an hour. He looked across at Helen. 'Is he a good policeman?'

'I think so.'

'OK, then.' Akhtar shrugged as if there was therefore nothing to worry about. 'So we have to trust that he will do a good job. A better job than his colleagues made of things, at any rate.' He went back to his magazine, turned the page.

'Sometimes it doesn't matter how good you are,' Helen said. 'How hard you work. You don't always get the result you want.' She waited, but he didn't look up. 'Do you know how many times I've had to watch while someone I know is guilty as sin gets away with it? Someone who's hurt children and who will go on hurting them.'

Akhtar closed his magazine. 'And you wonder why I no longer have any faith in the law?' He shook his head. 'Justice is a bloody joke, you have just made that very clear yourself.'

187

'Things don't always work out the way they should, I'm not saying they do.'

'I know that, believe me.'

'But that doesn't mean . . . this is right. What you're doing.'

'Right does not come into it. I know that this is not *right*, but in the end I did not have a choice.'

'Course you did.'

Akhtar stood up and took down a carton of cigarettes from one of the shelves. He brandished it, angrily. 'You know, I could be doing what everybody else does and driving across to France or Belgium and bringing thousands of these things over in the back of a van. I would save myself a fortune, but I always refused to do it because I never believed that sort of thing was right. You break a small law and soon the bigger ones become easier to ignore. So I always did things the correct way, I always obeyed every rule because the most important thing was that I could sleep at night. That mattered to me, Miss Weeks, however silly it might sound now. I never had to worry that someone would come knocking at my door in the middle of the night, you understand?' He tossed the carton on to the floor. 'I was stupid,' he said. 'I believed that the law would look after my son, that he would be treated fairly.' He took a deep breath and wiped the sleeve of his shirt across his face. 'And when he died, I believed, *stupidly*, that the person who was responsible would be found and would be punished.'

They both turned at the sound of a raised voice somewhere outside the front of the shop. They waited. Helen guessed it was just some copper shouting at a subordinate and shook her head to let Akhtar know there was nothing to get excited about.

He nodded and sat down.

'Sometimes people get it wrong,' she said.

'*I* was the one who got it wrong,' Akhtar said. 'Because I trusted in people who I thought were far cleverer than me. Who were supposed to be good at their jobs.' He picked up the gun then laid it down again. 'Now look where we are . . . '

Helen groaned as she shifted her position to relieve the ache in her buttocks. In an effort to ease the cramp in her calves she reached forward with her free hand and pulled back on her toes.

'Shall I try and find another cushion?' Akhtar asked.

'It's fine,' Helen said. She leaned back. 'You never answered my question.'

'Which?'

'What if all Thorne's efforts aren't good enough?' Helen stared at him, her face neutral, no more than curious. Thinking: what if you're just a misguided old man with a screw loose? And even if you're not, will it bring your son back? Will it bring Stephen Mitchell back? 'What if you don't get the answers you're waiting for?'

'Very simple. I keep waiting. I have plenty of time.'

'We can't sit in here for ever, Javed.' She nodded towards the shop. 'They won't let that happen.'

Akhtar shook his head and slapped his palm against the desktop. 'No, no, *I* am the one in charge here.'

'Yes, you are,' Helen said.

'Good, because everyone needs to understand that. You and the people outside.'

'They understand, believe me.'

'And you're doing well, yes?' He pointed at her. 'I'm looking after you OK?'

'Very well,' Helen said. 'Thank you.'

Akhtar seemed pleased and began searching eagerly through the pile of magazines on the desk. He asked Helen if she would like something to read, told her he always kept an excellent selection. He offered her *Hello!*, *Bella* and *Brides Monthly*. Helen said thank you and told him that she would look at them later.

They sat in silence for a few minutes, then Helen nodded towards her phone. It was sitting on the desk, plugged into the charger that Helen always kept in her handbag. 'Do you think I could make a quick call?' she asked.

'Who to?'

'My sister,' Helen said. 'I just want to see how my son's doing, you know?'

Akhtar looked suspicious, but his expression was almost melodramatic, as though he believed it was how he ought to look. 'I don't think that's a good idea. It's not what's supposed to happen.'

'Please, Javed. Only for a minute.' Her voice was barely above a whisper, but she kept it even at least. 'I want to check he's all right.'

'No.' Akhtar stood up. '*I'm* running this bloody show and *I* decide what happens.' He picked up the gun to emphasise his authority, but did not point it at her. He walked towards the shop then stopped in the doorway, calmer suddenly. 'Anyway, we need to keep the phone free in case Thorne calls.'

'I just wanted him to hear my voice,' Helen said. 'That's all.'

Akhtar looked at his feet for a while, then disappeared into the shop.

Helen closed her eyes and lay down.

A few minutes later, she could hear him crying again next door.

Sue Pascoe emerged from the toilet cubicle and crossed to the row of small sinks to wash her hands and splash some water on her face. She smiled at seeing that someone had written 'Wesley is a big knob' in black felt-tip on the mirror. Wondered if Wesley, who could be no more than eleven, would have the wherewithal to change 'is' to 'has'.

It was the first time all day that she had found a few minutes to herself or thought about anything other than the job in hand.

The first time she had smiled.

She looked at her watch. It was now thirty hours since Javed Akhtar had taken two people hostage at gunpoint. Donnelly seemed happy enough with the way things were progressing, though in a situation such as this one, that only meant that nothing bad was happening. Chivers was still making noises about the need for advanced technical support and Pascoe knew there would soon be pressure from elsewhere to relax the cordon so as to ease traffic congestion in the area, or at least make an effort to get the station at Tulse Hill reopened.

God forbid the commuters should suffer.

As things stood, none of this was her concern, but it soon would be if the whispers about resolving the hostage situation as quickly as possible grew any louder. If Donnelly started to listen. Then it would become Helen Weeks' concern too.

She dried her face and brushed her hair. She groaned at the amount of grey coming through and determined to get back to the hairdresser's as soon as she got the chance. She reapplied her lipstick, then stepped out into the school corridor feeling better. Passing one of the classrooms, she glanced in through the small window and saw a black woman talking animatedly to a WPC. The woman saw her and immediately stood up and walked towards the door.

Pascoe swore quietly and braced herself. She knew Denise Mitchell had clocked her, that there was now no possibility of walking quickly away.

The woman was pretty, with flawless skin and hair in cornrows, and she had begun talking before she had opened the door. 'Look, nobody will tell me what the hell's going on. I'm going mental stuck in here.'

'Everybody's doing everything they can,' Pascoe said.

'It doesn't feel like it,' Denise said. 'It feels like everyone's rushing around with serious faces, but nothing's actually happening.'

'I'm very sorry,' Pascoe said. 'Obviously if there was anything to tell you, I would.'

'Right.'

'Honestly.'

'Even if it was something I really didn't want to hear?' The woman's eyes were suddenly wet. 'Is that your job or do they give that one to somebody else?'

'Look, I think perhaps you'd be a lot more comfortable staying elsewhere. Has anybody talked to you about a hotel?'

A nod.

'Don't you think that would be a good idea?'

'I don't want to go on my own.'

'What about family?' Pascoe asked. 'There must be somebody . . .'

'There's just Steve.' Denise reached into the sleeve of her sweater and drew out a used tissue. She lifted it towards her face then stopped and crushed it in her fist.

'Everybody's doing everything they can,' Pascoe said.

'Yeah, you keep saying that.'

'Because it's the truth.'

'Really?' The woman narrowed her eyes and stared at the Met Police badge on the lanyard around Pascoe's neck. The WPC had appeared behind her in the doorway. 'What are *you* doing?'

Pascoe wondered if there was anything she could say that would make this woman feel better. *I'm the one being paid to negotiate with the man who has your husband. I'm the one whose job it is to keep him alive.*

Denise Mitchell did not bother waiting for an answer. 'It's not fair,' she said. 'Steve hasn't done anything.' Her voice cracked as she raised it. 'You should stop talking about it and get him out of there, because he hasn't *done* anything.'

Now, Pascoe really had nothing to say.

She watched as the WPC guided the woman back into the room, then turned and walked back towards the hall.

THIRTY-TWO

'You don't appear to be with us today, Mr Jaffer . . .'

Rahim looked up and stared at his tutor. She waited, as though expecting an explanation for his lack of attention or perhaps a précis of the topic she and the other students had been discussing for the previous few minutes. All Rahim could do was mumble an apology, feeling the blood rush to his cheeks while some of the others around the table laughed and shook their heads. The woman began talking again and Rahim did his best to listen. He scribbled a few notes on a page that was already covered with meaningless doodles, but within a minute or two the pen grew heavy in his hand and the tutor's words had become no more than background burble and hiss.

So rack that fucking big brain of yours . . .

Thorne's words were still ringing loud and clear though, the expression on the policeman's face vivid enough to tighten the cold and slippery knot in Rahim's guts whenever he closed his eyes.

I'm betting he had more than one secret.

He was squeezing the pen so tightly that purplish half-moons of blood had formed beneath his fingernails. He cast his eyes in the direction of his tutor and told his head to nod, while he tried to regulate his breathing. To keep the anger in check. He was not a child any more, and he hated being made to feel like one. He resented feeling ashamed and fearful when he had left shame and fear behind him, locked away back in his parents' house with the ugly carpets and the stink of patchouli.

The other students laughed suddenly. One of his tutor's bad jokes.

He laughed along, while he sat there and told himself that none of this was his fault. Not what Amin's stupid father was doing and not what had happened to Amin. He could never have foreseen that, or done anything to stop it, and nothing he could do or say now would change the fact that he was dead, would it?

Dead was dead, even if there was no need to rack that big brain of his. Even though he knew exactly what Thorne was after. Dead was dead, whatever his parents and their priests might have taught him, and did it really make any difference to anyone except one policeman and a crazy old newsagent how it happened?

Or why?

He was your friend ...

Rahim looked up at the mention of his name. Saw the look of concern on his tutor's face.

'Perhaps you should go home,' she said. 'You really don't look well.'

He did not need a second invitation. He stood and gathered his books, said something about a virus and hurried from the room without bothering to close the door behind him.

He was lucky that the toilet was only a few steps away.

Ten seconds later his books and papers lay scattered on the floor of the cubicle, as he dropped to his knees, clutched at the edge of the bowl and threw up.

Excited as he was by developments, Thorne had been at something of a loss as to where he should go after talking to Rahim Jaffer, so he decided to get some lunch. To share it with someone he could at least usefully discuss things with. It would not be the first time he had eaten in a mortuary, enveloped by the sounds and smells of the dead and those who worked on them. Thorne figured there were probably fewer germs around than in the average greasy spoon.

Phil Hendricks shared the small office at Hornsey Mortuary with three other pathologists. In contrast to the state-of-the-art lab and post-mortem suite along the corridor, the room was tired and grimy. Hendricks' desk was as cluttered as usual with olive-green arch files and folders, the only flashes of bright colour provided by the columns of curling pink Post-it notes around the computer screen and the obligatory 'Arsenal: Legends of the Seventies' calendar pinned to the wall above.

This month: Liam Brady with his 1979 FA Cup Winner's medal.

'So the kid was gay,' Hendricks said. 'You'd more or less worked that out anyway and it's still not much of a motive.'

'No?' Thorne held out the plastic bag containing the selection of sandwiches and snacks he'd picked up from Tesco on the way. Hendricks rummaged around, finally plumped for the ham and cheese and a bottle of apple juice. 'That was the one I wanted,' Thorne said.

Hendricks said, 'Good,' went back into the bag again and fished out a packet of crisps. 'OK, so there's always a few morons who enjoy taking their problems out on people with better fashion sense than them, but as a rule I don't think gay-bashers tend to be quite so ... imaginative.'

'It's definitely part of it though.' Thorne took out his own sandwich, opened a bottle of water. 'There's sex involved somewhere.'

'You're obsessed, mate.'

'*Me?*'

Hendricks had taken off his scrubs and was wearing jeans and a tight-fitting white T-shirt. Thorne took a quick inventory of the tattoos on display. There were none he could not recall seeing before, and as his friend usually celebrated each sexual conquest with a trip to the tattoo parlour, this probably meant that he wasn't getting much action. It was always possible that there was a new tattoo somewhere Thorne couldn't see it of course, but he doubted it. That would mean that Hendricks was getting his end away and keeping it to himself.

195

And he never kept it to himself.

'You thought about blackmail?' Hendricks asked.

'All the time,' Thorne said. 'Give me a thousand pounds or I'll go on Facebook and tell all your friends you're shit in bed.'

Hendricks flashed a sarcastic grin, teeth full of ham and cheese.

'Yeah, I've thought about it,' Thorne said.

'He sleeps with someone who'd rather it's kept quiet, tries to squeeze them for money.'

'Maybe.'

'You might want to look at the Muslim angle again.'

'Why?'

'They hate poofs even more than people who kill themselves.' Hendricks took another bite of his sandwich. '"When a man mounts another man, the throne of God shakes." Muhammad said that, apparently.' He chewed for a few seconds. 'I'm clearly not sleeping with the right men.'

They said nothing for a minute or two. Sat and ate and listened to the noises of the mortuary. The distant clanging of freezer cabinets and the squeak of trolley wheels in the corridor outside.

'This Rahim kid knows more than he's telling me,' Thorne said.

'Sounds like you put the wind up him.'

'I hope so.' Thorne aimed his empty water bottle at the metal bin in the corner and missed. 'I haven't got time to do things any other way.'

'How's that copper in the newsagent's doing?'

'Pretty well, I think,' Thorne said. 'She's tougher than they think she is.' He gathered the plastic packaging and empty crisp packets and shoved them into the plastic bag. 'It's that poor sod who works in a bank I feel sorry for. God knows how he's holding up.'

Thorne walked over and dropped the plastic bag into the bin. When he turned round, Hendricks was looking at him.

'You spoken to Louise lately?'

Thorne shook his head. 'You?'

He was not surprised when Hendricks nodded. He and Louise had grown extremely close in the two years she and Thorne were together

196

and theirs was a relationship of gossip, whispers and in-jokes that had often made Thorne stupidly jealous. Had made him feel excluded. There were times when Thorne had resented his best friend coming between himself and Louise, and others, somewhat less comfortable to think about now, when he had felt as though Louise were the one doing the muscling in.

'How's she doing?'

'She's doing OK,' Hendricks said. 'I mean it's not like you're any great loss, is it?'

'I suppose not.'

'You should call her.'

'Yeah, well she did accidentally manage to hang on to several of my Emmylou Harris albums.'

'Seriously,' Hendricks said.

Thorne nodded and lifted his leather jacket from the back of the chair. 'Listen, about this drugs thing.'

'I knew it,' Hendricks said, mock-offended. 'There was I thinking you'd just dropped in to have lunch.'

'A *working* lunch,' Thorne said.

'I told you, I'd get on it.'

'When, Phil?'

'Look, I just need to find a few hours to get my nose into a couple of books,' Hendricks said. He nodded towards the computer keyboard. 'Spend some time on the internet.'

'Soon as you can, eh?'

Hendricks pointed to the door, the post-mortem suite beyond. 'Sorry, mate, I've been a bit bloody busy. RTA on the Seven Sisters Road yesterday. Multiple fatalities.'

'They're not going anywhere,' Thorne said.

While Kitson brought him up to speed with the day's developments, Russell Brigstocke – ever the keen amateur magician – sat with a deck of cards, practising fancy cuts and shuffles. He listened intently while Kitson talked him through the interview with Peter Allen, the movement of the cards between his fingers helping him to relax and calm down after the call he had received ten minutes earlier from Martin Dawes' commanding officer.

'I just thought we should "touch base" on this Amin Akhtar thing,' the man had said. That one phrase alone had been enough to tell Brigstocke the kind of pompous tosser he was dealing with. 'From the sound of it, your DI is doing his level best to discredit the original inquiry, which I think is a real shame. It's not going to make him very popular and if he's not careful it's going to make my team look rather silly.'

'I think you've already made a decent job of that yourselves.'

Now, Brigstocke's opposite number knew what kind of man *he* was dealing with. 'Let's not make this about scoring points,' he said.

'Sorry, I must have got the wrong end of the stick.'

'I'm thinking about the Murder Command London-wide. The Met in general, if it comes to that. Nobody's going to come out of this well, certainly not once the media get hold of it.'

'Oh, I think you might come out of it a bit worse than anybody else,' Brigstocke said. 'From the sound of it, *your* DI should start thinking about traffic duty.'

'That's not exactly helpful.'

'It wasn't meant to be.'

'Look, if you're not willing to listen, I'm perfectly happy to go over your head.'

'Fill your boots,' Brigstocke said. 'In the meantime I'll pass your concerns on to DI Thorne, but I think he's got one or two more important things to worry about at the moment.'

'OK, well I was hoping you might be reasonable, but—'

'Really? I thought you were just touching base?'

'I can see where this bolshy DI of yours gets his attitude from.'

'Come back and talk to me when you're a superintendent,' Brigstocke said. 'Actually, I'll still tell you to piss off!'

Kitson had laughed when Brigstocke told her about the call. Said, 'Tom would be very proud.'

Brigstocke fanned out the cards on the desk in front of him, flipped them and brought the deck back together. 'So, is he on to something, do you reckon? I mean, I know what's going on down there is important and I'm happy for you and Dave to go chasing around for him, but you do have other cases.'

'Difficult to tell,' Kitson said. 'He sounds excited, but that might just be panic.'

Brigstocke picked up his cards and dropped them into a drawer. 'It's not very often I feel sorry for him,' he said. 'But Thorne's under the cosh with this one, because Akhtar's made it all about him. If anything happens to that woman he's holding . . .'

'It won't be Tom's fault.'

'Good luck trying to tell Tom that.'

They both turned as Holland knocked on the already open door and stepped inside. 'We've got a hit on Rahim Jaffer,' he said. 'A strange one.'

Brigstocke looked at Kitson. Said, 'Call Thorne.'

THIRTY-THREE

For the final briefing before the call that was scheduled for four o'clock, they gathered in a small room behind the stage in the assembly hall. There were large papier-mâché heads lined up on the window ledge and a row of brightly coloured costumes hanging from a clothes rail. Thorne guessed that most of the kids would be relishing their time off school, but that a few might be upset at missing out on performing in the school play.

One kind of drama cancelled out by another.

Donnelly asked Sue Pascoe to summarise her thoughts about Akhtar's state of mind and, from that, to give her opinion about the degree of threat posed to the two hostages.

'He's certainly emotional,' she said, looking down at her notes. 'Angry at times . . . petulant even, but these kind of extreme emotions don't last, certainly not once real tiredness kicks in. Other than that very first contact, there have been no threats of any sort against the hostages, no deadlines set. Javed hasn't talked directly about suicide and there's certainly no previous history of violence.'

'You make *Javed* sound like the Archbishop of fucking Canterbury,' Chivers said. He was smiling, but it didn't look good on him. 'Clearly we're all worrying for nothing. Guns going off are neither here nor there and Weeks and that other poor sod are having a whale of a time in that shop.'

'All right,' Donnelly said. He looked back to Pascoe.

'I don't see any increase in threat or volatility,' she said. 'And unless and until that changes, I would definitely recommend that we keep doing what we are doing. This is all about wearing him down.'

Donnelly turned to Chivers. 'Bob?'

It was the first time Thorne had heard Chivers' Christian name and he thought it suited him quite nicely. Just the one syllable, a 'Bob' and not a 'Robert'. Nice and easy to have tattooed somewhere handy in case he ever forgot it.

Thorne glanced at Pascoe, but she would not look at him. He told himself it was because she was afraid she might laugh.

'Well, you know what I think,' Chivers said. He nodded in Pascoe's direction. 'With all respect, I've probably been on a few more of these things than you have, and in the end the only difference between sitting it out and going in early is a lot of wasted time and effort. Usually the same result in the end.'

'Usually?' Pascoe asked.

Chivers clearly saw the question for the challenge it was. The invitation to state his credentials. 'In five years of these operations, my team has discharged their weapons exactly three times,' he said. 'One fatality, two woundings and no hostage so much as scratched. Good enough?'

Pascoe considered this. There no longer appeared to be too much chance of her laughing. 'I'm presuming that you don't regard that one fatality as any kind of failure.'

'Look, if you think I'd send my team charging in there without being convinced they could resolve the situation *without* the use of force, then you're wrong. But our hostage taker is waving a loaded gun about, let's not forget that. So I'm not going to sit here and pretend that his safety is every bit as important to me as the well-being of the hostages. Fair enough?'

'I'd like to get everybody out safely,' Pascoe said.

She was about to say more, but Donnelly cut across her. 'I think we're getting ahead of ourselves,' he said.

Chivers looked at Thorne. 'What about you?'

'I'm not a big fan of guns,' Thorne said.

Chivers nodded, but clearly thought this was akin to confessing to some outlandish sexual perversion. 'I was asking how your investigation was going,' he said. 'The business with his son.'

'Do you care?'

'In so far as you being in a position to give our hostage taker what he wants, which will have a direct bearing on the job I'm trying to do here, yes, of course I bloody care.'

'I think somebody murdered his son,' Thorne said. 'And I'm doing my best to find out who.'

'Timescale?'

The look on Thorne's face made it clear he thought the question was every bit as stupid as the last time Chivers had asked it. 'Ten minutes from now? Next week? Never? Still impossible to say, Bob.'

Donnelly stood up. 'For now, we'll carry on as we have been, but I'm taking everything I've heard into consideration and obviously we'll continue to review the situation. OK?'

Nods around the table, some rather more enthusiastic than others.

'Right, let's make the call.'

They trooped back into the hall and once everybody was in position and Donnelly had called for silence, Pascoe dialled.

Akhtar answered and Pascoe asked how he was. He thanked her and told her he was fine, so she asked if he would mind providing some proof that the hostages were doing equally well. Akhtar briefly passed the phone to Helen Weeks. She told Pascoe that she and Stephen Mitchell were tired but in good spirits and being well looked after, then handed the phone back to Akhtar. Pascoe thanked him and he asked her if she had heard anything from Tom Thorne.

Thorne leaned in towards Pascoe. Said, 'I'm here.'

Akhtar said nothing.

'I just got back from talking to more people about Amin, and I want you to know that I'm making real progress.' Thorne reached out for Pascoe's headset, but she seemed reluctant. They both looked for the go-ahead from Donnelly and were given it. Pascoe handed over the headset and Thorne took her seat. 'OK, Javed?'

'What kind of progress?'

'I need to talk to you.'

'So, go ahead.'

'In person,' Thorne said. He was immediately aware of the shock turning quickly to fury around him and of the frantic head-shaking. Donnelly hissed, 'No way,' and Pascoe raised a hand in warning.

'I don't see how that is going to happen,' Akthar said. 'I will not allow anyone in here and I hardly think I will be permitted to just pop outside for a . . . quick chat.'

'We can talk through the shutters,' Thorne said. He waited, trying to ignore the anger of the officers close to him and the pressure of the superintendent's hand on his arm. He stared at the image of the shopfront on the monitor, listened to the rasp of Akhtar's breathing. 'Just come to the door on your side of the shutters and I'll be on the pavement right outside.'

Akhtar grunted and swallowed. 'All right.'

'I'll be there in five minutes,' Thorne said.

THIRTY-FOUR

Donnelly spent almost half of those minutes shouting; making sure Thorne knew that whatever happened and however the situation ulti-mately resolved itself, he would make it a priority to have his balls for breakfast. Thorne stood and took the dressing-down, but could not resist pointing out that Donnelly would probably still be hungry after-wards. Then, he walked out of the school with Pascoe and Chivers in tow.

'This is stupid,' Thorne said. He slapped at the Kevlar vest Chivers had insisted on him wearing.

'Doesn't happen without it,' Chivers said. 'Simple as that.'

They crossed the road and walked towards the newsagent's. 'How's he going to take a shot at me from behind those shutters?'

'It's not open for discussion.'

'What do you think he's got in there? A bazooka?'

As Thorne moved closer to the shop, he was aware of eyes on him. Those of Donnelly and the many others watching on the monitors; of the uniformed officers still manning cordons a hundred yards away either side of him and probably unsure of what was happening. He was most aware, most apprehensive, about the armed officers who had been swiftly briefed and instructed to take up firing positions behind appropriately placed vehicles. Thorne knew that eyes were not the only things being trained in his direction.

'It's them I'm scared of,' Thorne said. He nodded back towards the helmets just visible above the bonnet of a Volvo. 'Not him.'

'Well, you'd better hope those shutters don't start to open then,' Chivers said. He seemed to be enjoying himself. 'And just remember whose bright idea this was in the first place.'

There was not much Thorne could say. He looked at Pascoe, but she was walking with her head down. She had not spoken to him since the call had ended.

They stopped a few feet from the front of the shop.

'Just talk,' Chivers said. 'That's it. On no account suggest that you go inside or that he comes out, because if those shutters do go up and he's got a gun in his hand, you're in all sorts of trouble. Clear?'

'Clear,' Thorne said.

Finally, Pascoe spoke. 'And if the conversation starts to move in a direction you're not comfortable with, back away. I've been working hard to build up his trust and I really don't want that compromised.'

'I'm not trying to step on your toes,' Thorne said.

'I never suggested that you were.'

'I just need him to know I'm doing what he wants and that I might actually be getting somewhere. He needs to trust me as well.'

'Can we crack on?' Chivers said.

Thorne stepped up and knocked on the shutters. There was a distant hum of traffic from the nearest main road, but suddenly everything went very quiet.

'I'm here,' Akhtar said.

It was strange, hearing the man's voice at close quarters. It was muffled by the glass in the shop's front door and Thorne had to lean in close to the sheet of ridged, spray-painted metal that separated them still further.

'Thanks for doing this.'

205

'Are you alone?'

Thorne saw little point in lying. 'No. Sue Pascoe is with me and so is the head of the firearms unit. That's just the way things have to be done, I'm afraid.'

'I understand.'

'But it's just you and me talking, Javed, so ...'

'What do you want to tell me?'

'I wanted to tell you in person that I think you're right,' Thorne said. 'I don't believe that Amin took his own life. It would be easy enough for me to say that anyway, whatever I thought, because I know it's what you want to hear, but I'm not just saying it. I need you to believe that, and to believe that I'm doing everything I can to find out who killed him. To get you the truth.'

There was a long pause, then Thorne heard Akhtar say, 'Thank you.'

'I've already talked to the authorities at Barndale and to Amin's friends. I've spoken to the boys and the relatives of the boys who attacked him a year ago, and to Rahim Jaffer.'

'Why are you talking to Rahim?' Akhtar asked.

'I'm talking to anyone I can think of.'

'You think Rahim knows something?'

'I think ... he might know things about your son's life that you didn't, that's all.' Thorne was choosing his words carefully. 'Sometimes we can talk to our friends about things we might not want to discuss with our parents.'

'He talked to us about everything,' Akhtar said.

'I'm sure he did.'

'There is nothing Amin could not come to us about.'

Thorne turned to see Pascoe and Chivers watching him. He could still feel the eyes on him and the telescopic sights of the sniper rifles. 'Javed, I need to know that you're ready to hear whatever I find out.'

'I don't understand what you're saying to me.'

'Listen, I know that you don't want to hurt anyone, or hurt yourself, so I'm asking you to hang on. To be patient, and to be prepared if the facts about what happened to Amin are not very pleasant.'

'My son was murdered,' Akhtar said. 'How could the facts be *pleasant*?'

'They might not be easy to hear, that's all.'

There was another long pause. Pascoe signalled to Thorne that he should step away. Mouthed: 'That's enough.'

Then Akhtar spoke, his voice a little louder suddenly, as if he too were leaning close to the shutters. 'The lies we have been told about Amin, about what happened to him in that prison, have torn our hearts out, Mr Thorne. Mine and Nadira's. They have sucked away my decency and turned me into the kind of man I despise. The kind of man who no longer has any respect for the law and would do something *unspeakable* like this.

'Lies have done these things, do you understand? So how can I be afraid of the truth?'

THIRTY-FIVE

Just a few seconds after Akhtar came back into the storeroom, a phone began to ring. They both looked at Helen's handset still sitting on the desk, then quickly realised that the noise was coming from the shop.

Mitchell's mobile, ringing in his pocket.

They sat and listened to it ring, then when it had stopped, Akhtar said, 'I meant to tell you this before, but I wrapped Mr Mitchell's body up as best I could. There were some black bags, so . . . '

'That's OK,' Helen said. 'I don't see what else you could have done.' She was already wondering when the body would start to smell. It would not be long, not in this heat.

Akhtar sat down. 'I am so ashamed that he is lying out there . . . like that, so very ashamed, but I promise you this, Miss Weeks. When all this is over, I will do everything necessary to make sure that he has a proper burial. It does not matter what it costs. I swear to do that.'

Helen just looked at him. The nodding, the earnestness. Did he really think that when it was over he would just walk out of here and go back to his old life? Home to his wife and dinner on the table and up again at half past four the next morning to open the shop? Did he really think there were any other options besides death and prison?

And what were her options?

She thought again about the price she was likely to pay for keeping Stephen Mitchell's death a secret, the career she had worked so hard for and had now jeopardised, and she felt a hot rush of anger for the man lying dead in the next room. Why had he not listened, why had he been so *stupid*? He was the one who had put her in this position.

Had made her lie and squirm and snivel . . .

When the anger had finally subsided, she felt every bit as ashamed as Akhtar did. The truth was that she would sacrifice anything, her stupid career included; that she would crawl out of this shop bleeding and limbless if it meant the chance to see her son again. And she knew that if she did, when she did, Stephen Mitchell would be carried out in a body-bag, stinking, in a shroud of bin-liners.

'Are you all right, Miss Weeks?'

Helen looked at him and tried to smile. 'Don't you think "Miss Weeks" is a bit formal? I mean, considering where we are and everything.'

'Yes, of course,' Akhtar said. 'Stupid.'

'It's Helen.'

He nodded and moved his chair a little closer to her. 'I think this might be over soon, Helen.'

'That's good,' Helen said. A genuine smile broke, unbidden, across her face and for the first time in many hours she forgot the numbness in her backside and the pain where the cuff had bitten into her wrist. 'That's really good, Javed.' She did not want to push it, to ask him what he and Thorne had been talking about at the shutters. She had heard Akhtar's voice but could not quite make out what Thorne had been saying. She was happy enough to wait until Akhtar told her.

Instead, he asked, 'How do you know Mr Thorne?'

'It's a long story,' she said.

Akhtar shrugged. 'I don't think either of us is going anywhere for a little while, at least.'

'My partner died, just over a year ago. Just before Alfie was born.'

209

'Ah,' Akhtar said, nodding. 'I had wondered why I never saw the baby's father. I would never have asked, of course.'

Helen swallowed, took a few seconds. 'Paul was . . . killed, and it was Thorne's job to find out what happened.'

'Like this, then?'

'I suppose so, yes.'

'So, did he?'

'Well, actually I found out the truth myself.' Helen shook her head, still not quite able to believe, a year on from it, that she had done the things she had. Taken such stupid risks. Putting herself close to gangs and killers like a kid poking at a wasps' nest and tearing around like a lunatic while eight months pregnant with Alfie.

She had felt proud of herself though, in the end, and vindicated because she knew how proud Paul would have been. It had helped her cope with the grief, and the guilt.

'Well, perhaps I should be asking *you* to find out what happened to Amin,' Akhtar said, grinning. 'And Thorne should be sitting where you are.'

'Sounds good to me,' Helen said.

Akhtar stood up and flicked the kettle on. There was a lightness to his movements suddenly, as he reached for mugs and spoons. A squareness in his shoulders. 'Yesterday, when he suggested swapping places with you? That told me something very important about the kind of man he is. Told me he was the right man . . . '

Helen suddenly remembered talking to Thorne a year before, at Paul's funeral. He had looked uncomfortable in a stiff collar and tie and had told her he was going to be a father. 'One on the way,' he had said. 'Not as far gone as yours but . . . on the way.' So just a couple of months, but that meant Thorne would have a baby of his own now.

Yet still he had offered to take her place.

When it came, Helen drank her tea and ate the biscuits that were given with it, feeling anything but proud. Because she knew that she would not have done the same.

THIRTY-SIX

With an insight gained solely from episodes of *The Young Ones*, Thorne still imagined that most students lived in glorious and chaotic squalor, with Che Guevara posters covering up the damp patches on the walls, washing-up growing mouldy in the sink and a note stuck to the fridge saying, 'Don't eat my yoghurt!' It was an out-of-date stereotype, but comforting. It served to water down the envy Thorne felt for those less than half his age, with three years free to enjoy a plethora of sex and freedom from responsibility. It eased his regret at never having been one of them himself.

Rahim Jaffer's flat would have made most people envious.

Jaffer lived a stone's throw from the Old Vic theatre, on the ground floor of a converted warehouse just off The Cut in Waterloo. After a curt exchange over the intercom system and a short staring match on the doorstep, Jaffer had shown Thorne into a sitting room that would not have disgraced an up-market design magazine.

'Nice,' Thorne said.

Jaffer said nothing.

The white walls were broken up with rows of framed black-and-white photographs; portraits of people who, with the exception of

Marlon Brando and Imran Khan, Thorne did not recognise. A lamp at the tip of a thin metal arc reached fifteen feet into the room from a marble block in the corner and hung above a coffee table shaped like a strand of DNA. Some Japanese designer, Thorne thought, though he could not remember the name. He was sure that nothing in the place had come in a flat-pack, and when he saw that all the electrical appliances were Bang & Olufsen – the TV, the stereo, even the absurdly shaped telephone – he remembered what Holland had told him about Peter Allen's flat, though he could not imagine that it was quite as tastefully done as this.

He sat down in a chrome and leather armchair that had clearly been bought for looks rather than comfort and watched as Rahim lounged on the matching sofa. The boy was wearing the same clothes Thorne had seen earlier in the day, though he had since dispensed with socks and the trainers had been replaced with soft red moccasins.

'You feeling better yet, Rahim?'

'Sorry?'

'I spoke to your tutor.'

'Why did you do that?'

'Well, for some reason you weren't answering your mobile,' Thorne said. 'So I tried the university. She was very helpful, actually. Told me you'd been feeling unwell. That you'd gone home early.'

'Yeah.'

'That must have come on suddenly.' Thorne shifted his position to try and get comfortable, then gave up. 'Not long after we spoke, wasn't it?'

'Some kind of virus,' Rahim said.

Thorne nodded then turned towards the stereo. 'What was that you were listening to before?' Rahim had turned the music off as soon as he'd shown Thorne in.

'You wouldn't know it.'

'Probably not,' Thorne said. 'Didn't sound like my kind of thing.'

Rahim just looked at him. Thorne could see that he was nervous but nevertheless unwilling to make casual conversation. Bright enough to know that Thorne was not there for that.

'You like music then? Go to a lot of clubs and stuff?'

There was a moment's hesitation. 'Not really.'

'Sure?'

Rahim sat forward, said, 'What's this about?' but it was clear from his expression that he already knew.

'You were arrested as part of a raid on the Crystal Rose in Brewer Street five months ago,' Thorne said. 'Cautioned for possession of cocaine.'

The boy was probably aiming for something like insouciance, but he could not control the nervous reflex. That soft red moccasin tapping fast against the floor. 'So?'

'So, were you there for the music?'

'It's a nice club,' Rahim said. 'I just went out with some friends.'

Thorne leaned forward, happy to see that Rahim leaned that little bit further away as he did so. 'I don't give a toss about the drugs,' he said. It was no longer a conversation, no longer casual. 'What's interesting is that it wasn't even the drug squad that made the raid. It was actually part of a vice operation. They'd been tipped off that certain individuals were using the Crystal Rose as somewhere they could go to pick up underage boys.' He waited, but Rahim just stared at the floor, both his feet now working together against the stripped and varnished boards. 'I'm talking fourteen- or fifteen-year-olds here,' Thorne said. 'You understand? Nothing disgusting enough to get the "dirty paedo" brigade too hot under the collar, but, unfortunately for some of the customers, illegal enough to do time for, and these are the kind of men who really can't risk a quiet stroll around the alleyways off Piccadilly Circus in the early hours. Professional types, you know what I'm saying, Rahim? *Respectable*. I mean, who in their right mind wants to risk getting ripped off, or having their head kicked in by some junkie, when all he wants is a quick hand-job from someone with nice smooth hands?

'So, somewhere like that club you were in ... well, it's a godsend, don't you reckon? The perfect place to find what they're looking for without any hassles. A few drinks and a slow dance, and no need for

213

money to change hands until they're safely back in their nice comfy "bachelor" pads or hotel rooms. Then the really sad ones can kid themselves that whoever they've brought home with them actually *wants* to be there. They can do what the hell they like then and take their time about it. They can relax and take off their business suits . . . and fuck teenage boys like you to their hearts' content.'

Rahim eventually raised his eyes from the floor. Now, he looked as unwell as he had previously been pretending to be.

'You remember what we talked about earlier,' Thorne said. 'So, bearing in mind that I'm pushed for time and that it's Amin I'm really interested in . . . I was wondering what you might be able to tell me about that.'

'Nothing,' Rahim said.

'Not good enough.'

'*I'm* not underage.'

'You *were*,' Thorne said. 'And so was Amin.'

Rahim stood up. 'I want you to go.'

'Considering what you haven't told your parents, I'm guessing that they don't know about your arrest.' Thorne stood up too, stepped towards Rahim. 'About the drugs.'

'So tell them,' Rahim said.

'I will if I have to.'

'I don't care.'

'Yes, you do.' Thorne stared until the boy's bravado began to fall away, until his head sank and it looked as though he might drop backwards on to the sofa. Thorne knew that he was being a bully. He had treated killers, rapists, better than this in the past, but then he had been granted the luxury of time, and a team behind him to gather evidence. He looked at the boy's face and hated himself, but he could not afford to spare anyone's feelings, and thinking about what Helen Weeks was going through, what Amin Akhtar had suffered, he fought the temptation to push Rahim against one of his tastefully decorated walls and press an arm across his throat until the boy told him what he knew.

'We went to parties,' Rahim said. 'Me and Amin.'

'What kind of parties?'

'Parties with men, OK?' He spat the words out. 'Like the ones you were talking about. Respectable men.'

'And these men paid you and Amin for sex?'

Rahim nodded slowly. 'Some boys did it because they needed drugs, but we just did it for the money. Our parents were not rich, do you understand? Most of the time the men were ... clean, and we were looked after.'

Most of the time.

Thorne waited.

'It was ... exciting too,' Rahim said. 'We liked it, the fact that we were not like the other Asian kids, spending every minute swotting to be doctors and lawyers and all that. Living to keep their mothers and fathers happy. We were in control, you know?'

'You really think so?'

'It felt like that.'

'Where did these parties take place?' Thorne asked.

Rahim hesitated. 'Different places. The City. A penthouse on the river. Highgate sometimes.'

'I need addresses.'

'I can't remember.'

'Tell me about these men, Rahim.'

'I've told you—'

'You need to give me some names.'

'No.'

'For Christ's sake,' Thorne shouted, 'one of these men might have killed Amin.'

The boy shook his head and kept shaking it, and Thorne's breathing grew more ragged with every refusal. He knew there was little point in dragging him down to an interview room, with no valid reason to hold him and even less chance of getting the answers he was looking for. Once again, he felt ready and willing to beat the information from him. The bruises would fade a damn sight quicker than grief, and Thorne would live with whatever consequences came his way.

Then, as quickly as the urge for violence had come over him, it went again, as Thorne looked into Rahim Jaffer's eyes and saw that he would be happy to take it.

Would welcome it.

Instead, Thorne lashed out at the brushed chrome shade of the lamp that hung low to the side of him. He sent it swinging and bouncing across the room on its spindly metal neck; the pool of light washing back and forth across the boy's face as Thorne walked out of the door.

THIRTY-SEVEN

Peter Allen spent a lot more time in the pub these days. He had always liked a drink, but lately it had been less about enjoyment and more like a simple need to get wasted. To sink into the beer or the cider or whatever and lose himself. Ironic, he supposed, considering how he'd earned the money to pay for it.

The Victoria on the Queensbridge Road wasn't quite his local. That honour belonged to an old man's boozer that stank of piss and brown ale, so he preferred to walk the extra ten minutes and drink with people who were a bit closer to his own age. Where there was a big TV if there was a match on and something to eat besides peanuts. This place wasn't flashy like a Wetherspoons or what have you, and Allen guessed it had been there since before he was born, because there were frosted-glass windows and old-fashioned booths that made it feel like you were getting pissed up in a church or something. There were a few stroppy locals who tried to stare you out when you first walked in, but there was usually a decent game of pool to be had, as well as live music some Fridays and a wide selection of fruit machines to pour his shrapnel into.

Best of all, it wasn't one of those Paddy places with shamrocks and shit everywhere you looked.

He'd started good and early, had a couple of cans at home before he'd gone out. But even after four pints of lager in the Vic, he was still sober enough come eight o'clock to be taking his third straight frame of pool off some shaven-headed squaddie type. The bloke had been winding him up since he walked through the door, looking and smiling and all that, and now Allen was enjoying making him look stupid.

He'd actually lost the first frame when he'd knocked the black in accidentally and was forced to watch as Corporal Cock winked at his slag of a girlfriend in the corner and said, 'Bad luck, mate.' Then, it had been a toss-up between breaking his cue across the arsehole's nose or sharpening his game up, and after thinking through his options Allen had decided to get his own back on the table. He reckoned it was probably the sensible thing to do, considering the terms of his licence. Besides, he knew he could always batter the bloke later on if he lost, or if winning didn't prove satisfying enough.

He sank the final black nice and slow, and was staring at the squaddie's pig-ugly girlfriend before the ball even dropped. Giving her a nice, big smile. He winked and said, 'Bad luck,' and as he was walking back to the bar, it struck him that he could have been talking about the game, or just saying it was her bad luck to be shacked up with such a loser. A double-meaning kind of thing.

He thought that was pretty clever.

Despite waving a twenty at her for at least half a minute, the snotty cow behind the bar ignored him and carried on gassing with some twat in a suit, so he moved to the other end of the bar and squeezed into the first gap he could find. He started waving his money again, then turned at the sound of a payout on the fruit machine and saw a face he recognised.

'Oi, knobhead!'

The boy at the fruit machine turned, his eyes cold and dead, then grinned when he recognised Allen, who had raised his arm and was now making wanking gestures. He scooped out his winnings and sauntered across, then, ignoring the angry looks of those he jostled on the way, he pushed through the crowd at the bar to Allen's side. He held out a fist. Said, 'What you doing here?'

Allen touched his fist to the boy's. 'Just getting hammered,' he said. 'Sweet . . .'

'What you drinking?'

He hadn't been particularly close to Johnno Bridges in Barndale. The kid was a Jock for a kick-off and Allen never really had much to do with the smackheads. On top of that, Bridges only ever hung out with the white kids, and while it wasn't like Allen was any big fan of the blacks or the Pakis, he'd preferred to give the gangs a wide berth and keep himself to himself. Safer that way in the long run, he reckoned. All the same, Bridges had never seemed like too much of a prick whenever their paths had crossed. That was a pretty decent character reference considering some of the idiots they'd been banged up with and was certainly a good enough reason to buy him a drink.

'How long you been out?'

Bridges thought about it. 'Not long after you. Couple of months, whatever.' He reached into his pocket and produced a string of blue, plastic rosary beads. He dangled them in front of Allen and smiled, showing a row of crooked and missing teeth. 'Secret signal,' he said. 'Come on then, let's see 'em.'

Allen nodded and produced his own beads from his jacket. All the boys at Barndale had been issued with them and it was accepted that, once released, they would always carry them. It was a way of acknowledging a shared history, establishing trust with one another on the outside.

No different from those secret handshakes all the coppers and judges had, that's what Allen reckoned.

He slipped the rosary beads back into his pocket and watched Bridges sip his beer. He had very short, reddish hair and wore a dirty denim jacket over jeans. His pupils were dilated and Allen could see that he had got himself high recently.

'Still on the gear, then?'

Bridges nodded slowly and raised his glass in a salute. 'Nothing cut to shite with laxatives either.'

'Where's the money for that coming from?'

Bridges nodded across towards the fruit machine. 'Them.'

'Piss off.' It was the same kind of story Allen had tried on those two coppers earlier.

'I swear,' Bridges said. 'I just drift around the pubs emptying those things once the punters have filled them up for me. I've got a mate works for the company, told me how to beat 'em.'

'For real?'

'Piece of piss, I'm telling you.'

'Yeah, well tell me then.'

Bridges put a finger to his lips and giggled.

While Allen downed the rest of his drink, Bridges rummaged in his pockets then slammed a fistful of change down on the bar. Ignoring the coins that rolled on to the floor, he turned to Allen as though he'd just had a revolutionary idea. 'Let's make a night of it.'

'What have you got in mind?'

'Let's get completely off our faces,' Bridges said. 'See if we can find a couple of birds who are up for it.' He reached for his rosary beads again and waved them in front of Allen's eyes like a hypnotist's gold watch. 'Come on . . . a great big "fuck you" to Barndale.'

Allen stared at him. He was starting to feel the booze kick in himself, but Bridges looked well out of it, and bearing in mind the day Allen had had, the mood he was in after his visit from those two smartarse coppers, he certainly fancied getting into the same state himself.

'Sounds good,' he said.

Pascoe and Donnelly sat drinking coffee in the small room behind the stage. There were no more than a couple of hours to go before the overnight team came back. One more phone call to Helen Weeks, a briefing for the new boys and girls and they would be away.

'You're doing well, by the way,' Donnelly said.

Pascoe looked at him, swallowed her coffee. 'Thanks,' she said.

'Just wanted to let you know.'

Pascoe turned away, not wanting the superintendent to see her blush, to see what the praise had meant to her. Almost immediately she began to wonder why he had told her. Was it perhaps because he fancied her a bit and was trying to gain favour? Or did he simply think she was the sort that needed reassurance?

Neither explanation made her feel particularly good.

'I'm pleased that's what you think,' she said. 'Don't think I'm not . . . but I just wondered why you felt the need to mention it. Is it because you don't believe I'm . . . confident?'

'No. I mean I think you *are*—'

'Because I am.'

Donnelly raised his hands in mock-surrender. 'I know, I know. Look, I just thought you were a bit nervous when you arrived, that's all, but you're doing a great job and I wanted to let you know that I'm impressed. That's it. No hidden agenda.'

'Sorry, I wasn't suggesting that.'

'I think it's part of my job to make sure everyone on the team's feeling positive about themselves,' Donnelly said. 'Every bit as much as they are about the operation. People work better, simple as that.'

'Makes sense.'

'So, are you still feeling positive? About what's happening?'

'Yes, I am,' Pascoe said. 'There's no increase in references to violence and no insistence on face-to-face negotiations. We've got a hostage taker demonstrating no more than mild to moderate anxiety and a hostage with at least basic training in dealing with her situation.'

'Right . . .'

Donnelly had grunted and nodded three or four times as Pascoe had been speaking, but she got the impression he had been looking for something other than chapter and verse from the hostage-negotiator handbook. 'I think it's looking good,' she said.

'You still think we should wear him down?'

'Absolutely.'

'Provided the state of play stays the same.'

'Of course.'

Donnelly nodded again, and not for the first time Pascoe saw an uncertainty that bothered her. She would have been far from happy had the officer in control of the operation been one of those hard-arses unwilling to listen to those around them, but she was nervous nonetheless. Donnelly was starting to look increasingly like someone who needed others to make decisions for him. Who took advice only because it meant he could duck responsibility if things didn't work out.

'It was impressive,' he said. 'The way you squared up to Chivers earlier.'

'I was just fighting my corner.'

'It was good,' Donnelly said, smirking.

'Was it?'

'I don't think he's used to people taking him on, you know?'

It *had* been good, and Pascoe smiled remembering the look on Chivers' face. Thorne had clearly been impressed too, and she in turn had enjoyed watching him give every bit as good as he got.

Still impossible to say, Bob . . .

Donnelly said he was going to have another coffee and asked if she wanted one. She handed her cup across. He filled it from one of the vacuum jugs and handed it back to her.

'Are you married, Sue?'

'Excuse me?'

'Just asking, that's all.' Donnelly slurped at his coffee. 'I mean I noticed there wasn't a ring, so just wondered . . . '

'I don't think *that's* part of your job, sir,' Pascoe said. 'Is it?'

THIRTY-EIGHT

Though Helen knew what time it was and that it would be dark outside, the light in the storeroom never changed. With no windows to
the back and the shutters down in the shop itself, the sickly white
wash of the flickering striplight had remained constant and, exhausted
as she was, Helen knew that once again there was little possibility of
sleep.

Akhtar was lying on his camp bed. He had one arm folded across
his eyes, but Helen knew that he was awake.

The most recent call with Sue Pascoe had been brief and unevent-
ful, which Helen knew was a good thing. It was becoming routine. The
woman was good at her job, Helen decided; businesslike, but as
friendly as she was required to be. Helen guessed that she could also be
firm if the need arose, but for now she was doing all that was necessary
to keep Akhtar calm and relatively relaxed.

Helen had once again reassured Pascoe that she and Mitchell were
fine and in good spirits and, when the call had ended, Akhtar had
thanked her for continuing to lie. He had made her more tea, asked her
if there was anything she would like to watch on the television, before
moving across to his bed and settling down.

Now, while he was still awake and feeling well disposed towards her, she decided to ask him a favour.

'Javed . . .'

He sat up and looked at her.

'Can I call Thorne?'

'Why?'

'I understand why you didn't want me to call my sister,' she said. 'But if I could speak to Thorne, then maybe he could call her. I just need to know that my son's all right.'

When Akhtar looked at the phone on his desk, Helen knew that he was going to agree. She was still surprised when, instead of pointing the gun and sliding the handset across the floor, he left the gun where it was and handed the phone to her. It was as close as they had been to one another since Akhtar had bent down to uncuff and then remove Stephen Mitchell's body.

'Thank you,' Helen said.

Akhtar nodded and returned to sit on the edge of his bed. 'So you can tell them how well I am treating you.'

Helen dialled and the call was answered every bit as quickly as she had been expecting. Thorne had obviously recognised the number.

'Javed?'

'It's Helen.'

'Is everything all right?'

'It's fine. Listen, I wondered if you'd be able to call my sister for me? I need to know that everything's OK with Alfie, that's all.'

'No problem,' Thorne said. 'What's the number?'

Helen told him. 'And tell her that I'm all right and not to worry.'

'I'll call you back when I've spoken to her,' Thorne said. 'Is that OK with him?'

Helen raised her head and asked Akhtar the question. He thought about it for a few seconds, then nodded. 'It's fine,' she said.

They sat in silence, waiting for Thorne to call back, occasionally catching one another's eye and smiling a little awkwardly like patients

224

in a waiting room. Helen's stomach rumbled loudly and Akhtar pretended not to hear.

Helen stabbed at the button the instant the phone began to ring. 'Tom?'

'Alfie's fine,' Thorne said, immediately. 'He's asleep now, obviously, but Jenny said he's in top form. Giving her the runaround by the sound of it.'

Helen's breath caught in her throat when she tried to speak. She managed to say, 'Thanks,' then took a few seconds. 'Is he eating OK, did she say that? Because sometimes he's fussy, you know?'

'He's *fine*. I promise.'

'OK ...'

'Probably hasn't even noticed you're not there,' Thorne said. 'You know what kids are like, right?'

Helen managed to laugh, but it felt tight in her chest. 'Yeah, she's probably spoiling him rotten.'

'Course she is.'

'Is *she* OK?'

'She's worried,' Thorne said. 'She's your sister. But I told her how well you're doing, and that you're going to be seeing her very soon.'

'Did she mention my dad?'

'Yeah, he's bearing up, she said. He's worried too, obviously, but your sister told me she'd send him your love and tell him everything was going to be fine. Helen?'

'Sorry, yeah ... listen, thank you.' She glanced up at Akhtar. 'I need to go,' she said. 'Thank you, really. I'm sure you've got better things to do.'

'I can't think of any,' Thorne said.

Helen laughed and this time it felt a little easier.

'And it *is* going to be fine, all right, Helen? So just hold on.'

When Helen had hung up, she held the phone out for Akhtar to take. He stood for a few moments, looking up at the striplight and shaking his head, then walked across to the same cupboard from which he had dragged the camp bed and reached inside.

'Let's see what we can do,' he said.

With a small cry of satisfaction, he retrieved a wooden table lamp with a torn green shade. He carried it across to the desk then fumbled underneath with an adaptor until he had managed to plug it in. As soon as he had switched the lamp on, he turned off the overhead light and considered the effect.

'Still too bright,' he said. Then, 'Wait.'

He stepped across and picked up one of the cushions that Helen had discarded after Mitchell had been shot. He pulled the cover off and held it up triumphantly, as though looking for her approval. Helen watched as he tried and failed to tear it, then walked across to the desk and took a large pair of scissors from one of the drawers. When he had finished cutting the cushion cover in half, he put the scissors back then carefully draped the square of dirty brown material across the lampshade.

'There,' he said, making final adjustments. 'That's much better. Not perfect, but at least you might be able to get an hour or two's sleep. Before, it was impossible, I know.'

'Thanks,' Helen said.

Akhtar went back to his camp bed and lay down. Helen still thought that the chances of sleep were slim, but the light was better, she had to admit that, softer. Diffused as it was through dirty cotton and dried blood.

THIRTY-NINE

Thorne had barely eaten a thing all day, so had made himself three pieces of cheese on toast as soon as he'd got home. Now, after finishing his conversation with Helen Weeks, he went back into the kitchen to make himself another couple.

He hoped it was a myth, the business about cheese and bad dreams.

It had been uncomfortable, lying to Helen on the phone, but it was not as if Thorne had been given a great deal of choice. Her sister's landline had been engaged every time he'd called and she had not been answering her mobile. Having sat and eaten in front of the ten o'clock news, Thorne had a fair idea of why that might be. However much those running the operation in Tulse Hill tried to keep a lid on it, the press was persistent and had deep pockets. Leaks were all but inevitable. During the latest report 'live from the siege', Helen had finally been mentioned by name, and Thorne guessed that her sister was now leaving her phone off the hook in an effort to avoid the media.

He bent to check what was happening under the grill.

There would almost certainly be a fair-sized scrum of hacks and snappers on the poor woman's doorstep by now.

So, in the end, he had said the things he felt sure he would have been saying if he had spoken to Helen's sister. The things Helen was clearly desperate to hear. It had not been easy listening to the emotion in her voice and he had fought to keep it from his own; letting her know simply that all those she loved and who loved her would be waiting on the other side of those shutters.

Waiting, with those who loved Stephen Mitchell, and Javed Akhtar.

When it was ready, Thorne carried his supper back into the living room. He opened a can of supermarket lager and ate while flicking through the channels on the TV.

Supersize v Superskinny, *Rude Tube*, golf . . .

I'm sure you've got better things to do . . .

He called Louise.

He was thirty seconds into leaving a rambling message on her answering machine when she picked up.

'Tom?'

'Sorry, I was just . . . I thought you'd probably gone to bed.' He waited for her to say something. 'Are you OK?'

'It's late.'

'I know,' he said. 'Sorry. I'm on stupid hours at the moment.' He told her about the situation in Tulse Hill. She had been following developments on the news, but was still surprised to hear that he was involved. Thankfully, as of yet, Thorne's name had not been mentioned.

'I would have thought this one was right up your street,' she said.

'Why?'

'Someone to catch *and* someone to save.'

'Yeah, well, we'll see about that.'

'Chuck in a dead kid,' she said, 'I reckon this just about ticks all your boxes. Probably not quite enough bodies yet, but plenty of strangers to care about.'

'Come on, Lou.'

'What?'

'Let's not get into that.'

There was a long pause, then Louise apologised. She told Thorne that she was still thinking about getting out of the Job and away from

228

London. Then, as if by way of explanation, she talked a little about the case she was working on. The kidnapping of a fourteen-year-old Romanian girl that had widened to become a major investigation into sex trafficking.

'It's hard to think of anything but the faces of those girls,' she said. 'The marks where they stubbed fags out on them.'

Thorne waited a few seconds. 'That's what used to piss me off,' he said.

'What?'

'All that stuff about me caring, when it was always perfectly bloody obvious that you care every bit as much as I do.'

'Yes, but I care a bit more about myself.'

'Listen, the reason I was calling,' he said. 'We've got this hostage negotiator in Tulse Hill ...'

'What's his name?'

'Her. Sue Pascoe?'

Louise hadn't heard of her and asked if she was any good.

'She's fine,' Thorne said. 'But you'd be better. Maybe if I talked to the superintendent ...'

'What, you think we can just arrange a job swap or something?'

'It might be worth thinking about.'

'Right, presuming he'd be happy for you to bring your ex-girlfriend in and the woman who's there already would be happy to step aside, and presuming I hadn't got anything better to do.' It was mock-outrage, nothing more, and there was lightness in her voice. 'Have you actually thought about this?'

'Well ...'

'It wasn't the reason you called at all, was it?'

'I suppose not,' Thorne said.

'Anyway, I'm pretty much burned out when it comes to all that stuff.' Louise laughed. 'After two years trying to negotiate with you ...'

Rahim fetched a knife from the expensive set in the kitchen, chopped out two fat lines of cocaine with it, then sat and stared at them. He raised the knife and licked the few grains from the blade. Let the metal rest against his tongue.

He had always known Amin was brave of course, he'd seen that for himself, but when he heard what Amin had done to himself at Barndale, that had been his first thought.

Then: I could never be brave enough to do that.

Even if what Thorne had told him was to be believed, it didn't matter that Amin hadn't actually killed himself. It still applied. His best friend had been so much braver than he was.

Amin had taken far more risks than Rahim had ever done. It had not mattered what he might have seen in the eyes of some of the men at those parties, what some of them had asked him to do. Some part of him had enjoyed the danger. He had taken all the chances and laughed when Rahim had talked about playing it safe.

'That's what nice Indian boys like us are *meant* to do,' he had said.

Yeah, well, Rahim thought, the anger rising up in him suddenly. Which of us is still here? Which of us has all this? He looked around at his expensive furniture, listened to the jazz whispering from his expensive speakers. The things that caution had bought him.

The drugs. The knife in his hand.

Amin had been the one that night, after it had all happened, who had come up with the story about the party. Rahim had been hysterical, had wanted to tell the police everything, but Amin had told him that they would be all right, that they just needed to stick to their story.

To stick together.

Rahim had never visited him in Barndale, never written him a letter. At the funeral, he had sat in the corner with some of the other boys they had met at the 'parties' and laughed at half-remembered stories. He had eaten samosas and drunk Kingfisher like a big man and had not been able to look Nadira or Javed Akhtar in the eye.

One of these men might have killed Amin.

The music finished and, in the few seconds of silence before the next track, Thorne's words came back to him.

230

Rahim turned the knife over in his hand, the wooden handle slick against his palm. He placed the edge of the blade against his wrist and began to press.

He cried out and jerked the knife away the instant it broke the skin. He pushed his wrist against his mouth and sucked. Why had he thought, for even one second, that he would have the courage? He stared down at his wrist and watched the scarlet line rise up again through the skin and begin to run.

He reached across the table for a banknote and rolled it, then when he lowered his head towards the first line of cocaine, he watched a drop of blood splash down into the white powder. He angled his wrist so that more would follow.

Rahim remembered his friend slipping as he bent to pick up the knife that Lee Slater had dropped, and screaming as he lunged. He remembered sitting on the ground and watching it all happen, his own arse wet and cold, and safe.

He stared down at the table, remembered blood on the snow.

FORTY

No 'birds' whatsoever had proved to be even remotely 'up for it' by the time Allen and Bridges left their fourth pub of the evening. They had tried their luck gamely in each place and Bridges called the latest woman to reject their advances a 'fat lesbian' before the pair of them stumbled out on to the Lower Clapton Road. Allen said, 'She wasn't fat,' which reduced Bridges to fits of hysterics and they were both still laughing fifteen minutes later when they arrived at Allen's front door.

'Nice place, pal,' Bridges said, when they got inside. He walked across to the stereo and whistled. 'Where did you get all this gear, then? It's like one of them shops on Tottenham Court Road or something.'

'Came into some money, didn't I.'

'Where from?'

Pissed as he was, and tempted to show off, Allen knew better than to say any more. He shrugged.

Bridges did not seem bothered. 'We could have had a major party in here if your ugly mug hadn't put all the slags off.'

'I think that was you, mate.'

'Bollocks!'

They both started laughing again. Allen's dog came running in from another room and they both made a fuss of it for a while.

'Beers?'

'In the fridge.'

'Go on then,' Bridges said.

Allen collected four cans from the kitchen, and by the time he came back in, Bridges had selected a CD and turned the volume up good and loud. They opened cans and stood grinning at one another, heads nodding in time to the music and fingers moving against the tins as though they were the necks of Fender Strats.

'Slayer,' Bridges shouted above the squeal of a guitar. 'Fucking excellent.'

Allen nodded. 'Top band.' He moved to nudge the volume down. Said, 'Neighbours can get a bit arsey.'

'Leave it.' Bridges sat on the floor and leaned back against the sofa. The dog jumped up and lay down behind him. 'Fuck 'em.'

Allen turned the volume down just a little, then joined Bridges on the floor and they sat and smoked and drank a couple each. They talked about their time at Barndale and other places. The screws they had hated, the scraps and the war stories.

'Like a holiday camp,' Bridges said. 'Barndale. Compared to some, you know?'

'No holiday camp *I'm* ever going to visit,' Allen said.

'They all get easier after a while.'

'Not going back, mate.'

'Right.'

'Straight up,' Allen said. 'Got a bit of dosh now, going to get things sorted out.' He picked up the empty cans and carried them towards the kitchen.

'Don't be such an old woman,' Bridges said.

Allen turned in the doorway, the empties clutched to his chest. 'Spent too much time in a pigsty,' he said. 'My place stays nice and tidy from now on.' He walked into the kitchen, dumped the cans into the bin and pressed his forehead to the cool glass in the back door. He stared at the outline of the plastic chairs on the dark patio outside and hoped that Bridges was not planning on staying too much longer. Allen was one more beer from slaughtered now and struggling to think straight. He just wanted to crash out, to curl up with his dog and get some sleep.

When he came back into the living room, Bridges was taking his works out of a battered metal tobacco tin. A syringe and a needle, a crooked and blackened tablespoon, a wrap of paper.

'Get us some water, would you, pal?'

Allen turned and walked back towards the kitchen.

'Got any lemon juice?'

'Who d'you think I am, Jamie fucking Oliver?'

'Vinegar?'

'Yeah, somewhere.'

'That'll do.'

He came back with a glass of water and a Sarsons bottle, sat and watched Bridges tip the drug carefully out into the spoon and drizzle a few drops of vinegar on it. Bridges filled the syringe with water, added it to the spoon, then heated the mixture over a lighter. He broke off the filter from a cigarette, dropped it into the bubbling brown mess and drew the liquid up through it into the syringe. Then he fixed the needle, the movements small and sure. He told Allen to take off his belt and once Allen had handed it over, he tied it around his arm, tapped up a vein and injected himself. His head nodded a few times and when he finally looked up and across at Allen, he looked as though he'd just come in his pants.

'Beautiful,' he said.

'How you getting home?' Allen asked.

Bridges held up the syringe, shook what liquid was still left inside. 'Come on, we'll do half each,' he said. 'Seeing as I'm feeling generous.'

'I'm fine, mate,' Allen said. 'You do the lot.'

'You scared?' Bridges showed as many ratty-looking teeth as he had left. 'You never shot up before?'

'Course I have. Just too pissed to enjoy it, that's all.'

234

'Come on,' Bridges said. 'That big "fuck you" to Barndale, eh? Like a celebration kind of thing. We're going to get out of it, let's get *out* of it!' He took the belt from around his forearm, leaned across and began tying it around Allen's. 'Half each, yeah?'

Allen stared at the syringe. Looked like a lot more than half left in there, but what the hell. He had always wanted to, had come close a few times, and he certainly wasn't going to chicken out in front of a prick like Bridges.

He nodded.

'Take you to the moon, pal,' Bridges whispered. 'Won't even be able to *remember* Barndale ...'

Allen sucked in a fast breath as the needle went in and watched as Bridges drew back the plunger. The skinny scarlet thread that twisted and bloomed in the barrel.

'Sweet, isn't it?' Bridges looked at him and smiled. 'That's how you know you've hit a vein, not just going to skin-pop, which hurts like fuck and doesn't give you the same hit.'

'Like a lava lamp,' Allen said.

'In she goes ...'

Allen instantly felt like someone had driven a bus across his chest. He struggled to breathe and wanted desperately to be sick, but before he had the chance to do either he heard a loud bang. He was still wondering what the hell it was as the blackness fell across him.

Bridges winced as Allen's head crashed against the floor, then watched, fascinated, as the eyelids fluttered and the eyeballs rolled around like hard-boiled eggs. He waited until Allen's chest had stopped heaving, then pulled himself up. He fetched a cloth and a bottle of spray-cleaner from the kitchen, then moved around the flat, carefully wiping down any surfaces he might have touched.

The heavy metal was still thumping from the speakers and he turned the volume back up, moving his head and hand in time to it as he sprayed and polished.

'I'll clean your place up good and proper, you fucking old woman.'

He wiped down the stereo and the CD case. He went into the

kitchen, rooted in the bin and wiped down each of the empty beer cans. He wiped down the syringe that was still dangling from Allen's arm then, last of all, he applied a delicate squirt to his tobacco tin. He would miss that, it had seen him through some hard times, but if everything was going to look kosher he would need to leave it behind and he knew these things had to be done properly.

The song was almost finished by the time he'd put the cleaning things back where he had found them, so he waited. He wheeled his arm around on the final chord, jumped in the air on the last deafening crash of drums and almost lost his balance. He steadied himself against a chair, giggling. It was very decent gear indeed and he was pretty far gone himself. He looked down at Allen's body.

Way too good for pussies like that, anyway.

The dog was looking up at him from the sofa, tail going like a bastard and tongue lolling out. He thought he might get a puppy himself, thought about taking this one while he had the chance, then decided that would be a stupid move, all things considered.

He spent a few minutes rubbing the dog's belly and tickling it behind the ears, then left.

He is lying in bed watching the news when he gets the call.

It's one of his greatest pleasures, stretching out between clean sheets with a decent malt close at hand, greater even than the pleasure he gets from some of the bodies he shares his bed with now and again. That, however, is never more than a temporary arrangement, an hour or so to get what he needs, after which there is no company he craves but his own. He would certainly never dream of letting any of them stay the night. He has never so much as entertained such an idea. It's not just that he could not bear to wake up next to one of them, he could not even contemplate going to sleep with anyone that close. An arm draped across him, or a foot against his own, someone else's hot breath on the back of his neck.

Just the thought of it makes him shudder.

It's not that he isn't . . . tender. He prides himself on being a considerate lover, but he just prefers his own company when the sex is over and he always sends them home in a taxi with a little something extra in their pockets to spend on whatever drug lights their candle. They come looking for him, some of them, because they know they'll be given a good time, in and out of the bedroom.

He is pleased that he has earned that sort of reputation.

He is watching the rolling news on Sky, which is nothing short of a godsend when something like this happens. Of course, it gets tedious after a while, with the same news – or lack of it – being tarted up a dozen different ways within the same programme, but it is oddly hypnotic nonetheless.

It will help him sleep, if nothing else.

There is one reporter standing just a few feet from the police cordon at one end of the street, a uniformed officer grim-faced behind him, while another –

a young black woman, who is clearly the junior of the two – delivers her reports from outside the railway station, which is still closed of course. She occasionally talks to a disgruntled and barely literate commuter, but otherwise her screeching monologues have none of the drama commanded by her colleague. He has a face you can take seriously. He has coppers in shot as well as the occasional emergency vehicle, which always ramps up the excitement, such as it is.

He lies there and chuckles to himself.

There are, after all, only so many ways of saying that nothing whatsoever is happening.

He sips his malt and asks himself again what on earth the man inside the wretched little shop could possibly be doing this for. Yes, a few questions asked, but to what end? Is the man going to get his son back?

He takes another drink. Not going to happen.

Now the black woman is wittering on about 'tension in the community' and, as the phone rings, he decides that she could only have got the job because of some positive discrimination quota, and would be better off presenting children's programmes . . .

'Just watching the latest at Fags 'n' Mags,' he says.

'What?'

'The newsagent's. These Indian places usually have some stupid name like that. Same as when they call a barber's Hair Today, Gone Tomorrow! Bloody ridiculous.'

'What's happening?'

'Silly bastard's still waving his gun about at some poor policewoman. Nothing to get excited about.'

'Yes, well, on a related matter—'

'Oh stop talking like a ponce, will you?' He sits up in bed, mildly irritated. He mutes the sound on the television. 'I get enough of that at work every day.'

The man at the other end of the phone sniffs and says, 'Fine. I just called to let you know that things have been sorted out. I thought you might like to know.'

'Our Scottish friend earned his wages then?'

238

'Well, I've only got his word for it, but he knows better than to try it on.'

'And he was careful?'

'Made a point of telling me just how careful he was.'

'Good. As long as he's careful enough to keep his own head down now he's done what was asked of him.'

'He's got enough money to disappear, so there shouldn't be a problem.'

'I want this to be the end of it.'

'Don't you think I do?'

'Where are you?'

The other man's voice drops. 'I'm at home. Downstairs.'

'Get yourself off to bed, man, for God's sake. Have a quiet wank, or better still give your wife a good seeing-to. Sounds like you need to relax.'

'Shall we talk tomorrow?'

'Well, I'll be seeing you at the party, I presume?'

'You think that's a good idea?'

'Like you said, things have been sorted out. We should enjoy ourselves a little.' On the TV, the male reporter hands back to the studio. Behind the two suntanned anchors is a large picture of a smiling Javed Akhtar. 'With any luck our newsagent friend will have done us all a favour and put that gun in his mouth by then. We can crack open a bottle of something.'

239

DAY THREE

THIS MAN WHO
WAS THE LAW

FORTY-ONE

Thorne had woken several times in the night and, after a few minutes lying there in the dark, he had somehow managed to drift away again, but now his chest was tight and it felt as though his heart was pulsing hard and fast against the bone. He knew there was no chance of getting back to sleep now, because this time his phone was ringing.

'We've got a body you might be interested in,' Holland said.

'I'm *always* interested.'

'I stuck a flag-up on the PNC. Everyone we spoke to the last couple of days, just in case. The on-call DI in Hackney rang me ten minutes ago.'

Thorne tried to think. Who was in Hackney? He found himself smiling when it came to him. 'Peter Allen?'

'Dead as mutton.'

'That's a coincidence and a half.'

'Isn't it though?'

'I'll be about forty minutes,' Thorne said. 'Make sure the body stays where it is until I get there.'

While he dressed, the eight-thirty news bulletin on BBC London told him that traffic was building up on the A40 into town, that the

Olympics were now seven billion pounds over budget and that there had been no significant developments overnight at the armed siege in Tulse Hill. Thorne had thought it best to check. He guessed that he would not be the first person Donnelly called if there had been.

Studying his reflection as he brushed his teeth, he realised that he had not shaved for the last couple of days. He had not showered either, but had gone heavy on the Right Guard and hoped he would get away with it.

Hendricks would be the first to let him know if he hadn't.

He spat into the sink, then stared at himself again. He probably looked a little less worn out than he felt, but there wasn't much in it. His hair was a good deal greyer these days, more of it on one side than the other, same as always, and creeping in at much the same rate that the line of his jaw was subsumed into flesh and the circles darkened into black smiles beneath his eyes. Hendricks had already mentioned all those things of course, had gone as far as giving him a selection of male grooming products the previous Christmas. They each remained unopened in the bathroom cabinet. It wasn't that Thorne thought them in any way effeminate, rather that he was still unconvinced that any of them actually worked. It was a smart move on the part of cosmetics companies, he reckoned, to start ripping men off in the same way they had done for so long with women.

Men were every bit as vain after all, and probably a damn sight more gullible.

The toupée, Bruce? Trust me, it's absolutely invisible.

He leaned in close to the mirror, a ragged rumble in his throat as he breathed. He reached up to wipe away the smear of condensation. Wasn't this about the time that men his age were supposed to start looking distinguished? Maybe that was just architects and film directors, blokes that knew about wine and read books nobody had heard of. Most of the coppers he knew who were pushing fifty just looked . . . fucked.

Were fucked.

Thorne walked back into the bedroom and picked up his leather

244

jacket from the chair in the corner. He examined the dark stain on the front and wondered if buying a new one in exactly the same style and colour would count as a minor addition to his list of lifestyle changes. He shoved the tattered slab of Amin Akhtar paperwork into his brief-case, then carried it to the bathroom.

He tossed in the can of Right Guard and turned towards the front door.

Holland was waiting on the pavement and raised a hand in greeting as Thorne pulled up. The entrance to the block had been tented off and stood guarded by uniformed officers, statue-still behind the fluttering line of crime scene tape that ran around the edge of the front garden. Holland was already wearing a blue paper suit and, as soon as Thorne was out of the car, Holland handed him one of his own. Thorne tossed his jacket into the back seat of the BMW and clambered into the suit, a hand on Holland's shoulder for balance, turning his face away from the small crowd of onlookers who stood watching from the other side of the street.

Nodding towards the newcomer and muttering to one another. Phones raised to snap pictures.

Some, Thorne knew, were waiting eagerly for a body – or better still, bodies – to be brought out, while others were looking around for cam-eras and faces they recognised, wondering who the star of the film was. The majority were almost certainly standing there purely because that's what other people were doing.

It was probably the most popular that Peter David Allen had ever been.

'Who found the body?' Thorne asked.

Holland turned towards the block. 'There was music playing all night. He had the same album on repeat at full volume, so the neigh-bours called the council.'

'*He* being Allen?'

'Well ... possibly. Anyway, the council sent the noise pollution job-sworths round and eventually they called us. They ran the address through the PNC and when the flag came up, the local boys put the door in.'

'No sign of forced entry?'

'Apart from that one, no.'

'What was it?'

'What was what?'

'The album.'

'Slayer. *Hell Awaits*, if you want to get really specific.'

'Definitely a suspicious death then,' Thorne said. 'Nobody in their right mind leaves that on repeat.'

'You don't think he could have overdosed accidentally then?'

'Come on, you've seen his records.' Thorne bent down to pull on the paper bootees that he hated so much. 'No record of intravenous drug use. Not so much as an arrest for anything even drug-related. To be honest, even if he'd been a Premier League junkie, I'd still think it was iffy the day after you spoke to him.'

Holland nodded. 'Easy enough to give someone an overdose if they've got no tolerance.'

'Right.' Thorne stood up and they began walking towards the flat. On the other side of the road a few more mobile phones were raised to begin shooting stills and video. 'Having said all that, I mean ... Slayer?'

'That's a decent motive in itself,' Holland said.

'Could easily have been a mercy killing.'

There were more pictures being taken in the now crowded room where Allen's body had been discovered, though the cameras were a little more sophisticated and, with the exception of the jury at any resulting court case, the films and photos were not intended for public consumption. The police cameramen moved easily around the crime scene examiners, weaving between assorted groupings of forensic scientists and fingerprint officers, each team intimately acquainted with the working practices of the others as they calmly went about their tasks.

Bagging, tagging, scraping.

Thorne could never watch any of them work without being

reminded of how clumsy his own efforts seemed by comparison. These were the men and women who did the real detection, while he blundered around hoping to get lucky and banging his head into a succession of brick walls. At its best, there was a kind of . . . grace to what they did, though this was not to say that their manner was always delicate, or necessarily deferential to the corpse around which they crouched and crept.

'Think anyone would notice if that hi-fi went walkabout?'

'Well, I'll keep schtum if I can have the wide-screen.'

'Seriously though, you seen some of the DVDs he had?'

'Yeah, he was a bit of a torture buff, clearly.'

'Gang rape and chainsaws and all that.'

'Did you know that nine out of ten people enjoy gang rape?'

Allen was lying on his side in front of the sofa. His eyes were half closed and protruding. His lips were blue. The side of his face that lay against the floor was swollen and purplish and there was a light coating of froth around his mouth.

'The other morning,' Holland said, 'when I said this case sounded like something different.' He nodded down towards the body. 'I suppose I meant that there wouldn't be any of *this*.'

Thorne looked at Peter Allen's pale fingers, clawed against the tatty carpet, and remembered what had been said on the phone the night before.

Another box ticked.

It was not the first time he had thought about Louise that morning.

It had seemed somewhat incongruous, barrelling through the rush-hour traffic towards Hackney and listening to Gram Parsons and Emmylou Harris. Roaring along bus lanes with the blue light flashing on the roof and jumping lights with his hand pressed to the horn, while those voices – one frail, one pure – snaked so perfectly around one another. Emmylou had always maintained that she and Parsons had never been lovers, but Thorne still found it hard to believe. You could hear it in the way they sang to each other, for each other.

He listened, and asked himself why he had really called Louise.

Had some part of him hoped that she would tell him how unhappy and lonely she was, what a mistake they had made? How would he have felt if she had actually said any of those things?

He had wanted to talk to someone who *knew* him, he could admit that much, however uncomfortable it might turn out to be. He had wanted to hear her voice. Yes, and perhaps he had needed to pick at the scab just a little. To open it up. All those changes that had been decided upon in the wake of the split were exciting in theory . . . fresh challenges, change of outlook, all that, but wasn't it possible that you could change too much and move on too quickly?

He would be stupid if he wasn't scared.

No time to dwell on it now, thank God.

Another box . . .

Thorne had put his foot down and pushed on across the round-about at Old Street, losing himself in the gorgeous noise of Gram and Emmylou, and the tightness in his chest was gone by the time he saw Holland raising a hand to him outside the crime scene.

Hemmings, the on-call pathologist, was a humourless piece of work Thorne had run into a time or two before. As he walked across to join Thorne and Holland, the look on his doughy face made it clear that having already conducted his initial examination of the body, he was not best pleased at being asked to wait until Thorne arrived.

'He's been dead at least eight hours. No more than twelve.'

'No time for hello?'

'I was told you were in a hurry.'

Thorne thought he could probably spare the few seconds it would take to tell Hemmings where to go and what to do to himself when he got there. He decided against it. 'Definitely an overdose?'

'Well, clearly I can't say if there was any underlying condition that precipitated it, but on the face of it . . . probably. There are no track marks to suggest he'd done it before.'

'So, not self-inflicted?'

'Not for me to say, but presuming he was right-handed, it's a little odd that he injected himself in his right arm. Then again, you're the detective.' The way he said the word, and the smile before he turned away, made it clear the pathologist thought much the same about what the likes of Thorne did as Thorne himself.

Blundering, clumsy . . .

'Arsehole,' Holland muttered.

'That's *Dr* Arsehole to you,' Thorne said. 'They like you to remember that.' They walked across to where a fingerprint officer was working at the hi-fi, passing a magnetic wand across the surface, then applying powder with a fibreglass brush as delicately as if he were restoring an Old Master. 'Anything?'

'Plenty,' the officer said. 'But I'm guessing they all belong to the victim.'

'Why?'

'Because there are whole areas that have no prints at all, lots of things that have obviously been wiped clean. Even the empty beer cans in the bin.' He nodded across towards the body. 'And the syringe, and as far as I know not many people can jack up without touching that.' He smiled. 'I mean, I don't want to tell you your job . . . '

'I wish more people would,' Thorne said.

'Whoever did it wasn't as clever as he thought though.' The officer laid down his brush and took a step across to a plastic box containing evidence that had already been earmarked for further examination. He reached inside and held up a plastic bag containing a bottle of cleaning spray. 'He didn't think to wipe this down after he'd used it.'

'D'oh!' Holland said.

'It gets even better.' The crime scene forensic manager, who had clearly been listening in, walked across and removed a second bag with one of the beer cans inside. 'No prints,' she said, 'but I'll bet we can still get DNA from it.'

Thorne looked at the two technicians, each proudly holding up their evidence bags like children waiting to be praised. 'Which is going to be quicker?' he asked.

They looked at one another.

Thorne knew that under normal circumstances the prints would probably come back faster than the DNA, but he also knew that there were a good many variables and that turnaround times for both could be significantly improved if the job was deemed urgent enough. If the samples were hand-delivered to the Forensic Science Service labs at Lambeth and prioritised. A matter of hours as opposed to days.

The forensic manager shrugged. 'Probably not a lot in it.'

'What about ADAPT?' Holland asked. He reddened slightly as everyone turned their attention to him. 'Accelerated DNA Profiling Technology. They reckon they can get a profile in under an hour now.'

'Where did you get that from?' Thorne asked.

'You know those memos and Job newsletters that you throw away every day? Some of us actually read them.' Holland looked to the forensic manager. 'DNA in a box, right?'

She nodded, then turned to Thorne, a hand raised. 'Under an hour is a bit of an exaggeration and anyway it's not cut and dried. It's enough to make an arrest on, but the level of identification is not strictly evidential. So, even if I got permission to run it, nothing I come up with would be admissible in court.'

'I'll worry about that later,' Thorne said.

'I can't promise anything.'

'See what you can do.'

The fingerprint officer took half a step forward. 'I reckon I can get the prints turned around in a few hours,' he said. 'If it's really important.'

Thorne knew that normally the forensic manager would be responsible for looking after both print and DNA evidence. For getting the samples to the lab then transferring the information to the relevant offender databases at Scotland Yard to see if there was a match. On this occasion though, he guessed that keeping them separate and encouraging a degree of competition would get him a result the quickest.

'There's a bottle of decent Scotch in it, OK?' Thorne looked to the fingerprint officer, who nodded. He turned to the forensic manager.

'Make it a case of Merlot and you're on,' she said.

'You get back to me before he does, I'll cook you dinner and drink it with you.' Thorne looked back to the fingerprint officer. 'That offer doesn't apply to you, obviously.'

As he walked towards the front door, Thorne barked instructions at Holland who was a step or two behind. 'I want *everything* done on the hurry-up,' he said. 'House-to-house, the lot.'

'I'll sort it.'

'And talk to the coroner. I want this PM done straight away, so put the wind up him a bit. Tell him there's a police officer's life at stake.' He began to strip off the paper suit. 'And I want Hendricks to do it.'

Holland watched him. 'So what do you think? If Allen was responsible for putting Amin on to the hospital wing ...'

'He was,' Thorne said. 'Someone paid Allen to do it, and now they've paid someone else to make sure he never tells us who.' He leaned against the front door and bent to remove the bootees. 'Whoever killed Amin wanted him in that hospital, because that was the only place they could really make it look like suicide. Whoever did it knows the prison. Knows it's not very easy to walk into someone's cell in the middle of the night and string them up. They organised the whole thing, and now we've started sniffing around they're ordering a clean-up operation.'

'If we can find him, it sounds like whoever killed Allen is our best bet.'

'One of them,' Thorne said.

He kicked off the suit, took out his mobile and walked towards the BMW, dialling as he went.

The call went straight to an answering machine.

'Rahim, it's Tom Thorne. Listen, I know you're already frightened, but I thought you should know that whoever was responsible for Amin's death has just had somebody else killed. If that scares you even more, then good. I'm sorry, but I don't really have time to care. Now, is there something you want to tell me?'

251

FORTY-TWO

Paul had always tanned more easily than she did on holiday. Not that they'd taken too many holidays together, a couple of weeks in Greece and two more at a falling-down villa in Majorca. But when they had, he was always the jammy so-and-so who ended up nut-brown, while more often than not she would look as though they'd been away to Iceland or somewhere, with shoulders and thighs the colour of a smacked arse unless she lathered on a fresh layer of Factor 30 every half an hour.

Paul would wind her up and she would get increasingly annoyed.

'It's not fair,' she would say on the last day. 'You look like you live here and I look like I've just got off the sodding plane.'

He would say something about wrinkles or not getting skin cancer, but it didn't help. Then she would look at him lying on the bed and grinning at her, unshaven and shirtless and more tanned than a hard-arsed London copper had any right to be, and it was impossible to stay angry for very long.

'I feel like one of those desperate women who's come on holiday on her own and found some local fisherman to shag her ...'

Alfie had thankfully inherited the tanning gene, and now, as the three of them walked along the beach, Helen cast a sideways glance at father and son, the same long legs and skinny chests, bronzed and beautiful in multi-coloured shorts, and for once the sun felt good on her face.

The sea was that colour you only ever see in the brochures.

Someone was cooking on the beach just up ahead, fresh fish for her and steak for Alfie and Paul.

They were all laughing . . .

Helen opened her eyes.

Akhtar turned from the sink where he was rinsing out the mugs they had drunk tea from half an hour before. 'I did not mean to wake you.'

'I wasn't asleep,' Helen said.

Akhtar nodded and wiped his hands on a grubby-looking tea towel. 'Yes, of course.' He turned and picked up the box of tissues from the desk, stepped across and held it out towards her.

Helen had not realised she was crying. She reached out to take a couple of the tissues and nodded her thanks. Her fingers brushed his wrist and his face was no more than two feet from her own.

It had been a while since he had picked up the gun.

Backing away from her, he nodded around the storeroom. 'It is definitely a lot more pleasant to spend time in your mind than it is in here,' he said. 'I have been doing the same thing myself.'

'What do you think about?' She needed to ask before he did.

'Just remembering things, that's all. Growing up, you know?'

'What part of India are you from?'

He sat down at the desk. 'Actually, I grew up in Aden. South Yemen.'

'Oh, right.'

'My family moved there from Bombay in the twenties and we did not go back to India until after the British left Yemen in 1967. Things became difficult. There was some trouble over independence, you understand?'

Helen knew nothing whatsoever about it, but nodded anyway.

'My father died at around the same time, so the whole family moved back to Bombay. He had his own business, you know? Importing rice and sugar from Australia.' He nodded to himself, remembering. 'Dropped dead at forty-two.' He clicked his fingers. 'Just got up from the chair and fell on his face. So, we went home ... everyone in the family still thought of Bombay as home ... and two years later I came to the UK. When I was nineteen.'

'Why did you come?'

'To make money,' he said, as though it were obvious. 'With my father gone, the family was relying on me and I could not make enough in Bombay, simple as that. We sold some of the furniture in my mother's house to pay for the ticket and that was it.' He smiled again. 'I went to Finchley! Straight from Heathrow on the train, because that was what everybody told me. Go to Finchley, because there are plenty of Indians there and somebody will help you. It sounds funny, I know, but they were right. I found a guesthouse on the first day and I managed to get myself some small jobs, washing cars and cleaning in a restaurant and what have you. And I remember being shocked ... really shocked to see British people *working*, doing the same things I was. Because back at home, we were the ones that did all the work.

'It was not easy to find anything better, because back then, in the early seventies, it was not always easy for an Indian to be accepted. There was still a lot of ... tension. Rivers of blood and all that carry-on. But eventually I was lucky and I got a good job in a bank on the Euston Road. Eight pounds a week, that was. Eight pounds a week and I was still sending money home, because there were fifteen or sixteen people relying on me back in Bombay. My mother and everyone else over there waiting for the money to arrive every month.' He waved a hand. 'But it was fine, you know? That was the reason I had come, after all.' He paused for a few seconds. Shook his head. 'I was at that bank for eighteen years altogether, though I should say the wages did go up a little, and after a while the family started coming across in dribs and drabs. My mother, my sisters, my uncles. I got them settled over here and got a small loan for a flat. A very small loan for a very small flat!

'Then, I met Nadira.'

Helen saw his face change, a wash of pleasure. 'How did you meet?'

'It was through someone at the bank. Someone senior to me. She was from a very well-off family, very respectable, so of course her father wanted to make absolutely sure I was suitable. He came to see my flat and spoke to people at the bank. It was not arranged, but it was *approved.*

'Thank heavens ...

'I stayed on at the bank for another year or so, but a cousin of mine had a shop in Bristol and after I had been to stay with him, Nadira and I decided that we would try to do the same. It was eighty thousand pounds plus the stock to get the shop and we could not get a loan, so we remortgaged our house. It was a big risk, but we had to take it.' He pressed a hand to his chest. '*I* had to take it, if you want the truth. I wanted my own business, the same as my father. We already had my eldest son and daughter by then and Nadira was pregnant with Amin.' He swallowed, tried again. 'With Amin ... '

'It can't have been easy,' Helen said.

'Not easy, no.'

'With a young family.'

'Nadira would have to bring the children in of course and I remember very clearly that she was working in the shop until the very last day of her pregnancy. Sitting behind that counter, the size of a house! Nowadays, she helps out if I need to go to the cash-and-carry, but most of the time it's just me and to be honest, that suits me fine. I have plenty of time to read and listen to the radio, or just to think about things, you know? Perhaps too much time, lately.'

'Don't you ever take a holiday or anything? I mean, you never seem to be closed.'

Akhtar shook his head. 'I get up at a quarter to four and get here an hour after that. I sort out the newspapers, do the paper round then get back to open the shop ready for the morning rush. I stay open until half-past six Monday to Friday, five o'clock on Saturdays, two o'clock on Sundays. No holidays.'

'Bloody hell,' Helen said.

'I think I have worked hard.' Akhtar's face had changed again. He leaned forward in his chair, angry suddenly. 'I thought that would make me the sort of person that deserved to be taken seriously. That would be respected. I thought I was the kind of person, that we were the kind of family, the law should be protecting.'

'I'm sorry,' Helen said.

'*Now* they are taking me seriously though.' He picked up the gun and pointed it. 'This thing gets you plenty of bloody respect.' He stared at her for a few moments, then looked at his watch. Said, 'They should be calling again soon.'

Helen closed her eyes.

She leaned her head back against the radiator and tried to forget about the metal cuff eating the flesh from her wrist, the stiffness in her back and neck and the terrible cramp in her legs.

She tried to empty her mind.

To get back to that beach, and her two beautiful boys.

FORTY-THREE

Thorne had called on his way back from Hackney, and while they were waiting for him to arrive, Donnelly, Chivers and Pascoe gathered for a pre-contact briefing in the small room behind the school stage. Pascoe listened while Chivers continued to press for technical support, arguing that the operation was not moving forward, that the information they were getting back from the phone calls was limited. Donnelly nodded and grunted, casting the occasional glance in Pascoe's direction. He had not been in the best of moods since they had relieved the overnight team a couple of hours before.

'Everything OK?' Pascoe asked.

Chivers looked at her, annoyed, as though he had almost forgotten she was there at all. Pascoe ignored it. She had been trying to do the same with him.

'Just the usual carry-on,' Donnelly said.

Pascoe waited.

'My boss is getting it in the neck from the Commissioner, who's getting it in the neck from the Mayor's office because Transport for London are kicking off.'

'So now your boss is giving you grief.'

'People need to get around.' Chivers slurped at his coffee. 'They want their lives back.'

'So does Helen Weeks.'

'It's not your problem,' Donnelly said. He turned back to Chivers and asked him to carry on.

'We get a Technical Support Unit in, let them do their stuff and see how it pans out,' Chivers said. 'I don't see what we've got to lose. At least with all that in place, we'll be in a far better situation if anything does happen and we need to go in quickly.'

'We're all hoping that doesn't happen though, obviously.'

'I said "if".'

'What exactly are we talking about?' Pascoe asked.

'Microphones in the walls. Maybe some cameras in there if we're lucky and depending on the set-up.' Seeing that Pascoe was about to raise her usual objections, Chivers steamed on. 'Listen, Akhtar won't have a clue what we're doing, all right? No need to worry on that score. Some of the gear these guys have got is so sophisticated they could slip a microphone in your knickers and you wouldn't know it.'

'You reckon?'

Chivers smiled. 'They're like ninjas.'

Nobody spoke for a long few seconds. The only sounds were the squawk of a radio from the hall and the rustle as Chivers adjusted the weapons belt around his waist. Pascoe saw that he had now added an M26 Taser to his personal armoury.

'OK, we'll see how this next call goes,' Donnelly said. 'If there's no significant change we'll bring in a TSU.'

Chivers nodded, happy.

'Is this just because they want the bloody station reopened?' Pascoe asked.

'Don't be ridiculous,' Donnelly said.

Pascoe knew she had overstepped the mark and looked away. A tiny, suspicious part of her thinking: *is this because I knocked you back yesterday?*

Donnelly stood up. 'Like I said, we'll see what happens when

Thorne gets here and we put the one o'clock call in. That might change things.' He gathered his notes together. 'From what Thorne told me on the phone, it sounds like he's planning to rattle Akhtar's cage a bit.'

Chivers said, 'Good,' and Pascoe said nothing.

She wasn't sure she liked the sound of what Thorne was planning at all.

FORTY-FOUR

Hendricks called as Thorne was on his way into the hall.

'Queue-jumping again?'

'Sorry?'

'Peter Allen.'

'It's important, Phil, and I don't think too many of your customers are likely to complain.'

'*I* can complain though.'

'And just so you know, I still need help with the drug thing. Amin Akhtar's overdose, I mean. Soon as you can, mate.'

'I'm starting to see why Louise dumped you.'

'It was mutual,' Thorne said.

Hendricks laughed. 'What, as in the two of you talking things over and mutually deciding you were a complete and utter cock?'

'Something like that.' Thorne nodded across to Donnelly, who was waiting with the others at the monitors. 'Call me when you're done, will you?' He hung up before the abuse became rather less good-natured, and walked across to join them.

He took Pascoe's seat and put on the headset while she gave him the usual instructions. Again she urged him to keep his tone nice and even when talking to Akhtar, to listen and to reassure, but Thorne could sense her uncertainty.

He told her that he was ready.

'Do we really think this is a good idea?' she asked.

'It's the only one I've got,' Thorne said.

'There's no way of knowing how he's going to react to this and that worries me.' Pascoe looked to Donnelly. 'Excitement, rage, guilt. None of them are exactly ideal.'

'He wants answers,' Thorne said. 'That's why he's doing this. That's why we're all here and why Helen's in there. We're only going to get the right outcome if I start giving him some.'

'Some,' Chivers said, quietly.

'Look, I can't give him the one answer he really wants, not yet, but surely it's important that he knows I'm close.'

'Are you?' Donnelly asked.

Thorne said that he was, and he meant it, but he had also lost count of those times when touching distance was as close as he got. When a killer had remained that all-important step ahead and a case had finished up as nothing more than a folder full of paper and an uncomfortable memory. Donnelly nodded, but Thorne knew he understood the way it worked as well as he did. 'I want him to know I've shaken things up,' he said.

Donnelly told him to make the call.

As soon as Helen answered, the sound quality told those listening that her mobile had been put on speaker. Thorne asked her how she was and, though her voice was a little smaller, a little flatter than it had been the last time he'd heard it, she told him she was fine. Ticking along. She told him she was being well looked after, but that she didn't want to see another bar of chocolate for as long as she lived, that she was desperate for a hot bath and something a bit stronger than 7-Up to drink. Donnelly signalled to him and Thorne asked her how Stephen Mitchell was, but Akhtar cut in before Helen could answer.

'Do you have any news, Mr Thorne?' He sounded almost as tired as

Helen Weeks. 'Or are you just calling to tell me how busy you are? To remind me once again that these things take time.'

Thorne remembered everything Pascoe had told him a few minutes earlier, her worries about Akhtar's reaction. But there seemed little point in going round the houses, and besides Thorne wanted the news to sound every bit as important, as shocking, as it was.

'He's killed somebody else.'

'Who has?'

'The man who murdered your son.'

There was almost half a minute of silence. Thorne glanced at Pascoe, but she was looking at the floor. Behind them, the doors to the hall banged as someone came in. They started to apologise and were quickly shushed.

'Who is he?' Akhtar asked.

There was no easy way to say it. 'I don't know,' Thorne said. 'But he is scared because we're getting close to him. He's *scared*, Javed.'

Though Pascoe had been unsure as to how Akhtar would react, Thorne had expected something approaching pleasure at the news. But when Akhtar spoke again, there was little sign of it.

'Who was killed?'

'Another boy from Barndale,' Thorne said.

'A friend of Amin's?'

'No, not a friend. I think he was the boy that attacked Amin.'

'I don't understand.'

'Someone paid this boy to attack Amin, because they wanted to make sure he ended up in the hospital wing. That was where they planned to kill him, so they could make it look like suicide.'

'That's what I *said*, didn't I?' There was anger creeping into Akhtar's voice. 'I said that to the police over and over again and I told everybody at the bloody inquest. I kept saying that my son would never have taken his own life.'

'Yes, that's what you said.'

'And you see what happens? You *see*?'

'Yes.'

'Now another boy is dead because nobody would listen.'

'That boy is dead because the man responsible was worried he could identify him.'

There was another long pause.

'So, if this boy is dead, how *are* you going to identify him?'

'I'm waiting for more information,' Thorne said.

'Waiting.' There was a snort of derision. 'There's been far too much waiting.'

'I know that sounds a bit vague, but I'm hopeful.' Even as he said it, Thorne realised that he was often guilty of confusing 'hopeful' with 'desperate'. 'OK, Javed? We're nearly there.'

Akhtar did not reply. Thorne exchanged a long look with Donnelly while they listened to the hiss and crackle from the speakers, something muttered which was impossible to make out clearly, Helen coughing.

'Helen?'

'Yes, I'm here.'

'You heard all that?'

'Yes, I heard. I hope you get the information you need.'

'It's going to be over soon, OK?'

'Thank you.'

'So, what are you drinking?' Thorne asked. 'I'll have a bottle waiting.'

'Right now, I'd settle for paint-stripper,' Helen said.

Then Akhtar's voice. Louder, as though he'd suddenly moved closer to the phone. 'Don't start planning your celebrations just yet, Mr Thorne. You have to find this man first. Then you have to catch him.'

The line went dead.

Thorne removed the headset and looked at Pascoe. 'All right?'

'Let's hope so,' she said.

Chivers nodded towards the monitors. 'She's every bit as good as you said she was. Weeks.' He looked back to Thorne. 'I reckon she could really help us.'

'Help us how?' Thorne asked.

'With information,' Chivers said. 'Once the tech boys have done their stuff, if we can somehow let her know that we're listening in, she might be able to send us messages.' He looked to Donnelly. 'We can slip it into a call or whatever. "TSU's set up" or something. She'll know what that means and maybe she can find a way to let us know where Akhtar is when the time comes. What might be waiting for us on the other side of that door if we need to go in.'

Donnelly nodded. Said, 'Makes sense.'

Thorne turned to Pascoe.

She was looking at the floor again.

FORTY-FIVE

Though she could not know it, Helen had been every bit as surprised as Thorne that Javed had not reacted more positively to what he had been told. To hearing about Thorne's progress. He had quickly grown irritable on discovering that he had been proved right and that he might soon know the name of the man who had murdered his son. When the call was over, he had spent a few minutes stalking back and forth between the shop and the storeroom, muttering to himself angrily. He had waved his arms around and slapped himself on the side of the head. Then, he had suddenly fallen silent and become morose.

Inconsolable.

As though he had just remembered something terrible.

Helen had said, 'Good news,' and 'Sounds like you got what you wanted,' but he had ignored her. She had asked for water and he had snapped at her, saying that he was not her bloody servant. Then he had brought it to her without a word.

Over the last twenty-four hours, she had begun to feel as though she understood this man who was holding her. That she could adjust to his reactions, handle things. She had not felt the need to keep pushing for sympathy or pity, to remind him that she was the mother of a small child, and when they had talked, really talked to one another, as they had only an hour before, there were moments when Helen might almost have been able to forget where they were. Now, watching him slumped in the chair with his eyes closed and the blood pulsing at his temple, she realised that she needed to sharpen up and remember exactly who and what she was.

What they both were.

Hostage and hostage taker.

She was well aware that her own emotions had been all over the place too, but reminded herself that she was not threatening to kill anyone. Yes, Akhtar had been genuinely horrified at Mitchell's death, but Helen also remembered the sound of him smashing things up next door and she could not forget the hatred on his face when he had turned round in the shop two days before and pointed that gun at them. She recalled those moments of dark rage and the keening sobs from the next room, the tenderness then the paranoia.

Like lights going on and off.

And the fear that had begun to fold away its wings fluttered back to life in her gut, as Helen asked herself if those running the operation outside were getting as nervous as she was.

FORTY-SIX

I'm waiting for more information.

Thorne waited, and as the time passed and no other useful option presented itself, the waiting sucked the energy from him as efficiently as any physical exertion. Sapped him. He sat at the trestle table in the school hall and stared, unmoving, at the monitors, feeling heavier and more useless by the minute.

More desperate than hopeful.

Donnelly was sitting outside in the newly arrived Technical Support vehicle, poring over plans of the building; discussing the thicknesses of walls, the locations of gas and water pipes and electrical cabling. Chivers was in the playground, talking through a variety of scenarios with key members of his firearms team. Thorne did not know where Sue Pascoe had gone.

Once the Technical Support officers had been busy for a few hours there might be other pictures to look at, but for now Thorne could do little but stare at that single, fixed image of the front of Akhtar's shop.

He stared, and began to drift.

For a few dizzying moments, despite the urgency, the tension that was clearly still ticking in all those around him, Thorne found his mind starting to wander. Staring at the monitor, there was something soporific about the picture: the occasional flicker across the image; the blurred swirls of dark graffiti against the grey shutters.

PAKI still the only word he could make out.

Akhtar's words: *Amin could come to us with anything.*

In that vague and comforting way that the past got wrapped up and presented to oneself, Thorne had always considered his own relationship with his parents to be reasonably open and honest, but just a few seconds of serious reflection was all it took to tear that wrapping away and reveal the truth.

Unvarnished and ugly.

Thorne had not told his mother and father he wanted to join the police force, not until it was too late anyway, when he was no more than a few days away from traipsing off to Hendon. He had not told them that he did not want to go to university. That he had no wish to take whatever exams he would need to become a lawyer or an accountant, or any of those other professions he knew would make Jim and Maureen Thorne so proud.

He had not told them that he was too afraid to fail.

He might not have dreaded their disappointment quite as much had he been telling them he was away to join the army. His father's older brother had been a soldier, he seemed to remember, or in the air force maybe. Yes, that would definitely have gone down better. There would have been tears from his mother almost certainly, but perhaps a grudging wink from the old man later on.

Or would it have been the other way round?

The police, though?

There was no *Dixon of Dock Green* dignity about the job back then, as there might have been in the fifties or sixties. None of the *Sweeney* swagger. Thorne chose to join up just as the chickens started coming home to roost. Too many coppers on the take and rape victims treated like sluts.

Not a good time for that particular career move.

Thorne had stuck to his guns though, safe in the knowledge there was nothing they could do to stop him. He'd shouted back, his eighteen-year-old sulking skills more than a match for theirs, and bitten back the terror that first night as a cadet. Lying awake in the jockstrap-stinking dormitories that by some bizarre quirk of fate now housed his own office.

He had never really talked to them about the job either, had taken good care to avoid it. The gossip and the funny stuff, but nothing that had actually mattered.

Not Calvert.

Three dead girls, smothered in their beds by their own father. Matching ivory nightdresses splayed like angels' wings and six tiny white feet.

Was that really the reason he and Jan had never had kids? Why he had felt so ambivalent about having a child with Louise? Some counsellor or other had said as much a few years before and Thorne had told her where to stick her Christmas-cracker theories. He had not quite been able to forget that knowing smile though, just before she'd looked back down at her notes.

His notes.

He was vaguely aware of footsteps approaching behind him. Heels . . .

Jan had a kid with somebody else now and Louise would probably end up doing the same, as soon as she found someone a little quicker than Thorne had been to admit he quite fancied the idea.

Lives moved on.

'Tom . . .'

Thorne turned, just as Sue Pascoe arrived with two cups of coffee. He could smell the cigarettes as he leaned forward and gratefully took the plastic cup she was proffering.

'I need to wake up,' he said.

They sat and drank their coffees in silence for a minute, then turned at the sound of Chivers' voice from the other end of the hall. He was talking to a pair of uniformed officers. There was laughter, some back-slapping.

'He wants the same thing as we do, you know,' Thorne said.

Pascoe looked at him. 'Let's hope so.'

'Just a different way of going about things.'

She blew on her coffee, her eyes still on Chivers.

'I'm sure he's good at what he does.'

'He is,' she said. 'I asked around.'

'There you go then.'

She shook her head. 'You're good at what you do, too.'

'Did you ask around?'

'I didn't have to.'

Thorne nodded, tried not to smile too much.

'But you still fuck up,' she said, looking at him.

'Sorry?'

'Same as everyone else does. Right?'

Calvert had been the big one, no question. There's always one that shapes you, that's what his boss had said at the time. You don't get a lot of say in the matter. Lucky or unlucky, result or disaster, all that. Why couldn't it have been talking someone down off a bridge though? Or saving a playground full of kids from some headcase with a samurai sword?

Someone to catch and someone to save. Right up your street.

Louise knew him well enough. Knew which of them he would pick if he could only choose one.

'Right?' Pascoe asked again.

Thorne looked at her. Unable, unwilling, to speak.

'Only problem is,' she said, nodding towards the other end of the hall, 'if he fucks up, so do I. So have I.' She turned back to Thorne. 'Chivers could shoot a hostage in the face, but in the end it would still be down to me. The hostage is mine to lose, do you see?'

Thorne sipped his coffee.

He could certainly see the intensity in Pascoe's eyes, but he was not sure if her concern was based on anything other than professional pride. Was she thinking only about doing her job properly, about her record as a negotiator? Or had she genuinely come to care about the

270

well-being of Stephen Mitchell and Helen Weeks? Of Javed Akhtar? Thorne supposed that it didn't much matter, that it might be all those things, but still he did not know what to say to her.

When his mobile rang on the table, he grabbed at it.

'DI Thorne?'

'Speaking.'

'It's Wendy Markham.'

Thorne waited, unable to place the name.

'I was running the DNA sample. The beer can in Hackney?'

'God, sorry. Thanks for getting back to me.' Thorne could feel a tingle of excitement. He sat up straight in his chair. He glanced across at Pascoe who raised her eyebrows.

'Am I first?'

'Yes,' Thorne said. 'You're first.'

'Good, because we've got you a nice cold hit. Jonathan Bridges, aged eighteen, record a mile long. He just served six months for robbing a junkie at knifepoint.'

'Bridges?' Thorne had seen the name written down somewhere. He struggled to remember. 'Served six months where?'

There was a pause as Markham consulted her notes. 'Barndale YOI.'

Even as Thorne had asked the question, it had come to him. The boy's name on a list along with ten others. The patients on the hospital wing the night Amin Akhtar had died, the boys that Dawes had questioned eight weeks ago. He swallowed hard, remembering what Hendricks had said a couple of nights before, his suggestion that one of the other patients had been responsible for Amin's death.

He was half right . . .

Thorne signalled to Pascoe, who quickly passed him a pen and a scrap of paper. He scribbled down the name.

'Will that do you?' Markham asked.

'That's fantastic, thanks.'

'So, what about this wine then? Dinner . . .'

'Absolutely,' Thorne said. 'But I'll need to get back to you. Merlot, right?'

'Yes—'

'I'll call you.' Thorne hung up and immediately began dialling.

'Merlot?' Pascoe said.

Thorne shook his head. Long story. When Holland answered, Thorne gave him the name of their prime suspect and told him to check with the Probation Service, the DSS, whoever the hell would be quickest with the most recent address for Jonathan Bridges. He told Holland to call straight back with any information, to ask Brigstocke to organise a support team on the hurry-up, and said that wherever Bridges turned out to be living, he would meet him there.

'Got what you needed?' Pascoe asked, when Thorne had hung up.

Thorne said, 'Both of us, I reckon,' and the two of them sat staring at the phone, willing it to ring.

FORTY-SEVEN

'I'm sorry about before,' Akhtar said. 'When I got so worked up. I could see that it was upsetting you.'

'It's fine, I understand,' Helen said.

'No, it's not fine.' He was still sitting at the desk, but the tension had gone from his face. He moved his chair a little closer to her. 'I seem to have lost control over the way I respond to things. Does that make any sense?'

Helen told him that it did.

'I always used to think carefully about things first, you know? Whatever happened, good news or bad news, it would take a while to sink in and feel real, but these days everything is speeded up. Everything is more intense, much brighter, much darker. I'm absurdly happy or far more miserable. Very much angrier ...'

'Your son went to prison,' Helen said. 'Then he died, was killed, so you're not going to feel normal about anything.'

'I suppose that's right.'

'Of course you're not.' She was still wary, aware that the mood Akhtar was in at that moment might not be the same one he would be in five minutes from now, but she needed to do everything possible to

273

keep him where he was. To maintain the calm. '*This* is hardly ... normal, is it?'

Akhtar shook his head, ran a hand slowly across the top of it.

'One man is already dead, Javed.'

He nodded, solemn. 'If I was reading about something like this in one of my papers,' Akhtar said, 'I would despise the person doing it. I would talk about what was happening with Nadira and in the shop with my customers, and we would all shake our heads and tut-tut and say how disgusting it was, asking ourselves what the world was coming to and so on. I would be thinking about the people being held against their will, nothing else, thinking about their families. I swear to God, I would not give a damn if the man who was doing such things lost his life. I would be happy for the police to do whatever was necessary.'

Helen pointed to Akhtar, then to herself. 'This ... is not you,' she said.

He asked her if she would like to watch the television for a while, but she said no. Much as she would have appreciated the chance to get lost for a while in something nice and mindless, she thought it was important to keep talking. At least until she was sure things were back on an even keel.

As even as it was ever likely to get, at least.

'You know, even on that first night when Amin came home, I did not get upset straight away,' Akhtar said. 'Nadira went to pieces as you would expect, the sight of all that blood, but I kept it all inside for a while, same as always. Even when I knew what had happened, when I discovered that this other boy was dead, I just *thought* about it. I was trying to *understand*, trying to work out what needed to be done and it was like all the emotions I should have been feeling were just laid to one side for later on.'

'People do that,' Helen said.

'When he was killed, I did not even cry like a father *should* cry for his son.' He shook his head. His voice had dropped. 'Can you believe that? I felt ashamed that I was not like my wife, like the rest of the family. Nadira wept enough for all of us of course, rivers of tears, but

274

still . . . I felt as though I was letting Amin down or something. Like I did not love him as much as I thought.'

'Someone has to be strong.'

'I did not feel strong, Miss Weeks,' he said. 'I just felt . . . inhuman.' He glanced at the gun and sighed, he looked exhausted suddenly. 'What's happening now, all these feelings like bolts of lightning, this blackness . . . I think maybe I am paying the price for what I was like back then. You are paying the price too, and Mr Mitchell.'

He stood up and walked to the toilet, and for a few minutes Helen was forced to listen to him voiding his bowels, shitting like it was water. When he emerged, Helen bit back her disgust and told him that she needed to go too. He took the key to the handcuffs from the table-top and stepped towards her.

'What about you?' he asked. 'When Paul was killed.'

Helen wished she had said yes to the television. 'I was like you,' she said, eventually. 'I didn't cry straight away. I wanted to, I felt like I should be crying, but it just . . . didn't happen. I made myself busy. I ran around like an idiot. I was trying to find out why Paul had died.'

'Yes, you said. This was when you met Mr Thorne.'

She nodded. 'And I had the baby to worry about. I had Alfie kicking the hell out of me, and I'd spent weeks crying for no good reason anyway because my hormones were all over the place.'

'You did cry though, eventually?'

'Eventually.'

'What did it feel like?'

'What?'

'Did it feel good, I mean?'

Helen thought about it, tried to remember. 'Like finally eating something when you've been starving. But it tastes foul. Sour.'

'Because I still haven't cried for Amin,' Akhtar said. 'Not for the right reasons, anyway. Not because I've lost a son.' He leaned towards her and offered the key. 'There will be plenty of time for that though. In prison, if that is the way this ends.'

Helen said, 'Yes,' and took the key, the 'if' ringing in her head.

'Everything is finished one way or another,' Akhtar said. 'After what I did to Mr Mitchell.'

'I'll tell them what happened.'

He shrugged as though it did not matter. As though he had already resigned himself to life in prison, or worse. 'I will cry for Amin before this ends,' he said. 'I'll cry for him when I know *why*.'

FORTY-EIGHT

'I'm just saying these things because someone needs to,' Holland told him. 'That's all.'

'Point taken,' Thorne said.

'We go in there half-arsed and it goes pear-shaped, Bridges' defence team will have a field day.'

Thorne drummed his fingers against the steering wheel. 'Not as much of a field day as the prosecution's going to have.' He continued to stare out of the car window, towards the row of houses opposite, the green front door of the run-down Edwardian conversion, the bay window of the ground-floor flat. 'All the forensics we've got . . .'

The SOCO who had been running the fingerprints from the Peter Allen crime scene had called Thorne on his way to Hounslow; the address Jonathan Bridges had provided to the DSS when he had last signed on. The officer had been disappointed at coming second to his female colleague, at missing out on the promised bottle of whisky, but Thorne had taken pains to let him know just how grateful he was for the information. If the ADAPT DNA match was unlikely to stand up in court, the fingerprint evidence certainly would.

These, though, were things Thorne would worry about later on.

Right now, he was more concerned with getting the information that might see Helen Weeks and Stephen Mitchell released than he was with putting anyone away for Peter Allen's murder.

'Never mind half-arsed,' Kitson said from the back seat. 'What if he's armed?'

Thorne glanced at his rear-view mirror. Kitson was sitting next to DS Sam Karim. 'Nothing in his record about firearms,' he said. He thought about the offence of which Bridges had most recently been convicted. 'Everyone's wearing stab-vests, right?'

'It would be nice to know what was waiting for us, that's all.'

'If he's even in there,' Thorne said. He was almost certain that their prime suspect would not be inside, but he understood Yvonne Kitson's concerns. She was speaking not just for herself, Holland and Karim, but for the support officers drafted in at short notice. The four other detectives sitting behind them in an unmarked Ford Galaxy and the two more at the back of the house had no knowledge of the connection between Jonathan Bridges and the armed siege in Tulse Hill; no understanding of the urgency or the disregard for standard procedure.

'Be nice to know that too,' Kitson said.

'What do you want me to do, Yvonne?'

'*Think*. Just think.'

Normally, there would have been a careful assessment of the premises front and back. Intelligence would be fed through to the officers on the ground via the kind of technical support that was being employed at Tulse Hill at that very moment. There would have been an open line of communication with senior officers back at headquarters, an adequate briefing and a cordon that amounted to rather more than a panda car parked at either end of the street.

There would not have been a strategy formulated on the hoof.

But Thorne could not afford to waste minutes, let alone hours. 'I think I'll just pop across and ring the bell,' he said.

Holland shifted in the passenger seat. 'Gives him time to get rid of anything he might not want us to find.'

'Nobody's coming up with any better suggestions.'

'If he is in there, he's probably off his face anyway,' Kitson said.

Thorne reached for the radio that was sitting on the dash then opened the door. 'With a bit of luck, I might not need you lot at all,' he said.

He zipped up his leather jacket as he crossed the road. Anyone watching from that bay window would have a clear view and Thorne wanted to hide the Met Police logo on his stab-vest. He walked slowly, aware that there might be eyes on him other than those of his fellow officers, conscious of the fact that he did not look a lot like the average delivery man and bugger all like a Jehovah's Witness.

A strip of paper beneath the top bell said *Dawson*. There was no name beneath the bottom one. Thorne rang it.

Waited.

If he had thought there might be anyone besides Bridges inside the property, Thorne would have made an effort to acquire the phone number. It was common practice to call the suspect inside and suggest that they come out of their own volition to avoid the possibility of other family members getting hurt. There was nothing to suggest that Bridges had so much as a girlfriend.

Thorne did not care a great deal about Bridges getting hurt.

He gave it another few seconds then took out his radio. 'Not a sound, Yvonne,' he said.

'Like I said, he might be out of it.'

'Makes our job even easier then, doesn't it.'

'I'm still not thrilled about this, Tom.'

'It's on my head,' Thorne said. 'Put the door in . . .'

A few seconds later, the doors of the BMW and the Galaxy opened simultaneously and half a dozen officers began running across the road. Two others moved quickly to the boot of the Galaxy then followed their colleagues carrying a metal battering ram.

A little less polite than Jehovah's Witnesses.

Thorne stepped to one side as they crashed first through the outer door and then through the door to the downstairs flat. Thorne was only a few steps behind them, but it was not a large flat and by the time he had heard the first officer shout, 'Room clear,' it had become obvious that the man he was looking for was not at home. He started to take off his vest.

'Bedroom clear,' Holland shouted.

It would have been nice of course, but Thorne had known that Bridges was unlikely to be sitting there waiting for them. He had made a decent attempt to clean up after killing Peter Allen, and whoever had employed him to do it would almost certainly want to do the same thing themselves. They would want Bridges well out of the way.

It had already crossed Thorne's mind that this might mean permanently. Sitting outside in the car, he had been forced to consider the possibility that there might be nothing but another body waiting for them. Another brick wall.

Back to waiting . . .

As he stood in the middle of the living room, he saw that someone had been living at the property until very recently. There were several empty pizza boxes by the side of the sofa, a TV listings magazine from the previous week, a pub-sized ashtray overflowing with butts. As the team filed one by one into the room, including those who had been ready at the back of the house, Thorne stared at the beer cans lined up on the mantelpiece, the labels all facing the same way. He remembered the neatness, the obsessive order of Antoine Daniels' cell at Barndale.

'What now?' Holland asked.

'Turn the place over,' Thorne said. 'We're looking for bank statements, bills, mobile phone records, anything.'

Holland didn't move. 'We need a warrant, sir.'

'Again, Dave, point taken.'

'Get a bloody grip, Tom,' Kitson said. 'He's right, you know that. Without a warrant, anything we find is almost certain to get thrown out and all you'll be left with is the shit you're going to be up to your neck in. Is it really worth it?'

Thorne swore and kicked out at one of the discarded pizza boxes.

He had requested the warrant as soon as he'd been given the address for Bridges, and though he did not need one to enter the premises, he was not permitted to search for evidence until it arrived having been signed by a magistrate. He watched as a couple of the detectives dropped happily on to the sofa. There would be time for a smoke now, time to read the paper. They might even be able to nip out for a bit of lunch.

'We're thinking about *you*,' Kitson said.

Thorne looked at his watch. 'It's nearly three o'clock,' he said. 'We should have this warrant here any time, I reckon, half past at the latest, all right?' He told Samir Karim to chase it up, then when Karim had stepped out, he said, 'But aside from the people in this room, who's to say what time we actually started searching? We do it now, but anybody asks, we waited until we had the warrant. Fair enough?'

Thorne studied the faces of the officers in the room. There were a few sideways glances, some awkward shifting from foot to foot. Holland kept his head down.

'Listen, you all know about this business in Tulse Hill,' Thorne said. 'You know that one of the hostages is a police officer.' There were nods. 'Well, what we're doing here might help to get her out, OK? I'm just asking you to trust me on that and do what I'm asking, because I'll carry the can, and the fact is we really haven't got time to sit on our arses waiting for a poxy warrant.' He paused. '*She* hasn't got time.' He looked around again. 'Anyone unhappy with that?'

If anyone was, they kept it to themselves.

'Right, let's crack on.'

Thorne and Kitson took the bedroom, and as Thorne dug through drawers and reached carefully into the back of the flimsy wardrobe, he thought about what he had said to Holland. He felt bad for snapping at him.

We're thinking about you.

He looked over his shoulder at Kitson, who was searching through the small cupboard beside the bed.

She shook her head. Nothing.

Thorne knew he was further out on a limb than he had been in a long time, but he could only hope, if his actions succeeded in getting Helen Weeks released, that the powers-that-be might overlook them. He was probably kidding himself, he knew that, with more than enough black marks against him already. The DPS had a file an inch thick with his name on, and the Rubberheelers wouldn't need much of an excuse to come for him.

But what choice did he have?

More choice than Helen Weeks, that was for sure.

From the wardrobe, he pulled out a stash of magazines. *Sexy Matures*, *Fit & Fifty*. Underneath, a few tattered leaflets for the Scottish Defence League, a far right rent-a-mob who protested against the spread of Islamism at every opportunity and always seemed up for a good scrap. Thorne glanced at the misspelled ranting and wondered if money had been the only motive for the part Bridges had played in Amin Akhtar's killing. It was something to bear in mind. It was not as if Amin had been one of Imam Shakir's brigade, or even been particularly religious as far as Thorne could tell, but to the likes of Johnno Bridges and his SDL mates, such minor details had probably not been important.

Paki meant towelhead meant terrorist.

Pornography – political and otherwise – aside, there was little else to get excited about. There was certainly nothing that could be described as 'evidence' and the search of the property could only be deemed successful if they had been looking for dirty underwear and used needles. Thorne asked a couple of the support officers if they would mind hanging back to take delivery of the warrant when it arrived. He let the rest go.

'Doesn't look like Johnno was one for keeping much in the way of records,' Kitson said.

Thorne led Kitson and Holland into the kitchen. It smelled of something that had burned recently and there was an inch of dirty grease in the bottom of a chip-pan. Thorne leaned back against the oven.

'What do I do now?' he asked.

'We put a watch on all the stations,' Kitson said. 'An all-ports alert.'

Thorne knew it made sense, but guessed that they were probably twelve hours too late. Bridges would almost certainly be back in Scotland by now, or France or Finland or fuck-knows-where.

Holland nodded. 'And if we can't get him, we get the information from somewhere else. Mobile phone provider, bank if he had one.'

'Little shitehawk like Bridges,' Kitson said. 'He comes into a decent amount of money, he's got to start spending it somewhere. Right?'

Thorne thanked them for their help. He told them to get back to the office and start chasing, but it was hard to summon much enthusiasm. He knew very well that nothing they had suggested would give him what he needed quickly enough, and as he followed Holland and Kitson out of the flat, Thorne could feel the excitement that had seized him only an hour before leaking from his body with every step.

The rush dissipating.

His mobile sang in his pocket and he answered it as he reached the pavement.

'I can't quite see what was so bloody important,' Hendricks said. 'Peter Allen was a textbook diamorphine overdose, end of story. Someone who'd never used, that amount of heroin could have killed him twice over. He was probably dead a minute or so after he was shot up.'

'So definitely not self-inflicted, then?'

'No chance, mate. No signs of previous intravenous drug use, plus the needle went into his right arm and he was almost certainly right-handed, so unless he was some kind of circus freak—'

'How can you tell that?' Thorne asked.

'The hair.'

'Come again?'

'Ninety-five per cent of right-handers have hair that grows clockwise from the crown. Another riveting seminar, that was.'

Thorne watched as Holland and Kitson walked towards the squad car at the end of the street. They were deep in conversation and he could guess what it was about. Who it was about.

'Doesn't mean it wasn't an accident though,' Hendricks said. 'Somebody does it for the first time, they often get someone else to do it for them. If his mate was already out of it, he could easily have got the dosage wrong.'

Thorne knew this was true, but explained that a mate who had accidentally given Allen an overdose was unlikely to have wiped everything down afterwards.

'So none of this is news then, right? You knew it was murder before they took the body away.'

'I needed it confirmed officially, so I could go after the man responsible.'

Hendricks laughed. 'You're *so* full of it.'

'Yeah, well, time's not exactly on my side on this one.'

'How's it going?'

'I think this is the kid that gave Amin the overdose.'

There was a pause. 'I said that, didn't I? I said it was one of the other prisoners.'

'He was just a willing pair of hands,' Thorne said. 'Someone set it all up, showed him what to do.'

'I take it you've not caught him yet then?'

'He's done a runner,' Thorne said. 'We're staying on it, but I'm not holding my breath, so now I really need to know how Amin was given that overdose. No pressure or anything.'

'Yeah, yeah, I still need to check a couple of things—'

'I'm getting desperate here, Phil.' Thorne watched as a panda car turned fast into the street, swerved past the squad car just as Holland and Kitson were about to reach it. He saw them turn to watch as the panda came to a halt a few feet shy of where he was standing. An Asian WPC got out and began walking towards him.

He told Hendricks that he would call him later and hung up.

'I'm looking for DI Thorne?'

'Me,' Thorne said.

The WPC nodded back towards the panda car. 'Someone who wants to talk to you,' she said. 'He rang 999, and when he gave them your name they patched it through to a temporary incident room in Tulse Hill. You know, this siege?'

Thorne nodded.

'It's taken us a while to track you down.'

Thorne walked up to the car and peered in through the back window. He opened the door, felt the excitement flood back into him as Rahim Jaffer climbed nervously out.

FORTY-NINE

Sue Pascoe was feeling less in control of the situation with every hour that passed. Mid-afternoon on the third day, she would normally have had some sense of how events were likely to pan out. At the very least she would have felt a little more ... *connected*, as though her own role in proceedings was part of an agreed and well-orchestrated strategy.

Normally ...

Who was she kidding?

She sat in the small room behind the stage with coffee and sandwiches and reminded herself that she could slide back in behind a nice tidy desk any time she wanted 'normal'. That it was its unpredictability that had attracted her to hostage negotiation in the first place. The training was vital, of course it was, but once you got out of the classroom, when it came down to the business end of things with guns pointed at heads, the job was all about reacting. Circumstances changed whenever moods did, so it was important to be flexible and to think on your feet.

That's what kept people alive and got her own heart beating that little bit faster.

She looked across at Chivers on the other side of the table. He crammed half a sandwich into his mouth then washed it down noisily with a slurp of black coffee. He reached for another one and took a bite without looking at it. The process seemed to be about nothing but taking on fuel.

Keeping his strength up. Staying ready for it.

'Obviously we're all hoping it doesn't come to that,' Chivers kept saying. 'If and when' and 'worst case scenario', but Pascoe was becoming increasingly convinced that the CO19 man would go home disappointed if he did not get a chance to draw his weapon.

One of his weapons.

Still chewing, Chivers glanced up and nodded. Pascoe quickly looked down at her coffee, watched the creamy globs of powdered milk floating on the surface.

She thought about Tom Thorne.

Usually, the lack of operational predictability stemmed from whatever was happening on the inside. The delicate relationship between hostage and hostage taker, a flash of temper, a sudden tumble into depression. A host of dreadful possibilities and acceptable outcomes. This time though, what was happening on the outside felt every bit as uncertain, as impossible to second-guess, as what was going on behind those scarred metal shutters. There was simply no way to exercise any degree of control or to impose order, when so much seemed to depend on a single copper charging around like a nutcase and hoping to get lucky.

It was rapidly becoming clear that however things turned out, it would have as much to do with Tom Thorne as it did with Javed Akhtar.

Either capable of ending it.

Each with as great a potential for chaos as the other.

'Nice job,' Chivers said, suddenly.

Pascoe looked up. Chivers was wiping his mouth with a paper serviette. 'Sorry?'

'Just wanted to say. Nice job you're doing with Akhtar. And with Weeks.'

287

Pascoe nodded. Bloody hell, was this another one who thought she needed bolstering up somehow? Did he actually think she might like him a bit more if he chucked a pointless compliment or two her way? Or was he trying it on, same as Donnelly had done? Even as she contemplated this last horrific possibility, she knew she was being ridiculous, that Chivers was probably the sort who lived alone and would go home to a cold shower having happily rubbed himself against pictures of some really shiny guns in *Massive Weapons* monthly. She watched him toss the crumpled serviette back on to the table and hesitated. Saying nothing might come across as unnecessarily antagonistic and 'Thanks' would sound a little too grateful.

She said, 'Cheers,' and turned as Donnelly came into the room.

'So, where are we?' Chivers asked.

'Getting there,' Donnelly said.

The Silver Commander had spent the last half-hour in the back of the mobile TSU suite parked up next to Teapot One, being briefed by officers and civilian technicians on their progress thus far. He now explained how an initial survey had made it clear the hostages were being held at the rear of the newsagent's, in a small room used primarily for storage. Access had been gained to the premises next door – a dry cleaner's with largely the same layout – from where they were now proposing to establish audio monitoring of the storeroom via the adjoining wall.

'One microphone in there,' Donnelly said. 'And maybe a second in the rear wall next to the back door.'

'Cameras would be even better,' Chivers said.

'I'm being advised that's not too clever.' Donnelly told them that the cameras involved a more complex install. That even accounting for micro-tools and fibre-optic cabling, the drilling still needed to be deeper and was that much more likely to be seen or heard from inside. 'They reckon we could probably get one into the main shop from the front, but what's the point of that? Just going to be looking at a smashed-up shop, right? I've told them to go ahead with these two microphones.'

'How long?' Pascoe asked.

'A couple of hours if we go as carefully as we should.' Donnelly looked at Pascoe. 'Any reason to think we need to get it done quicker than that? Any concerns for the hostages? For Akhtar's state of mind?'

Chivers sniffed. 'Other than the obvious ones, you mean?'

'DS Pascoe?'

Pascoe said she had no immediate concerns.

'In the meantime we keep putting the calls in as per normal,' Donnelly said. 'Maintain the routine.' He looked at his watch. 'Two o'clock?'

Pascoe nodded. Thirty minutes away. 'Any word from Thorne?'

'Nothing,' Donnelly said.

'He was certainly fired up earlier on. Someone in the frame for that overdose in Hackney.'

'I told him to call if he had anything worth sharing, so—'

'We better not be counting on Thorne,' Chivers said. 'I think we might all end up looking very stupid.'

Pascoe opened her mouth, but only long enough to push another sandwich into it.

FIFTY

Thorne led Rahim away towards the main road and around the corner to a Turkish café he had driven past an hour or so before on his way to Bridges' flat. The boy said nothing as they walked and Thorne was happy enough to let him. Happy enough to wait just a little longer. Thinking was what had finally driven Rahim Jaffer to pick up the phone and a few more minutes of it could not hurt.

Could only wind things up that little bit tighter.

Nothing spoken then and both kept their eyes on the pavement a few feet ahead, but all the way there Thorne was aware of Rahim breathing heavily next to him. A faint wheeze when he inhaled. As though he had just been running and urgently needed to suck in some strength.

The place was busy, noisy with chat and clatter from the kitchen, and Thorne ushered Rahim to a small table in the corner. A waiter followed them over. Rahim said that he was not hungry, but Thorne ordered for them both anyway; tuna mayonaise sandwiches and two cans of Coke. He looked across at Rahim who nodded, mumbled, 'Thanks.'

'You've got to eat,' Thorne said. '*I'm* bloody starving. Missed breakfast and that feels like almost a day ago.'

Rahim studied the tabletop.

Between them in the middle of the table, a wooden rack held the laminated menu. Thorne pushed it to one side, then slid the ketchup bottle and the salt and pepper out of the way. His view was clearer, but with a baseball cap pulled down low over the boy's brow Thorne still had difficulty making any sort of eye contact. 'Up and out to a murder scene at half past stupid, I was.' He grimaced. 'Not that a body first thing does a great deal for your appetite, mind you.'

'Don't,' Rahim said, quietly. He raised his head.

'What?'

'Bang on about it. I got your message.'

'Sorry about that.'

'I'm here, aren't I?'

'I'm very glad you are.'

'So . . . you know. You don't need to . . .'

Thorne sat back and folded his arms as the drinks were laid down. The waiter popped the ring pulls then turned to an adjacent table. Thorne watched Rahim reach for a can.

'What did you do?'

'Sorry?'

'*That.*'

Thorne pointed and Rahim quickly drew the can closer, obscuring Thorne's view of the sticking plaster across his wrist. He took a sip and shrugged, lowered his head again. 'Accident,' he said.

Thorne snatched a serviette from the dispenser and dabbed at the few drops Rahim had spilled. Looking around, he understood that the café was so busy because of the range of food it served. To one side of them, a large man squeezed into a shiny suit was making short work of a full English breakfast, while at another table a pair of young girls who might have been students picked at chicken salads. There was a Daily Specials board Thorne had not noticed before. He quite liked the sound of the Mediterranean omelette with feta and peppers, or the shepherd's pie with spiced lamb, but despite what he had told Rahim he was not feeling particularly hungry.

It had felt better to do this somewhere informal, that was all. To try and take the pressure off a little. Better than talking on the street or in the back of a panda car.

'Why did you call 999?' Thorne asked.

'I needed to get hold of you.'

'I gave you my mobile number.'

'I threw it away.'

'So, why now?'

'Because I was scared, just like you said.' Rahim looked up and stabbed a finger at Thorne. 'And don't say sorry again, because you know very well that's what you wanted.'

'It was the only way to get you to do the right thing,' Thorne said.

'You didn't think I would otherwise?'

'Well, you hadn't so far.' Thorne lowered his voice and leaned in. 'Come on, Rahim. You must have thought there was something dodgy about Amin's death. Even when you thought it was suicide, right?'

Thorne watched the judder and lurch of the boy's skinny chest, the rapid rise and fall visible even beneath the padded jacket he was wearing, and he saw tears welling at the corners of his eyes. Neither of them looked up as their food was laid in front of them and neither seemed inclined to touch it once the waiter had walked away.

On the pavement outside, a woman bent to slap a young child's legs.

A few tables away, the girls eating the salad were laughing.

Thorne said, 'Whatever it is you've come here to tell me, you need to get on with it.'

Rahim nodded and blinked slowly. He reached into the pocket of his jacket and took out an iPhone. He began to scroll through the menu.

'What?' Thorne said.

Rahim shook his head and pressed a few more buttons on the screen, then, when he had found what he was looking for, he laid the phone down on the table and slid it across to Thorne.

Thorne picked it up and was immediately looking at a photograph.

Decent quality, colour.

Three men.

They were standing close together, glasses in fists and arms on shoulders. A party. In the background there were others with drinks and smiles and a couple of men appeared to be dancing. There was a table with food.

Thorne glanced up. Rahim was looking away and nervously picking at the ring-pull on his can. Thorne pressed his finger and thumb to the screen, then eased them gently apart to enlarge the image of the group at the centre of the picture.

Three men . . .

They were all dressed similarly in open-necked shirts, though the one on the left was perhaps a few years older than the other two. The one in the middle and the one on the right both appeared to be laughing at something the one on the left had said. Having seen him so recently, Thorne recognised the man on the right straight away.

He grunted, felt a rush of anger, the breath heavy when he released it.

For obvious reasons, it took him just a little longer to identify the man on the left.

'Jesus Christ . . .'

'Yeah,' Rahim said. 'You see?'

Thorne stared at the picture and struggled to put the pieces into some sort of order. He asked himself questions and tried to answer them. He teased out the tangles, made reasonable assumptions.

There was a 'why' now, all sorts of 'whys'. Two-thirds of a 'who'.

'Is this Amin's phone?'

'Mine.'

'You took the picture?'

'Yeah, but Amin was there, at the party. He . . . went with one of those men. Not sure which.'

Thorne looked again. 'Did they know about the picture?'

'I don't think so,' Rahim said.

'Are you sure, because it could all be about this.' Thorne turned the phone round, held it up to Rahim's face. 'If they thought it was Amin who had taken it.'

'They didn't.'

'Did Amin know about it?'

Rahim shook his head.

'He could have been trying to blackmail someone—'

'No way. Look, they didn't even know I was taking it. See?'

Rahim pointed at the picture, and looking again, it seemed obvious enough to Thorne that the three men were not aware they were being photographed. That their focus was elsewhere.

Thorne turned the picture back towards Rahim and tapped a finger against the head of the older man on the left. The man it had taken him that bit longer to identify. 'Did Amin recognise him?'

'I don't know,' Rahim said. 'I never got the chance to ask him.'

'*You* did though.'

'Yes.'

'You didn't know who he was back then, at the party?'

'You never knew names or what anyone did,' Rahim said. 'Nothing like that. They were just punters, you know? And we were just ... whatever we were.'

'Must have been quite a shock when you saw him again.'

Rahim nodded, swallowed. 'I thought I was going to throw up, you know? I didn't know what to do, I just wanted to say what I had to say and get the hell out of there. I tried to forget about the whole thing. Then, when I found out what had happened to Amin, I figured it must have been connected.'

'Connected is right,' Thorne said. He stared down at the three men, their easy smiles, the arms draped across shoulders. 'It's all connected.' He pointed to the man laughing in the middle of the picture. 'Any idea who this one is?'

Rahim said he hadn't. He pointed to the man on the right, another man he had not seen since the picture was taken and started to ask Thorne the same question.

'Oh don't worry,' Thorne said. 'I know exactly who this gentleman is.'

'So which one of them killed Amin?' Rahim asked.

Passing the table and seeing their food untouched, the waiter stopped to ask if everything was all right. Thorne said they were just in a hurry. He slipped the phone into his pocket and took fifteen pounds from his wallet to cover the bill.

'I'll organise a car home,' Thorne said. 'Do you need somebody to stay with you?'

'I'm fine,' Rahim said.

Thorne pushed his chair away from the table, caught another glimpse of the plaster on the boy's wrist. Said, 'Let's do it anyway. For me, all right?'

FIFTY-ONE

Sue Pascoe was on her way out of the girls' toilets when she bumped into Nadira Akhtar who was on her way in. They swapped muttered 'hellos' as Pascoe stood aside to let the older woman pass. Then Pascoe exchanged a few words with the family liaison officer who stood waiting outside. She told her to go and grab some tea and that she would take care of Mrs Akhtar for ten minutes or so. When Nadira came out of the toilets, Pascoe smiled and said, 'I'm guessing you could do with some air. Cooped up in here . . . '

'That would be nice,' Nadira said.

They walked the length of the wide corridor that snaked around the school hall, and through a small cloakroom. Training shoes were arranged in wire baskets and the rows of low metal hooks were still festooned with brightly coloured bags and coats abandoned two days before. The back door was unlocked. They stepped out on to an enclosed play area, equipped with games and apparatus for younger children and looking towards a well-kept playing field. There were half-sized football goals and a running track marked out in white paint. A zigzag of red and yellow cones.

'I'm really surprised you're still here,' Pascoe said.

'I need to be close,' Nadira said.

'Even so.'

Pascoe knew that the policy in such situations as these was to get the relatives away from the site of the incident if at all possible. This could not be done against anybody's will of course, but once reassured that they would be kept fully informed at all times, friends and family would usually be 'forcefully encouraged' to relocate. More often than not, they would be taken to a hotel that was sufficiently close to have them brought back quickly if the situation demanded it, but far enough away so as not to impede the operation. Far enough to enable a dynamic entry to proceed without needing to worry about the impact it might have on the relatives of hostage or hostage taker.

Outside the range where gunfire might be heard.

Though she knew Nadira would have had all this explained to her already, Pascoe ran through it again. She changed the emphasis, talking about comfort and convenience and fighting shy of any suggestion that they might want anyone out of the way. 'Mrs Mitchell was taken to a nice hotel yesterday afternoon,' she said.

'Well, we could certainly not stay in the same hotel,' Nadira said. 'She and I had something of an altercation.'

Pascoe reached for her cigarettes and was about to light one. She glanced at Nadira and asked if she minded.

'Can I have one?'

'Oh . . . help yourself.' Pascoe offered her the packet. 'I didn't think, sorry.'

Nadira said thank you. She pulled out a cigarette and leaned a little awkwardly towards the lighter. Pascoe lit her own, then watched as the woman, who was clearly not a regular smoker, took her first drag and puffed out the smoke without inhaling.

'Javed would kill me,' Nadira said, quietly. She took another drag then smiled, cocking her head one way then the other, the irony of what she was saying obviously not lost on her.

'How do you think Javed is coping?' Pascoe asked. 'How is he . . . under pressure?'

Nadira stared at her through a ribbon of blue smoke. 'Pressure? I hardly think this is normal,' she said. 'This is not like the papers being late. It's not like having the credit card refused at the cash-and-carry.'

'I know.' Pascoe fingered her ID badge. 'I just meant generally. Is he the one that stays calm if something happens? Is he the one that starts to panic?'

'He was calm that night when Amin came home,' Nadira said. Her voice was suddenly a little quieter. 'Not straight away, but once we knew what had happened. He was ... measured, you know? I was all over the place, hysterical and whatnot, I'm sure you can imagine.'

'Tell me,' Pascoe said.

Nadira took another puff. 'It was because he was the youngest, I think. The most naive. That's why I was wearing out the carpet at half past one in the morning and talking to myself like some mad woman. I kept calling his mobile phone and telling him to call me back, telling him he was being selfish and trying to keep the panic out of my voice.

'Stupid, I know, because he was a grown man more or less, but common sense has nothing to do with anything when all you can see is your child's face and all you can imagine are horrors.' She looked at Pascoe. 'I was already blaming myself for the things I imagined had happened. We had known it was wrong, you see, that sixteen was still too young to be going into pubs, but he and his friend were only going for the quiz, so we let them go. He said he would not be drinking, that they needed to keep clear heads, and it made sense, him using all those brains God gave him to make a little money. He had shown me the cash they had won the last time, and he was using it to buy books for college, so we thought, where's the harm, you see?'

Another puff, then nodding as she remembered.

'Javed had been in bed for hours already and it was only a few more until he would need to be up. I was telling myself that Amin had missed his bus or whatever. Telling myself that when he finally came home I would rant and rave and give him a good talking-to and then climb into bed thinking about what I was going to make him for his breakfast.' She smiled, drew her thin scarf a little further forward on

298

her head. 'When I heard the key in the door I started laughing, because I'd been so foolish to worry.

'My God, when I saw his face . . .

'His eye was just a slit and his mouth looked like it had been chewed by a dog or something. I saw this dark stain on his jacket, which was buttoned right up to the neck and that made me very cross, I remember, because I'd told him it was cold and that he should have worn a sweater or something. When I asked him what had happened, he pushed past me and ran up the stairs. He locked himself in the bathroom and I followed him and that's when I shouted for my husband. Javed came out in his underwear, swearing and yawning.

'I tell him Amin is hurt and that he won't come out of the bathroom. Oh yes he bloody will, Javed says and he starts shouting and hammering on the door, saying, "Open this bloody bastard door before I smash it in."' She took a fast drag on her cigarette, puffed the smoke out almost simultaneously from her mouth and nose. 'Between the blows on the door, I could hear him sobbing inside, so I took hold of my husband's arm. We stood waiting there on the landing and, after a minute or two, Amin opened the door.' Her hand moved towards her mouth; the unconscious recreation of a movement she had made instinctively that night. 'That's when we saw all the blood. The same shirt I had ironed for him . . . crisp and white . . . his favourite shirt. Now it was pasted to him. It was sopping.

'I was screaming and I asked him where he was hurt, and Javed was asking the same thing, and we were both reaching out for him. He was crying and he cried harder when he saw how afraid I was. He said he was fine . . . he was fine, and he told me not to worry about the blood.

'"It's all right, Mum," he said. "It's all right. It's not mine."'

Pascoe looked around for somewhere to put her cigarette butt. Had she been alone, she would simply have flicked it away, but in this woman's presence she felt the need to dispose of it properly. To be seen doing so. She leaned down and dropped it into the inch or so of water that had gathered in the base of a plant pot.

'Would you mind?'

Pascoe turned to see that Nadira Akhtar was holding out what remained of her own cigarette. Pascoe took it from her and dropped it into the pot.

'You have any children?' Nadira asked.

Pascoe shook her head.

'Your job is too stressful for that, I suppose. Everyone counting on you all the time. Such a big responsibility.'

'Something like that,' Pascoe said.

'Do you also talk to those people who want to kill themselves?' Nadira gestured towards the far side of the playing field. 'Last week there was a man up on a bridge over there . . .'

'I have done,' Pascoe said. 'To be honest though, that's the sort of job they usually assign to someone with a bit less experience than I've got.' She was about to say more, but stopped herself, wondering why she felt the need to brag in any way at all to this woman. To sing her own praises.

She told Nadira it was probably about time to get her back inside.

Nadira nodded, staring out across the playing field. 'So what about you?' she said. 'How are *you* coping?'

FIFTY-TWO

'Stay strong . . .'

Pascoe had said that, whispered it at the end of the last call. Helen had told her that she needed to go – she was keen to get all the calls over with before anyone started asking about Stephen Mitchell – and Pascoe had said that she would call again in an hour. Then she'd said it, quickly.

Stay strong. Where the hell had that come from?

It sounded weird, oddly intimate, touchy-feely. Not the sort of thing Helen was expecting, had grown used to, not . . . *professional.* Then again, perhaps it was just Pascoe's job to make it sound exactly as though she really was Helen's closest friend. Maybe she reacted differently when the hostage was a copper.

Or maybe there was nothing strange at all about what Pascoe had said, and it was just another of the thoughts that had begun to reel and crash aimlessly around inside Helen's head. She'd looked into the faces of plenty of drunks and sky-high addicts in holding cells, met enough people whose minds were not functioning properly, temporarily or otherwise. She'd listened to the ramblings.

She recognised the patterns.

301

She was hot and it was sticky and she could not think what day it was without really concentrating. When she closed her eyes, the lights that swam around behind them exploded together and fused into faces: Jenny, Paul, her father. A man she'd seen on the train a few weeks before who'd smiled and who she'd fantasised about for several days. After a few moments, the lights trailed away like dying fireworks and the features began to dissolve. She tried to picture Tom Thorne, but couldn't. Just a sketch, a shape, somewhere between sad and scary.

She thought about Thai food and wine and a hot bath.

She thought about Paul's broken head and a bloom of blood.

She thought about Alfie.

It had been nine months, more, since she had last felt him sucking at her, having never really felt good about it, never felt relaxed or capable or natural like her sister had been. But now, thinking about her son's drool drying on her neck and his fat little legs, she felt an ache in her breast as though she might start to leak at any moment.

A pressure, building.

She thought about the gun on the desk and the scissors in the desk drawer.

Akhtar walked back in from the shop. He had cleared away the remains of their most recent meal: the crisp packets and empty cans, the ice-cream wrappers. He sat at the desk looking serious and for a few minutes neither of them spoke.

'It seems that we have finally run out of things to talk about,' Akhtar said eventually. 'Perhaps we should watch some television.'

Helen said she didn't mind, but Akhtar did not move. He stared at her and when he rubbed his face, his palm rasped against the stubble. He smoothed down the hair at the side of his head and she could see the dark patches underneath his arms.

'There are some programmes at this time of day you might enjoy,' he said.

'I told you it's fine.'

'I was thinking you might like it, that was all.'

302

'Whatever you want,' Helen said, fighting to keep the irritation from her voice.

Akhtar leaned across to switch on the television, then sat back clutching the remote. He flicked between the channels. The picture was far better on some than others.

'Nadira tells me about these programmes,' he said, sitting back. 'She watches them at home in the afternoon, all curled up with coffee and damned chocolates, like some kind of princess, you know? Antiques and holidays and people moving to the countryside.'

Helen nodded.

'That's all you get these days, isn't it? Reality programmes or murder mysteries. Reality and crime.'

Helen nodded again.

'I know, I know,' Akhtar said. 'You're sitting there thinking to yourself, look at where we *are*, for heaven's sake!'

Helen kept her eyes fixed on the screen, on the couple being led around a garden, tried hard to focus on the monotonous commentary. To distract herself.

Thinking: Alfie, gun, scissors, Alfie, gun . . .

'You're asking yourself, why do we even need the bloody television?'

Thinking: stay strong.

FIFTY-THREE

Thorne called Donnelly on his way to Barndale.

He told him about the empty flat in Hounslow and about the forensic evidence linking Jonathan Bridges to the murder of Peter Allen. He told him that when Bridges had been in the hospital wing he was almost certainly responsible for giving Amin Akhtar the drugs that had killed him. He told him about the photograph on Jaffer's phone.

Donnelly was keen to know why Thorne was not on his way back to the RVP. Was this not the information that Javed Akhtar had been demanding? Thorne explained that there was no point until he had all the answers that were needed, until he could name names. That he could not go back to Akhtar again and say that while he still had a fairly good idea why his son had been murdered and was almost certain who had actually done it, he could not yet be sure who was *ultimately* responsible. He told Donnelly that until he was in a position to give Akhtar the whole story, it was not worth giving him anything. The man had not reacted particularly well to Thorne's previous progress report and getting him worked up still further was definitely not what Helen Weeks needed.

'It's your shout,' Donnelly said. 'But the sooner you get the rest of it, the better.'

Thorne said, 'It's got to be all or nothing.'

He called Holland, told him who he was on his way to see.

Holland asked if Thorne was planning on making an arrest and Thorne said he was not planning on anything, that he would be in there making it up as he went along. The last thing he needed was that kind of formality, the time-suck of the process and the paperwork. Then, of course, there was the small matter of grounds, the absence of anything but circumstantial evidence, however damning it appeared. Holland apologised for being overly pessimistic then asked Thorne what he intended to do if the man he was going to talk to did not immediately feel like confessing. Thorne said he would have to beat it out of him. Holland said nothing for a few seconds and Thorne laughed and told him he was joking.

'Do you want me to come with you?' Holland asked. 'I can be there in forty minutes.'

Thorne said, 'I was *joking*, Dave. Half joking at any rate ...'

He called Helen Weeks.

They spoke for less than half a minute, but the strain was clear enough in her voice. She was hesitant suddenly, all but monosyllabic. She sounded oddly disconnected from events, as if the call had just woken her and she was not yet sure if she was still having a bad dream. Thorne could hear voices in the background and Helen told him she and Akhtar were watching the television. She and Akhtar and Mitchell. Thorne told her it was good to take her mind off things, that it made the time go faster. She was tired, she told him, but beyond sleep. She kept zoning out, but it worried her because she knew she had to keep her wits about her.

'Don't want to drift,' Helen said. 'Need to stay sharp.'

Thorne said, 'Think about Alfie.'

FIFTY-FOUR

He got to the prison a little before five o'clock, and the man he had driven there to confront, though surprised at first, seemed happy enough to see him. Thorne was shown once again into the man's office and his jacket was hung carefully on a metal hook behind the door. He was offered tea. The man sat down behind his desk and moaned for a minute or so about his heavy schedule and the day from hell he'd had already. He gave a 'what can you do?' shrug and said he would do his best to help, though he was a little pushed, and he wondered aloud what it was that Thorne had forgotten to ask first time round.

Thorne smiled and walked back to the door. He took down his jacket from the metal hook and reached into the pocket for the phone.

He was trying not to enjoy it.

But not very hard.

'Don't get to a lot of parties myself,' Thorne said. 'I mean there's usually a piss-up in the pub over the road if we get the right result in court, and every now and then the brass lay on some warm white wine and sausage rolls when they want to pat a few backs, but I couldn't tell you the last time I went to a proper party. Where you can really cut loose and let your hair down, you know. Like *this*.' He raised the phone and gave a little wave with it. 'You can see it on people's faces, can't you? You can see that they're just having the best time, because there's something like … *abandon* or whatever you call it in their expressions. They don't give a monkey's, you know, and the best time to see it is when they don't know they're being watched. Even better, when they don't even know they're being photographed. That's when you catch a glimpse of how people actually are, isn't it? When nobody's pretending to be something they're not, when it's all out there in the open and there aren't any inhibitions. I mean, when you think about it, that's the sign of a really great party, isn't it? When people can just be themselves.'

Thorne looked across at the man behind the desk, at the look of confusion on a face that was considerably paler than it had been just a few moments before. 'Oh sorry, here you go.' Thorne stepped across and pushed the phone across the desk. He watched as the man picked it up and stared at the photograph.

'Looks like you were having one hell of a night, Dr McCarthy.'

The doctor spoke without taking his eyes from the picture. 'Where did you get this?'

'I mean, I'm not sure if this was taken before or after you'd had sex with an underage boy, but either way it looks like you and your friends are enjoying yourselves.'

McCarthy said nothing.

Thorne leaned against the desk.

For almost half a minute there was no sound save for McCarthy's breathing, and his finger tap-tapping against the edge of the phone, and a few seconds of indecipherable shouting from one of the wards.

'So I was at a party.' McCarthy pushed the phone back across the desk at Thorne. 'I'm not an expert in these matters, but I'm not convinced there's a law against that.'

'Depends on the party.'

'I don't know what you think you can see in that picture.'

'Well, I can't see too many women.'

'Again, not illegal.'

'Men and boys.'

'My memory isn't quite what it was, Inspector, so why don't you remind me where that party was?' McCarthy waited. 'How about when it was?' There was the hint of a smile, cold and tight. 'You don't know, do you?'

'The person who took that picture knows.'

'You don't know anything, you don't *have* anything, so—'

'I know about Jonathan Bridges.'

'So, if there's nothing else, I'd appreciate the chance to get on with my work.'

Thorne leaned closer. Said the name again. Hissed it, like a threat.

McCarthy sat back and raised his hands. 'He was a patient here.'

'I know he was, and I know when.'

'Well good, because that saves me the trouble of looking it up.'

'In for something serious, was he?'

'Sorry?'

'In-growing toenail? Athlete's foot?'

'The patients' medical records are confidential.'

'Methadone, I'm guessing, but it doesn't really matter,' Thorne said. 'The fact that you admitted him is all that matters. The fact that he was in here at the same time as Amin Akhtar.'

'I was at home when Amin died, as you well know.'

'But Jonathan Bridges was here, doing exactly what you'd set him up to do.'

'Which was what?' The smile made its presence felt again, but now it was looking a little frayed around the edges. 'How exactly do you think Amin Akhtar was killed?'

'Why don't you tell me?'

'Because I haven't the faintest idea.'

'You're a liar,' Thorne said.

'What do you want me to say?'

'Did you have sex with Amin Akhtar?' Thorne picked up the phone, held up the photo. 'Did you have sex with him that night?'

308

'Certainly not.'

'On other occasions?'

McCarthy stood up. 'I think that's enough.'

Thorne was already on his way round the desk. 'Fucking sit down!'

The chair sighed as McCarthy dropped back into it and rolled a few inches away across the polished vinyl on squeaky wheels.

'Sit down . . .'

Thorne sucked in a deep breath that tasted of metal and bandages. He blinked away an image of himself jamming the phone into McCarthy's mouth, holding it steady with one hand and smashing it through the teeth with the heel of the other.

I was joking, Dave.

Instead, he held up the phone with his left hand, spread the fingers of his right hand around the back of McCarthy's head and slowly but firmly moved one towards the other. 'The man on the left, I know,' he said. 'You with me?'

McCarthy nodded.

His head moved a few inches closer to the phone.

'So who's the ugly-looking article in the middle?'

McCarthy said nothing.

'Name not coming to you?'

'No . . .'

A few seconds later, his nose was pressed up against the screen.

'I mean you look matey enough there,' Thorne said. 'So I presumed you knew one another.' McCarthy was pushing back hard against Thorne's hand, but Thorne kept the pressure on. 'The thing is, I've got a real sense that you're not exactly top dog in this particular set-up. Trust me, you get a feel for these things, Ian, and if I'm honest, I don't believe you were the one calling the shots. I'm not saying you weren't the one with the brains or anything like that, I mean you're clearly hugely intelligent and you may have been the one who planned the whole thing for all I know.'

Thorne felt the smallest movement beneath his fingers, a shake of the head, aborted.

'I'm just saying, you might want to think about being the one that names the names. That does it *now*, because it's the kind of thing that'll do you a favour when the sentences are handed out. And they *will* be handed out, Ian. I promise you that.'

Another shake of the head, firmer this time.

'No, you don't know his name?' Thorne asked. 'Or no, you're not going to tell me?'

'Take your pick.'

McCarthy raised his hand and grabbed at Thorne's wrist. There was a second or two of resistance before Thorne reluctantly loosened his grip and the doctor ducked smartly away. He was quickly out of his chair and moving into the centre of the room. Keeping one eye on Thorne as he backed away, rolling his neck around on his shoulders, then smoothing down the hair at the back of his head.

He turned to see a female PHO staring in at them through the window. He raised a hand and nodded. He stuck up a thumb. The woman looked Thorne up and down before moving away.

'Listen, I don't have to tell you a thing,' McCarthy said. 'I don't have to talk to you at all, in fact, because the truth is you've got nothing but a single, pointless photograph and a very sick mind.' He began to pick at the corner of his goatee. 'Actually, I think your options at this point are rather limited, don't you? I mean you're certainly not going to arrest me, because the fact is that you haven't got a shred of evidence on which to charge me with anything and you're only going to end up looking like an idiot.'

Thorne came slowly round the desk. He watched and listened.

'You're pissing in the wind, and you know it.'

It was not the worst attempt at a show of confidence that Thorne had ever seen, but the smile was now looking awfully ragged. The words had clearly been well rehearsed, but they were spoken a fraction too quickly and Thorne could hear how dry the mouth was.

'That business at the newsagent's,' McCarthy said. 'It was still going on, last time I checked.'

Suddenly, Thorne's mouth was equally dry.

310

'I mean we can take a trip to the station if you want, and I promise to come quietly. Might be quite an adventure. We can hang around and make small talk while I wait for my lawyer and then you can sit and listen to me saying "No comment" for a couple of hours, by which time those poor people being held at gunpoint may well be dead, and whose stupid fault do you think that will be?'

The PHO reappeared at the window, watching for a few seconds before gesturing at McCarthy that she needed to speak to him. He held up one finger to let her know that he would only be a minute, then turned back to Thorne.

'So . . . those options. Well, just the two really. You can waste a little more time asking me some more questions I'm not going to dignify with an answer. Or you can get the hell off my wing.'

FIFTY-FIVE

There was strictly no food or drink allowed inside the Technical Support Unit vehicle, so with a few minutes left until they were due to put the next call in, Pascoe finished her coffee walking around the playground. There was rain in the air, and it had turned a little colder, so anyone who did not need to be out here was back inside the school, but it was still busy enough. Kidnap, traffic, CO19. Uniform and CID. A situation like this was one of the few that brought a large number of different Met Police units together on the same operation. 'Suits' and 'lids' in something almost approaching harmony. They just needed Vice, Anti-Terror and the Royalty Protection branch, maybe a copper or two on horseback, and they would have pretty much the whole set.

Pascoe lit a cigarette, then walked across to a chalked-out hopscotch court and stepped slowly from square to square, careful to avoid the lines.

Not forgetting the one poor bugger from the Murder Squad, of course. Who, if he succeeded, would almost certainly receive no credit for his part in a successful outcome, and who she felt sure would blame himself if things did not turn out well. She thought about Tom

Thorne; grim-faced, a blue-arsed fly, desperately searching for answers with no guarantee there were any there to find.

His hand wrapped tightly around the shitty end of the stick.

She bent to pick up a smooth, flat stone and weighed it in her palm. She walked back to the first square of the court and told herself that if she could toss the pebble cleanly into the semicircle at the end, she would be drinking tea with Helen Weeks before the day was out. She crouched and prepared to throw the stone, wondered how many people as control-freakish as she was were also superstitious.

'DS Pascoe . . .'

She turned to see Donnelly beckoning her from the back doors of the TSU truck. She threw her cigarette away and slipped the stone into her jacket pocket as she crossed the playground to join him.

As she climbed up a small set of metal stairs into the truck, Donnelly asked her if she had thought about what to say, how to get the necessary message across. She told him how she was planning to handle things and he said that it sounded ideal. Clear enough, but still subtle.

'She's clever,' Pascoe said.

'So is he,' Donnelly said.

Pascoe took her place on a low stool on the left-hand side of the truck and picked up a headset. Donnelly settled in next to her and did likewise. A large pair of speakers were mounted above a line of TV monitors on the rear wall, while on the right-hand side a pair of civilian technicians – a twenty-something woman and a forty-something man – sat in front of a console that made the cockpit controls of a 747 look primitive.

'Can you get Radio 1 on there?' Pascoe asked.

The woman looked over her shoulder. 'Sorry?'

'Scott Mills is on in a bit.'

Donnelly managed a grunt of amusement, but the woman just shrugged as though Pascoe had been speaking a foreign language and slowly turned back to her bank of knobs and faders.

'We set?' Donnelly asked.

The man turned, said, 'Absolutely.' What was left of his hair was fine and sandy-coloured and his paunch was exaggerated by the tight black polo shirt he wore over neatly ironed jeans. His name was embroidered in red just above his left man-boob: *TSU: Kim Yates.*

Donnelly looked at his watch. 'About a minute.'

Pascoe nodded. She knew that the slightest break in routine could wreck many days of delicate negotiation and be enough to push a hostage taker over the edge. A change of voice at the end of the phone, or a call coming at one minute past the allotted hour.

'Off you go, Sue.'

Yates saw Pascoe take out her mobile and waved a hand. 'You won't be needing that again,' he said. 'It's programmed into our system as a speed-dial. More or less instantaneous, and obviously we've made sure that yours will still appear as the incoming number on Sergeant Weeks' handset.' He half turned back then stopped. 'If you've got any questions, feel free to fire away.'

'I think I've got it.'

Yates spun back round to his console and he and his colleague put on their own headsets. He stabbed at a button. 'Here we go.'

The ringing of Helen Weeks' phone immediately filled the van.

It was answered after three rings and Helen said, 'Hold on.' A few seconds later and the quality of the silence changed, as she switched the call on to speaker. 'Now Javed can hear,' she said.

'Of course,' Pascoe said.

Straight away, Yates and his colleague began making minor adjustments to their settings. The voices of Helen Weeks and Javed Akhtar would be relayed inside the vehicle via the microphones that had been carefully sunk into two of the storeroom walls. It was crucial, however, that this sound did not feed back to Helen's phone. That she and – more importantly – Akhtar were not able to hear their voices broadcast back at them through the TSU speakers.

Yates gave Donnelly and Pascoe the thumbs-up.

'It all looks very busy out there,' Akhtar said. 'Like Piccadilly Circus or something.'

'What do you mean?' Pascoe asked.

'We have got the television on with the sound turned down,' Akhtar said. 'We can see it all on the six o'clock news. All the reporters, the flashing lights and what have you. A lot of police officers.'

'This is a major operation, Javed.'

'There is a picture of me in the corner of the screen.' There was a grunt of shock or disapproval. 'Where did they get that? Did *Nadira* give them that?'

'Probably the passport service,' Helen said. 'DVLA maybe.'

'You're making the news, Javed,' Pascoe said. 'What you're doing.'

'I don't care about that.'

'Of course you don't, I know that, Javed. I know that this isn't about making headlines.'

'Not until my son's murderer is caught and sent to prison. Then I want to see big bloody headlines, believe me.'

'Of course.'

'Biggest ones they have.'

'Biggest ones they have, absolutely,' Pascoe said. 'But until then you can at least see how seriously we're taking everything.'

'Everybody looks very serious, that's for sure,' Akhtar said. 'Everybody seems very busy, but still there is nothing really happening. I have heard nothing more from Inspector Thorne.'

'He wanted me to tell you that he's still chasing that lead, Javed.' Pascoe glanced at Donnelly. 'A very strong lead.'

'The dead boy, yes I know.'

'He has more information now—'

'I'm getting *impatient.*'

Pascoe looked at Donnelly again. They did not need top-quality speakers and high-definition stereo to hear the anger in Akhtar's voice.

'That's understandable, Javed.'

'I will not be strung along, do you understand?'

Donnelly waved to get Pascoe's attention, pointed at his headset and nodded.

'That's not what's happening, Javed,' Pascoe said. 'You need to believe that. You need to know that there's support for you out here. A lot of support, for all of you. Can you hear me, Helen?'

'Yes,' Helen said.

'Whatever happens, you need to know that we're out here, that there's support here and that we're listening. OK?'

'OK,' Helen said.

'I do not want to be ... *fobbed off*,' Akhtar said. 'I do not want to be messed around.' The anger was blossoming now, his voice ranting and ragged. 'There has been far too much of that.'

'I will not mess you around,' Pascoe said.

'You give me your word?'

'Absolutely.'

'Good. OK. That's it.'

There was a second or two of silence before the line went dead.

'Nice,' Donnelly said. He took off his headset. 'You think she got the message?'

'Like I said, she's clever.' As Yates and his fellow technician began to confer about DBs and balanced output, Pascoe excused herself and stepped down from the truck into the playground.

I'm getting impatient ...

She thought about the textbook response to anger on the part of a hostage taker. The strategies she had been taught to deal with the increased threat of volatility. She considered the options as she walked back towards the hopscotch court and felt for the pebble in her pocket.

FIFTY-SIX

It was just beginning to get dark as McCarthy's silver Astra drove out of the Barndale car park and its headlights came on as the barrier was raised at the security checkpoint. The car turned on to the quiet country road towards the M25 and Thorne waited for another vehicle to pass before he pulled out of the unmarked track opposite, flicked on his own lights and began to follow. It would be easier to stay out of sight once they reached the motorway and until then it would just be a matter of staying far enough back. Thorne did not think there would be a problem. He guessed that Ian McCarthy would have more important things to worry about than whether or not he was being followed.

He hoped so at any rate.

Though not quite able to pull off 'blasé', the doctor had done his best to appear cocky, defiant even, and Thorne's first thought when he had left the prison almost an hour before had been to race back into central London and confront the person he believed had given McCarthy the coaching. He had quickly decided that he would almost certainly have even less luck with him than with McCarthy. So, with no idea who the third man was, he could do little for the time being other than stay close to the doctor and see what happened.

See where the weakest link in the chain would lead him.

Or to whom.

Thorne was now convinced that Amin Akhtar had been the victim of a conspiracy. He also knew that he could base this on no more than a single picture on Rahim Jaffer's phone, which actually proved nothing at all. The names and the reasons were what mattered now of course, were what would get Helen Weeks out of that newsagent's, but if those responsible were to pay for what they had done, Thorne would need evidence that the conspiracy had been maintained. He had to prove that the men in that photograph were still in contact with one another.

It began to rain as they drove past Chorleywood Common. The road straightened over the next mile or so, becoming wider and better lit as it approached the M25 roundabout. Thorne was three cars behind the Astra, doing fifty-five in the inside lane, when his phone rang.

'You sound weird.'

'I'm in the car.'

'Hands-free, I hope.'

'What is it, Phil?'

'I know how they did it,' Hendricks said.

Thorne's hands tightened on the wheel, just for a second, as he followed McCarthy's car across the roundabout, up on to the slip road, then southbound on the M25.

'We'd already established there was no way the killer could have got that many pills into Amin's stomach,' Hendricks said. 'Right? Those few pills in his mouth, on the bedclothes, they were just for show. They were the suicide indicator.'

'But there was enough Tramadol in his system to kill him?'

'Plenty, so there's only one other way it can have got there. It was liquid Tramadol and it was injected.'

'But Bridges did this.'

'It's just an injection, Tom, it's not rocket science. He takes the cap off the cannula on the back of Amin's hand and in it goes. Anyone could have shown the kid how to do it.'

318

Thorne told Hendricks exactly who had shown him.

'Right,' Hendricks said. 'So McCarthy gives Bridges a quick lesson on cannulas and needles, slips him the pills and the syringe—'

'We've still got a problem with these pills though,' Thorne said. 'How did he get as many as he did into Amin's mouth? How did he do it that fast? That quietly?'

'Because it wasn't just Tramadol in the syringe,' Hendricks said. 'This is what I've been trying to figure out. What the extra drug was.'

'You've figured it out?'

'Remember that Hamas agent? The one the Israelis killed in that hotel in Dubai a couple of years ago? This is the same drug they used on him. It stops the victim struggling, eliminates noise.'

'Go on then.'

'You might need to write this down.'

'Tricky,' Thorne said.

'Suxamethonium chloride.'

'I can't even say it.'

'You don't need the chloride bit.' Hendricks said it again, slowly. 'It's a neuromuscular blocker, OK? Basically a muscle relaxant, but incredibly powerful, incredibly quick. It's used in anaesthesia and intensive care, to make intubation easier. They used to use it in the US to paralyse prisoners before they got the lethal injection.'

'Jesus.'

'They stopped because of the side-effects.'

'I'm listening ...'

'As soon as it's administered, all the nerves start to fire and every muscle in the body begins to spasm like mad. The patient starts fitting basically, then a minute or so later he's completely paralysed and pretty soon the drug makes it impossible to breathe. But he's awake the whole time this is happening, so these days it's never given to patients who are conscious, not unless there's no other option. It's too dangerous.' There was a pause. 'Too disturbing.'

'Amin would have known what was happening to him?'

'Sorry, Tom.'

'It's OK.'

'It was the perfect drug,' Hendricks said. 'Sodding *perfect*. The fits were consistent with a Tramadol overdose . . . the tongue bitten off, all that. Then as soon as the paralysis kicked in, Bridges could put the pills into Amin's mouth, set up the overdose scenario and the beauty part is he's in and out of there in a couple of minutes. Job done.'

'Why didn't they find it at the PM?' Thorne asked.

'That's why it's so perfect. Unless you take a blood specimen within thirty minutes, the enzymes in the body start to break the drug down and eventually it becomes so degraded it's almost undetectable.'

Ahead of Thorne, the silver Astra was indicating, pulling across to the inside lane.

'So how the hell do I prove any of this, Phil?'

'*Almost* undetectable,' Hendricks said. 'And only when you're not specifically looking for it. Amin wasn't cremated, was he?'

'Buried.'

'No problem then. If we can exhume Amin's body, I'll find it.'

Thorne watched as the Astra began to indicate again, just shy of the first motorway junction. He followed the car as it came off at the exit then turned right at the roundabout following the sign for Maple Cross. Holland had already texted through McCarthy's address and Thorne recognised the name.

It looked as though the doctor was heading home.

Thorne pulled out to overtake a lorry and ratcheted up his wipers to handle the spray. He put his foot down. Now, he was happy enough to follow McCarthy all the way to his front door and he no longer cared whether he was seen or not.

FIFTY-SEVEN

The sound had gone back up on the television now, and as Helen watched, she imagined Pascoe and the others outside, huddled in their van, their eyes narrowed in concentration, with their headphones pressed to their ears, enjoying *Emmerdale*.

We're listening.

If anything, she was surprised that it had taken them this long. Perhaps it had been her presence inside that had delayed the decision to bring in technical support until now. The notion that, as one of the hostages was a police officer, they had 'ears' on the inside anyway.

We're listening.

The implication was obvious enough.

We're listening ... if there's anything you want to tell us. Anything you think might help. Something to give us the advantage out here, put us ahead of the game.

She leaned back against the radiator, took her eyes from the screen and looked across at Akhtar. He had no interest in the television. He was sitting with his back to the wall opposite her, his head lowered, staring down at the gun. He had been doing this a lot more since the previous evening. Picking the gun up, carrying it around for a while, putting a hand on it. He was not pointing it, or even waving it around, and it seemed to Helen that it was simply a question of reminding himself that he had it, and why he had it.

That *he* was the one ahead of the game.

Helen felt something tighten in her chest each time he reached for it.

However much she thought she understood Javed Akhtar, she could no longer be sure what he was or was not capable of, and she did not need to be reminded what a loaded gun could do. She hoped to God that she was imagining it, but several times in the last few hours she had thought she could catch her first whiff of the body in the next room. A sharp stab of something sweet. Only for a moment, but enough to make her stomach turn over and her eyes begin to water.

We're listening.

She felt as though she should say something to Akhtar, to warn him before he said the wrong thing, but she had no idea how. She could write something down perhaps – *DON'T MENTION MITCHELL* – but even asking for a pen and paper would probably sound suspicious to anyone listening in.

Inevitable in the end, she knew that. Same as the smell.

Now it was only a matter of time until they were found out. Until she was found out. A matter of time before the people on the outside stopped listening and took a rather more proactive approach.

Because of something they *hadn't* heard.

FIFTY-EIGHT

Thorne slowed and watched the silver Astra fifty yards ahead of him turn into the driveway of a modern, semi-detached house. He watched Ian McCarthy get out of the car and drag his briefcase from the back seat. He watched him walk quickly through the rain along a path paved in red brick, past nicely trimmed shrubs and well-tended flower beds, and step through his front door without looking back.

He gave him five minutes. Just enough time for someone to get their feet under the table, put the kettle on or open a bottle of something. Start getting comfortable.

When McCarthy opened the door he was still wearing his coat.

'Oh,' he said. 'No.'

'There's a third option,' Thorne said. 'You stop pretending you're big and brave and tell me everything you know.'

McCarthy moved quickly to close the door, but found Thorne's foot in the way, then his shoulder. A dog began to bark somewhere behind him and a few seconds later a Golden Retriever that looked anything but fierce forced its head through the gap. McCarthy tried to pull the dog back while keeping his weight against the door.

'It's finished,' Thorne said. His face was only a few inches from

McCarthy's. 'We're going to get Bridges eventually and he'll give you all up in a second as soon as he starts to need a fix badly enough. Let's not forget we're talking about two murders here, counting Peter Allen, oh ... and when we re-examine Amin Akhtar's body we'll find the Suxamethonium.'

McCarthy blinked.

'So, can I come in?'

The dog had retreated back into the hall, barking with less enthusiasm now, and as McCarthy opened the door Thorne saw a woman come through a doorway behind him, grab the dog by the collar and tell it to be quiet. She looked up at McCarthy as Thorne stepped past him.

'Everything all right?'

McCarthy closed the front door. 'Fine, love. There's a problem back at the prison, that's all.'

'What's happened?'

'Nothing very serious,' Thorne said. 'I shouldn't keep him too long.'

McCarthy moved to a closed door and nudged it open. 'Let's go in here.'

'Wherever.'

'Would you like tea or coffee?' the woman asked.

'I'll have coffee,' Thorne said, smiling. 'Only if you're making some.'

McCarthy switched on a light and disappeared through the door. Thorne watched the woman and the dog head off towards the kitchen, then followed him.

The room was pristine – the cushions on sofa and armchairs perfectly plumped and the Hoover marks still visible on the carpet – and Thorne guessed it was the living room the McCarthys kept for best. The one they might take coffee through to after a dinner party and where they played Trivial Pursuit or Risk once in a blue moon. There were framed degree certificates arranged on the wall and dried flowers in the fireplace, and the highly polished sideboard in one corner was topped with an array of family photographs.

Husband, wife, daughter, dog.

Perfect.

Thorne dropped into an armchair. Said, 'Very nice.'

McCarthy was already sitting on the sofa. 'What is?'

'All of this,' Thorne said. 'Your wife.'

'Don't,' McCarthy said.

Thorne sat forward. 'Here's the thing. I *was* thinking "conspiracy to murder", but the law's become very ... fluid these days, as far as all that goes. I mean, let's say you're part of a gang that attacks and kills someone. Even if you do nothing but egg somebody else on, even if you don't lay a finger on the victim, you can still go down for murder.' He let that hang for a few seconds. 'That's what the law says now. "Joint enterprise", it's called. Probably got a few up in Barndale been done because of that. You give someone a murder weapon ... the fact that you're miles away when that murder's committed is neither here nor there. You're as guilty of murder as they are in the eyes of the law.'

'I didn't kill anyone.'

'Knife, gun, syringe ... doesn't matter.'

'No—'

'You gave Bridges that syringe, and you showed him exactly what to do with it. Eager to learn, I should imagine. A decent wedge to spend when he got out, and the fact that it's an Asian kid he's doing is probably a bonus for a racist headcase like Johnno Bridges, right? You gave him the keys to get out of the ward and into Amin's room. You showed him where the cameras were.'

'Please—'

'And let's not forget who staged those thefts from the dispensary to make it look like those were the drugs that Amin Akhtar had taken. So, even though you were tucked up here in bed while he was being shot full of poison, you're the one who was ultimately responsible. You're the one who's looking at a very long time in prison, and it'll be somewhere a damn sight rougher than Barndale, I can guarantee that—'

'It wasn't my idea,' McCarthy said. 'None of it was my idea.'

Thorne sat back. It was like he had thought. The weakest link in the chain.

McCarthy's face was tight and bloodless, and he squeezed one hand with the other, methodically crushing the knuckles as though trying to distract himself with pain. The first pangs of remorse, or anguish at being caught, it did not much matter.

Thorne looked at him and felt nothing.

'The shit in that syringe,' Thorne said. 'The paralytic. They stopped using that in executions because of what it did. Because it was too cruel. Did you know that?'

McCarthy started to talk, quickly and quietly. 'The other men I was with at that party, the men in the picture. One you know, obviously, and the other one's called Simon Powell.'

The name meant nothing. 'What does he do?'

'He works for the Youth Justice Board. He's on the allocations team.'

Thorne thought about it and it made perfect sense. The second in the chain of three, the second in the process. It also explained something the governor of Barndale had told him two days earlier.

Sometimes these pen-pushers who allocate placements just like to try and make things awkward.

What else had Bracewell said?

I'm sure you've met the type.

The type. Thorne looked across at McCarthy.

'I didn't sleep with Amin that night,' McCarthy said. 'I swear. Not ever in fact. Powell might have done, or . . .'

He stopped speaking as the door opened and his wife came in with two mugs of coffee. She handed Thorne his, then gave the other one to McCarthy. 'You didn't say, but I guessed you'd want one.' She stopped at the door. 'What time did you say you were going out?'

McCarthy looked at her. Opened his mouth and closed it.

'I need to know what time to get dinner ready, that's all.'

'Don't worry,' McCarthy said. 'I'll get myself something later on.'

'It's no bother.'

'I'm fine, love, really . . .'

Thorne watched McCarthy's wife leave, wondering if she was simply playing the good wife for the sake of the visitor, and how things

326

were between the happy couple when there was nobody else around. If she had the remotest idea what her husband got up to in his spare time.

McCarthy waited for ten, fifteen seconds after the door had closed. 'I thought the whole thing was stupid,' he said. 'Worse than stupid.'

'By "the whole thing", you mean killing Amin Akhtar.'

The doctor nodded, slowly. 'It was all so . . . unnecessary.'

Just the man's choice of word made Thorne want to kick his face off, but he bit back the impulse, let him continue.

'Amin showed no sign whatsoever that he recognized me. Nothing, not a glimmer of it, in all those months. So why anyone else thought they might have been recognized, I don't know.'

'Anyone else meaning one man in particular.'

McCarthy nodded.

'He didn't want to take any chances,' Thorne said.

'I told the other two what I thought, that there was absolutely no need to take such a pointless risk, but my opinion clearly didn't carry the same weight as . . . some other people's.'

'And Simon Powell was happy enough to go along with it.'

'Not happy, exactly,' McCarthy said. 'Nobody was happy about it. But yes.'

Thorne thought about the man who, by the sound of it, had been orchestrating the trio's activities, both before and after the killing of Amin Akhtar. Who had led a conspiracy to murder first one boy, then another whose help had been enlisted in the killing of the first. Who was clearly a great believer in covering his tracks. Once again, Thorne asked himself what the chances were of finding Jonathan Bridges alive.

Did this man simply believe that he had that much more to lose than his friends? Or was he just that much more inhuman?

'When was the last time you talked to him?' Thorne asked.

McCarthy hesitated. 'Last night.'

'And when were you planning to see him next?' He saw the answer in McCarthy's face. 'Tonight? That's what's messing up wifey's plans for dinner, is it?'

'There's a party.'

McCarthy had only whispered it, but Thorne heard it loud and clear. There it was, the piece of luck that he was long overdue. He could not keep the grin from his face. 'Is Powell going as well?'

'I don't think so,' McCarthy said. 'Some of the parties, there's a different crowd.'

'Well don't worry, I'll make up the numbers.'

'What?'

'I'll tag along as your "plus one".'

McCarthy shook his head. 'No.'

Thorne dropped the jovial tone. 'Maybe we should just get your wife back in here, see what she thinks. Maybe she'd like to come along as well.'

McCarthy began to squeeze his hand again, muttered, 'Fuck, fuck, fuck ...'

'I don't know why you're so scared,' Thorne said. 'Because as things stand right this minute, *I'm* the one you need to be afraid of. You clear about that, Ian?'

McCarthy looked up. The smallest nod.

'Good. Glad we've got that sorted.' Thorne sat back and spread his arms along the back of the sofa. 'Like I said, been ages since I went to a decent party.' He took a sip of coffee and grinned. 'Might be quite an *adventure*.'

FIFTY-NINE

Kim Yates looked up from his 'extra-fiendish' sudoku and glanced across at the woman sitting a few feet away. She was concentrating on the same puzzle in her own puzzle book. He looked at his watch. He and Annette Williams had been working together as technicians for almost a year now, but it did not look as though either of them was likely to beat their personal best on this occasion.

Today, it was just going to be about who finished first.

In their headphones, from the speakers, the sounds of some drama or other. One of those set in a hospital. Bar a short exchange about tea – asked for by the hostage and curtly refused by the hostage taker – it had been nothing but television for the last hour or so.

Behind him, on the other side of the van, Yates was aware that the hostage negotiator had her nose buried in one of those magazines. *Hello!* or some rubbish. He knew what Annette would think about that.

He wondered if he should let her finish the sudoku first. Beating him would put her in a good mood and she might be more inclined to say yes if he finally plucked up the courage to ask her out for a meal. He would need to think carefully though. Taking the standings between them into account, the fact that he had now won six in a row, she was far too smart not to at least suspect that he had let her win, and her reaction to that could only really go one of two ways. Would she think he was being gallant, or patronising? Would she be angry with him? Or would she pretend to be offended, but only because she was secretly pleased?

Hell's bells, this was why he found women such a nightmare, he could never second-guess them.

He went back to the puzzle, filled in another couple of numbers.

Who was he trying to kid anyway? Like he was ever going to ask Annette out for a meal. Perhaps he should ask another woman what she thought. Yes, that was a sensible idea, he decided. Get a second opinion before deciding what to do next.

He would ask his mother when he got home.

Yates, Williams and Pascoe all looked up at the same time when the sound stopped suddenly. Magazines and puzzle books were pushed quickly aside.

'TV's off,' Pascoe said.

The two technicians made a few minor adjustments to the levels. All three listened. Pascoe looked back to where Donnelly was talking to Chivers in the playground, just beyond the back doors of the truck.

She shouted, 'Sir . . . '

Akhtar: *I think I have been very patient up to now, but I am running out of it. No more patience.*

More adjustments, to cope with the sudden increase in volume level from the hostage taker.

Weeks: *Please put the gun down, Javed—*

Akhtar: *I think I am being laughed at.*

Weeks: *That's really not true.*

Akhtar: *Inspector Thorne thinks I am a fool, that he can tell me this and that and string me along while I sit in here like an idiot making bloody tea! Well, that's enough.*

There was a pause. Half a minute. Donnelly and Chivers stepped up into the van.

Akhtar: *Does this have a camera on it?*

Donnelly looked at Pascoe as he grabbed a pair of headphones. She shook her head, no wiser than he was. They all listened, but for the next few minutes until Akhtar spoke again the only sounds were generated by Helen Weeks. A grunt as she shifted position, the rattle of metal handcuffs against the radiator pipe.

Akhtar: *There. Now we'll see.* Then, *Sorry about the smell.*

Weeks began to cough.

Akhtar: *I brought this. Should help a bit.*

There was a long hiss, then another. Donnelly looked at Pascoe.

'Aerosol,' she said.

Akhtar: *That's better.*

A few seconds later the television was switched on again. The channels were changed in rapid succession; music, football, canned laughter, before Akhtar – presuming it was Akhtar – finally settled on the same drama they had been watching a few minutes earlier. There were a few more coughs from Helen Weeks, then the sound of something – a remote control or possibly the gun – being dropped on to a table.

Then nothing.

'Hell was all that about?' Donnelly asked.

SIXTY

McCarthy told Thorne that there were perhaps a dozen different venues where the parties had been held, in the few years he had been in regular attendance. Locations and guest lists were confirmed last minute, he said. Despite having been to this particular place before, he had no idea who owned it, only that it would be an individual whose discretion could be relied upon absolutely. Someone who, because of their shared tastes and enthusiasms, was happy to entertain a few dozen high-flying professionals once every couple of months. Who would not mind too much if red wine, or anything else for that matter, got spilled on the soft furnishings.

Thorne craned his neck to look up. Thought, someone who's worth a good few million.

The venue for the evening's get-together could not have been any closer to the water. Housed within a sleek glass-and-silver crescent on the south side of the river between Battersea and Albert Bridges. Eleven storeys arcing back from the water's edge, with a horseshoe of duplex penthouses, light spilling from their tinted windows across a wraparound balcony.

'Nice place for it,' Thorne said.

'You're just trying to make it sound dirty,' McCarthy said. 'I'm not ashamed.'

'*What?*'

'Not of . . . the sex.'

Thorne turned in his seat, stared right at him. 'Listen, I don't care who you fuck, or how,' he said. 'Long as it's legal and you're not using anyone. Fact is though, Ian, I think it's all gone a bit beyond that, don't you?'

McCarthy said nothing, leaned his head against the window.

'I'm more concerned about you killing young boys than sleeping with them.'

Thorne had parked up on a narrow access road to the west side of the development. It was probably not a location mentioned on the estate agent's lavish description of the property. From the car, he could see no more than a dark sliver of Thames, and nothing at all of Chelsea Embankment twinkling on the other side of it, but he had a nice, unimpeded view of the entrance to the twenty-four-hour underground car park.

Since arriving fifteen minutes before, they had watched half a dozen cars turn in and drift slowly down the ramp. As many black cabs dropped passengers off at the main entrance. Now, another car approached. McCarthy checked, shook his head.

Thorne already knew what vehicle he was looking out for. 'He'd better be coming.'

'Why don't you just arrest him when he arrives?' McCarthy asked. 'Why do you need to go up there?'

'Because I want to walk in there and catch him sweating,' Thorne said. 'With his hands all over some fourteen-year-old. I want to see his face when he knows I've got him, same as I wanted to see yours. Then he's going to tell me the whole story. He's going to tell me *everything*, so I can tell Amin Akhtar's father.'

Through the rain on the windscreen, Thorne saw another pair of headlights emerge from the blackness. He watched as a dark-coloured Jaguar XJ slowed, and turned into the car park.

McCarthy nodded. 'That's him.'

Thorne could smell the fear coming off the man in the passenger seat, or perhaps it was something coming off himself. He could certainly taste the adrenalin in his mouth, the metallic tang in what little spit he was able to suck up. Tinfoil against his teeth.

He told McCarthy to stay where he was, and got out of the car. 'We'll give it a few minutes,' he said, before closing the car door. 'Let things get going a bit. No point being unfashionably early.'

Thorne jogged the twenty or so feet to the car that had driven in and parked opposite his own a few minutes after arriving. He climbed into the back of the unmarked Volkswagen Passat, then leaned forward between the front seats to talk to the two occupants.

'We're in business then,' Holland said. He too had recognised the number plate on the Jag, having pulled up all the necessary information from the Police National Computer several hours earlier, after Thorne had called him en route to Barndale. He had texted Thorne the details. The registration numbers for the Jaguar and the Audi Q7. The addresses of the flat in Marylebone and the weekend house in Sussex.

Yvonne Kitson turned from the passenger seat. 'So what's the plan?'

'I don't have one,' Thorne said.

'Making it up as you go along again?' Holland asked.

'Best way, I reckon.' Thorne told them that he would send McCarthy back out once he was safely inside. 'You hang on to him for me, and I'll call to let you know what's happening up there. If I need you for anything else. In the meantime, watch the exits and if anyone comes out of there before I'm finished, nick them.'

'Nick them for . . . ?'

'Anything you fancy.'

'What if we don't hear from you?' Kitson asked. 'How long do you want us to give it?'

'This won't take long,' Thorne said. 'I think the party's going to be winding down fairly soon after I get in there.'

As Thorne walked quickly back through the drizzle towards the

BMW, the message alert sounded on his mobile. He saw that he had been sent a text from Helen Weeks' phone. When he opened it, there was only an MMS attachment.

Unknown JPEG.

Thorne clicked to open the picture. Stopped and stared. He swallowed, wiping a finger across the small screen, and for a few seconds he could not be sure if it was rainwater he could feel creeping, slow and icy, down the back of his neck.

The gun went off for some reason, but nobody's hurt.

The image was slightly blurred, but Thorne could make out the waxy, bloated features well enough. The lips, pinched and so much paler than the rest of the face. The spatters of what looked like dried blood around the chin and neck, a few brown flecks near the hairline. It took him a few moments before he recognised the tattered scraps of shiny black that seemed to flutter around the head like bats' wings, but it made sense to him, once he had.

He was looking at a man he could only presume was Stephen Mitchell.

A dead face.

His body, wrapped in bin-bags.

Thorne took half a dozen steps towards the car, then turned and walked back again, his mind racing. Had Pascoe and Donnelly been sent the same image? If they had, then surely they would be calling to tell him. Thorne looked at the phone, waited half a minute . . . more, for it to ring.

He punched in the number for the RVP.

'Where are you?' Donnelly asked.

'I'm about to meet the man who organised the murder of Akhtar's son,' Thorne said. 'Actually, we've met before.'

'Well, quicker the better.'

'Something going on?'

'Akhtar's kicking off a bit,' Donnelly said. 'Waving the gun about, shouting about running out of patience.'

'What's Pascoe saying?'

'She's worried.'

'Tell her, when she speaks to him, to say that I'm getting exactly what he wanted. All the answers.' Thorne glanced up towards the shining half-moon of penthouses high above him, narrowed his eyes against the rain. 'Tell him this'll be finished tonight.'

'I hope so,' Donnelly said. 'And I *really* hope he listens. Chivers is getting decidedly jumpy, and I can't say I blame him.'

Thrusting the phone back into his pocket, Thorne walked back towards the car, asking himself why on earth Helen Weeks had not told those on the outside about the death of Stephen Mitchell. Was she simply being coerced into silence by the gun at her head? Or had she deliberately chosen to keep it quiet? As a police officer, she would have understood only too well how quickly a situation could escalate once there were fatalities. As a mother, she had more than just her own life to worry about. He remembered what Donnelly had just said about Chivers, and thought he could understand why Detective Sergeant Helen Weeks might have decided to say nothing.

Whatever the reason, now Thorne had done the same thing and kept the fact of a hostage's death from those running the operation. One more black mark against him, but it could not make things any blacker.

What else could he do?

Akhtar's kicking off a bit ...

Now, Thorne understood all too clearly that Javed Akhtar was not running out of patience. It had already been exhausted. The picture of Stephen Mitchell's body had been a simple enough message and one meant only for him.

Get a move on.

He reached the car and yanked open the passenger door. 'Let's go.'

McCarthy looked up at him. His face was pale and clammy under the sickly interior light. 'You said it was too early before. You said—'

'That was before,' Thorne said. 'And I've never been particularly fashionable.'

336

SIXTY-ONE

Donnelly had taken Thorne's call in the playground, shivering beneath a Met Police umbrella and helping himself to some slightly stale fruit cake from Teapot One as they had talked. Now, he walked quickly back to the TSU truck to relay Thorne's news. If they could contain the situation, keep the lid on things inside the newsagent's for just another couple of hours, then they might well see the result they all wanted before knocking-off time.

As soon as he climbed up into the truck, he could see that he had missed something.

'What?' he said.

Pascoe was pale, slumped in a chair. The two TSU technicians were looking at the floor. Chivers shook his head and said, 'Jesus.'

'I didn't think about it,' Pascoe said. 'It never even occurred to me.'

'*What?*' Donnelly asked again.

'She kept saying everything was fine.' Pascoe looked from Donnelly to Chivers. 'Every time I asked, she told me they were *all* doing fine. You heard.'

The sounds of the television in Akhtar's storeroom were still coming through the speakers. Donnelly asked the technicians to lower the

337

volume a little, then stepped across to Sue Pascoe. 'Exactly what didn't you think about, Sue? What never occurred to you?'

She looked at him.

The male technician – Yates – cleared his throat. 'Well, it was Annette who pointed it out.' He gestured towards the female technician sitting next to him; whip-thin with spiky black hair coloured red at the tips. He tentatively laid a hand on her shoulder. 'It was her idea, really.'

His colleague nodded and spoke quietly. 'I was just saying that we've been monitoring the conversations in there for about four hours now, and yes I know that the television's been on for a lot of the time and that nobody's said a great deal. It's just that in all that time we haven't heard anything from the second hostage. From Mr Mitchell.'

'Not a peep,' Yates said.

Donnelly stared at the speakers for a few seconds, as though willing Stephen Mitchell's voice to suddenly burst from them. 'Oh, Christ.' He turned and looked at Chivers.

'DS Weeks assured us that everything in there was fine.' Pascoe sounded as though she was talking to herself. 'Repeatedly.'

'You *told* us it was fine,' Donnelly said.

'Because I believed that it was.'

'All that guff about her voice being normal and no signs of coercion. "There isn't a problem," you said. That was your *professional opinion*, if I remember rightly.'

'That's the way I remember it, too,' Chivers said.

Pascoe looked as though the breath had been punched from her. 'This wasn't just me,' she stammered. 'Nobody else seemed too concerned about Mitchell.' She stood up, fumbling to straighten her jacket. 'It was not just me . . . '

Donnelly reached for a headset and threw it at Pascoe.

'Call her.'

SIXTY-TWO

Helen had been unable to say anything, to *do* anything but watch, when Akhtar had walked calmly away into the shop with her phone.

Does this have a camera on it?

She had fought to control her breathing as she thought about what he might be taking a picture of, struggled that little bit harder as she considered what he might be thinking of doing with such a photo. After a minute or so, she had finally managed to catch her breath and hold it. She had almost convinced herself she was being ridiculous, when the smell hit her and she knew that she had been right to worry.

He had torn open the bags.

Something like this had been coming for the last few hours, the signs had been clear enough. Or might have been, if she had been able to think clearly and focus for five minutes, if she had not been in such a state herself.

She suddenly remembered something Paul used to say. An expression he'd picked up somewhere.

Up and down like a whore's drawers.

He'd said it a lot – always in that comedy 'cockney wanker' voice he was so fond of – those first few months she'd been carrying Alfie.

When the hormone fairy arrived and the mood swings really kicked in.

She felt tears building and held her breath again, refused to let them rise.

She needed to concentrate . . .

It had been coming. Akhtar's hand on the gun, cradling it, the talk about being 'fobbed off'. Being 'ignored'. She had asked him for tea and he had snapped at her; her well-being or comfort no longer of any concern, no longer something worth worrying about. Not by him, at any rate.

And now he had done something stupid. Worse than stupid.

When he had finally come back in, apologising for the stink and squirting that air-freshener around, there had been this look on his face. Like he'd accomplished something. Triumphant, almost.

'There,' he had said. '*There*', like 'that'll show them' or 'now we'll see who gets fobbed off' and more than anything Helen had wanted to strike out hard and smash and claw at his face. To tear the smirk off and demand to know what the *fuck* he thought he was doing.

At that moment, she knew that she could hurt him.

She looked across at him. Sitting in his chair, his hand was on the revolver in his lap still, but his eyes were fixed happily on the television screen, as though he had done no more than simply cause a little mischief. Put the cat among the pigeons.

Helen knew that if Akhtar had sent a picture of Stephen Mitchell to anyone on the outside, there might not even be time to finish the programme he was watching.

She inhaled through her nose, so she would not have to taste it. The smell was still fierce, the cheap air-freshener no more than a top note, almost as sickening as the stench it was failing to mask. She breathed it in, because she had to.

Rotten meat and lemons.

SIXTY-THREE

McCarthy had punched in the code needed to access the private lift. It had been sent by text message the previous day. He and Thorne said nothing as the lift rose up towards the penthouse level, then just before they reached the top floor, McCarthy said, 'They're not always about the sex, you know?' He looked at Thorne. 'These parties. Sometimes it's just a question of meeting people and talking, without having to worry about what they're thinking. It's about having fun and not having to lie. You said it yourself this afternoon in my office. It's about being yourself.'

The doors opened.

'All very touching,' Thorne said. 'Except when "yourself" is nuts deep in an underage boy.'

The man who answered the door had the build of a nightclub bouncer, but his suit was somewhat better cut and Thorne doubted he ever had cause to turn people away for wearing trainers. He nodded his recognition at McCarthy then looked Thorne up and down.

'A guest,' McCarthy said.

The man at the door sniffed. 'Nobody said anything.'

'Sorry.' Thorne smiled. 'Should I have brought a bottle or something?'

'Oh come on, Graham, stop pissing around,' McCarthy said. 'He's with me, all right? And I'm gagging for a drink.'

In the hour and a half since McCarthy had told him about the party, Thorne had been thinking very carefully about the best way to get inside. To make his entrance. At this point of course, it would have been easy enough simply to produce a warrant card, to put a shoulder against the door and march inside shouting the odds. Thorne doubted very much that he would encounter a lot of resistance if he did, certainly none of an aggressive nature, but all the same he had decided on a rather more low-key approach. He wanted to walk in there with the not-so-good doctor and for it to be seen. He needed the man whose evening he was intent on spoiling to see clearly that the chain was broken and that McCarthy was *his*. To understand, as quickly as Thorne could engineer it, that no amount of wriggling was going to get anyone off the hook.

'Actually, Graham, we're both gagging for a drink,' Thorne said.

Graham rolled his eyes and stood aside. 'Enjoy . . . '

They laid their jackets down on a cowhide-covered chaise longue just inside the door. McCarthy took a glass of wine and Thorne helped himself to water from the tray proffered by a teenage boy with spiky black hair and pupils like piss-holes in the snow. Then they took three steps down into a large, open-plan living area.

Thorne smelled marijuana, amyl nitrate and aftershave.

Money . . .

The décor and furnishings reminded Thorne of Rahim Jaffer's flat and he wondered if it was all those evenings the young man had spent in places such as this that had given him a taste for the ultra-modern and expensive. Ironic, as they had certainly helped pay for it. Looking around – as though he were doing no more than admiring the art on the walls or the stylish light fittings – Thorne counted fourteen men in the room. Forty-ish and upwards and all dressed as though they had just come from one office or another, and while most had a drink in their hands, some had not yet been there long enough to loosen their ties.

There were at least the same number of boys.

While their prospective clients were just starting to relax and remained content to talk among themselves for a while, most of those who had been invited to provide a paid service did the same thing. They were gathered in twos and threes at the edges of the room. Whispering and giggling, moving in time to the low-level soft rock, or hovering near the long glass table where a cold buffet had been laid out.

Two distinct groups, for the time being.

There was plenty of eye contact though. Sizing-up being done on both sides. Sly looks and not so shy smiles.

The boys were white, black, Asian. A selection made deliberately, Thorne guessed, so as to appeal to all tastes. He wondered if the same consideration had gone into picking out the invitees according to their age. Thorne guessed that the majority were fifteen and up, but several were younger – or were at least trying to look younger – while two boys who stood close together near the food could not have been more than twelve.

Someone had probably agreed to pay a little more for them.

With McCarthy staying close to him as per instructions, Thorne wandered across the bleached-wood floor to stand near the vast windows that ran around half the room. A man with swept-back silver hair tapped a finger against the rain-streaked glass and nodded out.

'Shame about the bloody weather,' he said. 'Out on that balcony you get the most astonishing view.'

Thorne turned and leaned back against the glass, scanning the room.

The man nodded towards a skinny boy in a tight black vest who looked to Thorne as though he was not that long out of Spiderman pyjamas. 'Mind you, the view's pretty spectacular in here ...'

At that moment, Thorne got his first look at the man he was there for. He walked into the room from one of the two softly lit corridors running off on either side. Coming from the toilet, Thorne guessed, or perhaps a bedroom, though it did seem a little early for that. Thorne

343

watched the man help himself to a drink from another of the boys with the trays, then lean across, smiling at whatever the boy had said, to take something from the buffet. He popped the food into his mouth as he turned, and saw McCarthy.

He raised his glass and started walking towards them.

It took a few steps before the man got his first good look at Thorne, before the easy stride faltered, just a little. Thorne was impressed that he had been recognised so quickly. It had been eight months after all, and even then they had only been face to face for half an hour or so.

As long as it had taken for Thorne to give his evidence.

'Smashing party, your honour,' Thorne said.

The man stood close and stared hard at McCarthy, but McCarthy refused to meet the look, staring down instead into his wine glass. The man shifted his attention. Said, 'Thorne.'

Thorne was even more impressed that his name had been remembered. Then he realised that McCarthy would have been in regular contact with his colleague from the moment Thorne had turned up at Barndale two days earlier and begun asking questions. That the man in front of him was simply putting two and two together.

The quicker he made four, Thorne decided, the better.

'Your friend Dr McCarthy here has been great company,' Thorne said. 'And a *fascinating* storyteller.' He looked at McCarthy. 'You can toddle off now, Ian. My sergeant's waiting for you downstairs.'

McCarthy hesitated, but only for a second, and neither Thorne nor the other man bothered to watch him leave.

'So, who's waiting for me?' the man asked. 'Not a lowly sergeant, surely.'

The music got louder suddenly, and someone let out a whoop of excitement from the other side of the room.

Thorne did not blink.

'You're all mine,' he said.

SIXTY-FOUR

Helen Weeks' phone rang out. Ten seconds, fifteen. Twenty . . .

'They're not going to answer,' Chivers said.

'*They?*' Pascoe stared at him. 'What exactly do you think is going on in there?' Chivers started to answer, but Pascoe talked over him. 'Because two and something days is a bit quick for Stockholm Syndrome to have kicked in, you know what I mean?'

Twenty-five seconds.

'Neither the hostage nor the hostage taker is answering the phone,' Chivers said. 'I was stating a fact, that's all. There was no—'

The call was answered and, almost simultaneously, all five people inside the truck held their breath. Pressed hands to headsets. There were a few, crackly seconds of near-silence, then Helen Weeks said, 'Hello.'

'Helen, it's Sue Pascoe. I need to speak to Mr Mitchell.' Calm, but authoritative. The tone she reserved for particular types of crisis intervention.

'He's asleep.'

'I'm sorry, but you're going to have to wake him up.'

'Is there some sort of problem?'

'I need to speak to him *now*, Helen. I need to know that he's all right.'

There was a pause.

Chivers looked at Donnelly, turned his palms up.

'Helen?'

'Hang up now.' Akhtar's voice. Calm, but authoritative.

'It was an *accident*.'

'*Hang up!*'

The line went dead.

Pascoe removed her headset and dabbed fingers against the film of sweat on her ear. Donnelly and Chivers were already moving together towards the back doors, and their body language – their shoulders together, their heads low and close – made the manner of the conversation they were gearing up to have abundantly clear. Made it equally obvious that any further contribution from Pascoe would be entirely superfluous.

'Going in through the front isn't an option,' Chivers said.

'Right.' Donnelly began nodding.

'The shutters wouldn't be a problem, but we'd be too far away. He'd have too much time to react. The back door's the obvious entry point.'

'How long?'

'Best part of an hour to get set up. Forty minutes at a push.'

'So let's push it.'

Chivers jumped down from the back of the truck and immediately began shouting. Donnelly started talking to Pascoe. Something about how vital her role was going to be in this last hour or so, something about redeeming herself, but it took her a few seconds to focus. She was remembering something she had said to Tom Thorne.

The hostage is mine to lose.

And the nothing she'd had to say to Stephen Mitchell's wife.

346

SIXTY-FIVE

Looking at him, Thorne suddenly had a very clear image of His Honour Judge Jeffrey Prosser QC dressing before a trial. Transforming himself, enjoying the ritual. He pictured the man standing in front of a large mirror in his chambers, the smile widening and the blood rushing to his cock as he slipped on his purple robe and red sash. As he became empowered. The wig would be last of all, best of all. Stern and imposing suddenly, that blissful scratch of horsehair against the tender pink skin.

The smallest suggestion of punishment.

Bare-headed now and wearing a blue pinstripe, Prosser reminded Thorne of an old deputy headmaster he had not thought about in more than twenty years. A scrawny neck and sagging gut. Almost entirely bald, his face flushed with the effort those few stray tufts of grey were making in fighting their desperate rearguard action. Fierce, but ultimately ineffectual. The man Thorne remembered from school had made up for countless failings as a teacher with a manic adherence to a disciplinary regime that involved caning boys from eleven and upwards on a regular basis. Across the palm much of the time, but always the buttocks for the younger boys. Breathless by the end of it, and sweating.

Right, Thorne, now get out of my sight.

Thorne looked at Prosser. Perhaps the similarity was even closer than he had thought.

They had not moved from their positions near the window, except for Prosser stepping briefly across to a low glass table to set his tumbler down, after finishing his drink in two large gulps. Another half a dozen guests had arrived in the last few minutes and one or two of the boys had begun dancing together, showing themselves off to potential customers. The judge made no attempt whatsoever to disguise the fact that he was enjoying the show.

'I'm still not a hundred per cent sure why you've blundered into a private party without an invitation,' he said. 'One photograph is hardly going to give any of our friends at the CPS a hard-on, is it?'

'One photograph of you, Ian McCarthy and Simon Powell.'

'Whom I am not for one second denying that I know.'

'That's a good start.'

'I've dealt with Simon several times professionally and I met Ian socially a couple of years ago.'

'Somewhere like this.'

'I'm not disputing the fact that Ian, Simon and I were once at the same party.' He smiled. 'You have that photograph, so to do so would be ridiculous.'

'The person who took that photograph is willing to testify that Amin Akhtar was also at that party.'

'I go to a lot of parties,' Prosser said. 'I meet a lot of people.'

'I have a witness who puts you and Amin Akhtar at the same party just a few months before he was convicted. That's just a few months before you sentenced him to eight years in a Young Offenders Institution.'

'It's a small world.'

Thorne turned his head, nodded towards a man sharing a joint with a boy young enough to be his grandson. 'I bet *this* is. Same faces showing up all the time, I'd imagine. Same arses . . . '

'For God's sake—'

'Amin Akhtar.'

'It really means nothing.'

'Means everything if you had sex with him.'

'Now, I really don't see how you're going to prove *that*.'

A man in a cream shirt and brown velvet waistcoat approached and the smile indicated that he and Prosser clearly knew one another. He opened his mouth to speak, but Prosser shook his head, made it clear he was rather busy. The man raised his eyebrows and turned on his heel.

'McCarthy's not exactly playing hard to get any more,' Thorne said. 'He's made it very clear that he'll happily spill his guts in return for a nice bit of carpet in his cell, and there's no reason to believe that Powell is going to be any less of a pushover.'

'Thing is though, I'd like to hear it from *you*. Because you're the one it started with, that day eight months ago, when you looked up and saw Amin Akhtar in the dock in front of you. You're the one who made everything happen, the one who put the fear of God into your friends and called in a few favours ... so *you're* the one who's going to confess.' He leaned in close to Prosser. 'So that *I* can tell the father of the boy you had killed.'

'You're welcome to lie to him,' Prosser said. 'If you really think that will help.'

Thorne's mobile rang in his pocket. He dug it out and saw who was calling. It must have been obvious from his expression that it was a call he needed to take.

Prosser took two steps away, then turned. 'Don't worry, I'm not making a run for it,' he said. He picked up his empty glass from the table and waggled it at Thorne. 'Just getting a top-up ...'

'Just thought you ought to know,' Pascoe said, 'Donnelly's authorised a dynamic entry.'

'What's happened?'

There was the smallest of pauses, an intake of breath. 'We've got every reason to believe that Stephen Mitchell is dead.'

Every reason. So now Thorne knew for sure that they had not been sent the picture, that the RVP team had found out about the hostage's death in some other way. All the same, he could hardly admit that he had known and said nothing. 'That gunshot on the first night.'

'We don't know what happened,' Pascoe said. 'We can only assume that Weeks had no choice but to pretend everything was normal. I should have sussed there was something wrong, but I didn't.'

'You blaming *yourself* for this?'

'I fucked up.'

'How long until they go in?' Thorne asked.

'Under an hour.'

Thorne watched Prosser filling his glass. Still smiling.

'Where are you?'

Thorne told her, his eyes on Prosser as the judge walked back across the living room, moving calmly through a gaggle of partygoers. A nod and a wink to someone he recognised, something whispered, a hand laid on an arm. Watching, Thorne recalled how Ian McCarthy had reacted to those initial accusations. The doctor had tried to appear confident and fearless, but the anxiety had been all too obvious and Thorne had been able to smell the man's weakness, sharp as disinfectant.

Prosser, though, seemed genuinely unafraid of anything.

'Tom?'

'I'm still here,' Thorne said.

'Well anyway, I just thought you should know. If there's anything you might have that could persuade Akhtar to give up and walk out of there before Chivers and his mates go crashing in, you need to get back here with it on the hurry-up ...'

When Thorne had hung up, he walked across and took hold of Prosser by the arm.

Making it up as you go along again?

Prosser tried to pull away, but Thorne dug his fingers into the flab of the judge's forearm.

Thinking about the promise he'd made to Javed Akhtar.

The assurances he'd given Helen Weeks.

He prised the heavy tumbler from Prosser's hand, wondering – just

350

for a second – how it would feel to smash it against the table and grind the jagged edge into the mottled flesh of the man's neck. He set it down and guided Prosser none too gently towards the door.

'Hell are we going?' Prosser demanded, still trying to wrench his arm from Thorne's grip.

Thorne dug his fingers in harder.

He called Holland as soon as they were in the lift and told him that they were going to be swapping vehicles. Unlike his own car, the Passat was fitted with Blues and Twos and Thorne guessed that the siren might save him a few precious minutes. He told Holland and Kitson to call up a van, to make it two. He told them to get straight up to the penthouse party and start nicking people for fun.

Then he turned to Prosser.

'How do you feel about restorative justice?'

SIXTY-SIX

'I haven't been telling you the truth,' Helen said. 'Not that I've been lying, exactly, just not telling the truth, and I want to be honest. Here . . . like this. I need to be honest.'

Since they had called and demanded to speak to Mitchell, Akhtar had been prowling back and forth like one of those creatures in a zoo that have gone slightly mad. From storeroom to shop and back again. As though it were only a question of which way they were going to come for him.

Now, he stopped and stood a few feet in front of her, holding the gun.

Waiting.

'I can't say for certain that Paul was Alfie's father,' Helen said. 'That's it, basically.' She looked up at him. 'That's the truth of it. I know I've been talking as though he is, and that's the way I always talk, even to myself, but the fact is I can't be certain. Paul wasn't certain either, which was why things were so difficult between us when he was killed. He died not knowing one way or another.'

Akhtar backed slowly away until he reached the desk and lowered himself on to the chair. 'Why are you telling me these things?'

'I don't really know,' she said.

Why was she telling a man who had threatened to kill her, knowing full well that at the same time she was announcing it to whoever was listening in on the outside? Why did she feel the need suddenly to get this stuff off her chest? Did she really think she would absolve herself?

Because she knew that Akhtar was right and it was only a question of how and not when they would be coming in. Because although the men with the guns would do everything they could to avoid discharging their weapons and to keep her safe, things did not always go according to plan. Because people got over-excited and accidents happened.

Because she did not want to die without saying it.

'Because I need to tell someone,' she said.

Akhtar looked at her, cocked his head slightly. He rested the gun on his knee, the barrel pointing towards her. 'I am a newsagent,' he said. 'Not a priest.'

Helen's impulse was to smile back, but her mouth could do no more than say the words. Her tongue felt thick and heavy and her heart was thundering against her chest.

'I met a man on a course,' she said. 'A firearms officer, of all things. Right now, I'd be seriously thinking that he might be one of the ones out there with a gun in his hand, except that he moved away, after what happened to Paul . . .

'It was a fling, that's all. Stupid. Just half a dozen times in some hotel or other and I'm not saying that as any kind of excuse. I still did what I did, and at the time I wanted to do it. He was everything Paul wasn't, in all sorts of ways. I enjoyed it, I enjoyed being wanted that much. I'm just saying that I never actually thought about leaving Paul, that's all. He was the one who talked about leaving, when he found out. It was awful for a while and things never got back to how they'd been before, but we decided we were going to carry on.

'For the baby's sake.

'Things were said when it all came out. I'm sure I don't have to tell you. Horrible things, but I knew he was only saying them because he'd been hurt and because he wanted to hurt me back. I was happy to take whatever he was dishing out, because I knew I deserved it, and I thought everything would be all right because of the baby. I just kept telling myself that it would all be OK once the baby came along.

'After Paul was killed, guilt was one of the things that made me so desperate to find out what had happened. The main thing, if I'm honest. Just like I'd been kidding myself about the baby solving all our problems, I told myself that if I found out what had happened to Paul, if I found out the truth, I might feel a bit less guilty about what I'd done to him.

'Like I say, kidding myself.'

Helen was leaning back with her head against the radiator, her eyes fixed on a space a few feet above Akhtar's head, and she did not see him grimace and look away.

SIXTY-SEVEN

However unafraid Prosser might have appeared at the party, it was clear from his face, from the occasional whimper that escaped his lips, that he was a little less bullish when it came to being driven at seventy miles an hour through the dark of busy urban streets, with rain lashing against the windscreen, a siren wailing and a blue light flashing on the roof.

'You're a bit pale,' Thorne said. 'A bit quiet.'

Prosser turned to him. His left hand was braced against the dashboard and his right held tight to the seatbelt across his chest. 'I'm just trying to decide which lawyer I'm going to get to tear you a nice new arsehole.' He did his best to smile. 'Professionally speaking, of course.'

Thorne drove away from the river, pushing the Passat south on Battersea Bridge Road. In regular traffic, on a good day, they were no more than twenty-five minutes from Tulse Hill. The traffic was bad thanks to the rain, but with the blue light and the siren clearing the way Thorne was hopeful that they would make it in fifteen minutes or less.

'I spoke to Amin Akhtar's lawyer,' Thorne said, raising his voice to be heard above the siren.

'Congratulations.'

'He reckoned they had a good shot at winning the appeal. Getting the ridiculous sentence you handed out reduced. That can't have been good news.'

'Neither good nor bad,' Prosser said. 'It would have been the decision of another judge. I remain happy with the sentence I gave.'

'I bet you do.'

'A sentence that the law fully entitled me to pass. You should remember that.'

'Akhtar's lawyer told me he had grounds to pursue you for professional misconduct.'

'That's ridiculous.'

'For ignoring all the statements made about Amin's good character, the circumstances of his offence. For all that rubbish about "dangerousness" you peddled to the jury.'

'He stabbed a boy to death.'

'Bollocks,' Thorne said. 'The only person Amin was dangerous to was you.' He tore past a van that had been slow to pull over, swung the wheel to the left and accelerated into the bus lane. 'God, I'd love to be back in that courtroom. See your face when you got your first look at that boy in the dock. I'm betting you went as white as your fucking wig.'

Prosser sighed. 'I did not recognise the boy, because I had never seen him before. You see how that works?'

'Despite having been at a party with him. At least one party.'

'If you say so.'

'Or perhaps it was just that you didn't recognise him from the front.' Thorne was thrilled to see a flash of anger from Prosser, a glimpse of small white teeth biting down on his fat lower lip. 'Then again, it might have been the name that you recognised. I hadn't really thought about it until now, and I don't know if rent boys are in the habit of using their real names, but I suppose Amin might have done. I mean do *you* use your real name?' He looked at Prosser, shook his head. 'No, I doubt it very much. Do you have a special name you like to use when you're letting your hair down? A secret identity? Or do you just like the boys to call you "your honour" while you're fucking them?'

Thorne slowed to fifty around the one-way system at the southern corner of Battersea Park, then let the needle climb as he followed the Latchmere Road towards Clapham. The rain had worsened. Through the beating wipers, the brake lights and indicators of the vehicles in front were no more than smears of orange and red.

'You were probably putting it together before the trial had even finished,' Thorne said. 'The perfect three-part solution to your awkward little problem and the three perfect people to carry out the plan. Yes? Had it all worked out by the end of the first day, I reckon.' Another quick glance across at his passenger got no response. He shrugged. Thorne had never done a high-speed driving course and he told Prosser as much, then winced as he put his foot down and took the car across a busy junction on red.

'Jesus,' Prosser whispered.

'Once you've put Amin away for as long as you can get away with, it's just a question of making sure he gets sent to the right place. So that's where our friend Mr Powell at the Youth Justice Board comes in. He's the only one of the three musketeers I haven't had the pleasure of meeting yet, but it won't be long because he'll have been picked up by now. Probably sitting in an interview room next door to Dr McCarthy, while my sergeant takes bets on which one of them is going to start blubbering and shooting off his mouth first . . .

'Who would your money be on?'

Prosser's eyes were closed, the skin tight around his mouth.

'So . . . your friend Powell allocates Amin to Barndale, which conveniently happens to be the Young Offenders Institution where your mutual friend Dr McCarthy is the chief medical officer. Which means you can *watch* him. Because that's really what it's all about. Keeping an eye on the boy, making sure he says nothing, does nothing. Making sure there's one of you on the spot if he so much as hints at the fact that he sussed you out in that courtroom and knows exactly what the three of you get up to in your spare time.

'And it works. It all works very nicely until the boy decides he wants to do some course which isn't available at Barndale, which means he needs to be transferred. Which means you won't be able to watch him any more. Powell tries to block it, but the governor insists because he's trying to do the best thing for Amin ... and now you're in trouble. So, you decide to do what you would probably have done later on anyway when it was time for Amin to move into an adult prison. That's when you give McCarthy his orders and he puts a nice little plan of his own together with a couple of boys who are happy to earn some money before they get out. That's when he gives Jonathan Bridges a syringe.

'That's when you actually had Amin Akhtar killed,' Thorne said. 'But he was as good as dead the moment he walked into your court-room, wasn't he?'

Prosser shifted in his seat and looked at Thorne. 'I've got it.'

'Got what?'

'The name of that lawyer,' Prosser said. 'He's expensive, but it'll be worth it just to see you reduced to helping old ladies across the road.'

Thorne's knuckles whitened on the wheel and he nudged the Passat up to eighty on the long, straight road that crossed Clapham Common. Fifty yards ahead, a pedestrian beneath an umbrella was hesitating at a zebra crossing and though the lights and the siren were still going, Thorne leaned on the horn for good measure.

'Do you know what's really ironic?' Thorne asked. 'I don't think Amin would ever have said anything, because he didn't *know* anything. The simple, stupid fact is he didn't recognise you. You were just another punter he wanted to forget as quickly as possible. He never said a word to McCarthy, he never said a word to his long-term boyfriend at Barndale, he never said a word to anybody. He was just a seventeen-year-old boy keeping his head down and trying to do his time. He wasn't even the one that took that bloody photograph! I don't suppose we'll ever know for sure if you and your friends knew that photo existed, but even if you did ... even if it was one more reason why you thought you should get rid of Amin Akhtar, you got your Asian rent boys mixed up. Easily done, I appreciate that. You got the *wrong Paki.*'

'Oh for pity's sake—'

'You didn't need to kill him.'

Thorne blasted across the South Circular and pointed the car towards Brixton Hill. They were no more than a few minutes away.

'Where are we going anyway?' Prosser asked.

'You know exactly where we're going,' Thorne said. 'Thing is, I've never been a big believer in the whole restorative justice thing, but some people genuinely believe that when the perpetrator and the victim ... or in this case the victim's family ... come face to face, it can be hugely beneficial for both parties. On top of which, statistics suggest that it lowers the chances that the perpetrator will reoffend. Not really an issue as far as you're concerned, obviously.'

'You're wasting your time.'

'I don't care.'

'You should,' Prosser said. 'Because you don't have a great deal left. Not at your current pay grade anyway.'

Thorne turned to look hard at the judge for a few seconds longer than was strictly safe, all things considered. Long enough to see the blood begin to drain from Prosser's face. Then he turned his eyes back to the road. 'Listen, we've already established that Powell and McCarthy aren't very likely to tough it out and there's certainly no reason why either of them would want to do you any favours. Your two *co-defendants*, and I'm calling them that because that's what they're going to be soon enough, will roll over as quickly as one of those party boys when a punter starts waving his wallet around. So, my advice would be that you seriously consider your position at this point. Because, other than every effort I can possibly make to ensure you don't get within a hundred miles of a Vulnerable Prisoner unit, and that every hard case on your wing knows exactly who you are and which of their friends and relations, if any, you've put away ... I really don't see what else you've got to gain by being such a smartarse. Your honour.'

Prosser nodded, mock-impressed. 'Excellent speech, Inspector,' he said. 'Perhaps if you were to put that much effort in when you're giving evidence, a few less scumbags would get off.'

'One less will do for now,' Thorne said.

SIXTY-EIGHT

'They tried to give me an epidural when I was giving birth to Alfie, but they couldn't get the needle in and in the end it was like I just *screamed* him out.' Helen's fists were clenched as she remembered, her jaw tight as she lived through the agony again, but something soft all the same around her eyes. 'The pain felt pretty good in the end, can you understand that?'

Akhtar nodded.

'It felt honest. Like it was the only honest thing I had felt in a long time. It felt *earned*.' She took a breath and stretched out her fingers, used one to dam the tears just for a second.

'And he was ... perfect, you know? Whatever, whoever had made him, he was just this perfect little boy and it made everything else, all the horrible things and the hurtful things, seem unimportant. So I just got on with it. I found a new flat, and it was just the two of us twenty-four hours a day, and sometimes I'd look right into his eyes and I'd tell him he looked just like his dad. I'd be telling myself he was Paul's, because I wanted it so much. Because he had to be. Because that would be the fairest thing. Telling myself or telling other people that he had Paul's nose or his mannerisms or whatever else, and it was nothing but a lovely, stupid lie, because there'd be other times when I'd look at him and he looked nothing like Paul at all.

'When he wasn't so perfect.'

She reached across to rub at the wrist of her left hand, where the handcuff had taken away the skin. It had become a tic. 'There's other people that know. My sister and my dad. They know what happened and they know it was just before I got pregnant, and I know damn well they've wondered about who Alfie's father was. But nobody says anything. They just carry on as if I've got a husband or a boyfriend who's working in another country or something, or else my sister's trying to get me fixed up with some sad case that nobody else wants.' She shrugged, and for just a moment there was the hint of laughter, somewhere low in her throat. 'Nobody ever . . . talks about Paul. Only very occasionally, when they forget themselves or one of my sister's kids says something and even then it's like he's just some private joke. Like he's somebody I've made up. That's what makes everything so much worse . . . that hateful, pathetic fear of embarrassment, of saying something awkward, and I'm just as bad as they are, because I'm too embarrassed to tell them how shitty and awful it's making me feel. To tell them that sometimes it seems as if Paul can't possibly be Alfie's dad, because he was never there at all.

'I'm scared,' she said, quietly.

'I'm sorry,' Akhtar said.

'No, not just about all this. I'm scared about what I'm going to say to my son when he's old enough to want to know who his father was. I'm scared to find out the truth.'

Akhtar looked at her. 'There is some way to find out?'

'Paul was a copper, same as me. So his DNA's on record. I could get a test done, but I don't know what I'd do if it wasn't the right result.'

'Would it really be so bad?'

'I know there are worse things.' She looked at him. 'I know there are, but second to anything happening to Alfie, this would be my worst thing.'

361

'Thorne told me yesterday that I should prepare myself for the truth,' Akhtar said. 'He told me that it might not be particularly pleasant. Well, I can only say to you what I said to him. You have suffered, same as I have, and you must surely realise that the truth, however unpleasant, cannot compare to that sort of pain. That it can only make things more bearable in the long run.' He stood up slowly. 'Ignorance is not bliss, Helen. Trust me on that. Ignorance is torment.' He took a few steps towards the shop, then stopped and cocked his head towards the sound of a siren that was quickly growing louder.

Less than ten feet from where Javed Akhtar was standing – outside, on the rutted, overgrown path that snaked from a crumbling block of garages to the rear of the premises – Chivers was watching as his method-of-entry specialist knelt in the mud and carefully laid the last of the explosive charges at the base of the back door.

Five minutes from a 'go'.

Once the charges were in position, Chivers would brief each member of his team once more on the action plan. Each would have a specific function to carry out. One that would hopefully last no more than a few seconds, but which would prove crucial as part of a six-man operation and upon which their own lives as well as the lives of those in the building would depend.

The ballistic shield officer.

The baton officer.

The 'cover' officer.

The prison reception officer, responsible for handling the hostage taker until such time as he could be taken into custody.

The dog handler.

Following that final briefing, there would be a last-minute equipment check. Helmets, goggles, earplugs and body armour. All rifles, handguns and Tasers. The CS canisters and the 8-Bang stun grenades designed to create as much noise and chaos as possible, to distract and disorient the hostage taker in those first few seconds after breaching had been effected. A faulty bit of kit would always be a firearms officer's worst nightmare and with good reason. Chivers firmly believed that his men had been well trained and that equipment failure was far more likely than any human error.

Sadly, the same could not be said for others on the operation. There would certainly be an inquiry into why it had taken a trained hostage negotiator the best part of two days to notice that one of her hostages was dead.

Chivers doubted he'd be seeing DS Susan Pascoe again.

He had not even been aware of the siren until it became clear that it was somewhere very close. He immediately moved back towards the garages, well away from the earshot of anyone behind the door and called Donnelly on the radio.

'What's happening, Mike?'

'I don't believe this.'

The rain was noisy against his helmet, his body armour. 'Say again.'

'He's come right through the fucking cordon, almost took out a couple of the uniforms.'

'Who?'

'Thorne. Listen, Bob, you'd better hold off for the time being and get yourself and your lads back round to the front . . .'

SIXTY-NINE

As Thorne got out of the car and jogged around to the passenger side, he was forced to shield his eyes against the glare from a cluster of powerful arc lights that had been arranged on the pavement opposite the shop. In front of them was a line of emergency vehicles – ARVs, ambulances, rapid response cars – behind which the CO19 officers had taken up their firing positions earlier on.

Thorne's phone began to ring, but he knew very well who was calling.

He opened the door and dragged Prosser out. The light, bouncing back from the metal shutters of Akhtar's shop, washed across the judge's face, worsened its already sickly pallor. Thorne pushed him back against the side of the car. He pressed the flat of one hand hard into Prosser's chest, then answered his phone with the other.

'Mike.'

'What the hell do you think you're doing?'

'I've got what Akhtar wanted, so you can stand the CO19 boys down.'

'Who's that with you?'

Thorne guessed that Donnelly and the rest of the team were

gathered in the TSU vehicle, watching him on the monitors that carried the CCTV feed. He squinted up through the rain and stared straight at the camera mounted high on a lamppost on the opposite side of the road. 'This is the man who killed Akhtar's son,' he said. 'Who *arranged* for him to be killed.' He turned back to Prosser and looked him in the eye. 'He's the reason we're all here.'

'You need to move away from the shop, Tom.'

'I'm taking him inside,' Thorne said.

'Don't be ridiculous.'

'It makes about as much sense as sending Chivers and his mates in.'

'We'll talk to Akhtar,' Donnelly said. 'You tell him you've done what he asked. You tell him you've got the individual responsible for his son's death in custody and he walks out of there.'

'Never going to happen,' Thorne said. 'He doesn't trust us enough. He doesn't trust *me* enough.' He heaved Prosser away from the car and marched him towards the newsagent's. Just before he dropped the phone into his pocket, he heard Donnelly shout, 'Stay where you bloody well are.'

Thorne pushed Prosser back against the shutters, then began hammering at them, his fist smashing against the dirty metal, no more than a few inches from Prosser's face. He shouted, 'Javed, it's Tom Thorne. I'm out here with the man you asked me to find.' He banged again, Prosser flinching at every blow. 'Javed . . .'

He waited for a few seconds. He pressed his ear to the metal.

Looking up at the sound of footsteps to his left, he saw Chivers and five CO19 officers emerge at speed from the entrance to a small alleyway three shops down. They slowed when they caught sight of him and, after grabbing a ballistic shield from one of them, Chivers waved his team back behind the line of vehicles where they stood, looking somewhat bemused, waiting for orders. None the wiser himself, Chivers stayed where he was, in the middle of the road, thirty feet or so away from Thorne and Prosser.

Behind the shutters, Javed Akhtar said, 'I'm here.'

Chivers and Thorne both turned at the sound of more footsteps and watched as Donnelly, Pascoe and half a dozen others came running from the direction of the school towards the main road. All except Donnelly stopped at the line of arc lamps. He carried on that little bit further forward into the road, before stopping just a few feet away from Chivers.

A few feet behind him.

'Mr Thorne?'

'I've got him with me right now, Javed.' Thorne leaned close to the shutters. 'If I bring him in there, you have to promise me that once you have heard exactly what happened to Amin, you will give yourself up. No questions asked, OK?'

'I can't allow you to take a civilian in there, Thorne.' Donnelly was still struggling to get his breath back as he shouted. 'Not while Akhtar still has a loaded weapon. What are you thinking?'

'Not up for discussion,' Chivers said. 'Simple as that.'

The civilian in question, who up until now had remained relatively passive, suddenly became animated and began shouting. 'My name is Jeffrey Prosser, QC, and if you're the officer in charge you need to put a stop to this *now*.' Thorne pushed him back against the shutters and told him to shut up. Prosser struggled and shouted his name out again.

'Is this man under arrest?' Donnelly asked.

'No, I am not,' Prosser shouted. 'I have not been arrested, I have not been cautioned. This is kidnapping, plain and simple.'

The rain was heavier suddenly, hissing against the lamps.

From behind the shutters, Javed Akhtar said, 'The judge? My God, is it the *judge*?'

'Give the gun to Helen,' Thorne said. 'Give it to Helen and I can bring him in.'

'Wait,' Akhtar said.

The blue light was still flashing on top of the Passat and Thorne felt it move across his face every few seconds. He watched it dance across the windows of the cars opposite and the automatic weapons of the men crouched between them.

From further back inside the shop, Thorne heard the voice of Helen

Weeks. 'I've got the gun.' There was a pause and then she shouted it a second time.

Thorne turned to look at Donnelly and Chivers. 'Did you get that?'

'Changes nothing,' Chivers said.

Donnelly said, 'Hang on.'

'I want Nadira,' Akhtar shouted. 'I want my wife to hear this too.'

'No chance,' Chivers said.

Thorne turned back to Donnelly. 'Helen has the gun, Mike. What's the problem?'

Donnelly considered it for a few seconds, then brought a radio to his mouth and gave the order. Within a minute, a panda car was screaming down from the school gates and, when it had stopped near the line of emergency vehicles, a WPC helped a shaken-looking Nadira Akhtar from the passenger seat. She wore a headscarf embroidered with something that caught the light, and was all but lost inside a Met Police-issue quilted anorak.

Thorne called out to her.

When she looked over at him, Thorne waved and beckoned her across the road, nodding his encouragement as she took the first tentative steps towards him. 'There's nothing to worry about, Nadira . . . it's going to be all right. We're going to go inside together and bring Javed out.' The woman smiled nervously as she drew nearer to the shop, then Thorne saw the slow wash of recognition across her face. The confusion that quickly became alarm when she got to within a few feet of the man Thorne still had pinned to the shutters.

'I don't understand.' She pointed. 'Why is that man here?'

'He's going to tell Javed how Amin died,' Thorne said. He tightened his grip on Prosser's collar. 'He's going to tell both of you.'

Nadira shook her head slowly and continued to stare, and from behind the shutters, Akhtar called his wife's name.

'I'm here, Javee,' she said.

'OK, Javed . . . when I say so, you need to unlock the door to the shop and open it. Then you're going to raise the shutters.' Thorne became aware of Chivers and Donnelly whispering behind him and he could guess what was being suggested and by whom. If Akhtar no longer had the gun, then there was nothing to stop them rethinking their action plan on the spot. No reason not to . . . improvise a little. If the shutters were going to be raised, it would be relatively easy for Chivers to get in there and overpower Akhtar single-handed. One CS canister or an 8-Bang chucked in as soon as those shutters started to go up . . . job done.

'Just a few feet, all right, Javed?'

Behind him, the hissed exchange was becoming more heated.

'No need to open them any more than that. Then move back into the shop. Have you got that?'

Thorne turned and was relieved to see Donnelly raising his hands and Chivers shaking his head in frustration. He pulled Prosser away from the shutters, keeping one eye on the officers behind him.

'All right, Javed, off you go.' Thorne heard the key in the lock, then the sound of the bell as the door was opened behind the shutters. 'Right, open them up . . . '

The mechanised growl was painfully loud up close, but it took only a few seconds until the gap was big enough. Thorne banged and shouted, 'That's enough,' and the shutters juddered to a halt. He turned and nodded once to Donnelly then carefully helped Nadira to bend underneath. Once she was inside, he pushed Prosser down and followed him. Ducking quickly under the shutters, he heard Donnelly shout, 'Five minutes, that's all. If you're not out of there, we go back to the original plan.' Chivers shouted something after that, as Thorne stood up and his eyes began to adjust to the semi-darkness of Javed Akhtar's shop, but it was drowned out by the grind of the shutters coming down again and clanging shut behind him.

SEVENTY

It was the smell that hit everybody first.

Thorne moved across to Nadira who was leaning against the wall, moaning gently, a hand clamped tight across her mouth. He rubbed her back, shushed her like a baby. Then he walked across to Prosser. The judge had dropped to his knees the second he was clear of the shutters and stayed that way. He coughed and retched, his arms braced against the shop window and a string of drool running from his chin to his chest.

Thorne leaned back against the door.

'You'll never forget that smell,' he said. 'Never. And other people will smell it on you, long after you've left this shop, long after you think you've washed it off even. Because you'll actually absorb it . . . particularly through your hair and fingernails apparently. Believe me, for the next few days, you'll belch it and fart it and *breathe* it.' He leaned down. 'And I think that's only right and proper, considering. Don't you?'

He lifted Prosser to his feet, spun him around and pushed him towards the rear of the shop. Ahead, Thorne could see the figure of Javed Akhtar, waiting, in semi-silhouette behind the counter. Nadira was a few steps behind as they walked towards her husband.

369

The shop had been torn apart.

They moved cautiously, negotiating a mess of scattered magazines, sweets and crisps, the debris of tinned food and broken bottles. They stepped over the fridge which was lying on its side and were careful to avoid slipping on the small puddles of melted ice cream and sodden newspapers underfoot. The body of Stephen Mitchell lay close to the counter. The tattered black bin-bags in which it had been wrapped were submerged in shadow and only the face was clearly visible where the thin plastic had been torn open to reveal it.

'In here,' Akhtar said.

He nodded towards the room behind him. He held out an arm as if welcoming them to a drinks party or inviting a select group of friends into a well-appointed sitting room.

Thorne shoved Prosser through the doorway and followed. It took him no more than a few seconds to take in the tiny room. To his left, a desk and chair, assorted boxes, a sink and a small fridge, a kettle, a television. Ahead, the back door with a filing cabinet pushed against it, a small toilet.

He looked to his right, and nodded down to Helen Weeks.

A stupid thought: *her hair's different.*

He saw the blood on the floor and guessed that this was where Stephen Mitchell had died, the brown streak on the linoleum where the body had been hauled from the room.

'I don't understand what's happening,' Helen said.

'This'll only take a minute,' Thorne said.

Helen was holding the gun in her right hand. She lifted her left and rattled the cuff against the radiator pipe. 'The key's on the desk,' she said.

Thorne half turned to look for it, but his attention was seized by a loud *crack* from the doorway just behind him. He wheeled round to see Nadira Akhtar slap her husband again, the noise even louder this time, crying out with the effort of it. There was a fine spray of spittle as Akhtar's head snapped to the side. He righted it slowly and closed his eyes, then began to mutter something soft in Hindi as his wife stepped weeping into his outstretched arms and he eased her into the room with him.

The storeroom was crowded suddenly and though close proximity to the others in the room was unavoidable, people quickly did whatever they could to find themselves another few inches of space. Helen pulled her knees up to her chest, while Akhtar pushed the camp bed to one side so that he and his wife could stand against the rack of metal shelves at the far end of the room. Prosser had pressed himself against the back door, but Thorne dragged him away and stood him in the middle of the room, facing the Akhtars.

'Centre stage,' he said.

'This is stupid,' Prosser said. There was a laugh in his voice, but it was nervous, and he had not once looked at Javed or Nadira Akhtar.

'Wait,' Thorne said.

He took the key from the desk, knelt to unlock the handcuffs, then slowly helped Helen to her feet. She rubbed at her wrist, nodded that she was all right and leaned back against the wall above the radiator.

Thorne stepped up close to Jeffrey Prosser.

'Why is he here?' Nadira asked. The tears seemed to have stopped, but every third or fourth breath was catching. 'What's he got to do with what happened to Amin?'

Thorne dug an elbow into Prosser's ribs. Said, 'I'll kick things off, shall I, your honour? And you can chip in whenever you feel like it.' He looked at Akhtar. 'You need to know that your son was gay, Javed.'

'No.' Akhtar was shaking his head before Thorne had finished speaking, as though he had guessed at least something of what was coming. He wagged a finger. 'That is not true.'

'Yes, Javee, it is,' Nadira said. She took hold of her husband's hand and began to rub the back of it. 'Amin was how he was and it was fine. So you have to be quiet now, my love, OK? You have to shut up and listen to the rest of it.'

Akhtar blinked quickly and picked at a button on his shirt. He looked a lot thinner than the man Thorne had last seen on the steps of the Old Bailey eight months before. He was red-eyed and unshaven, his face almost grey.

'That was why he and Rahim were attacked,' Thorne said. 'They were coming from a gay bar. And sometimes they would go to parties, where older men would pay them. Pay to be with them.'

Akhtar moaned, low in his throat. Nadira gripped her husband's hand a little tighter.

'I'm sorry, but I said this would be difficult,' Thorne said. 'I warned you.'

'It's fine,' Akhtar said. He nodded, drew back his shoulders. 'Go on.'

Thorne nodded towards Prosser. 'Men like him.'

'He knew Amin?'

'Yes, he knew him.'

Akhtar looked at Prosser. 'You knew my son? *Before?*'

Prosser said nothing.

'He recognised him at the trial,' Thorne said. 'And he thought, wrongly as it turned out, that Amin had recognised him too. So, he conspired with the man responsible for deciding where Amin would serve his sentence, and the doctor at Barndale, and when he discovered that Amin was going to leave, he decided it would be safer to have him killed. They came up with a plan to make it look as though your son had killed himself.'

Akhtar's mouth opened slowly and hung there, as though the muscle that controlled it was no longer working.

'So,' Thorne said.

Nadira sighed and nodded. 'Thank you,' she said.

'This . . . *man.*' Akhtar took half a step towards Prosser, and Thorne could clearly see the pulse ticking at his neck. He could see the tremor that had taken hold suddenly in the man's hands and legs, as though a switch had been thrown and a current had begun to pass through him. 'This man who I put my faith in. This man who was the *law.*' He moved closer still to the judge and yanked his hand free from his wife's. 'My son was murdered in prison, because this man had been to a party . . . given him money.'

'The other two men are already in custody,' Thorne said. 'And all three of them will go to prison for a long time.' He could see that Akhtar was not really listening, that his eyes had not moved from Prosser's face. 'Javed . . .'

'Amin died because this man had . . .' Akhtar squeezed his eyes shut and the trembling in his hands increased and his face contorted as though something vile had risen up into his mouth.

'We need to go now,' Thorne said. 'You've got what you asked for.'

'I want to hear him say it.'

'Please, Javee,' Nadira said.

'I want him to tell me.'

Thorne put a hand on Prosser's shoulder and squeezed. 'Tell him.'

Prosser looked at the floor.

'Tell him what you did.'

Prosser shook his head.

Thorne was aware of Helen suddenly pushing herself away from the wall behind him. He was about to speak again when he heard the dull smack of the gun barrel being pushed into the back of Prosser's skull.

'*Tell him,*' Helen said.

The judge tensed and swallowed and began to gabble. His eyes were fixed on the floor. 'I had sex with your son, I was at a party and I paid him for sex and when I saw him in my courtroom I panicked and for God's sake you know the rest. Please, what else can I say . . . ?'

There was no need to say anything else. Thorne's failure to observe the correct legal procedure might well have done some damage to the case against Jeffrey Prosser, but there was no arguing with a confession, every word of which had just been monitored and recorded.

Helen Weeks left the gun where it was.

Prosser looked as though he were about to burst into tears, but when the sob exploded, it was from Javed Akhtar's throat and not his. Akhtar stepped then staggered backwards and only the steadying hand of his wife prevented him from crashing into the rack of metal shelves behind him.

'My sweet, sweet boy,' he said. 'I'm so sorry.'

'Stop it, Javed,' Helen said. 'It's not your fault.'

'Yes, it is.' Akhtar smiled at her, and looking at him it seemed to Thorne that the inside of his mouth was black, that he looked old and ill suddenly under the striplights. 'You see I was not strictly honest with you either, Helen. Not that I've been lying exactly, but ...'

'You did what you thought was right,' Nadira said.

'I was the reason he was in that courtroom in the first place, do you understand?' He was swaying slightly and his eyes were wide and wet, staring at Helen Weeks. 'I was the one that turned him in. I gave my own son up to the police, because I trusted in the law to do the right thing.' His words were coming in short bursts now, thrown up on noisy breaths. 'I told him that everything was going to be fine. I told him not to worry. He came home covered in blood, you see? It's all right, he told me. It's not mine, it's not mine.' He turned to his wife. 'You remember he said that?'

She nodded, clinging to him.

'Not my son's blood,' Akhtar said. 'Not his blood. Now, I am the one covered in my son's blood. Drowning in it.' He began to sink slowly towards the floor and his wife took his weight, and kissed his head and shoulders as she eased him gently down on to the canvas bed.

Thorne turned and took the gun from Helen Weeks.

He put a hand on Prosser's back, eased him towards the doorway.

He knew there was no need to shout.

'We're coming out,' he said.

SEVENTY-ONE

The light from the arc lamps outside flooded the shop as the shutters rose and once again Thorne was forced to shield his eyes against it. Through the curtain of drizzle he could not see anyone clearly beyond the lights, but he knew that there would be guns pointed into the shop. Trained on Akhtar, or perhaps even on him. With a loaded weapon still inside, albeit in theoretically safe hands, the Silver Commander would be taking no chances until everyone, hostage taker included, had been safely removed from the premises and was in custody or undergoing basic medical checks.

Or, in the case of Stephen Mitchell, on their way to the mortuary.

Thorne stood framed in the open doorway, a few feet back from the entrance, in the centre of the wrecked shop. Helen Weeks was to his immediate left while Javed and Nadira Akhtar stood close together on his right. Prosser was just behind them, sitting slumped on the over-turned fridge.

Holding the barrel between two fingers, Thorne slowly lifted the revolver high and squinted into the light.

He shouted, 'Emptying the weapon.'

He carefully released the catch that allowed the cylinder to swing out, then turned the gun, so that the unfired rounds spilled on to the floor. He leaned forward and tossed the gun out through the doorway. It skittered across the pavement and came to rest in the road, just a few feet away from the abandoned Passat.

'Here's how we do this.' Donnelly's voice was tinny through the loudhailer. 'We bring the civilians out first.'

Thorne was wondering if that included the surviving hostage, when Donnelly answered his question.

'Sergeant Weeks second, and then last of all Inspector Thorne can walk Javed out of there. Is that clear?'

Thorne said that it was.

'Right, let's have Mrs Akhtar and Mr Prosser front and centre.'

Thorne nodded to Nadira. She moved slowly away from her husband, her hands deep in the pockets of her anorak. Thorne turned and saw that Prosser was already on his feet, eager to be out of there.

'Now the pair of you start walking,' Donnelly shouted. 'Nice and steady, out of the front door and straight towards the lights. Is that clear?'

The judge and the newsagent's wife both nodded and began to move.

'There will be officers waiting to meet you.'

Prosser pushed past Thorne. In his hurry to leave he lost his footing in a tangle of plastic and paper, but regained his balance and stepped in front of Nadira, clearly desperate to be the first one out of the door.

She paused, let him go ahead.

Thorne doubted that there were still any weapons trained on the shop, but he understood nevertheless why Nadira Akhtar was raising her hands.

Thought he understood.

Then he saw the wink as the blade caught the light, and, as the arm came down, Thorne was already shouting out Nadira's name and driving himself forward. Trying to push her aside in an effort to get to the judge before she did. Taking her to the floor, then stumbling and crawling to where Jeffrey Prosser lay on his side, legs bicycling wildly and one hand flapping at his neck.

At the scissors that were sunk up to their yellow plastic handles into it.

Thorne heard cursing, running footsteps.

Someone screamed, *'Paramedics . . .'*

The blood bubbled up through Thorne's fingers and away, soaking into magazines and damp newspapers. Prosser gagged and began to shiver. He opened his mouth and the blood ran into it.

Then someone was telling Thorne to move and pulling him away from the injured man. There were uniforms and medical bags, a good deal of shouting. And some time after that, when the shouting had stopped, Thorne found himself sitting on the floor of the shop with his back against the wall, and he noticed that Helen Weeks was holding on to him.

A female officer leaned down and wrapped a space blanket around Helen's shoulders. Helped her to her feet. Helen kept hold of Thorne's hand until the last possible moment.

She looked down at her palm. 'You've got blood on you.'

'Always,' Thorne said.

THREE WEEKS LATER

LIKE A HOLIDAY

SEVENTY-TWO

'Got everything back then,' Thorne said.

Antoine Daniels was sitting on the edge of his bunk, leaning forward to stare at the TV screen in the corner and using a joystick to control a zombie or a soldier or an alien or whatever was noisily killing equally unidentifiable creatures on his PlayStation. His room was on the Gold wing and, though it had the same basic layout as the one in which he and Thorne had last spoken, the furnishings were a little less basic, presumably because the occupant was trusted not to smash everything up on a regular basis. As well as the television and games console, there was carpet of a sort on the floor and – surely the biggest perk of all – an ensuite shower. Though he instantly despised himself for thinking it, Thorne decided that he had stayed in marginally worse hotels.

Daniels shrugged. 'I'll lose it all again.'

'Why?' Thorne stood in the doorway to Daniels' bathroom. He could see the small tablets of soap and the bottles of shampoo all neatly lined up on a shelf above the sink.

'Because someone will say something that winds me up and I'll twat them.' The boy screwed up his face as he performed a complicated on-screen manoeuvre. 'Someone always says something.'

'About Amin?'

'About all sorts of things, man. Amin, yeah . . . '

'They know what happened?'

'Whispers going round, you know how it works. Doesn't matter to some of these boys how he died, why he was killed, any of that. He'll always be the "Paki poof", you know? *My* Paki poof.'

'Sorry.'

'No need,' Daniels said.

Thorne did know how it worked among the inmates, but though such things were rarely an enormous surprise, the reaction in other areas to the circumstances surrounding Amin Akhtar's death had been even sadder and more depressing.

There was talk of an official inquiry, but it remained muted.

Twenty minutes earlier, over tea in his office, Roger Bracewell had run fingers through his floppy hair and thanked Thorne for his sterling efforts in uncovering the truth. He took great pains to describe his profound shock and sadness at what had happened at Barndale. He said 'shocked' three times and 'saddened' twice.

Thorne had counted.

Several times he had simply said Ian McCarthy's name, then sat there shaking his head, as though momentarily dumbfounded at the actions of his former colleague. When he was being somewhat more talkative, he told Thorne that Barndale's peripatetic art teacher had initiated a special project in tribute to Amin Akhtar. Those boys who were contemporaries of Amin would be given the opportunity in class to create paintings or collages that summed up their memories of their murdered friend and their feelings about what had happened. The work would then be displayed in some of the prison corridors as a permanent reminder of tragic and unacceptable events.

'On the Gold wing, probably,' Bracewell had said. 'You know, if we want them to remain permanent . . . '

Daniels set his joystick down, though Thorne could not be sure if his game had finished or not. 'Did you come specially to see me?' he asked.

'You deserve to be told exactly what happened,' Thorne said. 'And I wanted you to know that the reason Amin never told you about that stuff in his past was because he was trying to forget about it. I think you were *helping* him forget.'

Daniels smiled, then looked embarrassed about it. 'The doctor and that other one are going to prison for a long time, right?'

'It's not up to me.'

'Definite though, yeah?'

'I hope so,' Thorne said. 'All three of them.'

While Prosser recovered slowly in hospital after life-saving surgery, McCarthy and Powell were on remand for conspiracy to commit murder. Rumour had it that Powell was already talking about a deal of some sort, but it was out of Thorne's hands now. He did know that when it came to a reduction in charge or sentence sought, both men stood more of a chance than Nadira Akhtar. She was in Holloway, awaiting trial for the attempted murder of Jeffrey Prosser, while her husband had been charged not only with kidnapping but with the murder of Stephen Mitchell. As things stood, both faced the possibility of life sentences, but there was at least a glimmer of hope for Javed Akhtar. Carl Oldman, who had offered to defend him, told Thorne that having seen the statement made by Sergeant Helen Weeks, the CPS were considering a reduction in the charge to one of manslaughter.

'I won't be able to keep him out of prison,' Oldman said. 'But bearing in mind everything that happened, I'm hopeful we'd get a jury that was sympathetic. Not to mention a judge, of course.'

Javed Akhtar would at least get the fair hearing his son had been denied.

'What about the kid that actually did it?' Daniels asked. 'The Scottish one.'

Johnno Bridges had yet to surface, but Thorne was confident that he would. 'We'll find him.' He stepped out of the doorway and walked over to where a row of drawings had been taped to the wall. 'It might well be dead behind a skip somewhere with a needle in his arm. But he'll turn up.'

Daniels leaned forward to pick up the joystick again. 'Good of you,' he said.

'What?'

'Coming back. You didn't have to.'

Thorne walked to the door. 'You got a year left, right?'

'Eleven months.'

'Then what?'

'See what happens.'

'Try and make sure you don't come back.'

'I hope he is alive when you find him,' Daniels said. 'The one that gave Amin the drugs. Be nice to get him back in here.' He glanced up at Thorne for just a second before he started playing his game again. 'Then I'd *definitely* lose my fancy room.'

Daniels was not the only boy Thorne had wanted to see on his return to Barndale. While talking to the governor, he had asked after the two boys he had met in the library last time he was here. He discovered that Darren Murray had been released two days earlier. 'Pleased as punch at becoming a father,' Bracewell had told Thorne with a knowing smirk.

Thorne guessed that the boy's maths had not improved, but decided that it was probably best that way for all concerned. The other boy, Aziz Kamali, was still an inmate, but as yet Thorne had not seen him. On his way to the Gold wing, he had put his head round the door to the library, but the boy was not there. Now, walking back towards the main entrance, Thorne watched as Shakir, the imam, came sweeping around a corner with a gaggle of eight or nine followers close behind him. Though now wearing the obligatory skullcap, and looking a lot more serious than he had done that day in the library, Thorne recognised Aziz Kamali among them.

On spotting Thorne, the imam and his followers changed course, veering towards him like an articulated lorry switching lanes.

Shakir told Thorne how pleased he was to see him. He talked about Amin in reverential tones and made the same sorts of noises the governor had made. Thorne waited politely for the priest to finish, then stared over his head and spoke directly to Aziz.

The boy would not look at him.

'Given up on the science then?' Thorne said.

SEVENTY-THREE

Eyes screwed tightly shut, he screamed up into her face, bouncing on the mattress in time to his keening and pulling hard at the edge of the cot. He leaned his head against the bars then rubbed his gums against the padded vinyl. He fell suddenly silent for a few seconds, as though he had forgotten what it was he was so upset about, then stared up at her, his lip quivering, and raised his arms.

'Come on then, chicken,' Helen said. She heaved her son up and placed his hot, sweaty head against her chest.

His cry was still the only thing that could rouse her – waking her almost instantly, completely – and three weeks on from it, she remained amazed that she was sleeping so well. Sleeping at all. Even that first night, she'd been spark out in the back of the panda car before it had arrived at her sister's place. Stretched out on the sofa an hour later, with Jenny still waiting not very patiently for juicy details and Alfie wriggling on her chest.

Sleep of the just, her dad would have called it.

She turned the dial on the musical mobile that was clipped to the edge of the cot. She murmured and shushed and padded around the

386

small bedroom on her bare feet. She rubbed and patted and Alfie's nappy was heavy against her hand.

'Right, chicken.' She carried him across and laid him down on the single bed. Leaned across for the changing bag. 'Let's sort you out.'

She smiled, remembering.

I slept like a baby last night. The pair of them in the pub with a few mates. Paul, a pint or two in, and on a roll. *Woke up every hour and shat myself!*

Releasing the poppers on the baby grow, she decided she was definitely going to call her DCI first thing. She was ready to go back to work, had been within a day or two if she were being honest. She felt fine and there was nothing she needed to 'come to terms' with. She did not need any more 'time and space to recover' and she was not up for introspection.

Not any more.

Imagining herself walking back into her office, the faces of her colleagues, she thought again about the things she had told Javed Akhtar. Those first few minutes after she was taken out of there, she had studied the face of every officer she'd come into contact with and wondered which of them had been listening in to her confession. How long it would take before the gossip spread as far as her own unit. By the time she was washing the blood off her hands, she had decided that she didn't really give a toss, that she had more important things to worry about.

She lifted Alfie's legs up. She pulled the dirty nappy away and dropped it into a nappy sack. She wiped him down, struggling to keep him still, then began to slather on the cream.

Within a day or two of her release, it had become obvious that nobody had told Donnelly or anyone else exactly what had gone on in that storeroom at the end. Nobody had talked about the gun being held at Prosser's head. She racked her brain, trying to recall if Thorne or Prosser had said anything while it was happening that would have given the game away to those listening in, and began to realise that she had got away with it.

Same as she had with Mitchell.

They talked about her bravery from day one, her *resilience*. Holed up in there with a gun to her head, knowing that she too could be killed if she let on that her fellow hostage had already been murdered. They talked about the strength of her character.

Mentioned a medal, for God's sake.

Tom Thorne had known that keeping Mitchell's death secret had been her decision. When they found their first moment alone together, he told her that he'd suspected it almost as soon as he'd been sent that picture of Stephen Mitchell's body. He hadn't said anything. He disposed of his mobile phone as soon as he had the chance. He had enough secrets of his own, he told her, so keeping another one was hardly going to get him into any more trouble.

Thorne did not seem overly burdened by guilt at the way things had panned out, which was fine, because neither was she.

Been there, done that, bought the hair T-shirt.

The way she heard it, Nadira Akhtar was not exactly overcome with remorse either and Helen had no real problem with that. She would never forget the look on Javed Akhtar's face though, when he had finally revealed just why his guilt was so poisonous and so all-consuming; why the ravenous cancer of it would never stop sucking at him. He had smiled at her and looked as good as dead.

'My sweet, sweet boy,' Akhtar had said.

Helen sat there on the edge of the bed as the music wound slowly down. She had a clean nappy in her hand, but she was happy enough just to sit and watch her son kick his fat little legs for a while.

SEVENTY-FOUR

There was light – grey and watery – creeping in through the gap where the curtains would not close properly. There were birds too – a couple of tone-deaf blackbirds with smoker's cough – and Thorne guessed it was somewhere around four, but his watch was on the dressing table and he could not be arsed to slide across to the other side of the bed and check the clock to be sure.

Whatever time it was, awake was awake and Thorne didn't fancy himself to get to sleep again any time soon. He hadn't been sleeping particularly well since the siege had ended. Some nights he would wake every couple of hours, his skin slick and his brain feeling as though it were about to overheat, his internal clock shot to pieces. Not that missing out on a few hours' sleep during the night mattered a great deal at the moment.

Not when he could catch up during the day.

'You should take the chance to get away,' Hendricks had said. 'Think of it like a holiday and do something you've always fancied.'

'I quite fancy doing sod all, which is handy at the moment.'

'Seriously. You could go to Nashville . . .'

389

'It's suspension without pay,' Thorne reminded him. 'I could barely afford half a day at Southend.'

'So, read a few books, go to a gallery or something.'

Thorne had watched a lot of daytime television.

Even before Javed Akhtar's wife had got busy with the storeroom scissors, Thorne had known he was likely to end up facing disciplinary action of some kind. Once Prosser had bled like a stuck pig all over last week's *Daily Express* and *TV Quick* there had been no question about it, but Thorne would almost certainly have been in big trouble anyway, just for taking him in there.

'There was always going to be some wrist-slapping,' Brigstocke had told him. 'Just for the way you did it. I know it's stupid and you didn't have a lot of choice, and I know that his being a judge should have bugger all to do with anything, but there you go. You might still have got away with it, but chuck in this business with the warrant and you're properly stuffed.' Brigstocke had at least looked genuinely upset, *was* genuinely upset, but it had not made it any easier to hear. 'I've gone out on a limb for you before, Tom, you know I have, but not this time. Nothing I can do to help you, mate.'

In the end, the illegal search of Jonathan Bridges' flat had put the tin lid on it and by the time the dust had settled, at least three different DPS teams had worked themselves into something of a frenzy. Whatever else happened, Thorne was determined to find out which job-pissed arse-licker had grassed him up about the warrant. To make his displeasure plain and painful. He knew, were this to happen before the brass had decided his fate, that it would not be doing his cause a great deal of good, but such things could not be helped.

Might as well be hung for a sheep as a judge.

Thorne lay listening to the birds getting louder and remembering the look Antoine Daniels had given him earlier that day, hinting at a revenge of his own.

Then I'd definitely *lose my nice fancy room.*

Plenty of people had lost a great deal more than that.

Stephen Mitchell, Denise Mitchell, Peter Allen.

Javed Akhtar . . .

Akhtar had lost his son, his wife, everything he had ever worked for. Once the body had been removed and the forensic evidence gathered, a FOR SALE sign had gone up outside his shop and those dirty metal shutters had come down for the final time.

The word *MURDERER* now legible underneath *PAKI*.

One thing Thorne *had* decided to do with the free time so generously granted him by the Directorate of Professional Standards was try and get the flat in Kentish Town shifted. The estate agent was talking about dropping the price a little further, but Thorne wanted to try tarting the place up a bit first. A lick of paint, the smell of fresh coffee, all that. Though the change of direction job-wise would now need to be put on hold for the immediate future, or more likely would be decided for him, he could at least make an effort as far as domestic circumstances were concerned.

Not that there hadn't already been major changes in that area.

'Sorry, did he wake you?'

Thorne looked up to see Helen in the doorway, carrying the baby. 'I was awake already.'

'Do you mind if he comes in with us?'

'Course not,' Thorne said. 'It's your bed. Are *you* all right with that though? I mean . . .'

'Fine with me.' She folded back the duvet and laid Alfie down. 'I mean we'll have to see how jealous *he* gets.' She grinned as she climbed in. 'And believe it or not, he snores.'

'I think I can live with that.'

'Then again, so do you.'

'That's rubbish.'

'*And* you talk in your sleep.'

'What?'

'Should have heard yourself the other night. "Phil, Phil . . . "'

'You're hilarious,' Thorne said. Thinking about it, he probably had talked a good deal about Phil Hendricks since he and Helen had begun spending time together, that friendship one of the few things in his life he could still count on. Actually, they had talked about all sorts of things this last couple of weeks, the job not included. Laughed a lot too, which never hurt. 'I don't though, do I?'

'Well it's only been four nights.' Helen turned on to her side and looked at him. 'Didn't Louise ever say anything?'

Thorne shook his head.

Four nights. Many bottles of wine . . .

The baby had begun to grizzle a little and Helen drew him close. Thorne moved gradually across to close the gap and found himself enjoying the feel of the small warm body against his own. The hand that flopped on to his arm or the swaddled foot that dug into his ribs. 'He's got a decent kick on him,' Thorne said. 'We could do with him at Spurs.' He turned on to his side and looked at Helen. 'Did Paul support a team?'

Helen's turn to shake her head.

They lay in silence for a while, but Alfie refused to settle and began to cry again. Helen said that three in a bed was a stupid idea. That she was happy to take the baby back to the spare room, so that Thorne could try and get to sleep.

'Stay here,' Thorne said. 'It's not like I've got anything to get up for, is it?'

'What do you think they'll do?' Helen asked.

Thorne knew that the DPS had plenty of options. 'Depends how public they want to be about it,' he said. 'I could always save them the trouble and knock it on the head.'

'You don't mean that.'

'It's good to think about doing something else every now and again,' he said. 'Don't you reckon? Something nice and simple and boring.'

'I suppose.'

'Apparently, there's a newsagent's for sale just up the road.'

Helen began to giggle, and when she lifted her leg across his, Thorne reached over the baby to stroke her neck. 'Let me take him next door,' she said. 'I can get him off in ten minutes and come back.'

Thorne nodded, grinning. 'Then you can get *me* off,' he said.

That was when Alfie chose to start kicking him again.

392

Acknowledgements

I am enormously grateful to the many people without whom this book would be as good as dead . . .

First and foremost, I am thankful to Dilip Gaglani for his kindness, his patience and a memory almost as astonishing as the life it recalled in such amazing detail.

Simply put, there would be no book without him.

As far as the book's other major location is concerned, I could not have created a YOI as dysfunctional as Barndale without seeing how one should be run properly. I owe a huge debt to Emily Thomas (governor), Sara Pennington (deputy governor), the fabulous Stieve Butler and all the staff at HMP Cookham Wood, whose attitude towards the boys in their care is truly inspirational. Further thanks are due to Debbie Kirby of HMP Press Office for arranging my trips inside and to my good friend Martyn Waites for guidance and great stories.

A born storyteller with an enviable amount of material, Ivor Ward was hugely generous with his time and advice, as were Caroline Haughey and Carl Newman, whose legal expertise was invaluable. Thanks to Michael Jecks, who has forgotten more about guns than most people will ever know, to Tony Fuller who saved my bacon innumerable times and to Premiership forensic experts Professor Dave

Barclay and Dr James Grieve. They all answered more stupid questions than anyone would consider reasonable.

Ten years ago, the incomparable Dr Phil Cowburn provided the spark that brought the first Thorne novel, *Sleepyhead*, to life. This time round, his champagne moment was every bit as important.

I owe you, Phil . . .

As always, the book would be the poorer were it not for the eagle eye of Wendy Lee, the enthusiasm and expertise of David Shelley and the team at Little, Brown and the immaculate furnishings of Sarah Lutyens.

And Claire, who makes *everything* better.